LIFELESS EYES

A white hand came down and clamped itself on the handle of her car door just as she was about to thrust the key into the lock.

Dorothy screamed. He clapped a hand over her mouth. His palm was as cold and hard as ice. The fingers of his other hand dug painfully into her shoulder.

He started to drag her toward the trees. He made no sound. Now she felt earth under her feet instead of asphalt. He was taking her into the trees, and once he got her there, all hope would be lost. She thrashed, and then went suddenly limp.

The tactic worked; when she fell, he lost his grip. She screamed before she hit the ground. *"Help! Somebody help!"* But he was hauling her back up before she could roll and try to run. He jerked her from the ground as easily as if she were a baby.

Suddenly she was looking into his face, and for the first time she could see his eyes. They were pale and lifeless, blind eyes that rolled unseeing in their sockets like a pair of colored marbles. They made her fear worse than rape.

They were eyes that no longer saw things from a human perspective. . . .

LIFEBLOOD

Lee Duigon

PINNACLE BOOKS
WINDSOR PUBLISHING CORP.

To my wife, Patricia,
who kept the wheels from falling off

PINNACLE BOOKS

are published by

Windsor Publishing Corp.
475 Park Avenue South
New York, NY 10016

First printing: May, 1988

Printed in the United States of America

PROLOGUE

He couldn't bury her, not just yet. He left the dark room, with his bride's dead body stretched out on their marriage bed, and went out to sit in the sun.

Later he would pray. He couldn't now, lest he provoke a crisis of faith, a rift between him and God. The sun pressed down on him. He hoped it would bake the pain dry.

The pueblo let him sit in silence. Later there would be time for condolences. Now there was confusion. Benejah Thornall had come to the pueblo to comfort its people, to reassure them that God was with them. Now that he was the one who needed comfort, they didn't know how to approach him.

Thornall sought refuge in confusion. For the moment it was less unbearable than his pain.

He had married her only a week ago, and she was dead. Vital as a sunbeam, as a swiftly rushing mountain brook in his native Vermont, as a bright bird flying . . . and she was dead. Esperanza Díaz Thornall. Seventeen years old, with the glow of childhood still on her, his bride. The companion of his labors for the rest of his life. Dead.

5

The rest of his life stretched before him like a dirt track leading into a yawning desert. He was not yet twenty-two.

Early death was not unknown in Pueblo Cielo. Thornall had seen it many times, in many forms. Snakebite. A swarm of endemic diseases. Stillborn babies, mothers who died in childbirth. Hunting accidents. Woodchopping accidents. Infection. Death had easy hunting here.

Yet he had never seen anything like the death that claimed his Esperanza.

She woke up pale and listless, complaining of pain in her joints, in her head—and she had gone to bed with him that night completely healthy, eager for the next day's work. She'd never been sick, not since she was a baby. In the chill of the dawn sweat dampened her pillow. Thornall went to fetch the doctor, a fellow New Englander named Taylor.

But Taylor wasn't in. His housekeeper didn't know where he was. He'd been called out late last night on an emergency in one of the other pueblos, she didn't know which one, and he hadn't returned yet. She couldn't reach him; there were no telephones in the country. *Señor Doctor* would come when he could, possibly sometime this evening. Thornall hurried back home.

Esperanza lay moaning on the bed. He held her hand and wiped her face with a damp cloth. He knelt beside the bed and prayed. She didn't seem to know he was there.

The darkness in the room oppressed him. He got up and pulled the curtain from the window. A shaft of sunlight fell across the bed.

She screamed.

God showed Thornall a sign.

He saw the bed, but the room was dark again, as dark as night. He shouldn't have been able to see the bed, but he did. He saw Esperanza, too, sleeping peacefully on her back. And he saw—not clearly—a dark, bulky form bending over her. The vision dissolved before he could make out whose form it was.

Suddenly the room was bright again, and Esperanza was still screaming, and he was still standing by the window, and Maria Goya was coming through the door. Her lips were moving, but he couldn't hear her above his wife's shrill scream.

Maria shoved past him and flung the curtain back across the window. Within seconds Esperanza's screams abated, her tortured writhing ceased. She lay back and panted like a fish tossed to the bottom of a boat after a long and killing fight. Maria went to her and felt her forehead.

It took some moments for Thornall's mind to get back into gear and interpret the questions that Maria hurled at him in rapid-fire Spanish. He felt drained and weary, as he often did after the Lord showed him a sign.

"No, Maria. I went to Dr. Taylor, he wasn't home." He answered in the rural dialect that was second nature to him now.

"My God, señor! She sweats like this, yet she has no fever. What's wrong with her?"

Thornall came away from the window and sat at the foot of the bed, looking down at his bride. Her face was the color of old newspapers left in an attic.

"I don't know. She was fine when we went to bed. She was like this when we woke up. I don't understand it."

"I came running when I heard her scream." Maria was fat. When she sat on the bed she made it creak painfully. "You poor man, you were standing by the window like a statue."

"It was so dark. I wanted to let in some light."

"She was screaming that the light was hurting her. Didn't you understand, señor?"

Thornall shook his head. No one in the pueblo knew that the Lord had given him second sight. They'd be afraid if he told them. He hadn't even told Esperanza yet. . . .

"I think I must have been in shock," he said.

"Damn that doctor," Maria said. "He's never here when he's needed."

"He has too big an area to cover."

"Listen, señor. Don't be angry, but I'm going to send Pedro to San Carlos for the priest. Maybe Father Melendez can help."

Thornall wasn't angry. These people had Romanism in their blood, generations of bowing to the priests and bishops. It would take years even to begin to change that. For now he was thankful they'd accepted him as a neighbor and a servant of God, albeit one with nothing like the authority of a Roman priest.

"Thank you, Maria. Father Melendez is a good man. I'll pray while I'm waiting for him."

Thornall prayed, and Father Melendez came and squeezed his shoulder. He sat on the bed and felt Esperanza's pulse, lifted her eyelids and looked into her eyes, and shook his head. He tried to question her, but she was oblivious to his presence. Later her mother and father came, but the priest sent them away when Señora Díaz fell to loudly sobbing. Maria went with them.

Peace descended on the room. Melendez's presence was a comfort. When Thornall had first come to the pueblo, he had expected the priest to view his missionary efforts with disfavor. But they were laborers in the same vineyard, the priest had been the first to point out, and between them there had never been rivalry.

"I am sorry, my son. I have never seen anything like this. Maybe Dr. Taylor can help."

"If he ever gets here," Thornall said. The priest sighed and ran his fingers through his steel-wool beard.

"My friend, I am sorry to bring this up at such a time. But Esperanza is Catholic, and there are certain things that I must do now. You understand."

8

Thornall nodded. Esperanza had defied her parents to marry him. Privately Melendez had given them his blessing; publicly, he could not endorse the marriage. They'd had to go to Guatemala City, where they'd found a Mormon missionary who was willing to administer the sacrament. In time Thornall hoped that the community would come to accept the marriage as they had come to accept him.

"I understand, Luis. I'll wait outside."

"We can pray together, Benito. God will hear us."

She languished all day without recovering consciousness. Taylor didn't arrive until after sundown.

Benejah Thornall felt no joy in seeing him. Strangely, he had never felt at ease in the doctor's presence, never had a desire to seek out the man's company, despite the two of them being the only New Englanders for hundreds of miles around.

Dr. Emerson Taylor was a Boston man; Thornall came from a little town in the White Mountains that nobody in Boston had ever heard of. Taylor had gone to Harvard and to Trinity Physicians College, had had articles published in the *New England Journal of Medicine,* and was a respected member of his profession. Thornall's only college was the Bible; no established church acknowledged him as its missionary, and he knew only what the Lord permitted him to know. And Taylor was twice his age.

Thornall's friends in Pueblo Cielo included a Papist priest, many campesinos and their wives, full-blooded *indios* who hunted in the jungle, the district police captain, and even old Ernesto, the village idiot. With any one of these Thornall would have preferred to pass the time rather than with his countryman, Dr. Taylor. He didn't know why this should be, and it troubled him. But he had never done anything about it because Taylor was the only American-trained doctor in the area and was seldom available socially. Even if he had wanted to befriend the man, Thornall reflected, Taylor seemed to have no time for friendship.

He was a big pale mountain of a man with thin silver hair and flat brown eyes. Whether it was Guatemala that had aged him, or something else, he looked much older than the forty-odd years to which he admitted. He had been in Guatemala for some years, said the campesinos, although he'd only been in Pueblo Cielo a little longer than Thornall. He had left the New England winters behind to study tropical parasites (as he had explained to Thornall briefly when they'd first met), and stayed on the government's good side by doubling as a kind of medical missionary. He had a sharp nose and a clumsy smile, and an iron handshake that took one by surprise because his hands looked soft and flabby.

He crunched Thornall's hand and apologized for not coming sooner. "I was up in Ocho Rios doing the best I could for an inflamed appendix," he said. "Let's see the patient, Ben."

Thornall led him into the bedroom. Overhead, the tin roof rattled as the resident tarantula did battle with the gigantic tropical cockroaches. A small lizard clung to one of the bedposts like a guardian spirit, but fled into the shadows when Taylor approached the bed.

Esperanza was much worse now. She hadn't moved for hours, except to gulp air through her mouth. Her eyes were sinking into their sockets, making her face look like a skull.

Taylor set his black medical bag on the bed beside her and bent down to feel her pulse. He opened the bag, took out a stethoscope, and listened to her heart. He looked into her eyes, her ears, and her mouth, and palpated her chest and limbs and neck.

Thornall stood by silently, fighting off a bitter nausea

that had seized him suddenly. He felt somewhat dizzy, too, and would have liked to sit down, but he remained standing. He felt sure he would pass out if he didn't stay on his feet.

Taylor questioned him, learning nothing because Thornall knew nothing. The disease had come like a thief in the night.

"She really ought to be in a hospital," he said, "but I don't know whether she's fit to be moved. If she doesn't improve within twenty-four hours, I'm afraid we'll have to risk it."

"What is wrong with her, Doctor?"

Taylor shrugged. "Nothing that I'm familiar with. It isn't snakebite. It isn't yellow fever, or malaria, or encephalitis, meningitis, typhus, or anything else whose symptoms I recognize. I'll have to take some blood and saliva samples. Maybe something'll turn up under the microscope."

He drew blood with a large needle and scraped the inside of her cheek with a stainless steel spatula. He packed the samples carefully and returned his instruments to the bag.

"I'm reluctant to give her any medicine," he explained, "since I don't know what I'm dealing with here, and the wrong medication could be disastrous. On the positive side, she's a strong and healthy girl. Her body's natural defenses may be able to pull her through.

"I hate to tell you this, but I have to be in Cienflores tomorrow, probably all day. Possible cholera outbreak, has to be seen to immediately. But I'll get right to work on these samples, and hopefully I'll have something to work with when I return tomorrow evening. In the meantime, I suggest you pray."

Thornall thanked the doctor and escorted him from the room. He sat on his front step and felt the nausea and dizziness recede. When his head was clear, he went back inside.

Esperanza died at midnight.

As he sat alone, simmering in the noonday sun, he lost his sense of time. Over the low rooftops of the pueblo stretched the blank green rampart of the jungle like a prison wall. For no conscious reason he rose on stiff joints and returned to the bedroom. He sat at the foot of the bed and was surprised to feel hot tears trickling down his cheeks; he couldn't remember when he'd started to cry. He made no effort to hold them back.

He had never loved before, never even aspired to it, longed for it, imagined it. He hadn't left his home valley to look for love. He'd asked for nothing from life but to serve God.

When Esperanza came into his life, it was like discovering a part of himself that he hadn't known existed. Suddenly there was more to him. He was like a dormant seed exposed to sun and water. He grew; he blossomed in his love for her. Nor did it detract from his devotion to the Lord. There was more of him to be devoted.

Now that part of him was gone, the green shoot withered. He knew he would never love again.

Esperanza stirred.

One pale hand trembled; one set of stiff fingers plucked awkwardly at the sheet.

Thornall sat and stared, his mind gone suddenly blank.

He had never doubted she was dead. There'd been no room for doubt. At home, and here in Pueblo Cielo, he'd seen death often enough to know what it looked like. There were ways to find the tiniest secret flutter of a heartbeat, the least little whiff of exhaled breath. Thornall knew them all and had tried them all. Father Melendez and old Maria, who'd been present at more deathbeds than they could count, came separately when Thornall sent for them and separately assured him that his wife was indeed dead, there

12

was no possibility of error. By the time he left the bedroom, the incontestable fact of her death was stamped onto his mind like the image on a coin.

Yet she stirred. Now the other hand . . .

He thought of Jairus' daughter on her bed of death, and Lazarus in his tomb, and how the Lord raised each of them to life again. But those were miracles, wrought by the Savior's own hand when He walked the earth. Moreover, the bereaved had earnestly entreated him to make their loved ones live again.

Thornall had made no such prayer. He'd begged for Esperanza's life; but when it had been taken from him, he'd prayed for her salvation. It would have been presumptuous to pray for a miracle, and he hadn't even imagined one. His faith was strong. He knew it would see him through his time of grief, if he clung to it firmly enough.

For a moment, seeing the twitch of his bride's dead hands, Thornall felt dread blow through his heart like an icy wind.

But then his heart leaped, because human beings were fallible and three of them could be mistaken when they found death in a body that still lived. He, the priest, and old Maria had been wrong. That was the only explanation logic would allow, and Thornall's mind embraced it more quickly than it was possible to frame it into words.

He uttered an inarticulate cry of joy and seized his wife's hands, squeezing them hard. They were cold, but the fingers moved.

"Esperanza! Can you hear me?"

Her head lolled. Her lips moved silently. She was alive.

He pressed an ear to her breast. He heard no heartbeat, nothing but his own blood pounding excitedly within his head, and his own breath coming in quick, frenetic gasps. He bent close to Esperanza's face and framed her cold cheeks in his hands. He was suddenly sweating like a fever victim.

13

"Esperanza, you're alive! Can you hear me?"

It was dark in the room with the curtains drawn, too dark to read her eyes when the lids flew open. They seemed to shine like black pearls from deep within their unfathomable sockets. They shone at him but told him nothing. He wondered if she could see him. There were many maladies that struck their victims blind.

He would take her blind, though. He would take whatever God would give him, and rejoice. His heart sang.

Tears blinded him as he felt her hands move up his body to clutch his shoulders. Her grip was surprisingly strong, almost painful. He gloried in it.

"Esperanza—"

She jerked him down on top of her and clamped her teeth in his neck.

The pain was inexpressible. Her hands tore him cruelly, her teeth savaged his skin. He floundered, too startled to push himself away. Her body was cold and hard. Her lips chilled him even as the pain shot through his body like a jet of fire. Finally it drove him to break from her. He needed all his strength to do it. He heard her teeth gnash as they lost their grip on him and her jaws clashed shut.

He looked down at her and saw her mouth and chin smeared darkly with blood, his blood. Her hands shot up toward his neck, fingers hooked like claws.

He tried to restrain her, but she was too strong for him, too quick. It was all he could do to pull away again and throw himself clear of the bed. His knees wobbled crazily as he tried to stand.

She sat up and grinned at him, bloodily. Her white teeth shone.

"In the name of God, Esperanza, don't you know me?"

Clumsily, but with a fixity of purpose that appalled his soul, she tried to free herself from the sheet and climb off the bed. His blood glistened on her cheeks.

Holy Savior, hear my prayer—

14

She gained her feet and lurched toward him. Her cold fingers tugged at his clothes. He wriggled free and backed out of the room, terror blotting out all thought. She followed him.

He pumped his jaws to scream, but no sound emerged. He eluded her and charged out of the house, to trip on the step and fall face-first onto the hard-packed earth. Before he could get up again, she was upon him.

A shrill scream burst from his lips. He tried to crawl away, but she held him firmly. Her fingers were like iron bands. Her teeth raked his scalp. Her weight pressed his mouth into the dust and stopped his screaming.

Suddenly she seemed to weaken. He shook off her hold and rolled free of her.

She lay on her back, bloody jaws snapping feebly, crazed eyes staring into the sky, fingers clenching and unclenching. She made no sound, not even a gasp. Villagers came running, only to be stopped short by the unnatural spectacle.

Thought came flooding back into his brain: disarticulated fragments of reason, jumbled together into chaos. He stared at Esperanza as he struggled to find a rational thought.

Surrounded by astonished campesinos, she had virtually ceased to move. Her eyes fell shut. A tremble ran through her body, shaking it like a rat in the jaws of a terrier. Then she was still.

He inched toward her on his hands and knees, but Maria seized his shoulders and held him back.

"She's alive, don't you see?" he babbled. "My wife! I have to go to her."

The campesinos crossed themselves. No one made a move toward the girl who lay stretched out in the dust.

A carrion reek drifted into Thornall's nostrils and made him violently ill. The Lord's mercy permitted him to faint.

* * *

15

He awoke in a strange bed, with a lantern burning fitfully and Maria dabbing at his forehead with a wet cloth. Behind her stood the priest, Melendez.

"He's come back to us, Father."

"Esperanza—" Thornall tried to say.

Melendez sat beside him. "She's dead, my son. I'm sorry."

"We thought she was dead before. We were wrong. In God's name, Luis!"

Maria hushed him with a finger on his lips. Sorrow etched deep lines in her plain, flat face. He reached up and felt bandages on his neck. His own touch made him wince with pain.

"She's at peace now, God rest her soul," Maria said.

"I don't understand. She . . ." Thornall shook his head wearily. His arms and legs felt leaden.

"I don't know how to tell you this, señor, but I must. And I can only say it simply. Señor, your wife was bitten by a vampire."

"Maria!" Melendez hissed. Maria shook her head.

"It's true. I have never seen it in my lifetime, but I know from things my mother told me. The person who is bitten by a vampire becomes a vampire. But the light of the sun, when she chased you out of the house, destroyed her. It freed her soul, but it destroyed her body. She had to be buried at once."

"Maria, be still!" The priest pulled the woman from the bedside and knelt by Thornall's pillow. "My son, you must not listen to such things. Our people are superstitious, they don't know any better."

"I'm telling the truth, Father, and you know it!" Maria said. Melendez glared angrily at her until she lapsed into a defiant silence.

"But I was bitten, too," said Thornall. "Doesn't that mean . . . ?"

"We will know when the sun comes up tomorrow," Ma-

16

ria said. "But you don't seem very sick just now. I think maybe the saints have seen fit to spare you."

The priest escorted her firmly out of the room. When he returned he prayed quietly, comfortingly, until Thornall fell asleep.

When the sun rose in the morning, Thornall crept outside and took no hurt from it.

I. STIRRINGS

MILLBORO
New Jersey, The Present

One

The crazies were coming back.

The detective sergeant pointed to the defaced tombstone and said, "Look at that, Chief. Same as last time."

Van Wyck, the police chief, shook his head, remembering. He doubted he would ever forget.

They took off their clothes and flogged each other with strips cut from old inner tubes; angry red welts streaked their bodies. They assaulted each other sexually, too. Pain is pleasure, pleasure is pain. *All of them were high on angel dust. Their radios blared, making a heavy-metal din that drowned out the agonies of the dog they'd tortured for its blood. The blood they drank . . .*

"Chief?"

"I'm all right, Randy."

It was a small cemetery, less than half an acre, and had been abandoned so long ago that its proper name was lost. Every now and then the Historical Society came by and tidied up; otherwise the place would soon be overgrown. The woods encroached on it, putting out feelers of brush and brambles, surrounding it, cutting it off from Richmond Hill Road. The nearest inhabited building was over half a mile away, the road so riddled with potholes that few motorists chose to come this way more than once. All the land around was tied up in endless litigation, with no party able to establish title, so it was safe from the builders. All in all, an ideal place for kids to get together to fool around and smoke dope.

Only it went much farther than that.

The stones, so recently cleaned by Historical Society volunteers, had been defiled again, spray-painted with upside-down crosses, pentagrams, and Satanist slogans. The weedy ground was littered with cigarette butts, beer cans, and used condoms. Clumps of black wax showed where candles had been burned on the tombstones.

Randy Musante, the detective, made a face. "Why do they do it?" he said. "What's this township coming to?"

Van Wyck didn't know why they did it, although he knew all the easy answers. They did it for kicks. They did it because they were made insane by drugs, or by their pathologically antisocial music, or both. They were possessed by the Devil. Van Wyck knew all those answers and didn't accept them. They didn't explain why a fifteen-year-old kid from a nice family would want to be whipped until his skin was raw and dapple his face with dog's blood. Nothing explained the things he'd seen the last time he raided this place, over two years ago.

Ed Van Wyck, a big, rugged, ginger-haired man with a gunslinger's moustache, felt sick to the roots of his heart because he had two teenage kids, a boy and a girl, and could neither advise them nor protect them. After the divorce his wife took them both, moved to Philadelphia, and married a lawyer who had more money than brains. He saw his children only two or three times a year and spoke with them on the telephone only to the extent that Helen and her officious little prick of a husband would allow. (*"Hello, Jeff.*

Hi, Lindy." "*How's it goin', Dad?*" And if he was lucky they'd talk for two or three minutes before Helen came on the line and put an end to it. "*Bye, Dad.*") Van Wyck had no idea whether his children were being raised properly, with love and firmness. He suspected that they weren't.

"You know what's wrong with these kids?" Musante said. "They never got a good swift kick in the ass when they needed it. Hey, give Junior whatever the fuck he wants—right? You wait and see, these crazy little bastards are gonna kill somebody someday."

That was precisely what Van Wyck was afraid of.

Dorothy Matthiesen hung up the phone and stood in the middle of her empty house.

Same old shit. "Sorry, honey, I won't be home for dinner, something came up, we gotta have a meeting, I just hope it won't run past eight o'clock."

It was happening twice a week now, on the average, and she was getting tired of it. Throw in the surprise interruptions of the bus service, the inevitable delays, and the special rush jobs that couldn't wait until tomorrow, and Chris was hardly ever home on time to sit down at the dinner table with her. And when he finally did get home, he was hardly fit for anything but to watch the news and fall asleep in his contour chair. He made her feel abandoned and unloved.

For two cents, Dorothy thought, *I'd go out and have an affair.* She wondered if Chris was having an affair in the city. Look what happened to Kathy Vanko: never suspected what Charlie was doing with his time until the guy came down with AIDS. All those nights he was supposed to be working late, he was playing Madame Butterfly.

But Chris always answered his phone when she had to call him at the office, he came home every night no matter how late he had to stay, and he never told her a story that

21

didn't ring true. All of which was probably just what Kathy Vanko would have said, had you asked her before she got the bad news. But it was bad enough just having an absentee husband without imagining him romping around the leather bars.

As for an affair of her own, it'd be like trying to get up a strip poker game in a nudist colony. Why bother? All the men she knew in Millboro were commuter workaholics, just like Chris—or worse.

She sighed and went back to her typewriter.

There is no truth to the rumor that the coaches of the three Little League teams with the worst won-lost records will be publicly hanged at the conclusion of the season. The truth is that they will be privately hanged.

"We have a right to expect our kids to be winners," said (Name Withheld), parent of a twelve-year-old shortstop on (Team Name Withheld). "It's a coach's responsibility to make them winners. They have to learn to win now, while they're young, so they can be winners later on in life. I'm a winner, I want my kid to be a winner."

"Well, I'm a loser," admitted (Name Withheld), father of catcher (Name Withheld). "I drink like a fish, I can't get it up anymore, my boss despises me, and I voted Republican in the last municipal elections. But by gum, I'll be damned if I'll sit back and let that schmuck (Coach's Name Withheld) turn my kid into a loser!"

According to (Name Withheld), (Team Name Withheld) (Coach's Name Withheld) is "the worst. My little (Name Withheld) is the best hitter on the team, but does he ever get to bat with the bases loaded? Not a chance! (Name Withheld) and (Name Withheld) are deliberately placed in front of him in the batting order, and" (Rest of Story Withheld)

Twice a month Dorothy wrote, edited, published, and distributed *Tales from the Developments*, two or three mimeographed pages of satirical insights into the mores and folkways of Millboro Township. It had started out as a column in one of the local weekly shoppers, *The Ad-Venturer*. When the paper went down the pipe financially, so many of Dorothy's neighbors told her that they missed her column that she decided to continue it on her own.

Tales kept her busy: attending public meetings on nights when Chris was either working late or just too groggy to miss her; carefully reading the Millboro news in all the local papers; sometimes even interviewing someone.

Ostensibly her motive was to nudge readers out of their apathy. Millboro was a big suburban sprawl with a high residential turnover and no sense of community identity. "The idea," she would explain when asked, "is to get us all laughing at the same things." Whether *Tales* was succeeding in that or not, she was in no position to know.

But the real reason for her continuing with *Tales* was to keep herself from going brain-dead. Unless you could keep your gray cells alive on a diet of TV soap operas, nail salons, tanning salons, poolside gossip sessions, and Chris's spousal shortcomings, she thought, intellectual starvation was a distinct possibility.

Every now and then she submitted a sample column to one of the real newspapers in the area, but so far there hadn't been any takers.

Felix Frick grinned as the express carried him in triumph back to Millboro.

Felix should have been an investigative reporter, or even a detective; but he was content to think of himself as a concerned citizen. His civic duty was his life.

He was grinning because he was about to pull off a major coup. After untold hours of pawing through Department of

State paperwork, after shelling out hundreds of dollars in fees, plus train tickets and cab fare, he finally had the information that would nail Mayor Ron Leib's scalp firmly to the wall.

The search began at Township Hall, right after Leib's swearing-in on New Year's Day. Millboro required its public officials to file statements disclosing all their financial assets and interests, for examination by any citizen who asked for it. Felix assumed there would be some deception involved: a politician was, almost by definition, a man who betrayed the public trust. But that was because the public allowed them to get away with it. The ordinary citizen was too busy working at his job, taking care of his family, and keeping a roof over his head to have any time left for ferreting out these often subtle and convoluted betrayals of his trust.

But Felix had the time. He had nothing but time. He was a retired high school teacher who had toiled like a quarry slave to put his rotten son through college and support him until he became a fabulously successful architect who was married to an equally successful lady doctor. Elroy felt guilty about the sacrifices his father had made for him, so Elroy bought Felix a nice house in Millboro and paid all the old man's bills. They never saw each other, but that was the way they both wanted it. And it allowed Felix to put all his pension and Social Security money into his new career as a concerned citizen.

When he read Ron Leib's disclosure statement, he was surprised by its modesty. According to the statement, the mayor owned his house, his local law practice, savings, checking, and retirement accounts, some stock in a few high-tech companies, and a couple thousand dollars' worth of bonds. Felix didn't believe it for a minute. There had to be more.

So he kept his ears open and asked around, and he soon picked up a rumor that the mayor was buying up potentially valuable properties all over the township. The mayor's bitterest political enemies believed this, but they couldn't prove it and they couldn't say how Leib was doing it. Leib might be well-heeled, but he hardly looked like he had the equipment to be a big-time real estate speculator.

Day after day, Felix went to Township Hall and checked the tax map, and then double-checked at the County Hall of Records. Millboro was a big township, and there were thousands of property owners; but it wasn't long before Felix saw a means by which the mayor might be able to snap up quite a bit of land cheaply and without fanfare.

Tax sales, that was the angle. When a property owner didn't pay his taxes, the property could be auctioned off by the county after a waiting period. The successful bidder would pay the taxes and acquire a lien on the property. The original owner would then have to pay the debt to the lienholder, plus interest—and if he failed to do that, the lienholder would eventually assume title of the property at a skimpy fraction of its market value.

When Felix checked at the Hall of Records, he saw that many of the tax sales in Millboro were made to corporations—faceless entities with cryptic names. Anyone could form a corporation.

But the corporate charter was held by the state, and the names of the corporation's principals were on record in the capitol. All you had to do was go down there and do some digging.

Felix dug, and what he uncovered was a list of dummy corporations, all of them fronts for Leib, all of them involved in the acquisition of tax-delinquent properties. According to the record, Leib held liens on more than two hundred acres scattered throughout the township.

It was a clever little scheme, and the mayor seemed to be having a lot of fun with it. He gave his corporations clever little names: Jo-El Realty, for his two kids, Joan and Ellis; Ripco for his dog, Rip; Barsan Properties for his ex-wife,

Barbara, maiden name Santangelo. Nor was he listed as the principal partner in all of them. He had one corporation headed by his grandmother, another by his sister-in-law.

It was more than just an inside joke, however. As mayor, Leib also sat on the planning and zoning boards and on the public utilities authorities, water and sewer. With developers poised to build, a small change in the zoning could turn an insignificant piece of property into a gold mine overnight. The same would apply to any decision to extend the sewerage facilities.

In short, Leib would know ahead of time which properties were likely to become valuable, and he could use his political clout to influence decisions favorably affecting property that nobody knew he owned.

It was a sweet scheme, and knowing that he would be the ruin of it made Felix Frick feel like Samson getting ready to pull down the Philistines' temple. He looked out the window of the train and grinned some more.

Far from the expensive developments that housed the township's white population, Alabama Road wound its way through the woods that cloaked the borders of Dutchman's Bog.

Here one house out of four made do without running water, and two families out of three lived on property owned by a landlord whom they had never seen face-to-face, or even spoken with on the telephone. Two out of five blocks had no sidewalks; nor did the township's sewer system extend to this neighborhood. Three out of eight buildings were abandoned and falling into disrepair; one out of four streetlamps didn't work; one out of three men were out of work. But it was a peaceful neighborhood, and most of its residents had been born there—as opposed to the high-priced developments, where two out of three residents had been born in Queens or Brooklyn.

Toby Hicks took his dog for a run in the woods and found a dead man.

Two

"This day sucks," Van Wyck muttered, looking down at the corpse.

It lay face up on a bed of ferns, swelled and discolored by decay and smelling so evil that Musante started tossing his cookies even before he came in sight of it. Toby Hicks, who had been sick already, stood beside the police chief and said, "Amen."

"Know him?" Van Wyck asked.

"Are you crazy? I wouldn't know my own mother if she was all messed up like this."

Musante caught up, took one look at the corpse, and threw up again.

"I thought you cops were used to things like this," Hicks said.

"We don't see too many things like this in Millboro. Take another look, Mr. Hicks. Maybe you recognize the clothes."

The body was clad in faded blue Levis and a black-and-white checked shirt, with worn-out Sears sneakers on its feet. Hicks thought the clothes were in a lot better shape than their owner, although the swelling of the body had popped the buttons from the shirt.

"Anybody could be wearing clothes like that," he said. "Why don't you see if he still has his wallet? That'll tell you who he is."

"I think I'll leave that job to the medical examiner," Van Wyck said. He turned around to face Musante, who was slumped against a tree. "Randy, do you think you might be ready to do your job so we can get out of here?"

"Sure, Chief." The detective pulled a handkerchief from his pocket and held it over his nose and mouth as he trudged over for another look at the body.

"Don't move around, guys," he said unnecessarily. "There might be fibers caught in the bushes, other stuff the crime scene crew might be able to use. Just stand still and look."

All three men looked; but for all they could see, the dead man might have been dropped from the sky.

"I can't see any indication of the cause of death," Van Wyck said.

"Neither can I. We'll have to wait for the autopsy." Musante bent a little closer to the body, but not too close. "He was a young male caucasian, age thirty, plus or minus a few years, and I don't see any wounds on him. Course, I ain't gonna turn him over to get a look at his back. But it sure doesn't look like anything but natural causes. It's funny, though—you'd think the bugs and animals would've chewed him up a lot, but it looks like they hardly touched him."

Having said that, Musante suddenly turned ashen-faced again and had to back away.

"Any poisonous snakes around here, Mr. Hicks?" the police chief asked.

"I saw a copperhead once, but mostly it's just water snakes and garters."

"How well do you know this area?"

"Pretty good. I used to play here when I was a kid, and I still take my dog out here once or twice a week."

"Have you noticed anything unusual lately? Seen anybody who didn't belong here?"

"Nope. Same as always, until today."

"Can we go call the coroner now, Chief?" Musante said.

* * *

Waiting for the medical examiner's team and the county's mobile crime lab, Van Wyck and Musante sat on Hicks' front porch and took his statement—what there was of it.

The witness, Tolbert Dale Hicks, 25, of 2602 Alabama Road, Millboro Township, a veteran of the United States Army and currently unemployed, found the unidentified caucasian male decedent while taking his dog for a walk in the woods approximately half a mile from his home. Hicks immediately returned and called police, whom he then led to the site. He claims not to recognize the deceased, nor is he able to speculate as to the deceased's identity. He further claims to have seen nor heard nothing unusual in the area during the past several weeks.

"Doesn't tell us a hell of a lot," Musante said.

"I don't know a hell of a lot, Sergeant."

"What do you do with your time, Mr. Hicks?"

"I'm studying for my degree in accounting over at the county college. G.I. Bill. I got a good job waiting for me when I get it. How about you, Chief? What do you do with your time?"

Van Wyck sighed. "I wish I had some."

Felix shuffled his papers, rechecked his figures, and prepared himself for his speech at the next night's Township Council meeting.

They hated it when they saw his name on the list for Citizen's Voice. They never knew what he would question next: a line item on the municipal budget, the fees charged for recreational programs, a clause in a proposed ordinance, a slipup by a township official, or some rip-off perpetrated by one of the builders. They knew he was the watchdog and they hated it. He loved it.

He anticipated the various defenses Leib might use. The mayor could claim he hadn't listed his corporations on his disclosure statement because they didn't have any real assets. He could claim it was an oversight that would be immediately corrected. He could point out that most of what he had was liens, many of which would be paid off and yield only a small cash profit. He would wriggle like an eel in a net.

Well, he could wriggle all he pleased; Felix had him. In point of fact it was a violation of the township's administrative code not to list *all* assets and business interests in the disclosure statement. With that point alone he could skewer the mayor. And then there was another whole can of worms: Leib's motives. Was he using his position in government to further his personal interests? Was he using his inside knowledge to decide which tax sales to bid on? *Let's see him wriggle out of* that, Felix thought.

Felix loved to see the mighty fall. He loved to shrink big heads down to size. All those years he'd stood up in his lousy Jersey City classroom like a target in a shooting gallery, trying to impart some knowledge to a horde of adolescent Cro-Magnons; the endless hours spent individually tutoring morons and punks who couldn't write a proper English sentence if you put a gun to their heads; all the guff he'd had to take from ignorant parents looking for a free ride for their stupid rotten kids; dealing with all the overpaid, underworked administrators who had their wooden heads thrust firmly into the sand—thank God it was all behind him now.

Tomorrow night he would stand before the mayor of this township and cry, *"J'accuse!"*

"How was your day, honey?"

Chris came tooling in at quarter to ten, hunched over like a beaten dog, clutching his briefcase in both hands. Dorothy couldn't help thinking it was all an act to make her feel guilty, that in reality he had a jolly time at work and chose to be there rather than with her.

And it worked: she did feel guilty. Chris's labors paid for

30

everything. House, cars, insurance, groceries, utilities. He was making a pile.

How often had she offered to get a job, any job, so she could share the expenses and give him a chance to find a less demanding job closer to home? She'd lost count. And the answer was always the same: "Do what you want, Dot. But as long as I want a good job in the publishing industry, Manhattan is where it's at. This is my career, I can't abandon it."

As long as he stayed where he was, they wouldn't *need* any money she could make, and this took the edge off her job hunting. Maybe, though, it was time to start sending out résumés to the newspapers. Even a part-time reporter's job would help stave off the tedium.

He gave her a sexless peck on the lips, laid his briefcase on the carpeted floor, and collapsed into his easy chair.

"Chris," she couldn't help saying, "do you know what the word *workaholic* means?"

"C'mon, Dotty, lay off. I'm not a workaholic."

It was old ground, so often traveled that it sickened her to be going over it again. But she was under a compulsion and couldn't stop.

"What else would you call it?" she said.

He tilted the chair backward. "The fact is," he said, "that Bob Benton came all the way down from Maine today to discuss the final proofs of his new book, and I had to spend some time with him. That's the kind of racket it is, Dotty. Things come up."

"I'm having an affair," she blurted out.

The chair lurched forward, and he stared at her with the look of a man transfixed by a javelin. She couldn't go through with it.

"Relax, dummy, I just said that to get your attention."

"Jesus Christ, Dot!"

"You have two jobs, you know, Chris. One of them is being a husband. You work hard at it, but you only work

31

at part of it, and not even the most important part. If you went about being an editor like you go about being a husband, you wouldn't last a week."

"What do you want me to do? Junk my career? Go to work for some little diddly-shit publishing house in Secaucus for ten thousand a year?"

They went around it and around it as they always did, until they couldn't go around it one more time. Chris had a beer, watched the late news, and went to bed, where he fell asleep immediately. Dorothy went back to the living room and stared at its four walls.

Three

"Toby, I don't want you goin' in the woods no more. It's dangerous."

If he could see himself through his grandmother's eyes, Hicks reflected, he would probably see a spindly ten-year-old boy, not a grown man who'd been to the Korean border and been shot at. But that was Gramma's way, and he was used to it.

"A dead man can't hurt me, Gramma. It was probably just some poor guy who dropped dead from a heart attack or something."

"I had a bad dream about those woods last night."

"Dreams can't hurt you neither, Gramma."

"Boy, you'll know better when you get older. You're part Indian, like me. Indians don't dream like white folks. They dream true dreams."

One of Hicks' best friends in his platoon had been Bobby Gene Smith, a full-blooded Cherokee. If he'd ever suggested to Bobby Gene that he, Toby Hicks, was even a little teeny bit Indian, Bobby Gene would've busted a gut laughing.

But it was probably true. Toby didn't look part Indian, but Gramma had honey-colored skin that seemed to lighten as she got older, and high cheekbones, too. No Indian had been born in this part of the state for better than a hundred years; however, Gramma's roots went deeper than that. Exactly how deep, nobody knew. Back before the Revolutionary War, though, for sure.

"There's spots of bad ground in those woods," she said. "And there's wicked things in the swamp, they been there since before the Indians was here. Mostly they lie still, 'cause they're so old. But they ain't dead. They don't ever die. And they're dangerous. Look what happened to that poor man you found."

Toby had heard Gramma's superstitious old tales before, and didn't feel like hearing them again just now. "Gramma, there are doctors who are gonna do an autopsy on that body, and they're gonna find out exactly how he died. And it won't have anything to do with evil spirits in the woods."

Gramma said "hmf" and fell silent. She didn't believe in autopsies any more than her grandson believed in evil spirits.

For want of anything better to do, Dorothy went to the municipal swimming pool at lunchtime and sat on a towel in the sun with some of the women she knew slightly. She didn't really know anyone in Millboro well, not even her next-door neighbors. She often wondered how many times you could sip drinks and barbecue steaks with your neighbors without ever getting to know them. Poolside gossip sessions, friendly (and not-so-friendly) confrontations on the tennis courts, a chance meeting in the shopping mall—these didn't do the trick, either.

She could understand how the men might wind up isolated. They were locked into their jobs, many of them spending three or four hours a day commuting, and they didn't have the time to develop close friendships. A lot of them weren't even all that chummy with their wives and children.

But so many of these women didn't have to work. Why couldn't they get closer?

Today she sat with Eve Milsap, from two doors down the street, and two other women who were more than acquaintances and would have had to be described as friends, for want of a better word: Nancy Kruzek, one of the township's Democratic committeewomen, and Barbara Feldman, whose husband sometimes sat next to Chris on the commuter bus. They all wore two-piece swimsuits and looked good in them. The day was unseasonably warm and sunny for late spring, but still not warm enough for swimming. The point, though, was to be seen in a swimsuit. *Very silly,* Dorothy thought.

They were talking about new neighbors. There were always plenty of new neighbors in Millboro, what with business transfers, rising taxes, and an aggressive local real estate sales force.

"You should *see* the guy who moved in next to me this weekend!" Barbara Feldman said. "What a hunk! I said to Howie, just kidding, 'You'd better be mighty nice to me from now on, because you've got competition.' And you know what that smartass says to me? 'Maybe we could get together and do a little swapping!' I could've belted him!"

"Well, I've got a *doctor* on my street now," said Nancy Kruzek, as though the presence of a doctor conferred a higher status on every resident of Whittier Avenue. "He's retired, though; he won't be hanging out his shingle. Still, it's always nice to have a doctor handy—all that free medical advice."

"How do you know he's retired?" Dorothy asked. "Did he say so?"

"His wife told me. I met her just the other day and we

had a nice chat. She used to be his nurse. Unfortunately the poor man's health isn't all that good and he isn't up to active practice anymore. Nothing serious, she says, but he does have to take it easy. So he's into research now, and he's thinking of writing a book. Something scholarly, not for popular consumption. Only doctors'll read it.''

"What's his name?'' asked Eve.

"Emerson, Dr. Winslow Emerson. And his wife's name is Blanche. She looks like a nurse, but she's well-spoken.''

Barbara interrupted. "Look! Ronnie's going to dive!''

She pointed to the diving board. Mayor Ronald Leib had just climbed onto it and was psyching himself up to plunge into the April-cold water.

"I just *love* that swimsuit!'' Barbara said, leering.

Leib wore a pair of sky blue trunks that were so tight and so brief that he would have better served modesty by appearing at poolside naked. He looked more like a male stripper than a mayor, only the male strippers Dorothy had seen on TV were big men with lots of muscles. Not that Leib didn't have a good body. It just wasn't as good as he probably thought it was. From the way the other women ogled him, though, Dorothy suspected she was alone in this opinion.

He crowhopped to the end of the diving board, sprang himself into the air, and sliced into the water as smoothly as an arrow.

"If he wasn't so short,'' said Barbara, "he'd be something else!'' Lost in admiration, she shook her head.

"It isn't that he's short,'' Nancy Kruzek said. "It's that he's so head over heels in love with himself. I went to high school with him back in Brooklyn; I know. He always acted like he shat rose petals.''

"Did you ever date him?'' Eve asked.

"No.'' Something about the way she delivered the one-word answer discouraged further inquiry.

Dorothy wondered whether she ought to yield to the temptation to write a piece about the mayor's swimsuit for

Tales from the Developments. Leib might never speak to her after that, but it might be worth it.

When the township clerk called his name, Felix Frick marched to the floor microphone like a champion bullfighter entering the ring. He wore a gray suit with a black tie and carried his notes and cue cards in a manila folder.

"I have a few questions for the mayor."

Leib, nattily attired in iridescent blue with a scarlet tie, nodded down at him. "You have the floor, Mr. Frick."

"Thank you, Mr. Mayor. As you know, the township's administrative code requires our elected officials to file statements disclosing all of their financial assets and business interests. These statements are available for public examination at the clerk's office. Mr. Mayor, I have examined your statement and found it to be deficient."

Leib kept his cool, saying nothing. Felix continued.

"Mr. Mayor, the following are corporations in which you and members of your family are principals. This information is on file with the Department of State, so you know it's accurate. Before I list the corporations, I wish to point out that none of them are mentioned on your disclosure statement. Furthermore—"

He got no further. Councilman Richard Phelps, the mayor's lackey, was waving his hand and appealing to the council president.

"Mr. President, this is a political statement and it has no place at this public meeting!"

But the only Republican on the council, Neal Irving, said, "The hell it doesn't! I want to hear this!"

Council President Tom Thurlow, a Democrat who liked to make a pretense of being independent from the mayor, rapped his gavel for silence. When he finally got it, he spoke.

"I will ask our township attorney whether this is a proper

subject for discussion at a meeting of this nature. Mr. Attorney?''

The attorney, a Democratic Party hack named Wiler, had to cough up the truth.

"Mr. President, in view of the fact that Mr. Frick is alleging a violation of our administrative code, I believe he has a right to make his statement. Mayor Leib, however, has no obligation to answer him, under the circumstances.''

Thurlow pointed the gavel at Felix. "Please make it brief, Mr. Frick. We have a big agenda tonight.''

Felix basked in the glow of victory. "Thank you, Mr. Council President.'' He turned again to Leib. "Mr. Mayor, these are the corporations in which you and members of your family are the principals. Jo-El Realty. Ripco. Barsan Properties. Millboro Investments. Modco Realty. Ralcorp. Mapaco. I would like to know why none of these is listed on your disclosure statement.''

Leib paused before answering. In front of the press and a hall full of township residents, he had to know he couldn't afford to stonewall it.

"Mr. Frick,'' he said, "those are paper corporations. They are vehicles by which I conduct business from time to time. They have no real assets. That's why I didn't bother to include them in my disclosure.''

Felix suppressed a grin; Leib had obligingly given him an opportunity to expose him as a liar.

"Mr. Mayor, I have to disagree with you there. It is a matter of public record that *all* of these corporations have been active bidders—and frequently successful ones—on various tax sales throughout the township. According to public record, your corporations have acquired in excess of two hundred acres of property in Millboro via the tax-sale procedure. But none of these holdings appears on your disclosure form.''

Was that a flash of anger he thought he saw in Leib's

eyes? Felix hoped so. Nothing would hurt the mayor's position more than if he lost his temper here.

"That is where you're wrong, Mr. Frick. But it's a common error. Let me enlighten you.

"When you bid successfully in a tax sale, you do not acquire a piece of property. What you acquire is a lien against that property. The reason the property is put up for a tax sale is because the owner has been delinquent in paying his taxes. Once you acquire a lien, *you* pay the delinquent taxes. And then the owner is obligated to pay the debt to you, plus a small amount of interest. So what I have, Mr. Frick, is not two hundred acres. What I have is a lot of paper, which may or may not turn a small profit for me in the future. And there's nothing improper about that."

Leib sat back in his seat, satisfied, but Felix wasn't finished with him.

"A small correction, Mr. Mayor. You have liens on *some* of those properties. But according to the record, other properties have actually reverted to your ownership—or rather, ownership by your corporations—due to the original owners' failure to make good the debt within the time allotted by law. So in point of fact, Mr. Mayor, you *do* own property which you haven't listed in your disclosure statement."

That set the hall humming, and Phelps crying protests, and Irving calling for an immediate investigation. Thurlow hammered with his gavel and threatened to have police clear the hall unless order was restored. When the clamor finally subsided, Wiler raised his hand.

"Mr. Attorney?"

"Mr. President, in view of the fact that we are dealing with an alleged violation of our administrative code, I suggest we table discussion until such time as we have a formal hearing on the matter."

"That won't be necessary, Mr. President," Leib spoke up. "It was my feeling that I didn't have to list tax-sale certificates and paper corporations on my disclosure state-

38

ment. But if the township attorney will give me a written opinion that I do, I'll be happy to update the disclosure statement to include all this information. The only reason it isn't in there now is because I simply didn't think it was required. So I'd like Mr. Wiler to study the ordinance and let me know exactly what *is* required."

Wiler said, "I'll be happy to do that, Mr. Mayor."

"All right, then—"

"Mr. President!" Councilman Irving fairly screamed. "For Pete's sake, we're talking about a major problem here! You can't close the discussion yet. The mayor is in flagrant conflict of interest here!"

All the councilmen started gabbling at once, and Thurlow rapped angrily and in vain for order, and the people among the audience who had political axes to grind—and that was most of them—ground them noisily.

Satisfied, Felix turned from the microphone and walked slowly out to the lobby. He knew the reporters would follow him, and he was looking forward to answering their questions.

On his police chief's salary, Van Wyck never could have bought the home in which he lived. But the house had been in his family for three generations, and he paid nothing on it but the taxes. It nestled comfortably on a shady one-and-a-half-acre lot, all that was left of the farm that had been sold off by Ed's father, and by Ed himself, piece by piece. He'd sold the least few acres to raise the money for a settlement that freed him from any further claims by his ex-wife, Helen.

He was sipping beer and watching the tail end of a Mets game when the call came from the medical examiner's office.

"Chief Van Wyck? This is Dr. Schneider, I'm the deputy medical examiner. They gave me your home number at police headquarters. Normally I wouldn't bother you until

39

tomorrow, but we've completed the autopsy on your John Doe, and—well, frankly, we feel we know less now than we did before the autopsy.''

"He's still John Doe?'' Van Wyck asked. "He had no identification on him?''

"No wallet, no papers. Bupkiss,'' the assistant coroner said. "We hope we can find out who he is eventually, but unless his fingerprints or dental records are already on the crime computers, it could take a while. Unless you've got something for us?''

"Afraid not. We're working on it. Do you have a cause of death?''

"No.''

"No?''

"N-O. Looks like we'll need some outside help with this one.''

"What's the problem?''

"The problem is that we haven't been able to find anything,'' the pathologist said. "The man was in his early thirties, fit and healthy. Healthy as a horse. If some disease killed him, we haven't been able to identify it. Ditto for drugs and poisons. Oh, we picked up some traces of cocaine, but only traces. We're sure he wasn't high when he died. There are still a lot of tests to be run, but for the time being we've ruled out all the common toxins.''

"But he was a cocaine user?''

"A casual user. Believe me, Chief, he didn't die of a drug overdose.''

"No external injuries?''

The doctor sighed. "This is where it starts to get weird.''

"How weird?'' Van Wyck asked.

"Very. You see, we found a small but fairly deep cut on the inside of his left wrist, deep enough to nick the vein. It was made with a sharp instrument, probably a scalpel. Some bleeding occurred, but nowheres near enough to cause death.''

40

Van Wyck had a feeling he was about to hear something bizarre.

"We also found some premortem bruises on the arms," Schneider said, "which indicate that the deceased was forcibly restrained when this small wound was inflicted. But those were the only injuries. We found no injuries that could have caused this guy's death."

"You're confusing me, Doctor," Van Wyck said.

"Good, that makes two of us."

"You're telling me that somebody held him down and cut his wrist, but didn't seriously hurt him."

"That's right."

"And how long ago did it happen? Can you say how long the man was dead before we found the body?"

"I wish I could," said Schneider, "but that's where this damned thing gets *really* confusing!"

"It looked to me like he'd been lying around for at least a week," Van Wyck said. "He looked pretty far gone. I'm no expert on decomposition, but that wasn't a fresh corpse we sent you."

"I know. But the contents of its stomach was fresh."

Van Wyck couldn't answer.

"His last meal was a tuna fish sandwich," Schneider added.

"You're losing me, Doctor."

"I'm lost, too, Chief. See, when a person dies, the body starts to decompose. The stomach contents decomposes, too. Some digestion continues after death, due to stomach acids which remain chemically active; but that doesn't go on for long. Normally, if the corpse has decomposed, the stomach contents has decomposed, too. But not in this case. In fact, the body seems to have had about a week's head start on that tuna sandwich. So either John Doe had a sandwich after he'd been dead for several days, or something happened that we flat out don't understand."

Van Wyck had had a tuna sandwich for lunch that day,

and the discussion was beginning to make him feel vaguely queasy. The pathologist hit him with a few more conundrums.

"Did you notice, Chief, that the man's clothes were in excellent condition? Hardly what you'd expect on a dead body that had been exposed in the woods for any length of time. And there was hardly any damage from animals and insects."

"Couldn't that mean that the body was kept somewhere else for a while, and then dumped in the woods?" asked Van Wyck.

"That may well be. Only in this case we can't be sure of anything."

They talked a little while longer without reaching any conclusions. Van Wyck promised to put more men on the case, but he had a feeling that it wouldn't do any good.

He was up late that night and dreamed troubled dreams that he couldn't remember after his alarm went off and woke him in the morning.

Four

Felix never got a chance to read all about it. The reporters started jangling his phone before his morning paper was delivered.

They all wanted to get his reaction to the council's decision to hold a hearing on the mayor's alleged improprieties, but not to open the hearing to the public. They'd decided this among themselves, after the meeting was formally adjourned and Felix had gone home.

"How can they do that?" Felix wondered. "Isn't that a violation of the Sunshine Act?"

But the state's Open Public Meetings Act was ultimately unenforceable, Jerry Carey of the *Asbury Park Press* reminded him. "Anyway," the reporter added, "they'll just get their tame attorney to write them up an opinion that they can do it that way."

"Have they actually scheduled the hearing?" asked Felix.

"No, not yet. Wiler has to do some paperwork. I suppose he has to find some legal basis for whatever they want to do."

Felix knew when he was being baited to make a dramatic public statement, but he certainly didn't mind.

"That's the trouble with allowing the laws to be written by lawyers," he said. "I'm sure if they wanted to declare Ron Leib the Sultan of Millboro, their attorney could give them a written opinion justifying it in law. Just as I'm sure, now, that they'll twist the administrative code around to say Leib did nothing wrong. The mayor set up corporations to buy land in this township, and there wasn't a hint of it on his disclosure form. Nobody knew he was doing it. If that's honest, the council must be speaking a different language from the rest of us."

He spent the morning dispensing equally quotable quotes to his friends from the *Register,* the *News Tribune,* and the *Independent.* Even the *Star-Ledger,* from all the way up in Newark, wanted a piece of this story. It was immensely gratifying. Leib's stooges on the council might be able to save him from the legal consequences of his slippery doings, but the newspapers would see that he incurred the full political consequences.

And the next time the watchdog barked, they'd listen.

The doorbell rang at noon, just as Felix was making himself sardine sandwiches for lunch. When he answered the door, he wasn't altogether surprised to find the deputy mayor, Jim Haskell, on his threshold.

Haskell stood six feet tall, and if he weighed a hundred

and twenty pounds dripping wet, it was five pounds more than Felix gave him credit for. His lavishly curly dark hair and beard made him look slightly top-heavy. As the mayor's gofer, and the most junior partner in the mayor's law firm, he commanded slightly more respect than a beggar.

"Hi, Mr. Frick," he said in his boyish way, which Felix didn't find at all ingratiating. "May I come in? I'd like to talk with you."

He fidgeted and looked about as anxious to have this talk as he was to swim the Bering Strait. Felix therefore let him in.

"I was about to have my lunch," Felix said. "I'd ask you to join me, but I'm afraid I have none to spare. We retired schoolteachers have to live according to a strict budget."

"It's okay, I'm not hungry."

Felix took Haskell to the kitchen. He sat at the table while Felix stood over the counter, putting the finishing touches on his sandwiches.

"What can I do for you, Mr. Deputy Mayor?"

"Well, I'm just here to ask you a simple question, Mr. Frick . . . on behalf of Mayor Leib and Council President Thurlow."

"They didn't have any ribbon-cuttings for you to go to today, huh?" Felix said. Haskell's face darkened slightly. The only time you ever saw that face in the papers was when its picture was taken at some public function that the mayor thought too trivial to attend himself. Haskell was the boy they sent to represent the regime at the Junior Woman's Club bridal fashion show or the opening of a new poodle-grooming parlor. It lent little to his prestige.

He ignored Felix's dig and continued, probably trying to wrap up the business in a hurry.

"As you may know, Mr. Frick, the council has decided to hold a hearing on Mayor Leib's alleged violation of the administrative code. Our attorney has advised us not to open

44

this hearing to the public, for reasons which we think are obvious. It'd just turn into a political occasion. Unfortunately, some will see this as a kind of cover-up."

Felix closed his sandwich, poured himself a glass of skim milk, and joined Haskell at the table. "If I may be candid, Mr. Deputy Mayor, it's bound to look like the mayor and council have something to hide. But I'm sure Councilman Irving won't let the proceedings stay under wraps for long—unless they make a point of scheduling the hearing for some night when he has to be out of town on business."

Haskell sighed. Neal Irving may have had the IQ of a bulldog, but he also had the tenacity to go with it. As the solitary voice of opposition on the governing body, he never got a chance to do much more than cry "Foul!" But he cried it loud and long.

"Mr. Frick, nobody wants to be accused of trying to stage a cover-up. To avoid giving any appearance of that, both the council president and the mayor would appreciate it if you attended the hearing, too. Consider this a formal invitation."

Felix was pleased, but not so pleased that he couldn't see Leib's fine hand at work.

They'd want him at the hearing in any event, so they could question him about the research he'd done into the mayor's corporate holdings. He'd also be a valuable witness to use if they had to deny a cover-up. Whatever they did to get Leib off the hook, as long as they could whip up some legalistic mumbo jumbo to back it up, Felix wouldn't be able to prevent it. They wanted him for window dressing, pure and simple.

But the hook was baited irresistibly. The fact that he was important enough to be invited to a closed hearing would add greatly to his credibility. He knew there were those who thought of him as a babbling old crank. Some of them were newspaper reporters. *Well, old cranks don't get invited to closed-door council meetings,* he thought.

45

Felix grinned at Haskell. "You tell your bosses," he said, "that I wouldn't miss it for the world."

Dorothy had hoped to run into Ron Leib at the pool, but he didn't show up today. It was not surprising, after last night's fun and games.

Chris had worked late again, so Dorothy had gone to the council meeting and been flabbergasted when that old fart Frick set off his bomb. She remembered Felix from one of the municipal budget hearings, back in February, when he hogged the mike for ninety minutes grilling officials on line items as small as twenty-five cents. ("Madame Business Administrator, is it really necessary to pay a quarter apiece for ordinary lead pencils? I *know* you can get them cheaper than that!") *Here,* she thought at the time, *is the crank to end all cranks.* The officials and the reporters—they had no choice but to stick it out for the entire meeting—were fuming dangerously by the time Mr. Frick was done with his inquisition. Watching their faces was the only thing that made it endurable.

And so she was astonished when Felix actually came out with something of importance. It only took her a second to grasp the implication of what he was saying. The mayor had not only put himself in a position where he could use his inside knowledge of the township's government to turn a profit; it was also a position where the chance to turn a profit might influence his decisions as a municipal official. *Say, fellas, what say we open up the zoning over here (where my dummy corporation just happens to own a few parcels of land that I can make a killing on, selling them off after we make the area attractive to developers)?* Since he was hiding behind his paper companies, no one would know what Leib was up to.

Well, she had to hand it to Frick for sniffing that one out. She wanted to talk to him, maybe write him up in a special issue of *Tales from the Developments.* But she was more immediately interested in seeing how the mayor would wriggle out of the trap.

She went to the pool with Nancy Kruzek, the only one of her acquaintances who was interested in talking politics for any length of time. As a Democratic committeewoman, Nancy must have already felt some of the repercussions from last night.

"You bet your ass there'll be repercussions," Nancy said, as they lounged on towels to improve their tans. "If Ron turns out to be an embarrassment to the party, we'll have to dump him in a hurry."

"What if he doesn't want to be dumped?" asked Dorothy.

"Then it's tough noogies for him. Listen, Dot, you're not going to quote me in that little paper of yours, are you?"

"That would be crossing the border into journalism, heaven forbid. You know I'd never quote any of my friends, Nance. But I may want to write up Mr. Frick. Do you know him?"

"He's my next door neighbor. I like him as a neighbor, but in public life he's nothing but a nosy old prick. He makes a big thing about being independent from politics, but that's so he can sit on the sidelines and take potshots without having to commit himself to anything positive."

"I was hoping the mayor'd be here today," Dorothy said. "I'd really like to get his reaction to all this."

"You couldn't print it."

"Of course, it isn't an election year. There's time for this to blow over. Look what happened when it came out that he was having that affair with Kathy Luebke. You'd think it'd be awful hard to elect a mayor whose wife ran out on him and then divorced him, but Ron won pretty easily."

"That's because the Republicans are assholes," Nancy said, "and they nominated the biggest asshole they could find to run against him. Besides, people can sort of look the other way if a man like Ron likes to run around with

47

women. It sort of fits with his personality. But they won't be so understanding if they think he'll sell out to the developers so he can line his pockets."

That was for damn sure, Dorothy thought. Having staked their claims to the township, the new arrivals didn't want to see any more new arrivals. Millboro was currently defending several lawsuits brought by developers who wanted to build apartments. It seemed like a hopeless battle; the State Supreme Court, after all, had long ago ruled that every municipality had to allow a certain percentage of every type of housing, including apartments. But having gained the suburban sanctuary of Millboro, the fugitives from the dying cities wanted to pull up the gangplank. The litigation dragged on like the Civil War after Gettysburg.

And Leib had ridden to reelection as the hero of the obstructionist crusade.

Five

As it turned out, it wasn't really so difficult to identify the body after all.

Working from the corpse, a police artist managed a pretty realistic portrait of what the man must have looked like when he was alive. The picture was published in all the newspapers and posted in public places, along with a description of the clothes found on the body. Within twenty-four hours of the dead man's return to his refrigerated drawer in the county morgue, the relevant law enforcement personnel knew his name.

Arthur George Volden, thirty-three. Last seen alive in a bar on Route 35, just three days before Toby Hicks and his dog found him dead in a bed of ferns in the woods near Dutchman's Bog.

Van Wyck studied the reports that the county had passed on to him and watched the case get hairier with every word he read.

First there was the problem of what Arthur Volden's remains were doing in Millboro in the first place.

The man's address was a cheap apartment way up in the Port, a dozen miles away from Millboro. He'd had lots of buddies but no close friends, and he'd moved around quite a bit: he'd only been at his last address since January. He had worked on a loading dock in Woodbridge. He had spent most of his spare time at various bars and most of his money on pot and pills. No one had bothered to report him missing because he had a habit of dropping out of sight from time to time. It had cost him several jobs. He'd also been known to skip out on his rent. So it had come as a shock to his associates to see his picture in the paper coupled with an announcement of his death.

"There's no connection with Millboro," Van Wyck remarked to Musante. "None at all."

"Whoever iced him, dumped him on us," Musante said.

Van Wyck hoped that would turn out to be true. As soon as it did, the Millboro Police would play a minimal role in the investigation.

Musante scanned his copy of the report. "It says here," he said, "that Mr. Volden was last seen leaving a place called The Playpen, a singles bar on Route 35 in Old Bridge. He was trying to pick up a chick and not having any luck. I think they're gonna find he went to another bar after that, probably several bars. Maybe he finally got together with one of our faithful Millboro taxpayers."

"Whoever he met," Van Wyck said, "killed him and dumped him in the woods—where the body did a week's worth of rotting in three days."

Musante added gloomily, "And never mind that they

can't even say *how* he was killed, let alone who did it. They're still running tests, huh?''

"Yeah. Testing for every toxin they have a test for—which is tough, because some toxins dissolve in the body without leaving a trace, given enough time. Something they might be able to find today, they won't be able to find tomorrow.''

"This one's starting to look like one of those cases that just won't be solved," the sergeant said. "Hell, if they don't have the cause of death by now, they'll never get it. Mark my words.''

On his last night alive, Arthur George Volden had visited a bar called Close Encounters. The place was the pits, and Arthur George would never have gone there if he hadn't come up dry everywhere else.

He hadn't liked it, because it attracted an older crowd, and he hadn't been ready yet to lump himself in with the old codgers, not by a long shot. He liked his pussy young and sweet. The younger, the better. He preferred a place like Brother Jonathan's, where they looked the other way when underage chicks came in and ordered drinks. Here at Close Encounters everyone was over thirty. It made him feel like he was getting old, even though he was thirty-three himself.

But it had been Close Encounters or go to bed hungry. He'd hit all the other bars that night, and the chicks had treated him like a leper. Sometimes that was just the way it went. He'd almost connected with a nice little blonde at The Playpen, but then she had seen Pete Soanes and she had forgotten all about Arthur George Volden. He had gotten pissed off when Pete winked at him, and had stormed out alone.

The old bags at Close Encounters wouldn't be so choosy. He only came here when he was super hard up, and so far he'd never had to leave empty-handed. All he had to do was find a table and sit there with his shirt unbuttoned halfway down his chest. The old broads would practically throw themselves at him.

Tonight was no exception. He wasn't halfway through his first beer when the first cow plumped herself down at his table.

"You're a handsome young man," she said, smiling at him boldly. "How would you like to earn a hundred dollars?"

He could use a hundred bucks, but he wasn't sure he could use it that badly. He stared at the woman. She had to be fifty, at least: a real fossil. Hair going gray, thirty pounds overweight, wrinkles around the eyes, glasses. No wonder she had to offer money.

Still, a hundred bucks was a hundred bucks. One night with this old bat had to be better than two eight-hour days of loading and unloading trucks. What the hell, it wasn't like she was actually decrepit.

"What have you got in mind?" asked Arthur George.

"My husband is away on business, and I'm getting a little lonely." She smiled at him, as bold as brass. "You know perfectly well what I have in mind."

Arthur smiled back. "I guess I do."

"How about it, then? I feel like I've been here for hours. Let's go home."

Arthur made his decision. When it came right down to it, he needed the money.

Because of nosy neighbors, they had to go through a lot of rigmarole: leaving his car way the hell out in the parking lot at the Woodbridge Center shopping mall and driving back to Millboro in her car. She'd take him back to Woodbridge in the morning. Arthur didn't feel too good about leaving his car like that, but the lady insisted and he wanted his hundred, so he humored her. Anyway, his car wasn't worth a hundred.

He never asked her name, she never asked his: it was that kind of arrangement and it suited him just fine. Not that he would've told her his name. He wouldn't want her getting a thing for him and trying to see him again. By keeping it anonymous, they made sure it'd be a one-time-only deal.

She lived in an expensive, fancy house, but before he could begin to admire it, her husband stepped out from behind the door and grabbed him by the wrist.

Arthur turned and let him have it right in the jaw; but other than making his hand sore, it accomplished nothing. The old man didn't even flinch.

Then he tried to jerk himself loose, but he might as well have been handcuffed to the bars of a jail cell.

"Look, mister, I don't want no trouble. You just let me go and I'll book on out of here and you'll never see me again. Honest to God, I didn't know she was married."

The old man only grinned at him, and Arthur George was suddenly weak in the knees and hurting in the guts. Looking into the old man's eyes was like looking at the lids of two coffins torn from muddy old graves to be opened by ghouls. The grip on his wrist was as cold as a manacle.

Something snapped in Arthur's mind and he attacked again. He hammered on the old man's face and chest and kept it up until all his strength was gone. Unhurt, the old man seized his other wrist and began to pull him across the slate floor of the foyer. When he tried to resist by falling down, the old man yanked him to his feet with a jerk that nearly tore his arms from their sockets.

Arthur whimpered and threw his head back and forth, pleading to be let go, but the old man ignored him. His eyes were so full of tears that he could hardly see. He was dragged bruisingly down a short flight of stairs and heard a door slam shut behind him.

Now the broad from Close Encounters was with them, not saying a word, not smiling anymore. The old man held one of Arthur's arms away from his body. The woman took a sharp blade of some kind and made an incision in the wrist.

The cut was painless, but when he saw the blood he writhed and jerked and screamed. The old man held him like a straitjacket.

"You might as well relax," the old man said. "I'm not going to hurt you, but if you keep struggling like this, you'll probably hurt yourself."

Arthur stopped fighting. His brain had turned into a handful of useless mush. It couldn't help him for the time being. There was no way out of this.

He groaned when the old man bent over and began to suck the blood from his wrist. It made him faint and dizzy. He tried to struggle some more, but all he could manage was a feeble twitch. After another second or two, he passed out.

He suffered through terrible dreams from which he could not wake—visions of his soul as a white, tenuous thing, like a form shaped by smoke, being drawn out through his navel, through the wound on his wrist, through the top of his head. Out of his body and into black nothingness, sped on its way by indescribable pain. The dreams were endless, timeless, infinitely repeated; but the pain never dulled through repetition.

And then a new pain burned the dreams away, a pain that was like a heavy sheet of red-hot iron being pressed down on his face, shriveling the brain within the skull.

At the same time, a nameless compulsion came over him, an urgency that could not be expressed in words. He had no words for anything. He knew nothing. He was like a whale being driven ashore, to his death, by some irresistible, indefinable command that overrode his terror of the shallow water, of the hard, hot sands that would serve as the anvil to gravity's hammer as it smashed his ribs and smote the breath from his lungs. He tried to obey the compulsion; but whether he actually succeeded in getting up and stumbling forward a little way, or only dreamed he walked, he couldn't know.

When he opened his eyes, the light of the sun was like flaming lances thrust into his skull.

His skin burned. His brain could generate no commands to give his muscles. He lay where he was and burned, understanding none of it, absorbed by a need that he lacked the strength to fulfill and the knowledge to define.

It could not be said that death claimed him, because he had ceased to live twelve hours ago.

II. POLITICS

One

Van Wyck didn't have to go out to Alabama Road to interview Toby Hicks again, but he wanted to.

He felt more at home there—a white cop in a black neighborhood that was poor enough and black enough to be called a ghetto—than he felt among the white people in the affluent developments. For all its poverty, Alabama Road was an integral part of the township. It had history, tradition, memories. It wasn't so easy, anymore, to find people who'd been born and raised in Millboro. The natives were selling their farms, they were being driven out by rising taxes. But the people on Alabama Road had nothing left to sell, and so they stayed. They had their church and they had their consciences; and if you didn't count the public drinking by some of the jobless men, and the sporadic, almost listless vandalism done to some of the derelict buildings in the neighborhood, they had the lowest crime rate in the county.

Van Wyck had his reasons for wanting to remain involved in the Volden case.

Whatever had happened to Arthur George Volden, his body had turned up in Millboro Township; and Van Wyck suspected it had been put there for a reason. Its condition strongly argued that Volden hadn't died in the middle of

Dutchman's Bog, but had been brought there after death and found almost immediately by Toby Hicks' dog. Someone had gone to a lot of trouble to drag that corpse into the woods—not to mention the risk of being seen doing it. And it hadn't been an effort to conceal the body. The body hadn't been concealed at all. Sooner or later someone was bound to find it. So whoever had put it there, maybe, had meant it to be found in that particular spot. Why?

Van Wyck wondered whether the proximity of the black neighborhood had had anything to do with it.

People who didn't know any better—and that meant most people—were already latching onto the idea that Volden had been killed close to the spot where his body was found. That he had come to Alabama Road and been murdered by some person living in the neighborhood. His wallet had been missing. Most of the people here were poor. The unspoken assumption was that black people habitually killed white people for their money. Didn't it happen every day in the big cities? No reason it couldn't happen here.

There were a lot of white people who'd fled to Millboro because they'd felt that their old neighborhoods in the cities weren't safe anymore. Most of them would have described themselves as liberals, politically. They observed Martin Luther King's birthday as a holiday and voted for liberal politicians. But when they saw a black face up close, they were afraid of being mugged. And they were the people who held most of the power in the township.

Well, now they had a white man found dead in the black section of their own town, their refuge from the black violence of New York and urban Jersey, and it scared them. They had no contact with Alabama Road. Up until the discovery of Volden's body, a lot of them hadn't even known that Millboro had a poor black neighborhood. They knew nothing about the people living in that neighborhood: only that they were black, and therefore to be feared.

Unless the Volden case was solved convincingly, and

soon, Van Wyck didn't like to think about what it might do to his township.

He sat on the front porch with Toby and his grandmother, Emma Plews, who teetered placidly in her rocking chair.

"Honest, Chief," Hicks was saying, "I never heard of the guy and I never saw him here. You ask around, you'll hear the same thing. Nobody knew him. He wasn't from around here."

"Ain't so many white folks droppin' in on this part of town," the grandmother said, "that we can't keep track of 'em. No offense, Mr. Van Wyck. But the whites mostly stay away."

"Especially since I found that body," Hicks added. His mouth hardened as he spoke. "Except for the cops, nobody's seen a white face around here since that story hit the papers. Racist assholes."

"Toby, you watch your mouth. Your momma didn't bring you up to talk like that."

"It's true, though, Gramma. They find a dead white man they figure a black man must've killed him. That's what they're saying. You ask Chief Van Wyck, Gramma."

"I can't help what ignorant people think," Van Wyck said. "They're city people, their minds are set a certain way. They don't know anything about the people who live in this neighborhood. But I still have to deal with them."

"They pay your salary," Hicks said.

"Mr. Hicks, the township pays my salary. Alabama Road is part of this township. I work for Alabama Road as much as for Royal Oaks or Triangle Mountain."

"We know it, Mr. Van Wyck," Mrs. Plews said. "You and your men are always welcome here. Don't you mind Toby, he's just upset."

"I'm upset, too. That's why I'm here."

57

"Ain't we lucky we got such *liberal* policemans?" Hicks said, laying it on thick. Van Wyck decided not to argue with him.

"That area of the woods, Mr. Hicks, where you found the body—is it really all that isolated? If you hadn't come along, would somebody else have been likely to find it?"

"I don't know. I guess so. Kids are always playing in the woods. I suppose somebody would've found it pretty soon."

"Kids oughtn't to go in there," the grandmother said.

"Why not, Mrs. Plews?"

"There's evil in that woods."

"Gramma!"

"Hush up, Toby. If you can't mind your manners, you might as well go for a walk."

"What kind of evil, Mrs. Plews? What do you mean?"

She looked across the street, beyond the houses on the other side, to the trees. Whatever she saw there was hidden from Van Wyck.

"The Indians knew about it," she said slowly. "They knew where all the bad spots was, and steered clear of 'em. But there ain't no more Indians now, and nobody can remember where the evil was. Indians didn't leave no maps behind.

"But there's places in that swamp where you can step on a patch of soft ground and sink right down to the bottom of the world. And there's places where you can step on hard ground and it'll suck the life out of you. I know of folks who came out of the woods and just laid down and died, and not a thing anyone could do for 'em. And they was strong and healthy.

"There's other places where you can stand still and listen, and you won't hear a bird sing or a cricket chirp, and no wind rustlin' in the leaves. And if you stand there and listen hard, you can hear the voices whisperin'. The Indians didn't know what the voices were, or what they were sayin'. Only that the whispers got inside your head and made you crazy from then on. And maybe they can drive a good man to drink and fornication, or even murder. Like Deacon Phillips, when I was a little girl. The night he come out of the woods, he got himself roaring drunk and he choked his wife to death with his own two hands. Took three or four strong men to pull him off her. You look back in some old newspapers, you'll see it happened just the way I tell it.

"Nobody ought to walk around them woods, Mr. Van Wyck. There's a danger in 'em. Folks don't believe in it no more, but that don't mean it ain't true."

The woman had lived in the shadow of those woods for all her long life, Van Wyck knew, and her roots went deeper than his. She told stories that were old when the British came marching up from Trenton. She claimed to be part Indian, and she looked it. More than one family in her neighborhood carried Indian blood, and they preserved traditions that were older than Columbus.

Van Wyck didn't believe in evil spirits and haunted spots of bogland. All the same, he wouldn't have been happy to take a hike through the woods just now. His own roots in Millboro went deep enough to give him pause. There had still been some Indians living here when his own people came down from the Hudson valley during the confusing interregnum between Yorktown and the ratification of the Constitution. The Van Wyck family had its share of what Ed's grandpa used to call "spooky-spookies." Like the legend of the strange tracks, like those of an elephant-size crow, that turned up on old Cornelius Van Wyck's front yard one snowy morning . . .

And there was the fact that the contents of Arthur Volden's stomach had been so much fresher than the rest of him. A fresh tuna sandwich in the belly of a rotting corpse. Was that any worse than haunted swamps and monster birds?

* * *

Hicks caught up to him as he was about to swing himself back into his car.

"Hold on, Chief—got a minute?"

Van Wyck hefted his keys in his hand. "What is it, Mr. Hicks?"

"I wanted to . . . well, I want to apologize. I gave you a lot of shit, and I'm sorry. It wasn't right."

"I won't pretend I wasn't offended. But I accept your apology. No hard feelings."

They were separated by the front of Van Wyck's car. He could have used an official car, but he saved that for his visits to residents who wanted to see their tax dollars at work. It was his own car, a gracefully aging Ford Escort, that was parked here. Hicks walked around it so he could stand in front of him.

"You were polite to my gramma while she was telling those old stories of hers," the younger man said, "and I appreciate it. But I don't want you to think she's just a superstitious old lady, even if she does like to spin a yarn or two."

"I don't think she was spinning yarns, Mr. Hicks. I don't think she was trying to pull my leg. And I wasn't just trying to be polite. Your grandmother knows things that we'll never know."

Hicks grinned. "Chief, I *know* you didn't believe those stories!"

Van Wyck made a decision that he'd been tempted to make for the last hour or more.

"Mr. Hicks, you saw the body. You remember what kind of shape it was in."

"Shit, man, I ain't likely to forget it!"

"What if I told you that the dead man's stomach contained almost perfectly fresh food? Food that couldn't have been in him for more than twenty-four hours."

"I'd say you were bullshittin' me," Hicks answered. Van

Wyck let the silence hang for a moment. Hicks looked him in the eye, and then looked away and shook his head.

"C'mon, man, that can't be right!"

"It's true, though. At least as far as the medical examiner can say. They ran all kinds of tests in their lab to back it up."

"I didn't see anything about it in the papers."

"It hasn't been in the papers," Van Wyck said. "It isn't going to be. We're all supposed to keep quiet about it."

"Then how come you're telling me?"

"Because you live here. People might say things to you that they wouldn't say to me. You might see something I would miss. You're an intelligent man, Mr. Hicks. You've been in the army, you've seen a lot more of the world than most. I could use your help."

"How much are they paying informers these days?"

"I'm not asking you to be an informer."

"Gee, it sure sounds like it."

Van Wyck could have grabbed him by the shirt and shaken him until his teeth rattled, but that wouldn't have been productive.

"Mr. Hicks, I'm not offering you any money. I'm not asking you to spy on your friends. I'm just trying to find out whether anything *else* is going on in the goddamn woods. If there is, the people in this neighborhood have the best chance to find out about it. And I told you about Mr. Volden's stomach contents so you could see what I'm up against. I don't know what we have to deal with here, but I know for damn sure that it's something they don't teach you at the police academy."

Hicks leaned against the fender and thought it over.

"Let me get this straight, Chief. You're saying that the food they found in that stiff's stomach was *fresh?*"

"That's right."

"And all you want is for me to let you know if I see or hear anything peculiar going on in the woods around here?"

"Right."

Hicks folded his arms, looked down at his shoe tops, and shook his head. "I guess Gramma's stories didn't sound so strange to you, after all," he said. He looked up at the trees. "What was it they found in the guy's stomach, anyway?"

"A sandwich," said Van Wyck. "Tuna on rye, with to-mato and mayonnaise."

"Jesus!" said Hicks, as his own stomach began to do a roll.

Two

The kid was trying to look like a tough inner-city punk, but his clothes were too new and too clean, his cheeks too plump with good feeding, to be convincing.

Not that Sergeant Polly, the lucky SOB chosen by fate to be Millboro Township's juvenile officer, was any kind of expert on inner-city toughs. He was a conscientious juvenile officer, and he kept up-to-date with all the literature, attended all the conferences. He read and was told about what went on in the big city, and what he read and heard appalled him. When you came right down to it, he'd actually be *afraid* of some of those kids they had to deal with in the Bronx, South Philly, or Newark. Those kids were animals. They'd fuckin' kill you.

But Sergeant Dave Polly was safe in the suburbs, and he reminded himself of that whenever he caught himself hating his job.

Sergeant Polly was the first fork in a road that often led to juvenile court, the county detention home, and prison. If he could, he would divert the young pilgrims onto the path that led back to home, family, and sanity. Much of the time it ws up to him to decide whether an offender should be processed into the juvenile justice system or sent back to his parents with a stern warning. And he couldn't flip a coin. If too many of the kids he sent home went on to get into worse trouble, he could wind up losing his job. And if he sent too many of the little darlings down to Freehold, the good people of Millboro Township would beat a path to his door, break it down, drag him out, and lynch him. Occupying such a delicate position, Sergeant Polly found life very stimulating.

Now he sat in his office with Nicholas Bernstein, Jr., fifteen, the son of a prosperous stockbroker and a Democratic executive committeewoman from Triangle Mountain. Junior had been pulled in for spray-painting swastikas and upside-down crosses on the rear wall of the Millboro A&P. He described himself as a graffiti artist.

Polly had already been to the high school to discuss the case with some of Nicky's teachers and the school staff. The picture they'd painted of the boy was anything but encouraging: a nasty little shit who bullied the straight kids, was failing most of his classes, was universally suspected of petty theft and vandalism, and ran with a bunch who claimed to be devil worshipers. A few phone calls to some of the Bernsteins' neighbors did nothing to lighten the picture.

"What're we going to do with you, Nick?" he said, to open the conversation.

"Why ask me? You've already made up your fuckin' mind," said Nicky.

The old juvenile officer, Sergeant Moorehead, would have dropped the hammer on Nicky right then and there; but Polly didn't want to be hasty. He had, after all, a bachelor's degree in sociology. Patiently, he employed a favorite tactic that had occasionally worked for him in the past

"Y'know, kid, you aren't going to be fifteen years old forever. Whether you like it or not, you're going to have to

63

find a way of getting through the next fifty or sixty years. Have you ever thought about that?''

"I don't know.''

"Believe it or not, and you'd better believe it, some of the things you do now are going to determine what your life will be like for the next sixty years. The jails, the hospitals, and the shelters are full of old men—sick, toothless, half-blind old men, some of them as crazy as bedbugs— who've been paying all their lives for things they did—or didn't get around to doing—when they were kids like you. They're too old to turn over a new leaf. They don't know how. You want to be a sick old man who doesn't have two dimes to rub together, Nick?''

"Balls.''

They never believed you at first. You had to work on them. Polly continued with his work.

"Maybe it's too hard to see that far down the road. Okay, let me put it this way. In five years you'll be twenty. That's not so far off. Where do you think you're going to be at twenty, Nick? What kind of life do you think you'll have five years from now?''

"I don't know.''

"Think about it. I want to know.''

If the kid has any brains at all, Polly thought, *he'll know I'm the one who can save him a trip to court and maybe a few long years on probation. He can cooperate now and save himself a lot of hassle later.*

Apparently Nick Jr. was bright enough to come to the same conclusion, for he finally muttered something about going to college. Polly pounced on it.

"You? College? Don't make me laugh! With the kind of grades you've been getting so far, you'll be lucky if you make it through high school.''

"*Everybody* makes it through high school, man!'' said Nicky.

"Only because they want to get kids like you off their

64

hands with a minimum of fuss,'' said Polly. ''They'll let you graduate, maybe, just to get rid of you. But any college you apply to, they'll know all about that. They'll only take you if your father is willing to pay plenty. Which he might do—to get you out of his hair, and in hopes that a miracle will happen and you'll somehow straighten out while you're in college. But it'll cost him a lot. Do you think he'll stick it out for the whole four years if you keep embarrassing him by getting busted?''

''What else is he gonna do?''

''Would you shell out ten or fifteen grand a year for some wise-mouth kid who was nothing but a pain in the ass for you?''

''My old man doesn't even notice. I could be Hitler, he'd never know the difference.''

Polly recognized the element of truth that lay at the core of the boy's statement. It was a common motif. The trick was to get the juvenile to take charge of his own life. It was a big, big trick.

''What about your mother, Nick? Does she notice?''

''Are you kiddin'? All she cares about is *politics.*''

''She's a Democratic committeewoman, I understand.''

''Yeah. Big deal.''

''I wonder what the other people on the committee will think when they hear you were pulled in for spraying nice big swastikas all over the A & P.''

The boy grinned and said, ''That's her problem!''

''It won't go over too big, will it?''

''Hell no, I guess not.''

''What about your father? When the men he works with brag about their sons, and their good grades, and the good colleges they'll be going to, how do you think he'll feel?''

''He'll just tell 'em a bunch of lies about how good I'm doing, too.''

''But he'll know they're lies.''

''Fuck him.''

"So by flunking school and getting caught doing vandalism, you really stuck it to your mom and dad, didn't you? Made them look like a couple of jerks who don't know how to raise their own kid. Really showed 'em up."

Nick liked the idea, liked it a lot. "Yeah," he said. "I guess I did."

Polly shook his head. "You're no smarter than the other kids who wind up here, Nick. You're just another dumb sucker."

The boy stared at him, not getting it. Polly explained.

"Suppose you keep on messing up, Nick. Maybe you can't go to college, after all; or you do go, but you can't finish, or else you get a degree that doesn't mean anything. Maybe instead of college you wind up in a juvenile program. Maybe even jail. And you turn out to be just another poor, sick, sorry old geezer. Your mom and dad won't like it, not having anything to brag about as far as you're concerned; but the day you turn eighteen, they're off the hook. *You* do the time in jail, Nick. *You* get hassled by the cops. *You* freeze your butt off in the winter. *You* can't afford a doctor when you get sick. Not Mom. Not Dad. Do you hear what I'm saying? Mom and Dad don't pay the price. You do. You're the fall guy. You're the sucker. It's *your* life that turns into a ball of shit, not theirs."

Polly was inwardly congratulating himself for making the point so effectively when Nick surprised him by laughing in his face.

"You're so full of it, man, I almost feel sorry for you! Shit, man, none of that stuff's gonna happen to me! I got Satan."

There was nothing in the sociology texts about kids who had Satan in their corner. Polly groped for an adequate response. "Tell me about that," was the best he could do.

"Satan's the Prince of this World, man. He's the Power. And he does right by his people. He makes sure they come

66

out on top. Y'know what I mean? Y'know Bloody Sunday?''

Polly shook his head, confused. Why was the kid suddenly talking about the Russian Revolution?

''Y'know, the dudes in Bloody Sunday are *really* into Satan.'' *He's talking about a rock group;* Polly understood now. ''They're all millionaires. They live in these incredible mansions, they got Rolls-Royces, they get all the chicks they want. The got *fame,* man. Anything they want, they just snap their fingers and they got it. They got the best cocaine money can buy. And you think they got all that by bustin' their asses in school and keepin' their noses clean? Man, *Satan* gave it to 'em! He gave 'em everything they have! That's where it's at, you dig? I'm not the sucker, man. You are.''

Polly knew just enough about the music industry to know that you got to the top by working like a dog for years and years, and once you got there, you had to work even harder to stay there. You played the bars along the Jersey shore, where they paid you just enough to keep you in guitar strings, and you went to bed hungry every night forever. For every group that made it, a hundred sank into the tar pit of failure.

''Satanism's just part of their act,'' he tried to argue. ''Now that they're on top, they can say peanut-butter-and-jelly sandwiches got them there. It doesn't matter what they *say.* They still had to learn their instruments. They still had to create an act that worked and rehearse it thousands of times. *They* put themselves where they are today, Nick. The Devil had nothing to do with it.''

''You don't know what you're talkin' about.''

''I'm told that you and some of your friends claim to be active Satanists. Why don't you tell me about that?''

''You mean why don't I squeal on my friends?''

''You don't have to name names, Nick. I really want to know about this. I'm really interested.''

"You want to know so bad, why don't you find a coven and join up?"

Polly tried to imagine himself naked under a black robe, chanting obscenities while some jerkoff broke a crucifix over his knee. He couldn't.

"Do you have regular meetings?" he asked. *"Services,* for want of a better word?"

"Course we do. Only we call 'em Sabbaths."

Polly thought of the old Richmond Hill cemetery that had been desecrated so many times, and the arrests that had been made there a couple of years ago, and wondered if he might not be onto something that the detective division would want to know about. But he wasn't allowed to pursue the inquiry.

There was a knock on his door. When he said, "Yes, who is it?" the door swung open and a well-dressed man with curly white hair was ushered into the room.

"Allow me to introduce myself, Sergeant. Maxwell Bruder, of Bruder, MacArlin and Stern. Mr. and Mrs. Bernstein have retained me to represent their son in this matter."

Reluctantly, Polly shook the man's hand. The lawyer turned and introduced himself to the boy, shaking hands with him, too.

"Now, Nicholas, we're going to fight this thing, you and your family and me, all of us together; and I advise you not to say any more to this police officer. I'm here to see that your rights are respected."

Polly could have groaned. "Mr. Bruder," he said, "you know there's going to be a juvenile court hearing unless I can recommend to drop the charges, after interviewing the juvenile. But if I'm prevented from doing the interview, I can't recommend anything. I can't stop the case from going to court."

Bruder smiled a syrupy smile at him. *"You* can't, Sergeant, but perhaps I can. I'm happy to report that the store

68

manager has agreed to drop the charges against this young man, in return for a settlement with his parents."

"*We* can still press the charges, sir."

"You go right ahead and press them then, Sergeant. As he is a first offender charged with only a minor misdemeanor, I'm sure the court won't make too big a thing of it. Meanwhile, I'd like to return Nicholas to his parents' custody, if I may."

Polly couldn't stop him. The lawyer left with the boy, who flashed Polly a triumphant sneer as he went out the door.

One more sick old man, thought Polly, *coming right up.*

Three

The council had a caucus room adjoining the meeting hall. Thanks to the Sunshine Act, regularly scheduled workshop meetings were open to the public. They didn't attract much of an audience, since there was no obligation to allow members of the public to speak at caucus meetings, but Felix still attended as many of them as he could. The only thing he didn't like was that smoking was still allowed in the caucus room. Whenever Councilman Rich Phelps saw Felix there, he lit up a cigar.

Armed with his facts and figures, Felix entered the caucus room fifteen minutes early and settled into a comfortably padded chair. He said nothing as he watched the parties to the special hearing come filing in: attorney, clerk, and business administrator; the mayor, dapper in a new forest green suit; Council President Thurlow, in a pale lilac suit, of all things; and Phelps with his regular Democratic hatchet men, Councilmen Hayes, Schreiber, and Goldman. The lone Republican, Councilman Neal Irving, came puffing in at the last minute. Felix had taken the liberty the other day of making sure Irving knew about this meeting. Somehow the clerk hadn't gotten around to telling him when it was scheduled for.

Deputy Mayor Haskell had been left out altogether.

Thurlow lost no time getting down to business. "We all know what was said at the April 19 council meeting. Our purpose tonight is to decide whether any violation of the administrative code took place, and if so, what to do about it. Mr. Attorney?"

Wiler cleared his throat. "I just want to make clear the difference between the administrative code and the law, Mr. President. You can violate the administrative code without breaking the law. So we are not talking about criminality in this case. In a sense, we are dealing with in-house regulations, such as a business might have. Whatever we ultimately decide, we must bear in mind that no law has been broken."

Typical lawyer talk, Felix thought. *When is a crime not a crime?*

The attorney read aloud the provision of the administrative code requiring the township's elected officials to file disclosure statements with the municipal clerk and keep them up-to-date. The regulation seemed clear enough to Felix; but then Wiler began to interpret it six ways from Sunday, and soon all clarity was lost.

The councilmen took turns questioning the mayor. Since five of the six councilmen were Leib's political bedfellows, the questioning struck Felix as somewhat less than rigorous. Only Irving, the Republican, tried to play the inquisitor.

"I don't understand your reasoning, Mr. Mayor. The code requires you to list your business and financial assets. How could you possibly think that meant tax-sale acquisitions didn't count?"

Leib was taking it in stride; Irving's questions didn't ruffle him. Doubtless the township attorney had put him through his paces several times beforehand.

"Councilman, when I win the bidding on a tax sale, I acquire nothing but the hope of picking up the interest when the property owner repays his debt. What I expect to gain is *cash,* not property. And nowhere in the code does it require us to list our *cash* holdings. We may be public officials, but we do retain some right to privacy. The way you seem to be interpreting it, we'd have to submit our private bank statements and credit records."

Irving appealed to Felix. "But Mr. Frick has the records!" he said. "And according to the record, you and your dummy corporations have acquired *property* this way! Why weren't those property holdings disclosed?"

"As I've explained many times before, Councilman, when you acquire a lien on tax-delinquent property, the last thing you expect to get is the property. Most of the liens are paid off. Anyway, I admit that I should have disclosed those unexpected acquisitions. I just never got around to it. I have agreed to update my disclosure statement. What more do you want?"

What Irving wanted was the mayor's scalp; but it was obvious he wasn't going to get it. Felix could see how it was shaping up. The Democrats were stirring the whitewash, and nothing would stop them from slapping it on.

When it was Felix's turn to be questioned, Phelps and company lit into him like prosecutors, hoping to trip him up somewhere; but Felix had kept it too simple and straightforward for that. He'd done nothing but examine the public record, as any citizen had a right to do. Phelps made a halfhearted effort to charge him with maliciously invading the mayor's privacy, but dropped it when Wiler ruled that he was out of line.

"Mr. Frick's motivations are immaterial," the attorney ruled. "I'm completely satisfied that he has done nothing improper."

"I think he deserves an official vote of thanks," Irving said. "We never would've found out about this if he hadn't brought it to our attention."

"Are you making a formal motion, Councilman?" Thurlow asked.

"You bet I am!"

"So moved, then. Is there a second?"

Hayes seconded, and it was carried unanimously. Felix wasn't surprised. It was all part of the whitewash.

Nor was he surprised when they let Leib off with a mild reprimand, upon his promise to update his disclosure immediately. Irving held out for a formal censure, but that was a motion for which he couldn't find a second.

"Neal, you're just being vindictive," Thurlow said. "All we want to do here is see that everybody conforms to the code. We're doing it. A censure of the mayor serves no purpose whatsoever. As a matter of fact, I have to admit that my own disclosure statement could use a little updating. And I'll be surprised if I'm the only one."

"That portion of the code ought to be rewritten, anyhow," the attorney said, apparently forgetting that he was the one who wrote the damned thing in the first place. "As it is, the disclosures really only have to be updated at the beginning of each year. As we've seen, that leaves plenty of room for oversight."

"Why don't you get to work on that for us, then?" said Thurlow.

When Felix emerged from the room, the reporters were waiting. As the first man out—the officials had remained to discuss, they said, some matter that was currently under litigation, which allowed them to dismiss Felix gracefully— he had first crack at the press. He wanted to take advantage of it, but the council's formal resolution to thank him made it hard to take shots at them without sounding like an ingrate.

"What about the potential for conflict of interest here, Mr. Frick?"

"As long as *all* of the mayor's land holdings are fully disclosed," Felix said, "I don't see how any conflict could arise. The potential for skulduggery existed when nobody knew about those holdings. With the information out in the open, now it'd be like trying to cheat at checkers."

"What do you think the mayor was up to, Mr. Frick?"

"You'll have to ask him."

"Do you think a reprimand is enough?"

"The council thinks so. Besides, according to the township attorney, you can't be kicked out of office for neglecting to update your disclosure statement. So there's no punitive measure they could take that would mean anything."

"You're starting to sound like a regular member of the team now, Mr. Frick. Are you thinking of running for office?"

"You wound me, miss. I'm just a concerned citizen whose pleasure it is to do his civic duty. I have no interest in selling my soul to politics."

On that note, they let him go.

A woman followed him out and caught him just beyond the lobby.

"Mr. Frick!"

He waited for her. She was a little breathless when she got there.

"You have the advantage of me, young lady. I thought I knew all the reporters who cover this town, but I'm sure I never saw you before."

She smiled prettily. "I'll bet you never saw my paper before, either," she said. "I'm not a bona fide reporter.

73

I'm Dorothy Matthiesen from Chaucer Drive. I put out a little mimeographed freebie, *Tales from the Developments.*"

Felix took a closer look at her. Now that he wasn't trying to identify her as one of the press corps, she began to look familiar.

"You're a friend of Nancy Kruzek's, aren't you?" he said. "I think I must have seen you in her backyard a couple of times. She's my next-door neighbor, you know. Come to think of it, I'm sure I've seen your little paper once or twice. It's more in the line of an old-fashioned satirical broadside, isn't it?"

Dorothy liked the allusion; in fact, it had crossed her mind before, but she'd judged it would've been pretentious to mention it herself. But it put her in the tradition of the old Colonial pamphleteers. Tom Paine's *Common Sense* was a freebie handout, too. She decided she liked Felix.

"I was at the council meeting when you first brought up that tax-sale issue," she said. "I was quite impressed. I've wanted to meet you ever since."

Felix was flattered: he couldn't feel blasé about a young, attractive woman wanting to meet him. He didn't read anything into it, but he did enjoy it.

"I hope you weren't planning to satirize me," he said. "I'm afraid I'm much too easy a target." When she blushed, he knew he'd hit the bull's-eye. "It's all right. Anyone who puts himself in the public eye also walks into the satirist's cross hairs. Anyway, I know a lot of people in this township laugh at me. But I taught for thirty years in the Jersey City school system, so I'm used to it."

Dorothy felt more than a little guilty. At a distance it was easy to write the man off as a figure of fun; up close, she couldn't maintain the perception. It was one of the reasons she hung back from getting into straight journalism. Reporters and editors had to work too closely with the people they covered. How could you urge the voters to run a man out of office after you'd had a drink with him in his living room and watched him kiss his kids good night?

She knew, now, that she could never put Felix in the pillory. That he could be a stubborn old prick sometimes was evident from his career. That he could also be pompous and self-important was implied. But he also seemed a lot more interesting than most of her contemporaries.

They wound up having a beer together at the Hearthstone, a tavern about a mile down the road, swapping sketchy life stories and political anecdotes, laying the foundations for a friendship. She was careful to keep her marital problems out of it, and for the time being, Felix asked no questions that had to be sidestepped.

III.   THE PHYSICIAN

One

Blanche did not fear the Master. He was death, but more than a few lay molderin' in the grave because Blanche had put them there. This began long before she met the Master.

It began as a kindness. Blanche felt sorry for the dying who couldn't die, who lacked even the strength to beg for release from torment. They lay in their white hospital cocoons, and their doctors battened on them like parasitic flies, sucking money from the patients' families and insurance companies, conducting their experiments, playing God. The insurance companies could afford it, but for the patients' kin it was devastating. So Blanche freed them. There were ways to do it without getting caught, and she knew them all. Like a great chess player, she never made a move without completely studying it out beforehand.

This contented her for a few years. The thanks of the dying could not be spoken, but Blanche heard it in her heart. The living tried to hide their relief, but she saw it shining through the masks of grief they wore. She rejoiced to be of service. At the same time she gloated inwardly over the doctors' discomfiture. She cost them uncounted thousands in uncollected fees, and they never knew.

But her pleasure went beyond even that. Looking at her—

and hardly anyone spared her a second look; she was plain and dowdy—one would never guess the power that she wielded. And the more she wielded it, the more pleasure it gave her. She and death were partners.

So she mapped out subtle ways to make the partnership more active. As long as she planned carefully, it was easy. Death would grant her favors in return for all the offerings she made, and the exercise of her power brought joy.

The Master called her to a private conference one night. At the time it didn't occur to her to wonder why. Doctors were always laying too much importance on minor matters: violations of hospital etiquette, trivial irregularities of procedure. Maybe he wanted to ask her what the nurses were saying about him behind his back. Blanche knew there was talk, but she never lowered herself to engage in gossip.

He sat behind the desk, massive and strange. She'd had little contact with him before, and never a face-to-face discussion. Now that she was alone with him, she wished she'd paid more attention to the other nurses' whispers.

"Sit down, nurse."

His greeting smile had no life in it, and it lingered on his waxy lips like a taste of bad wine. Under the fluorescent light, she saw that the skin of his hands and face was mottled unwholesomely. And was that makeup on his cheeks? She thought so.

He sat as though he had been piled onto the chair, pound by pound, with a shovel. There was a smell on him that suggested uncleanness. To mask it, he wore an abundance of cheap cologne. In the confined space, it was almost stifling.

His eyes were muddy stones, devoid of light and unreadable. She had never noticed that before; but then, this was the first time she had ever seen him without glasses.

She lowered herself into the chair in front of the desk.

"May I call you Blanche?" he said. She nodded, wondering what he was getting at. Nobody called her Blanche

78

anymore. To the doctors she was Nurse, to her colleagues she was Milliken.

"How many patients have you liberated from this vale of tears, Blanche?"

Her mind stopped as if he'd shot her in the brain; then it raced, silently but frantically.

He was relatively new to the hospital. He didn't send many patients and was never seen here more than once or twice a week. And she was sure she hadn't terminated any of his patients.

Was he an investigator posing as a doctor, someone hired by the hospital to flush her out? If that had been the case, he would have summoned her to one of the administrators' offices and accused her in front of the brass, with a policeman on hand to arrest her.

"Take your time," he said. "I know this must be difficult for you."

"You'd be speechless, too," she answered, "if someone leveled such a preposterous accusation at you."

His strange smile crept back to his lips. "But it's not preposterous, is it, Blanche?" And he went on to recite the names of her last half-dozen victims, and how she'd killed them. He knew everything.

"Don't be afraid," he added.

Strangely, she wasn't. She should have fallen into despair, envisioning relentless public exposure, trial, and endless years in prison if not death in the electric chair; yet her imagination called forth none of these things.

"I'm not afraid," she said. "But I don't see what you're driving at."

"Do you want to waste time trying to deny the facts?"

"You wouldn't believe me if I did. What's your game, Doctor? What do you want from me? I don't have any money."

He laughed, or rather emitted a sound and semblance of laughter. She waited for him to stop.

"My dear, keep your money! I wouldn't touch a penny of it. But we'll need it. We can't stay here. Your secret won't be safe much longer. I haven't breathed a word of it, and I don't intend to. But I've heard a few things. Suspicions are beginning to crystallize. If you stay, they'll crystallize around you. I'm offering you my protection. I advise you to take it."

The situation was quickly getting beyond her. "How did you know?" she asked. "How did you find out?"

"You covered your tracks admirably," he said, "but I was looking for someone like you. I've been looking for quite some time. I know your techniques because I've used them myself. You might say I'm a specialist—which naturally gives me an advantage over any other doctors who might venture into the field of inquiry. And why should they? Hospitals prefer to assume their staffs include no individuals like you. Only with great reluctance, and when forced by circumstance, will they ever turn a thought to the possibility. Otherwise they choose not to contemplate it. But in your case it's gone on for too long. You've forced them to take notice. The time has come for you to move on to better things."

He had denied any interest in blackmail, but she couldn't fathom his motives. She believed in his promise not to inform on her: if he meant to do that, he would have done it by now.

"Why are you warning me, Doctor? You want something from me. What is it? You might as well say so."

He smiled torpidly at her. His eyes revealed nothing of his thoughts, and even less of his emotions.

"I want you to come with me and be my servant," he said. "I need someone like you. In return, you'll have my protection. You'll share my work. There may be more in it for you than you think. I have a feeling that our association will be a fruitful one for both of us."

80

"You're only confusing me, Doctor. What work? What are you talking about?"

He trained a long look at her. It was like being stared at by a clay statue.

"I may as well tell you now as later," he said. He laid his big pale hands on the desk.

"I am a vampire," he said.

She had to go along with him because he knew all about her and could destroy her if he wished. Not that she didn't have a hold on him, too: the AMA was bound to take a dim view of any one of its members who claimed to be a vampire. But that would be a Pyrrhic victory.

He took her to a part of the city she had read about in the newspapers but never visited, and showed her a wino sleeping on a pile of trash in a dark alley. He opened his black bag and took out a scalpel and a white china cup. In one deft motion he slashed the man's throat; in another he filled the cup with blood. In the dim light it looked like black coffee.

He raised it to his lips and drank.

There was a dreamlike quality to it all, an air of surrealism that stripped the scene of its horror. Blanche watched and waited calmly, telling herself that what the doctor was doing here was essentially no different from what she did in the scrubbed and disinfected precincts of the hospital.

He drank three times, then wiped the cup and the blade with a piece of discarded newspaper and returned them to his bag. The newspaper he threw away.

"That'll hold me for a while," he said. "We'd better go on to your place and get your things. And then I'll have to lie up while you make our travel arrangements. I can't get around during the daytime."

Blanche looked at the dead wino, who lay like a pile of dirty laundry among the scattered trash.

"How often do you do this?" she wondered.

81

"As often as I have to. It's better to kill them outright, rather than to take some blood and let them live. You'll come to understand why."

In time she came to understand many things. But for the moment she was at a loss to understand how the insupportable din of heavy-metal rock in the living room could aid the Master in his research. It made the ashtray rattle on the coffee table, and Blanche's teeth rattle in her mouth. When she could endure it no longer, she turned the volume down to a whisper.

"Please!" she cried. "My head is pounding! Is it absolutely necessary to play it *that* loud?"

The Master looked up, seemingly having forgotten she was in the room. His lips twitched in a way she'd learned to recognize as the closest he could come to a spontaneous smile.

"I didn't mean to give you a headache," he said. He, of course, could never get a headache. There was no sound loud enough to pain his ears, and few soft enough to go unheard by him. "But that's the way *they* play it, isn't that right? They like it turned up to an earsplitting volume; and I can see why. This stuff is pretty hopeless, otherwise. Play it loud and it's an awful hymn to Satan. Play it soft and it's childish drivel."

He was listening to an assortment of LP's she'd bought for him during the day. She had asked the clerk for the most popular and most shocking ("I mean offensive to conventional middle-class morality," she had clarified) records he had in the store; seeing the way he gawked at her, she couldn't help adding, deadpan, "They're for my boyfriend. He's really into heavy metal." For Blanche maintained a matronly facade.

The clerk had certainly come through on the offensive part. Here she was, a murderer many times over, and the songs offended her. The lyrics touted incest, abuse, even child molestation. Suicide. Drugs, drugs, drugs. And devil-worship, too. Blanche's religious sensibilities could not be described as highly developed, but she hoped she would never sink as low as devil worship.

"I don't see how you can listen to them so calmly," she said to the vampire. "Those songs are disgusting. I'm glad the windows are closed. What would the neighbors think if they heard us playing this garbage?"

"With stuff like this available to them, I certainly wouldn't want to try raising teenage children nowadays," the Master said. "Still, if we're going to be dealing with a certain element, it'll help us to understand their psychological state."

The Master had been very active these last few nights, between midnight and sunrise, reconnoitering the township. Because he was tireless, could move without making a sound, and could see in the dark, he had learned much. And Blanche had learned just as much during the day, keeping her ears open, reading the local papers carefully, and striking up a conversation here and there.

There was a rumor of unease in Millboro, based on vandalized cemeteries, satanically oriented graffiti found on the walls of public buildings, and a belief that certain things that had happened in the recent past were happening again today.

"They're afraid of their own children," was the Master's conclusion. "Positively terrified."

They had studied Millboro closely before buying a house there, and had observed it closely since, getting a feel for the sociology of it.

"Look at it," the Master went on, ignoring the music that still played softly in the room. "These people are strangers to their children. In most households, both parents work. The husband is likely to have a long commute every day, getting home fairly late and having neither the

83

time nor the energy to get involved with the kids. The wife works locally, but she still has to run the home, which is another full-time job in itself. Once the children are old enough for school, she looks to the community to take them off her hands.

"Hence the plethora of after-school activities, summer enrichment courses, and all the youth programs provided by the township: soccer, Little League, Pop Warner football, Summer Fun Club at the swimming pool, and so on. Millboro parents wind up spending a minimum of time with their children without having to worry about a lack of adult supervision.

"But there are children who get older and ultimately fall off this treadmill of supervised activities, and they're the ones who interest me. They hardly know their parents. They never learned how to organize their own play without some adult doing it for them. Now that they're on their own, they're bored. They're ripe for any novelty that comes along. They turn to drugs and sex and satanism. I think we can use them, Blanche."

"Kids are kids," she said, but without much conviction. She had never had any children of her own.

"I remember when that was so," said the Master, "but it certainly isn't so anymore. Children these days have no innocence. Haven't you listened to these records I've been playing?"

Blanche didn't want to use these children, not because her conscience balked at it, but because she didn't trust them. She liked the idea of settling down in a comfortable home in a prestige development, and she wanted to stay there for a while without risk.

"You should watch more television," the Master said. "When I was a boy, all we had were the old penny dreadfuls. I suppose they were bad enough, but compared to the continual assault on innocence by television and rock music, they were laughable."

"I don't see how we can afford to get involved with a bunch of drug-crazed teenagers," Blanche said. "They'll talk."

"No one will believe them. Besides, we'll make sure they have compelling reasons to remain silent."

"If it were up to me, we'd just sit back and enjoy what we have for a change."

"It's not up to you."

"I wish you'd listen to me."

The Master sometimes took her advice, but on this point he was adamant. When it came to his research, nothing would hinder him. "I want to be able to walk in the sun again," he would say, "without fear." To that end he directed all his inquiries.

"I'm getting a bit too old for this," Blanche said. "My bones ache when I get up in the morning on a rainy day. Sometimes I'm afraid you're just going to use me up and let me die."

The record came to its end. The needle rose automatically. The room was silent.

"I have your service," the Master said, "and you have my promise. Do you think I'll break my word?"

She did think so, frequently, but she couldn't bring herself to say it. As long as she was strong and capable, and useful to the Master, he would take care of her. But he was beyond time, and she was still a prisoner in it.

"Blanche," he said, "believe me: it will cost me nothing to keep my word to you. But for a while longer, I need you as you are. If you become as I am, then we'll both need live servants. But we've had this discussion before."

We're getting to be like an old married couple, she thought, *haggling over where we should have spent our honeymoon.*

"Tomorrow," he said, "I want you to see if you can find out where these children meet. We need to know their names, and where they live. And would you please turn the record over so I can hear the other side? You can set the volume as you please."

Two

Bruce Randall made a point of looking like Young America personified. To the Millboro High School baseball coach, he was a young Tom Seaver. The football coach, who was older, thought he looked more like the original Golden Boy, Paul Hornung. And the track coach had wet dreams about coaching Bruce to a gold medal in the Olympics. But the coaches could only dream: Bruce was coming to the end of his junior year and had never tried out for any of the sports.

His parents were proud of him. He was respectful, tidy, as handsome as a boy could be, and he got excellent grades. All he asked—or rather, insisted on—was that his room be strictly off limits to both of them. It seemed a small price to pay for the satisfaction of having a son who was the envy of all their peers, and both his mother and his father paid it gladly.

He never bucked the rules and regulations of the school, never shirked his homework, and was well-behaved in class, alert and cooperative. In spite of these virtues, however, his teachers had serious doubts about him and the school administrators tried to keep an eye on him.

Bruce hung around with scumbags.

In his neat collegiate clothes, his gleaming gold hair tastefully shaped by a stylist who knew when to quit, he would sit in the cafeteria with the punks and the potheads. He looked like he should have been student body president; his friends looked like they should have been in juvenile court.

And not a few of them had been. It seemed a miracle that Bruce had not yet sunk to their level, but some of his teachers suspected that Bruce's record was only clean because he'd been too smart to get caught.

Bruce knew they couldn't touch him as long as he made the right moves. He knew they were frustrated because they hadn't been able to get anything on him. They had only a year left in which to try. Then they'd have to graduate him with honors, and he'd have won the game.

Today he spent his lunch period listening to Nicky Bernstein tell how he'd gotten out from under a vandalism rap.

"You shoulda seen Sergeant Pollyanna's face when that lawyer barged in," Nicky said. "Man, he was fucked and he knew it. I don't know what kinda shit that lawyer pulled behind the scenes, but it musta been wild. Blew the fuckin' pigs right out of the water."

Everybody had a laugh, but not for long. They quieted down when they noticed Bruce wasn't laughing with them.

"Nicky," he said, "are you sure you didn't tell the police anything about the Old Religion?"

Nicky squirmed uncomfortably. "Hell, no, man! Like I said, that's when the lawyer came in, just when Polly started to ask about it. Mr. Bruder didn't give him a chance to find out nothin'."

Bruce thought it over. His friends stayed quiet, waiting for his word. Nicky knew what was coming down and could only hope it wouldn't be too heavy.

"You know you're going to have to do a penance," Bruce said, after a long pause. "For getting caught."

"Give me a break, man! The cops didn't find out nothin'!"

"Only because your lawyer got there when he did. What if he'd had a flat tire, Nicky? What if he ran into traffic and got there fifteen minutes later? We can't expect Our Master

87

to look out for us if we don't look out for ourselves. It's good to spread the word, but don't get caught spreading it. One of these days, somebody might get hauled in and wind up telling the pigs what they want to hear. So the trick is not to get hauled in. You'll have to do a penance as a reminder to everybody else. You can appreciate that.''

Nicky nodded his head slowly, sadly, knowing he'd get no sympathy from the others. Bruce knew it, too. They really got off on penances; they wouldn't follow a leader who didn't dish 'em out regularly. And there was a trick to it. You had to put on a good show, but you couldn't make the penance so heavy that it'd drive the offender out of the coven. It had to be like a fraternity hazing, something you would put up with if you really wanted to belong to the group. Bruce's old man had told him all about frat life; it'd please him if his son joined good old Eta Delta when he went to college, following in his daddy's footsteps. Bruce didn't know whether he'd join a fraternity or not. In the meantime, he put the knowledge to good use as master of the coven.

He'd already decided what Nicky's penance would be. The fool would have to take a golden shower, everybody doing it to him at once; and then he'd be ordered to do a job on Mr. Gambi's tires. That'd go over big, because Gambi had recently given a few of the coven members failure notices in Algebra Two. Nicky would be rewarded if he pulled it off—and it ought to be a simple enough job to do, even for a dim bulb like Nicky. And everybody would be happy.

There had been a coven a few years ago, when Bruce was still in junior high, but the cops broke it up. The members were all gone now, graduated or dropped out, so Bruce and his friends only knew fragments of the story. But they knew that the old coven had gotten a bit too carried away with

S&M and stealing neighbors' dogs and cats for sacrifices. Unavoidably, when parents started finding bloodstains on their kids' underwear and sheets, and taxpayers started bugging the cops about their missing pets, there were a lot of questions raised, and a lot of pressure was put on the police and the school staff to find the answers. The old coven came to an end when the cops raided a Sabbath at the old graveyard on Richmond Hill Road. The authorities had taken pains to keep the story out of the papers, but a lot of it had gotten into print anyhow.

The new coven was floundering when Bruce joined and took over as master. Somebody had to take charge. Bruce was the obvious choice. He was the biggest, the strongest, and the best looking, and the only one with any brains. The others messed up what brains they had with drugs and alcohol. They needed Bruce to do their thinking for them.

He pumped his old man for fraternity stories and used the information to get the coven organized. He introduced initiations, dues, and secret signs. Rewards and punishments. Clearly delegated responsibilities. He took the rituals they had already, did some reading up on satanism and black magic, and made the rituals more structured, more impressive. But most importantly, he established himself firmly in command. Nothing was done without his advice and approval. Consequently, the coven's activities were better planned and members were seldom caught or even identified.

To mete out Nicky's penance, they assembled that night in a little clearing they'd found in the woods a couple of hundred yards off Van Dorn Road, down in the scantily developed southeast corner of the township. As much as they would have liked to return to the Richmond Hill graveyard, Bruce held them back. He was sure the cops were watching it, and he encouraged them to keep watching it by periodically sending out parties to litter the ground and deface the tombstones. Let the pigs think the coven was holding Sabbaths there. It'd make it that much harder for them to stumble across the clearing.

They brought beer and grass and partied for a while, with the appropriate music accompanying them on a portable tape player. Nicky had to sit off to the side, forbidden to join the fun until he'd redeemed himself. Bruce stayed straight while the others played sex games and got high. He wouldn't let them get too high. Just enough to fill their bladders and peak their receptivity to his suggestions. He sat aloof, nursing a beer and getting his kicks knowing they'd do anything he commanded.

When he judged the time was ripe, he stood up and held up his hand. They stopped the party and turned off the music.

Bruce explained why they were here, went through the usual invocations of Satan and his demons, and wondered how many of the brethren actually believed this shit. Then he raised his arms and his voice: "Let the penitent come forward!"

Nicky shuffled into the middle of the clearing, head hanging. The coven formed a ragged circle around him.

"Brother Nicholas, by allowing yourself to be arrested by the police, you jeopardized the secrecy of this our brotherhood. You failed to exercise proper caution. You neglected your responsibility to your brothers and sisters, and to our Dark Lord, Satan. Do you acknowledge these faults?"

Nicky nodded. Bruce had to tell him to speak up. He raised his head and said, "Yeah, I'm guilty."

"Do you repent sincerely?"

"I repent."

"Are you ready and willing to do penance?"

"I am."

"Take off your clothes and put them aside."

Nicky stripped and tossed his clothes out of the way. As yet he didn't know what the penance would be. Bruce was always coming up with something new. The best, so far, was the night he'd had Sue Meltzer wait blindfolded while the rest of the coven noisily hawked phlegm into a tin can. Then he gave her another can with a couple of raw egg yolks in it and told her to swallow the contents. Everybody got a blast out of that one, and Sue never fucked up again. They thought Bruce was a genius for coming up with it, but it was just an old fraternity hazing stunt his old man had told him about. It was ideal, though: it blew the penitent's mind without doing any detectable harm, and it entertained the others royally.

Sometimes, Bruce thought, it was almost too easy to get over on these jerks.

When Nicky was undressed and apprehensive, Bruce told him to lie down on the ground. Then he took his own clothes off. They were all naked now. He told them what he wanted them to do, and they grinned like dogs. Nicky screwed his eyes and mouth shut and took it about as well as could be expected. They washed him off with a bucket of cold water and let him dry himself with an old towel. He was shivering by then, so Bruce let him put his clothes back on.

"You'd better take a shower and a shampoo when you get home," Bruce said. He went on to tell Nicky how he could complete his penance by puncturing Mr. Gambi's tires tomorrow in the school parking lot. "All *four* tires, Nicky. Don't slip up." Nicky said he'd do it, thanked Bruce and the others for correcting him, and went home alone.

Bruce smoked a joint and had sex with Judi Myers, who took it as an honor and went along enthusiastically with whatever he wanted to do with her. Judi hadn't palled on him yet, but he knew she would in time. In fact, he was a little worried that the game was going stale.

Felix seldom got asked to parties. He believed it was because his relentless pursuit of the public interest made him too hot to handle, politically. That he was old, physically unattractive, out of the swim of things, and too smart for his yuppie neighbors had nothing to do with it, in his opinion. It just wouldn't make sense for anyone to pal around with Felix Frick unless he didn't mind crossing the powerful, influential people Felix offended by his watchdogging.

Felix got along just fine with all his neighbors. His son paid for Lawn Doctor to come by regularly to tend the yard, so there were no problems with dandelion seeds blowing onto adjacent properties. (In this neighborhood, the prestige-housing development known as Royal Oaks II, they had fistfights over that sort of thing. Felix had seen one: Neal Silverman and Howard Klein grappling in the driveway until Roz Klein turned the hose on them.) Felix would have liked to grow vegetables that he could eat, instead of a chemically bathed green lawn that he could only look at, but the contract his son had arranged with Lawn Doctor left no room for that. It was just as well. Evergreen shrubs and a couple of flower beds were acceptable, but Felix knew a few lawnarchs who would raise holy hell about cucumbers, peppers, and squash breaking up the grassy symmetry. So that potential source of friction was left untapped. Nor was there any trouble with children or dogs. On Whittier Avenue, neither kids nor pets were suffered to run free. The dogs and cats were kept indoors, the kids were bundled off to organized recreational programs.

Living in this neighborhood, Felix sometimes thought, was like living in a goddamn cemetery.

He was surprised when the Kruzeks invited him to one of their backyard barbecues.

The invitation came about as a result of his mentioning to Nancy Kruzek that he was afraid he might be going deaf in his left ear.

"Suddenly I'll hear a kind of whistling or ringing sound," he told her, when they chanced to meet in the housewares section of the local A&P. "And when that goes away, after a few seconds, I can't hear anything at all on that side of my head. It comes and it goes. At the moment, my hearing seems to be normal in both ears. But I'm afraid this one—" he tugged his left ear—"is finally calling it quits."

"Why don't you drop over tomorrow evening?" Nancy said. "We're having a little get-together around the barbecue, and Dr. and Mrs. Emerson will be there. I'm sure the doctor wouldn't mind having a look at you. He's retired from practice, but he may be able to give you some good advice."

Felix accepted the invitation and thanked her handsomely. He could be a courtly old man when he was in the mood.

He knew the Emersons by sight only. Since their arrival on Whittier Avenue they'd kept mostly to themselves, the old doctor especially. Felix had only seen him once, a hulking fat man with silver hair and a doughy, pale face, coming out to glance briefly at the sky one evening just after the sun had set, and then going right back in. The word around the neighborhood was that the doctor wasn't in the best of health and had to take it easy. Felix wondered how a doctor could ever have allowed himself to become so ponderously obese. *You'd think a medical man would know better,* Felix thought.

He'd seen Mrs. Emerson tooling around in her little green car on various errands. She seemed a plain and pleasant woman. They hadn't actually met yet, but Felix had waved to her on several occasions, and she always smiled and waved back. Blanche Emerson didn't look at all like your typical doctor's wife; most of the doctors Felix knew preferred women who were decorative, if nothing else. Felix heard that Blanche had worked as a nurse for Dr. Emerson for many years before becoming his wife. Felix approved of such a commonsensical marriage and wished he had made one himself. Maybe if he had, he'd have a son who would let him grow vegetables.

Hours before he was due at the Kruzeks', Felix found himself wondering about the Emersons. A big, fat doctor with a plain, plump wife: it was so far off the pattern that there had to be a story in it somewhere. Probably several stories.

Felix knew more about his neighbors than any of them ever would have guessed. Some of it he picked up by chance, just because he kept his eyes open. If you went for walks late at night and were willing to crane your neck and prick up your ears a bit, you were bound to find out about Ellen Silverman's manic drinking, Ginny Allen's habit of throwing crockery at her husband, and Art Vernick's steamy little games with various teenage baby-sitters. You couldn't help seeing and hearing things.

But with Felix it didn't stop there. The more he learned about people, the more he wanted to know. To this end he had purchased a pair of Zeiss binoculars and peered through them for several hours a week, the upper floor of his house offering a number of excellent vantage points. Thus he discovered that Doug Gromek liked to try on his wife's underthings, that Laura Mueller had a thing going with the sixteen-year-old boy next door, that Jennifer Rice liked to sunbathe in the nude within the privacy of the high red cedar fence encircling her inground pool.

Nor was Felix averse to paying a little something under the table to be kept up-to-date on various police activities in which his neighbors were occasionally involved. He knew about Nancy Kruzek's arrest for shoplifting at Alexander's, in the Millboro Mall: the charges were dropped, and Felix believed that word of the incident had never reached Walter Kruzek's ears. Felix knew who was stopped for drunk driving, whose kids were picked up for vandalism or smoking pot, and other items that never came to trial or hit the local papers. His friend at police headquarters kept him well informed.

It was his hobby, and there was no harm in it. He wouldn't have dreamed of revealing any of this information, or trying to exploit it.

But about the Emersons he knew nothing, and it nagged at him all day.

Up close, he didn't like the look of Dr. Emerson at all.

The doctor and his wife came late, when it was already getting kind of dark to be starting a barbecue. Walt grumbled about the delay until the phone rang and Mrs. Emerson told Nancy that the doctor hadn't had a good afternoon, but had since rallied and wouldn't make them wait much longer.

"What's he got, anyway?" Walt said. He'd had the coals ready an hour ago. Now he had to add some more.

"Some kind of disorder of the nerves," said Nancy. "I don't know the technical term."

"Did his wife tell you that?" asked Felix. But Nancy couldn't remember where she'd heard it. *That's the problem with most people,* Felix thought. *They don't pay attention.*

The Emersons arrived just as Walt was turning on his new electronic bug-zappers. Nancy, who enjoyed playing hostess, made some cheery introductions.

The doctor's hand, when Felix shook it, was as cold as clay. It looked soft and flabby, but it was hard. The fingers seemed stiff. Not awkward, not disabled. Just a little less motile than they ought to be.

95

Emerson was a huge man, a pyramid of flesh. The evening was warm enough for Felix to be in short sleeves, but the doctor wore a lightweight sports jacket, cream-colored, over a white shirt with brown pinstripes. A brown bow tie was gathered at his throat. He was overdressed for a backyard barbecue. *He must be cold,* Felix thought. What the hell, though; Felix knew plenty of elderly people who could never get warm. And the man's sense of smell had to be on the fritz, too. Otherwise he'd never drench himself in bargain-basement after-shave the way Emerson had. Felix was glad the get-together was outdoors.

It was Emerson's face that Felix didn't like.

Sure, if the guy's nervous system was shot, it'd explain why his facial expressions looked like they had to be assembled first, piece by piece, before they could be displayed. Felix wasn't an idiot; he knew how the human body worked. Muscles moved the face, and nerves were the wires that connected the muscles to the brain. Deterioration of the wiring was bound to lead to problems.

Emerson might have been a handsome man when he was young, and certainly a striking one. Tall and sturdy, with a commanding profile. But now his bones were loaded down with flesh, and his face had lost its shape.

The eyes, though . . . The eyes gave Felix the heebie-jeebies. They never seemed to focus on anything; they just sat in their fleshy sockets like bits of colored glass. *Only glass reflects light,* Felix thought. These eyes sucked light in, reflecting nothing. Whatever personality lay behind them, they revealed nothing of it.

"How do you like your burgers, folks?" Walt said. They all answered at once, and Walt got to work over the grill. Nancy went back into the house to fetch drinks, which Emerson politely declined.

"But you have to have something, Doctor!" she said.

He lowered himself stiffly onto a picnic bench. "I'm afraid my system won't tolerate alcohol of any kind," he said.

96

"We have lemonade."

"Thank you, Mrs. Kruzek, you're most considerate. But I don't think I'll have anything to drink right now. Maybe later."

"All right, if you're sure . . . and please! Call me Nancy."

Felix sat at the opposite end of the bench so he could start a conversation. He found it made him uncomfortable to look Emerson in the eye, so he avoided it.

"I understand you had a bad day, Doctor," he said. He didn't consider it prying. Most people would go on for hours about their ailments if you gave them the slightest encouragement.

But all Emerson would say was, "No worse than some."

"Some disease of the nervous system, I understand?"

"A degenerative condition. It's controlled by medication," Emerson explained, "so it poses no immediate threat. It just restricts my activities somewhat, that's all. It runs in my family."

"So it's a genetic disorder, something like that? What is it, Doctor? Maybe I know someone else who has it."

Blanche Emerson stood behind her husband and laid her hands on his lumpy shoulders.

"It's a very rare condition, Mr. Frick, and I'd just as soon spare you the medical jargon," Emerson said. "It's one of those things that can't be meaningfully discussed in layman's terms."

"How's your own health, Mr. Frick?" Mrs. Emerson put in. Before Felix could answer, Nancy was back with the drinks and Walt was ready with the burgers. Emerson liked his very rare, Felix noticed. Juice trickled out when he bit into it, sprinkling pink stains on his cream-colored trousers. He didn't seem to mind. They all sat around the picnic table and ate, their talk punctuated by the sporadic sizzle of the bug-zappers as moths and mosquitoes kamikazied themselves into the charged screens around the blue lures.

Nancy dominated the conversation, basking in center stage. She spoke for the Emersons' benefit, introducing them to the folkways and personalities of the neighborhood. As a Democratic committeewoman, she couldn't help dragging in some politics: who was elbowing whom out of position, who was going to get a nasty surprise in the party primary, and so on. The rest was strictly neighborhood gossip. Felix could have corrected her any number of times, but he held his peace. He collected information for himself, not others. The less you said about people, the more you learned.

Blanche Emerson listened as attentively as a college student at an important orientation session, but it was impossible to tell whether the doctor was listening, too, or just woolgathering. A retired physician afflicted with a nerve disease, it seemed to Felix, wouldn't be too interested in Gloria Sweynson's efforts to fit into a swimsuit that was two sizes too small for her. But Emerson neither fidgeted nor looked away. You just couldn't tell whether the information was registering or not. His eyes were barriers to speculation. And he sat so still that he reminded Felix of a reptile: a heavy python coiled torpidly on a rock, or a lizard perching motionlessly upon a branch. A mammal or a bird would move from time to time.

Walt made more burgers and fetched more drinks. Emerson declined second helpings and continued to decline offers of anything to drink until the Kruzeks stopped asking. Walt and Nancy imbibed enough to get visibly high, and Blanche Emerson downed her share of vodka gimlets. Felix stuck to beer and nursed it, staying sober.

It should have been pleasant to sit outdoors in the cool of the evening, snacking and drinking and sharing gossip; but for some odd reason it wasn't, especially. Not for Felix.

There was something about being in the doctor's company that kept him ill at ease.

Nancy startled him by suddenly blurting out his name.

"Oh, Felix! I forgot all about you. I'm sorry! Doctor, Mr. Frick has something he wants to ask you about. Something about his ear."

Felix had forgotten about the ringing in his ear, which hadn't bothered him all day. Now he felt reticent to bring it up, but Nancy prodded him until he described his symptoms. Emerson trained his eyes on him and Felix looked away, vaguely troubled by the doctor's unique stillness. It made him feel like an insect being stared at by a chameleon.

"I don't practice anymore, Mr. Frick," Emerson said when Felix was finished, "so I can't treat you or prescribe treatment. Have you discussed this with a physician?"

"No. Not yet. It, well . . . it sort of crept up on me."

An awkward smile slowly crossed the pale face.

"These things always do, Mr. Frick. And when we're old, we grow reluctant to see the doctor for something that seems just a minor annoyance. He might look into it and decide it isn't so minor, after all! And then it's off to the hospital, and no telling how it'll all turn out."

Felix smiled back, but not comfortably. "You read my mind," he admitted. It was true. When he was young he used to put off taking his car to the mechanic, who always seemed able to turn the slightest little knock and ping into a major repair job. Now that his body was knocking and pinging, he didn't trust doctors any more than he used to trust mechanics.

"But in your case," said Emerson, "I wouldn't worry. How old are you, Mr. Frick?"

"Seventy-two."

"Well, then. . . . The human body is like an engine, Mr. Frick." (Oh, no! thought Mr. Frick.) "Its parts wear down with age. That's fate. Maybe your ear just needs a good, professional cleaning. Your doctor can do that at his office. At worst you'll have to get a hearing aid. From what you've told me, I doubt a trip to the hospital would be in order, so there's nothing to be afraid of.''

What with malpractice lawsuits being a dime a dozen these days, Felix could appreciate any doctor's aversion to committing himself too definitely; but for a retired M.D. at an informal get-together, Emerson was playing it awfully close to the vest. Gawd, you didn't have to be a medical genius to know that the human body deteriorates with age.

''What about the ringing sound, Doctor?'' Felix asked. ''What is it that causes that, precisely?''

''It can be symptomatic of a number of things, Mr. Frick. Have you experienced any difficulty sleeping?''

''Not at all.''

''How's your appetite?''

''Normal.''

''Any dizzy spells? Feelings of disorientation? Have you been tripping or stumbling or bumping into things more often than usual, lately?''

''Nothing like that.''

''Headaches?''

Felix shook his head. Emerson asked a few more questions, ruling out cosymptoms such as nosebleeds, lapses of memory, fleeting interludes of nausea, or distortions of time sense.

''Well, Mr. Frick,'' he said, ''it doesn't look like you're about to have a stroke, at least. Nor does infection seem indicated. I think you'll just have to visit your general practitioner and have him clean the ear for you. That should do the trick.''

''I wish you could clean it for me, Doctor.''

''So do I, Mr. Frick, so do I. But my condition prevents me from practicing even the simplest hands-on medicine.''

100

"It's too bad," Felix said. "Were you in practice long? Do you miss it?"

Emerson shook his head slowly. Around the table, Nancy had seized Mrs. Emerson's wrist in her fingers and was leaning close to her to babble excitedly into her ear about Laura Mueller's flirtation with the teenage boy next door. (*Flirtation?* thought Felix. *Lady, you don't know the half of it.*) Walt had dropped out of the conversation to devote himself to some serious drinking.

"I had my own practice for over thirty-two years, Mr. Frick. And no, I can't really say I miss it. Medicine can be a very demanding profession."

"May I ask where you went to medical school?"

"Trinity Physicians College. You've probably never heard of it. It's a small private institution."

"Where was your practice?"

"Here and there. I've moved around a lot. Wanderlust, you might say. New York, Boston, San Francisco, New Orleans, Chicago. And I've been abroad, too: South America and the Caribbean. Did some medical missionary work down there for a couple years. I've been a rolling stone, Mr. Frick, and I haven't gathered much moss. But my rolling days are over, I fear. I expect we'll be neighbors for quite some time."

"Well, that's nice," said Felix. "Myself, I haven't been out of New Jersey since I was in Italy with Mark Clark's army. I think I must've spent a hundred years teaching school in Jersey City until I retired. I'm sure my life hasn't been anywhere near as interesting as yours, Doctor. You've really seen the sights, I'll bet."

"More than I could ever tell you, sir." Emerson fell silent and didn't seem inclined to say any more. Walt created a distraction by elbowing his wife and saying, "Will you knock it off with the gossip already? You're boring the hell out of our guests!"

Blanche hastened to insist that she wasn't bored at all,

101

but Walt was drunk and Nancy had imbibed enough to be heartily ticked off at him in front of everybody. After a few minutes of it, the Emersons made their excuses and went home.

"See what you did?" Nancy shot at her husband, after they left.

"See what *I* did? You're the one who won't let anyone get a word in edgewise! It's a wonder you didn't put 'em to sleep."

Felix tried to play peacemaker. "Please, folks! Dr. Emerson is not a well man. Naturally he couldn't stay much longer."

"Felix, you be the judge," said Walt. "You're impartial. Can Nancy talk the wheels off a car, or what?"

"Don't listen to him, Felix. He's drunk. We sit down to have a nice civilized barbecue with a few friends, and he decides to get loaded. Tell him what you think of *that!*"

Much as Felix would have liked to admit that there was truth to both claims, he opted for discretion.

"I can't stay, either, folks. I'm too old for protracted revelry. But I'm very glad you invited me, I had a very nice time."

"Do you have to leave so soon?" Nancy seemed distraught about being left alone to battle it out with her husband. Felix regretted not being able to stay and watch, but he had other things he wanted to think about just now.

Four

It was Felix's habit to check things that people told him, for the simple reason that people seldom told the truth if they could avoid it. They embroidered the truth, or they pruned it, or rearranged it, or discarded it altogether; but no one ever told it exactly as it was. And they never realized that a lie could be even more revealing than a baldly stated truth.

Felix had never heard of Trinity Physicians College, where Emerson claimed to have earned his degree in medicine. Ordinarily he would have let it pass. Emerson, however, hadn't satisfied him during their talk at the Kruzeks' picnic table. The man had been downright evasive about his own illness—which to Felix seemed so eccentric as to be unnatural. Who the hell could resist talking about his own afflictions? If there was anything a headhunter from New Guinea and a Supreme Court justice had in common, it was the sheer inability to resist the temptation to tell you what was wrong with him.

Furthermore, Felix had never met a doctor who was so bashful when it came to trotting out the medical terms. The thing that made a profession worth having was the jargon. Even *teachers,* for God's sake, liked to buffalo the layman with the jargon of their profession, on the time-honored principle that opacity of language equals profundity of thought. But Emerson hadn't used a single word to indicate that he possessed a specialized vocabulary, and it left Felix wondering whether the man knew anything more about medicine than he himself did.

It'd be funny as hell to find out that Emerson was not and had never been a doctor. Now that the flap over Ron Leib's tax-sale shenanigans had disappointingly fizzled out, Felix was looking for another juicy puzzle to occupy his time. Of course there was no harm in Emerson saying he was a retired physician, as long as he wasn't treating or advising anybody. If it was just a false front he was putting on to wrap a little prestige around his old age, Felix would keep the secret for him. But it'd still be fun to penetrate the deception.

He took a bus the following morning and spent the day

103

at the Rutgers Library of Medicine and Science, thumbing through the *Directory of Medical School Admission Requirements* to see what it said about Trinity Physicians College. He went through the library's five back issues without finding a listing. Since the directory was complete for both the United States and Canada, Trinity, if it existed, should have been in there.

But don't go off half-cocked, he told himself. *Emerson's an old man; Trinity might have closed up shop since he got his degree there.* He brought the last copy of the directory back to the reference desk and spoke to the librarian.

"Do you have older copies of this publication?"

"I'll check." She consulted a file and shook her head. "I'm sorry, we only keep these going back five years."

Felix explained, "I'm trying to look up a medical school that might have gone out of business some years ago."

"We might have some other resources for you." The librarian checked again. "Yes, here's something. *Medical Schools in the United States at Mid-Century.* It came out in 1953. Would you like me to get it for you?"

"Yes, please."

But Trinity Physicians College wasn't to be found in this book, either.

He tried to estimate Emerson's age. Given the state of his health, the man couldn't be much older than seventy. If he had been graduated from medical school at twenty-five, that'd put it almost fifty years ago. Even if he'd been precocious, and finished med school at twenty, it would mean that Trinity had been open during the 1930s.

They had a few lists on microfilm going back that far, but again the search was fruitless. No Trinity.

Felix grinned. It was beginning to look like a good bet that the place was purely imaginary and Emerson either a fraud or a quack. Felix took pride in his thoroughness, however. There were still some other alternatives to consider.

104

First—and least likely—Emerson might be somewhat older than he looked. What if he were in his eighties? Then he could have earned his degree sometime in the 1920s. If he were in his nineties, he could have attended Trinity during the teens.

But that was really stretching it. Felix couldn't see how the man could possibly be a day over seventy. Seventy-five, tops. Felix had never known an obese octogenarian, much less a truly fat person in his nineties. Fat people just didn't live that long. And Blanche Emerson couldn't be much older than fifty-five. Unless she were only posing as Emerson's wife—to what purpose, Felix couldn't begin to imagine—it was hardly likely she would be more than twenty years younger than her husband.

Another possibility was that Trinity had been a nonaccredited, fly-by-night medical college—a school for quacks, in other words. If so, it would never have appeared among the listings of legitimate institutions.

The puzzle was getting to be more intriguing every minute. Felix was glad he'd started it.

"Do you have any listings going back to the nineteen-teens or earlier?" he asked the librarian.

"Nothing that's complete."

"I'd still like a look."

She trotted out more microfilms. Felix studied them for hours.

To his intense gratification, he finally found Trinity included on a list.

The year was 1901.

He could have hugged himself for joy. If only he had a Watson to whom he could whisper urgently, "Come at once, the game's afoot!" He chewed on it mentally, like a dog worrying a tasty bone, all the way home on the bus.

Trinity Physicians College, Cambridge, Massachusetts.

A name on a list dating from the turn of the century. A fact delicious in its obscurity.

Why would Emerson claim to be a graduate of such a place? Why not claim an alma mater that still existed, or at least one that wasn't quite so long defunct? Why not some-place that was totally fictitious? No doubt Emerson had a reason for picking Trinity. But what that reason might be defied conjecture.

The library hadn't had any other information on the school. "You might write to the AMA," the librarian suggested. "They might be able to tell you more about it."

Felix would write that letter as soon as he got home. But how would he proceed while waiting for the response?

He would watch the Emersons' house from his upstairs bathroom window. After focusing his binoculars and turning out the bathroom light, he settled down to see what he could see.

All of the windows were closely curtained; he couldn't see inside the house. The lights were on in the living room. Blanche's car, one of those Japanese models, was probably in the garage; the garage door was closed.

People watching was like bird watching. Most of the time there was nothing much to see. If you didn't have the patience to wait for something to happen, you'd better find another hobby.

Felix had patience. He was content to gather information little by little, and slowly. Tonight it seemed unlikely that he'd learn anything more illuminating than at what time the Emersons turned out their lights and went to bed. Not much, but more than nothing. And he could use the time to ponder the puzzle.

In his letter to the AMA, he'd asked for any data they might have on Trinity Physicians College. In particular he wanted to know when they'd closed their doors, and why,

106

and for how long they'd been in business. And from where might he obtain annual lists of the school's graduates? (After all, there might be a simple explanation. Maybe Emerson's *father* had attended Trinity. Or an uncle, or whatever. That'd explain why Emerson had chosen to hang his phony doctor's hat on the vanished college: he'd know enough about it to add convincing details to his pretense, in case anyone asked.) Felix also requested any information the AMA might have on Winslow Emerson, M.D.

At this point he was prepared to rule out any possibility that Emerson had actually studied at Trinity Physicians. The man just couldn't be that old. It was obvious, then, that he was making a false claim. The reason for it was bound to be interesting.

From time to time he had to put the binoculars down, lean back, and rest his eyes. His elbows got sore from leaning on the windowsill. His back got stiff, so he had to get up periodically and move around.

From the bathroom window he couldn't see much of anything but the Emersons' house, so he couldn't divert himself by training his lenses on more active targets. This wasn't Jersey City, where there was always something to watch on the sidewalks, be it a live mugging or just a mincing queer taking his poodle for a walk. The streets and sidewalks of Millboro were strictly for transportation.

Felix watched the Emersons' house. It was like watching a test pattern. The light stayed on in what he assumed was the living room; the rest of the house stayed dark. You'd think lights would go on and off somewhere else in the house as Emerson or his wife visited the refrigerator or went to the bathroom, but nothing doing. Felix began to think they must have gone out and left the light on.

107

He had no way of knowing, of course, that the Emersons were at this very moment discussing him.

Their living room light was still on when he finally went to bed a little after 1 A.M.

IV. JUVENILE OFFENDERS

One

Blanche was surprised at how easy it was to become a substitute teacher in Millboro.

All she had to do was fill out a form, lie about her credentials and experience, and she was in. This late in the school year, she doubted they'd ever get around to checking on her. Maybe next year, when the county board of ed looked into it, they'd find out that she'd lied about her teaching background—which of course was nonexistent. But so what? She'd be just another middle-aged housewife who told a fib because she needed to earn a little extra money.

For the time being, she looked wholesome and motherly and was bound to be believed, wherever she went, whatever she said. It was her appearance that had preserved her from suspicion, long ago, when patients on her floor were dying left and right. It was an asset, the Master always said, that made her irreplaceable.

"You're sure you don't want me to put you on the list for the elementary schools, too?" the clerk at the school board office said.

"Thank you, no. I'm only looking to work a day or two a week, and I'm at my best with older children or young adults. I haven't any grandchildren. It's been so *long* since I've dealt with little ones, so *many* years. . . ."

The clerk, an inexpertly made-up girl in her twenties, smiled gushingly and said, a little clumsily, "Aw, c'mon, Mrs. Emerson, you don't look any older than *my* mom!" Blanche thanked her and was put on the list of substitutes for Millboro High School.

Her first assignment came by phone a few nights later.

"I'm nervous!" she complained to the Master. "I've never done this sort of thing before."

"I'd do it, if they had school after sundown," the vampire said. He was sitting comfortably on the living room sofa, reading the current week's *Independent*. "Relax, Blanche. All you have to do is tell the students to keep working on whatever their regular teacher has them working on."

"Fat lot *you* know about it! You haven't set foot inside a classroom since they had one-room schoolhouses."

"That doesn't mean I'm ignorant. I read the newspapers and magazines. I watch television. But that's beside the point. All they ask is that you maintain order until the regular teacher comes back. You can do that, surely."

"I have to substitute for a math teacher. Damn it, all I know is basic arithmetic. Not algebra, trigonometry, or God knows what. I mean, I haven't used my higher math since I was a kid in school, I've forgotten all of it—"

"Blanche, nobody will care. It's not important. You're only doing this to gather data for my experiment. You're my field researcher. Don't worry about anything else. And please sit down! How can I concentrate with you pacing back and forth like that?"

To Blanche, nowhere else did Millboro flaunt its wealth so gaudily as at the high school.

The building was big enough to get lost in; when she

arrived, she had to ask directions to the main office. She thought there must be literally thousands of students here. How could the administration keep track of all of them? But she was afraid to ask about such things; she didn't want anyone to think she was a hick.

The office itself was huge and equipped with computers, telephone switchboard, copiers, and other costly extras. A clerk had everything waiting for her: schedule of classes, substitute lesson plans prepared by the teacher, student rosters and seating charts, and a list of rules and regulations to which a new substitute could refer for guidance. She gave Blanche directions to her classroom and sent her on her way with a smile. Blanche forced herself to smile back; she felt more like running away.

The halls were thronged. Blanche was startled by the liberty allowed students vis-à-vis their personal appearance. Side by side, rummaging in their lockers, there were neat, clean, well-dressed young people and kids who looked costumed for Halloween. A girl with a bizarre hairdo and garish makeup wore a clinging T-shirt emblazoned with the message *I'm on the Pill*. A boy had his hair done to resemble the Statue of Liberty's spiked crown—plus earrings in both ears. Blanche felt a twinge of resentment against the Master for sending her into such a place. Hell's bells, there were kids here who looked like they'd come from other planets. She felt relieved when she reached her second-floor classroom without being assaulted.

All the lesson plans required of her was to assign the students to solve certain problems in their textbooks, the work to be handed in to the regular teacher tomorrow. Blanche wouldn't have to do anything but preside over each class. She would be free to concentrate on being the Master's field researcher—damn him. Couldn't he just steal drinks of blood and live in peace and quiet for a change? Him and his stupid experiments.

An electronic bell rang, the halls filled, and her first-period class came in and took their seats. Blanche introduced herself, took the roll, and announced the day's assignment. Most of them got right to work on it. A few bent their heads together and spent the whole period gossiping like a gaggle of Irish washerwomen. Blanche began to relax. This wouldn't be so bad after all. Indeed, she could put up with a lot worse for forty-five dollars a day.

In the third-period class, Plane Geometry, there were a couple of smart alecks who tried to give her a hard time.

"I don't understand, Miz Emerson, we *done* these problems already!"

"Are you sure we're supposed to do 'em all? Mr. Bailey always assigns us just the even ones, or the odds."

"Mrs. Substitute, I just don't get this freakin' theorem on page one-fifteen. Whatta they talkin' about, this stuff with the radius makin' a right triangle with the tangent or somethin'?"

Blanche put up with it for a while, trying patiently to explain that she had read the words of the assignment exactly as the teacher, Mr. Bailey, had written them. When she finally realized that they weren't really confused, that they were only baiting her, she glared so poisonously at one of them that they all subsided. She was imagining the overgrown lout screaming and thrashing as the Master cut his wrist and drained a cup of his blood, and herself looking on with satisfaction. Something of her thought seemed to communicate itself to the class.

"It says on this list of regulations," she told them after a long and weighty pause, "that any student sent to the principal's office by a substitute teacher shall be automatically suspended. Is that understood?"

Silence.

"I'm not here to be the butt of your adolescent jokes," she added. "I'm here only to see to it that you do the work your teacher left for you. If you have questions about it, save them for him."

Blanche, who had murdered more hospital patients than there were students in this classroom, won her point. Those who still didn't feel like working muttered harmlessly among themselves, and she was content. But she made a point of consulting the seating chart to memorize the names of the troublemakers.

She took her free period in the nearest teachers' lounge, where she relaxed and fell to chatting with a couple of the staff. She was infinitely more comfortable with adults than with teenagers.

"Really," she said, "it's been so long since I was in a classroom, it's going to take a while to get used to it again. But I can see that times have changed. It's not so bad, but a few of the kids in my third-period class were actually snotty to me."

"Welcome to the club!" said a woman named Carol Something, with a laugh. "There are a lot worse schools than this one, but we do have our share of snotty kids."

"I wonder if you know these individuals," Blanche said, and trotted out the names she'd memorized.

"Oh, them!" a man with horn-rimmed glasses said. "Don't feel bad, Mrs. Emerson, you haven't been singled out. You just ran over some of our rotten apples. Those three give everybody trouble."

"I'm a little surprised the school allows them to dress like rock stars."

"Haven't you heard? Dress codes went out with simple literacy," the male teacher said. "Seriously, though, the only reason they cultivate such an outlandish appearance is to get attention. It's strictly for shock value. You learn to ignore it."

"I'm sure you know what you're talking about," Blanche

113

said. "Still, I've always believed that a person's appearance reflects his inner beliefs and values. Some of which are pretty suspect, if you ask me!"

"They're not really bad kids," said an older woman. "They just like to dress like punk rockers. Monkey see, monkey do."

"Yeah," said the younger woman, Carol, "but there *are* a few characters who're definitely headed for trouble, if they haven't gotten there already."

"Frankly," Blanche said, "I did have some second thoughts about taking this job. I've heard a few things that daunted me. The usual stuff about drugs and sex and liquor—you know. But some people also said things about there being some kind of underground *satanist* thing going on here. Like a cult. That really alarmed me."

None of the three teachers responded to that, and for a moment Blanche was afraid she'd tipped her hand too soon. But her statement lay before them like a duelist's glove, and they couldn't leave it.

"Wild talk like that," said the older woman, "is bad for the school."

"I was hoping it was only talk," Blanche said. "Just a lot of alarmist gossip. I'm glad to hear there's absolutely nothing to it."

"Hold on—nobody said that," the man with glasses said. "It's obvious you came here with the wrong impression, but I don't think it'd be right to let you go home with an equally wrong impression."

"Herman!" the older woman said warningly.

"Well Jesus, Anne, we shouldn't *lie* about it! That can only make things worse." He turned to Blanche. "But you understand, Mrs. Emerson, that this is kind of a sensitive subject. The administration doesn't want to hear a lot of loose talk about it. Next thing you know, it gets into the papers and you've got a bunch of fundamentalists picketing the school board meeting."

"Remember when the Right to Lifers came down on our sex education program?" Carol said. "All because we acknowledged the *possibility* of abortion!"

Blanche didn't want to get sidetracked. "So there *is* something to this devil-worship thing?" she said.

"Mrs. Emerson, a lot of our kids are just plain overacculturated," Herman said. "If the rock stars suddenly started singing about how cool it was to solve quadratic equations, believe me, my job'd be a lot easier. Whatever the kids see on TV or get from their music, that's their big concern.

"Consequently, we have a small number of students who like to shoot their mouths off about satanism and black magic, crap like that, because it's in the music that they like. I'm sure you've heard some of this bullshit, pardon my French. About being able to learn spells and incantations by playing a certain track on a record album *backwards,* at a different speed, and so on. I'm sure some of these kids do just that. And they leave satanist graffiti on the bathroom walls, and call their gang a coven, and spout a lot of garbage about being able to summon up demons and all. Once again, it's a typical teenage attention-getting device. And it's blown way out of proportion. It's no different from the punk hairdos or the bizarre clothes. Just a bunch of dumb kids trying to make an impression."

"Only some of them," Carol interrupted, "are genuinely nasty."

"You take them too seriously," Herman said. "Too many adults do. Honestly, Mrs. Emerson, there's nothing to be afraid of. The administration has its eye on those few kids who might get carried away. Take it from me, Millboro High is not the blackboard jungle."

The Master was in his basement workroom, safe from the sunlight, when Blanche came home. Her report pleased him.

"A few more days at the school," he said, "and you should be able to identify our target individuals. Then it ought to be relatively easy to find out where they meet."

'I don't want anybody to think I'm a bug on high school devil worship," Blanche said. "Besides, the teachers don't know where these kids hold their Black Masses, or whatever it is they do."

"Once we have the names and addresses," the vampire said, "I can locate the meeting places easily enough. You've done well, Blanche."

"Thanks loads. You should see some of those kids. It's like an invasion of barbarians."

"Why don't you have a drink and lie down before you eat? And then go to bed early. I'm going to feed tonight, I won't need you."

"I wish you'd feed on a few of *them*. Snotty little brats!"

She moved toward the stairs, but he called her back.

"There's one little thing I'd like you to do for me, when you get a chance. It's not urgent, probably not important— but it could be in the future."

"What's that?"

The Master looked up from his microscope.

"Our neighbor, Mr. Frick, has been spying on us, my dear. With binoculars. I happened to see him the other night when I glanced out your bedroom window. He was sitting in a dark room, with no idea that I could see him, peering at our living room window through his glasses. I'm sure he hasn't discovered anything dramatic, but all the same, I'd like you to make some discreet inquiries. It may be he's just the neighborhood Peeping Tom; but whatever the case, I'd like to know for sure."

"I'll ask around," Blanche said.

Two

Blanche learned the name of every student who made trouble in her classrooms, as well as the names of those who looked capable of making trouble. There were more of them than she ever would have imagined—not like when she went to school. There had only been two or three really rotten kids in her high school class, and parents and teachers saw to it that the good kids kept their distance from them.

The Master helped her, teaching her to recognize certain occult signs and symbols when she saw them scrawled on a desk, on the blackboard, or on the cover of a loose-leaf notebook. Once she knew what to look for, they seemed to be everywhere. You'd think the whole damned student body was worshiping the devil.

She pumped the teachers for information on individual students and secretly wrote down what they told her. She had to proceed with care, so as not to attract attention. It would have been stupid to bring up devil worship every time she sat down in the teachers' lounge. She had to go about it in a roundabout way. "This one girl, Grace Whatsername—the one with the purple hair. I never heard such a foul mouth on a teenage girl. What's her story?" And if she was lucky, one of the teachers would tell her the story.

She could talk to the kids, too, if she was careful. "What's that symbol on your notebook, Robert? I never saw anything like it before. Does it mean anything?"

Responses varied. A churlish shrug, an inarticulate mutter. "Naw." "Nothin', I was just doodlin'." And the ever-popular "I don't know." They peppered their speech with "you know," using the phrase as random punctuation, and when you asked them a question, it was always "I don't know." Surly little shits they were, a lot of them. But every now and then she got an answer. Maybe the sign was something they copied from the jacket of a rock album. A few

117

would come out and say it was a sign of Satan, or this or that demon. And some said flatly, "It's a secret."

As she became more acclimated to the school environment, she relaxed a little and was less apt to snap at students for trivial infractions. She grew used to the punk hairdos and the slovenly clothes. Just because a kid's head looked like he'd combed his hair with an eggbeater and sprayed it with shellac didn't mean he was a satanist. For most of the punk types it was just an unofficial uniform, signifying nothing deeper than a desire to run with the herd, a passive rebellion against their parents' and teachers' middle-class values.

She kept lists: possible satanists, suspected satanists, and children who were most likely satanists. There weren't as many names on the third list as she'd hoped to get. It made her wonder whether she was doing something wrong.

"You're doing fine," the Master would reassure her. "Keep up the good work. We don't need all the names. Just a few."

"But I still don't know what they actually *do,*" she would say, "or where they do it."

"Just keep at it, my dear. We'll find out."

"But the school doesn't know where these kids meet! If they did, they'd do something about it."

"Let me worry about that."

Blanche persevered, but there was one incident that almost made her lose faith in the youth of America altogether.

Just out of the blue, two of the seediest-looking girls—regular slatterns, both of them—disrupted her class when they jumped out of their seats and started fighting in the aisle: clawing, scratching, punching each other, and swearing like a couple of drunken longshoremen. As Blanche cried out in vain for order, they fell to the floor and grappled, causing their classmates to scatter to the perimeter of the room. Cheers went up, and coarse teenage laughter, and cries of encouragement and advice to the battlers. Bedlam.

118

For some seconds Blanche stood paralyzed, not knowing what to do. But then she found herself.

"Don't just stand there!" she hollered. "Pull them apart before they kill each other!"

Some of the students still hung back, but others charged eagerly into the fray, whooping as they vaulted over desks and chairs, and soon each girl was firmly in the grasp of several of her peers. They struggled in vain, a pair of disheveled harpies with bile on their lips. They didn't shut up even when Blanche placed herself between them. It took all her self-control not to slap them into silence. She could only wait until they ran out of profanities, which took several minutes.

"I have never seen a more disgusting display of outright hooliganism," Blanche said. The girls glared at her like a pair of rattlesnakes whose heads were pinned to the ground by forked sticks. Half of one girl's shirt was torn away, and she hadn't been wearing a bra. The boys leered at the exposed breast. The other girl's face was bleeding from a jagged scratch. It all reminded Blanche of those old newsreel films about the troubles in the Congo.

All the money they spend on this school, thought Blanche. The brand-new up-to-date weight-and-fitness room, like a regular Jack LaLanne spa; computers in the classroom; enough video equipment (for a course entitled Modern Media) to produce a weekly soap opera; a roomful of hi-tech simulators for driver ed, to supplement the usual aging Chevy with the dual controls; science labs that'd do credit to some county hospitals Blanche had known . . . and it wasn't just equipment. They had extracurricular activities out the wazoo, everything from aerobic dancing to Zen. When Blanche went to high school, you got Pep Club, the school newspaper, and Chess Club (for the outcasts, the scrawny kids with foreign names and heads that looked like light bulbs, the fat kids with the squinting eyes and bottle-bottom glasses), and that was it. Short of going to the moon or waging war, these kids could do *anything*. The taxes on their parents' six-figure homes pumped oceans of money into the school district.

And this was what they got for it: a couple of sewer-mouthed bitches trying to tear each other's tits off. As a taxpayer, Blanche was almost too furious to speak.

"You don't belong in a classroom," she was able to say, "neither of you. For the time being, I'll let the office deal with you. I hope they have the common sense to expel the both of you."

Getting them to the principal's office, though—that was the tricky part. She couldn't just order them to go. Either they'd go over the wall the moment they were out of sight, or else they'd fall to fighting again. Blanche could deliver them in person, but if they went for each other's throats, she wasn't sure she could pull them apart. And to call the office and ask them to send the vice principal to pick them up—well, that'd look like she couldn't handle them herself, wouldn't it?

She picked a pair of likely-looking boys to be her escort: a squat, brawny kid whose center of gravity was probably somewhere in China, and a tall blond preppie type whose golden good looks and flawless classroom deportment had fascinated her from the moment she first saw him.

"You and you, Newman and Randall—I want you to help me conduct these two—" she was about to say "brawling floozies," but thought better of it—"these two persons to the office. The rest of you, back to your seats." She glared at the students until they were at their desks again. "When I come back, I want to see every single one of you with his nose buried in a book. And I don't want to hear a pin drop. Is that understood?"

With one boy taking each of the girls by the arm, Blanche led her convoy down the hall. The girls were sullen and silent, like prostitutes being led to prison. The brawny boy, Newman, seemed ill at ease, but the tall blond, Randall, carried himself like a state trooper. Blanche was thankful for him. He was proof that there was still some hope for the younger generation.

Later, in the teachers' lounge, she described the incident and was told that the two girls involved were suspected druggies.

"They've been in fights before," one of the veteran teachers said, "but their parents have a lot of clout, so there's nothing anybody can do about it."

"That whole class would be better off on Alcatraz," Blanche said, "except for a few. There's one boy in it who really impresses me. Bruce Randall."

She was shocked when Herman Franks, the math teacher with the horn-rimmed glasses, threw back his head and laughed out loud.

"Oh, boy!" Herman said. "So he's conned you, eh?"

'What do you mean?''

"Only that Bruce Randall is about the slickest piece of work in the whole damned school. Actually, I kind of admire him. I *know* he's up to no good—we all know it—and there's not a blessed thing we can do. Bruce is the original Teflon Kid. Nothing sticks to him."

She listened sadly as one teacher after another chipped away at her illusion. Golden Bruce was suspected of everything from being a drug dealer to masterminding juvenile crimes for his less intelligent peers, but the only thing they could prove against him was his constant association with known drug-users, vandals, and worse.

"He's laughing up his sleeve at all of us," Herman said. "One of these days, Mrs. Emerson, you'll be reading about him in the papers. You'll be seeing his face and hearing his name on the six o'clock news. Only it won't be for doing anything that does credit to this school, or to his teachers. You wait and see. He's one of those up-and-coming young men who keep on coming up until they find half a dozen teenaged girls rotting away under his living room floor.''

"Jesus Christ, Herman!" One of the older woman teachers scowled at him. "That's morbid!"

"Maybe. But I sure as hell won't be surprised if it turns out to be true."

Three

Trinity Physicians College graduated its last class in May of 1918, then closed its doors forever.

Well, ain't that a kick in the head? Felix said to himself as he sat at his kitchenette table contemplating the letter from the American Medical Association.

Furthermore, the AMA had no Dr. Winslow Emerson listed in its current membership files, and its computer hadn't been able to regurgitate any such name from the organization's past. They had checked back fifty years without finding the name, their letter said.

Felix reread the letter. It gave a brief history of Trinity Physicians: founded in 1882 by a former Union Army surgeon and his associates, turned out 2,112 graduates during its financially troubled thirty-six years, finally absorbed by Harvard Medical School. Its most famous graduate was Dr. Harvey Holbein, Class of '01, senior medical advisor to one of Admiral Byrd's expeditions to Antarctica. The school's records were kept at the Harvard Medical School Library, from whence further information might be available.

Felix was almost sure this was a blind alley, but it wasn't as if he were a police detective under pressure to solve a crime. He went to his typewriter and drafted a letter to Harvard asking for a list of Trinity's graduates. Maybe they'd had an Emerson or two, from whom Millboro's Dr. Emerson might be descended.

It was a good puzzle, and it was getting better. Why would anybody claim to be a *retired* physician with a degree from a school that had gone out of business in 1918? What conceivable purpose could it serve?

Felix could hardly wait to find out.

"I hate to gossip," Blanche said.

"Terrible habit," Nancy Kruzek agreed.

They were sitting on lawn chairs on Nancy's patio, sipping weak drinks under the springtime sun. Blanche had come over to ask a meaningless question about township politics—the primary campaign had just started, and Democratic fur was flying in every direction—and hadn't found it hard to get herself invited to stay for a drink or two. She had already pegged Nancy as a woman who loved to talk, about anything or anyone.

"I mean," Blanche went on, "it seems like such bad manners to talk about a person behind his back. But sometimes that's the only way, right?"

"Can't be helped."

"Nancy, have you ever noticed . . . I mean, have you ever *thought* that Mr. Frick is kind of a busybody?"

Nancy laughed. "Oh, don't mind Felix! We've all learned not to take him seriously."

"I know he's a friend of yours."

"I wouldn't say he was a *close* friend, though. Frankly, he can be a royal pain in the ass sometimes." She went on to fill Blanche in on Felix's self-proclaimed mission as tribune of the people and gadfly to the municipal government. Blanche listened carefully, taking mental notes. The Master would be very interested in Frick's investigation of the mayor's corporate dealings.

123

"Don't tell me," Nancy said; "he's been bugging you about something. He can be an awful pest."

"It's nothing like that. Oh, you're going to think I'm being silly, I shouldn't have mentioned it."

"Now that's not fair, Blanche—getting me interested in something and then snatching it away. What's Felix been up to?"

"I really shouldn't say. You'll tell him, it'll turn out I was dead wrong, and there'll be bad feelings."

"I'll do no such thing! Anyway, I don't get too many chances to talk to Felix. C'mon, I'm dying of curiosity!"

Blanche hemmed and hawed a little, whetting Nancy's appetite.

"It's just that I think he's been . . . well, *spying* on me. With those binoculars of his."

"Binoculars?"

"Yeah. I swear I've seen him peering out his window with binoculars, and they sure look like they're trained right on my house. Oh, dear, that sounds paranoid, doesn't it?"

"I never knew he had binoculars," said Nancy thoughtfully. *The old buzzard, that'd be just like him. I wouldn't put it past him for a minute.* "Probably he was looking at a bird or something," she added.

"I'm sure you're right," Blanche said. Obviously Nancy didn't know a thing about Frick's binoculars. "It just gave me the jitters, that's all. I mean, I don't know him at all well . . ."

The Master sent her to the Millboro library to look at back issues of the local papers, then thought over what she reported to him. She waited silently, worrying about being driven out of this nice neighborhood before they'd even truly settled in.

"This man," he said, breaking his pause, "is willing to go to a lot of trouble to satisfy his curiosity. It would be a mistake to take him lightly."

124

"He certainly surprised the mayor, coming out with all that stuff the mayor thought he kept a secret," Blanche said.

"For all practical purposes, Mr. Frick is an experienced investigator."

"What're we going to do?"

The Master smiled. "There's a state psychiatric hospital in this township. Mr. Frick could easily win accommodation there, if he went around telling people that his neighbor across the street is a vampire. But I doubt it'll come to that." He paused to think some more, his cogitations uncluttered in a way that no living man could know. "As I see it, the only thing he can find out about me is that my medical alma mater became extinct too long ago for me to have been a graduate, as I told him I was. It's also conceivable he'll discover that I'm living here under an alias. I wonder what he'll make of it."

"I don't think I want to wait and see," Blanche said. The Master sometimes exasperated her with his confidence in his ability to make things come out right. She had never known him to be seriously mistaken, but that made it all the more exasperating. "One of these days," she told him, "you're going to wake up and find yourself with a stake through your heart because you wouldn't listen to me. Something has to be done about that man. I don't want to think about him staring at me through his binoculars every time I walk past a window. I don't like to think about him pawing through a bunch of dusty old records, trying to find out who you really are."

"Tut-tut, Blanche. Mr. Frick is our neighbor. If the predator scatters blood and bones near the mouth of his lair, he makes the task of the hunters that much easier. I won't molest Mr. Frick unless he poses a clear and present danger."

"Have you thought about *me*? What if he decides to dig up dirt on me? I've got a few skeletons in *my* closet, you know!"

"There's nothing against you on the record," the Master said. "He'd need a crystal ball to get a look into your past."

But Blanche had frequent visions of someone sitting down to pore through the records at her old hospital, studying case notes that had gathered dust for all these years and suddenly putting two and two together. *Hey, Farnsworth, c'mere a minute! Look, we had a couple dozen patients die on us in just eighteen months, way back when, and all of 'em when they weren't supposed to go. Even the ones that were terminal, they croaked when their doctors least expected it. And y'know what? The only thing they had in common was this one nurse, B. Milliken, took care of all of 'em! Huh? You bet your sweet life I'm gonna call the FBI!* Blanche dreamed about it sometimes: the knock on the door, the two hard-faced cops who looked like the guys from "Dragnet" standing there with the warrant in their hands.

The Master didn't understand. He never dreamed; he never even truly slept. He'd been a vampire for too long, he couldn't remember what it was like to fret about your past jumping out of nowhere and murdering your future.

"Blanche, don't worry. I'll keep an eye on Mr. Frick. But surely you must realize that, for the present, he's less dangerous to us alive than dead."

Blanche snorted. "They're always better dead," she said. "Sooner or later you're going to have to do it. And later might be too late."

"Poor timing," said the Master, "was never one of my shortcomings."

126

V. A SCIENTIFIC EXPERIMENT

One

They smoked a few joints, drank a little beer and wine, and filled the woods with discordant music from a portable tape player the size of a suitcase—just a bunch of kids coming together to party.

The Master waited patiently in the shadows, invisible to them. They had a small fire and several battery-powered camping lanterns, but they wouldn't see him unless he chose to reveal himself.

Finding this place had been simple, once Blanche had given him enough names from the high school.

"My name is Dr. White, young man. I'm a professor of sociology at Rutgers University, and I'm doing research on the growth of grassroots religions in the Jersey suburbs. I understand there is a budding satanist movement here in Millboro, and that you belong to a coven."

"Get lost. You're either a cop or some kind of faggot."

The Master smiled indulgently and slowly drew a plump wallet from the inner pocket of his jacket. He opened it to show the boy a thick sheaf of bills.

"Naturally, I'll pay for any information I receive. And I'll hold it in strictest confidence. I realize that the established authorities are hostile to religious ventures such as yours. You have to be careful."

The boy's eyes fastened on the money and wouldn't let go.

"How do I know you're not a cop, man? Undercover cops, they got all kinds of fake ID. You prove you ain't a cop, maybe I'll tell you something."

"I'll be happy to do anything in my power to convince you that I'm not a police officer," the vampire said.

The boy made a suggestion that no police officer would dare to go along with, but the Master accepted readily. It was a shame, he thought, the kinds of things that filled young people's minds these days. And it was obvious, moreover, that the boy had done this sort of thing before. He knew a place where they wouldn't be interrupted. They went there.

"Shit, man! How come you're so freakin' *cold?*" the boy complained. But he didn't object when the Master suggested that they forget about completing this part of their transaction. The whole idea had only been to place the adult in a deeply incriminating position, and as far as the boy was concerned, that had been done.

"There's still money for you, if you'll tell me about the coven."

"Hold the phone, man. First I get paid for what I let you do to me."

The Master handed him ten dollars, which was clearly far below the going rate for what they had just attempted to do. But he didn't let the boy finish his protest. "There's ninety more, if you'll answer my questions."

"All right. We can talk here, nobody'll bother us."

When the Master finished his interrogation, he set about ensuring the boy's silence in the least troublesome manner he was able to devise, administering a drug that would prevent the boy from ever telling anything to anybody, ever again.

He resisted the temptation to feed, but only barely.

Well, it had worked out as planned. The boy was presumed to have overdosed himself, his parents and the authorities collaborated to keep the matter out of the newspapers, and the Master learned the location of the coven's meeting place, as well as many other things. Now he hid among the trees and watched the unfolding of the Sabbath.

He recognized the tall blond youth from Blanche's description of Bruce Randall and wasn't surprised when Randall turned out to be the leader of the group. He called them to order and led them in a series of chants and invocations that the Master recognized as basically nonsensical. Drugged and excited, and poorly equipped in background and intelligence, Randall's followers seemed to accept the gibberish as true mysticism.

Having done this, the young man set loose an orgy.

The Master watched, shaking his head. Blanche would have a fit if she could see this. For a multiple murderess, she had some surprisingly straitlaced attitudes. The Master was more tolerant. In his transition from mortality to vampirehood, he had lost the ability to become emotionally involved in anything that didn't directly impinge on his survival. Only small traces of that ability remained in him. He felt them now, trivial ripples in his pool of self-awareness. There was a time when he would have been appalled by what he was seeing. These were children from good homes, the heirs to an enlightened civilization. Just now, that civilization's prospects seemed rather dim. The Master was sorry to see what it was coming to.

The tall blond boy remained aloof from the frantic couplings of every possible variation that were assayed around

129

him. He was the only one with his clothes still on, the only one still standing. The Master admired his shrewdness. By remaining clothed, by taking no active part in the revelries, he placed himself on a higher level than the others. He stood among them like an idol.

But he was more like the shaman of a primitive tribe. The Master had known several such men. Whether or not they themselves believed in the ritualistic medicine they dispensed to their people, each was more powerful within his own sphere than any civilized religious leader could ever be in his. To the tribesmen the shaman was an object of awe and mystery, almost like a god himself. The Master thought of Jonestown, in Guyana, where several hundred worshipers drank poison because their shaman ordered it. You didn't have to be a poor Indian in a breechcloth, the Master reflected, to belong to a benighted tribe and believe in a shaman.

He decided, as he watched, to choose the blond boy as the object of his great experiment. The rest of these children were chaff; Randall was the kind who swept them in any direction he pleased. To choose any of the others would be a waste of time and effort.

The young shaman turned off the tape player, abruptly choking off the music and plunging the clearing into silence. Within seconds his followers were on their knees, waiting for him to speak. Their parents and teachers, the Master thought, would never believe they could be such a respectful audience to anyone. He saw the familiar pattern of habitual rebels setting up their own tyrant to have vastly more authority over them than they would ever have granted to family, church, or state.

"My brothers and sisters—" there were more brothers than sisters here tonight, the Master noted—"our Dark Lord will give us power over the things of this world. He will give us as much power over the world as we give him

130

over ourselves. That is our covenant with him. And it must be sealed in blood!''

It always comes down to blood, thought the Master. *As well it should.*

The boy went on for a while about all the delights the Devil had in store for them, then reached into a cardboard box and brought out a large white rat, holding it aloft for all to see. The rat was tame and didn't struggle.

''To symbolize our devotion to him, let us now shed blood. And let this blood be only a token of our debt to him, and a sign of the great feast which he has promised us!''

The boy strangled the rat. When it was dead, he took a knife from his pocket and slit its belly. Still on their knees, still naked, the worshipers dabbled their tongues with rat's blood.

Simple, the Master thought, but effective. No risk involved in sacrificing a rat. By this point in the ceremony, the worshipers were psychologically prepared to receive the sacrifice as a thing of high significance. Maybe when they grew older and more jaded they'd demand a white goat or a human being; but for now they'd be content with rat's blood. He couldn't help smiling as he thought of Blanche again. She couldn't abide rats or mice. This would kill her.

When they had all tasted blood, their leader threw the dead rat into the bushes and pronounced a benediction in the Devil's name. He seemed to have invented his own liturgy, his own version of the ritual: a good idea, the Master thought. Tailor your performance to your audience. Since none of these children were profoundly religious, anyhow, it would have been lacking in force to concentrate on perversions of Christian or Jewish ritual. Classical satanism could only take hold among people raised in a strong tradition of conventional religion. The blond youth had intuitively grasped that. He had great natural gifts, it seemed.

The Sabbath had come to an end. The children put on their clothes and spent a few minutes picking up the empty beer cans, wine bottles, cigarette butts, used prophylactics and their wrappers, and any other litter that might give them away should someone come hiking through this corner of the woods. According to what Blanche had heard, the police had been able to break up a similar group two or three years ago simply because they'd met in a cemetery—a dead giveaway—and left it cluttered with telltale litter. The new shaman had certainly learned from that mistake.

Two

The Master got between the boy and the road. In spite of his bulk he moved along the trees as noiselessly as a fox. None of the young people heard him. They made more noise on the path than he made off it.

As he'd expected, the tall blond youth was the last to leave the clearing. He wasn't like a Protestant minister chatting with his congregation after services. He wanted to be seen as the high priest of some awful mystery, the giver of dark gifts. He'd have to wait for a more appropriate time if he wanted to go to McDonald's with the gang. While the ceremony was fresh in their minds, he'd have to keep acting the part. The Master understood: between the shaman and the tribe, some distance must always be maintained. When you were on speaking terms with evil spirits, you gave up your right to be one of the boys.

Twelve teens left the woods. A couple of them pedaled away on bicycles, a couple had mopeds, and the rest drove off in a wheezy old car. When it was quiet again, the young shaman took a small flashlight from his pocket and began to make his way down the path alone. The Master stepped out from the trees and waited for him.

The boy seemed to sense him standing there in the dark. He stopped, and the flashlight beam quested amid the shadows until it froze on the vampire's broad chest.

The Master could see perfectly well in the dark, but the artificial light could not baffle his eyes. He waited patiently as the boy played the light over him from head to toe. The youngster was clearly startled, but he hid it well.

"Who are you?" he demanded. He kept the light pinned insolently on the Master's face, but the vampire neither squinted nor turned away. He smiled.

"A friend," he answered. "One who would do you good."

"You were watching us."

The Master nodded. "Naturally. And I must say I liked what I saw. You handled that ceremony very well. You're obviously a superior human being, deserving of great gifts."

"You still haven't answered my question. Who are you, mister? And what do you want? If you're thinking of telling the cops about us, you'd better think again. You're already in trouble for spying on us."

"Your caution is admirable," the Master said, "and I like your spirit."

"Who the fuck are you?"

The Master smiled as best he could. His face could never be as mobile as a living man's.

"I'm surprised you don't know who I am, my boy. Aren't you a student of black magic? Don't you regularly invoke Satan? You shouldn't be too astonished to meet me."

The boy hesitated. His thoughts were as clear to the Master as if they were printed on a white page. Here was a shaman who didn't believe in his own magic, and only used it to gain ascendancy over his peers. But any trace of true

133

belief in such hocus-pocus would have been a major disappointment. The Master wanted the boy for his intelligence, not his credulity.

"You can't scare me, mister."

"I believe I can," said the Master, "but that's not my purpose. I don't want to scare you, or threaten you, or do anything but promote you to a higher state than any you could ever attain without me."

"If this is some sex thing, you can forget it."

The Master laughed his empty laugh. It made the boy cringe.

"My dear young man, nothing could be farther from my mind! I'm beyond sex. In fact I'm beyond hunger and thirst, fear and sadness, illness and injury—and more. But you're too intelligent to take me at my word. Come closer and make a trial of my strength. I promise I won't hurt you."

Any of the others would have turned and fled, but this boy was made of better stuff. He studied the stranger in his path and assessed his chances. If the man tried to hurt him, or violate him, could he defend himself? Could he escape unharmed? He was tall and strong, built like an athlete. The man was tall, too, but he was old and fat. If it came to it, the man would never be able to catch him if he ran.

"I don't know what your game is, mister, but I'm not afraid to play. If it gets too rough, you'll be sorry."

The Master held out his right hand. "Come here and take my hand," he said.

The youth mustered up his courage and advanced. He reached out from a safe distance and took the hand. His grip was firm, but mortal.

"Now squeeze," said the Master, "and as hard as you can. Don't be afraid; you won't hurt me."

The boy squeezed. He put all his strength into it, and he was as strong as he looked. He hunched his shoulders. The

134

muscles of his neck stood out like taut cords. He ground his teeth.

Then the Master squeezed. He used only a small portion of his power, but still the boy gasped and shuddered. The Master took care not to subject him to insupportable pain. Just enough to make his eyes water.

"Now try to get away," he said.

The boy threw his weight back, twisted, flung his weight forward. He dropped the flashlight and seized the Master's wrist with his free hand. He tried to twist the Master's arm, but twice the strength he had wouldn't have sufficed for that. He could not have been held more securely if he'd thrust his arm into a trough of cement and allowed it to harden around him.

He began to curse and threaten, but the Master maintained his hold. In his desperation he punched his tormentor in the face, in the body, all to no effect but to bruise his fist. He lashed out with his foot and kicked the Master solidly in the groin.

When that tactic failed, he collapsed to his knees and pleaded for release. The Master let him go.

He swallowed back a sob and cradled his aching hand. He glared up at the Master.

"I'll get you for this! You bastard, you broke my hand!"

"Your hand will be all right, my boy. But how do you propose to 'get' me? You tried as hard as you could to hurt me, and I trust you saw that nothing you did was effective. For my part, I could have hurt you terribly. I could have literally crushed your hand. How would you have stopped me?"

With a slowness that the Master would have pitied, had he been capable of pity, the boy reached into his pocket for the knife with which he had cut the white rat's belly. It was a switchblade; otherwise he wouldn't have been able to free the blade.

"Ah, yes—your knife. It does you credit that you re-

135

member it, in spite of your pain. Very well, let's see what your knife can do." The Master held out his hand. "I hurt your hand; it's proper for you to try to hurt mine. Go ahead."

The boy was hurt and scared, but he still balked when it came to using the knife. The Master doubted he had ever used it except on helpless animals.

"I appreciate your reluctance to do me an injury," he said, "but I must insist on this final test. Use your knife. If you don't, I'll squeeze your hand some more."

The boy slashed wildly, and missed. He was still on his knees. The Master kept his hand presented as a target.

"Come now, you can do better than that. I won't try to dodge the blow. Here, aim at my open palm."

Goaded, the boy slashed again, this time with his eyes open. The sharp knife sliced a neat furrow across the Master's palm. The boy dropped the weapon.

"Pick up your flashlight, young man. It's on the ground by your left knee. Shine it on my hand. I want you to see this."

The boy retrieved the flashlight and turned it on. When he looked at the Master's hand, his eyes went wide with horror.

"You're not bleeding!"

"Correct. But look closely. You'll see that you did indeed cut me."

The boy forced himself to look. He began to tremble violently. The hand holding the flashlight fell nervelessly to his side. When he tried to speak, he could barely whisper.

"You're not human!" was all he could say.

"I was, once," said the Master. "Now I'm something more. As you'll be, too, in a short time."

The Master raised Bruce Randall to his feet and gently steered him back to the clearing. All the fight was out of him. He trod numbly and would have tripped and fallen without the Master to support him. They sat down together on a fallen log.

"You're frightened, my boy, as is only natural. But I haven't hurt you so far, have I? Your hand should be feeling better already."

The blond head nodded listlessly.

"If you were to take that knife and plunge it into my heart, it would admittedly to be a serious annoyance," the Master said. "But if you were to pull the knife out, I would stand up and be as strong and active as if nothing had happened. And I wouldn't bleed.

"If this were a winter's night, and it was snowing, and all the water was frozen hard as rock, I could sit through it all as naked as a baby and never even shiver.

"If I were at the bottom of a lightless cavern, I could open a book and still read every word. If I were waiting in the deepest mine, a mile below the surface of the earth, I would be able to hear birds singing in the tallest trees.

"I will never know sickness, pain, or fear. I will never stand before a judge, no matter what black deed I have a whim to do. No jail can hold me, no man can stand against me, no law can restrain me. I will never die."

The boy felt his own death very near, however; the Master discerned that much. He offered comfort.

"I don't say these things to threaten you, my friend. On the contrary, I hold them out to you as an offering. A gift. With a little courage, you can be like me.

"Think of it! A fleeting moment of pain, and then no more pain forever! Only power. Only strength. And freedom from fear forever. Don't you want it?"

The youth muttered unintelligibly, having sunk deep into the depths of terror.

"The choice is yours," said the Master. "You can accept what I have to offer, and become what I am, or you can die. But I can't sit here and debate it with you. Choose now!''

He wasn't running out of patience, but he was running out of time. The boy's cooperation was desirable, but not indispensable.

The boy looked as though he might start crying. The Master subscribed to the attitude that male tears were a mark of shame. It was fascinating, he sometimes reflected, how many of one's preconceived notions survived the great transformation. Intellectual capacity and memory remained virtually intact, while the strong emotions withered down to almost nothing. Someday he hoped to understand the process scientifically.

''I don't *understand!''* The youth's voice quavered, proof of the struggle he was waging against horror and despair.

''Do you want to be a vampire?'' said the Master. ''I hate to use the word, because it's so bound up with all kinds of superstitious hogwash, but it'll have to do for now. I am a vampire, and I'm offering you the chance to become one, too.''

The boy goggled at him and stammered out, ''You mean . . . and drink blood?''

''Actually it's rather pleasant. Very refreshing.''

The boy's face went deathly pale. He shook his head. ''Oh, God, I can't believe this! It's like a horror movie!'' He stared wide-eyed at the Master. ''You're going to suck *my* blood, aren't you? That's how you turn into a vampire: a vampire bites you first.''

''You aren't much of a satanist, are you, young man? Under all the playacting, you're just a conventional, middle-class, suburban *boy.''* The Master turned the last word into a sneer.

He was glad when the youth showed signs of being offended. Obviously he had worked hard to make himself awesome to his peers, and it got his back up to hear that work belittled.

"Time's wasting," said the Master. "Make your choice. Shall I make you a vampire, or shall I kill you?"

The boy sat up straighter and said, "Mister, I still don't know what you are or what you want from me, but I know one thing for sure. I'm dead no matter what I say or do. But if it makes you happy, go ahead, make me a vampire."

"Unbutton your shirt, please."

Almost defiantly, the boy undid his shirt. The Master had his knife, having picked it up where he'd dropped it.

"This will be almost painless, provided you don't resist. As you can see, I don't have fangs. That's Hollywood. I'm going to make a small incision in the base of your neck and suck out a small quantity of blood—not enough to do you any harm. Then I'll instruct you as to how to survive the transformation when it comes."

The boy stared straight ahead, trying to face death bravely, imagining that it was all that was left to him. He only winced a little when the Master expertly made the incision in his neck.

The Master held him and pressed his cold lips to the wound. The blood burned and tingled going down, like strong whiskey.

The Master had deemed it necessary to feed earlier— much earlier than usual, and to satiety. He didn't want to succumb to the bloodlust now. He'd had Blanche drive him to a nearby city, where he found a homeless old woman in an isolated alleyway, killed her quickly, and drank several cups of her blood. Without it, he ran the risk of losing control of his experiment.

He still didn't know how much blood he had to take from a subject to ensure a transformation, but that was one of the things he was hoping to learn. Actually, he suspected that the duration of the contact between himself and his victim was a more critical factor than the amount of blood consumed. If his theory was correct, the longer the contact, the better the chance of a complete transformation. So he took his time, and the boy's blood trickling into his system brought him a feeling of contentment like that engendered by sipping fine wine.

Except for the frenzied beating of his heart, the boy sat perfectly still. The Master had his arms around him, and there was no possibility of escape. Because he wanted the boy's mind to be as clear as possible afterward, he was gentle—almost tender.

When his only intention was to feed, the Master liked to be fast and efficient: slash a vein, catch the spurting blood in a cup, and be gone before the corpse began to cool. Over the years, he had observed that this method never resulted in a transformation of the victim. Thus he came to believe that close contact with the vampire was essential. He was proud of having come to that conclusion through empirical observation—which had led him to a hypothesis that he could test by experimentation. Once a scientist, always a scientist.

After a time that must have seemed endless to the victim, but in reality had lasted less than thirty minutes, the Master broke the contact.

The boy was ashen-faced and trembling, and on the brink of fainting; but he rallied when the Master withdrew his mouth from the wound. Relief shone in his eyes. His hope of surviving the ordeal was visibly rekindled.

"That was only the first step," the Master said. "The rest is up to you. To survive, you'll have to do exactly as I tell you. The next twenty-four hours are crucial. Do you hear me?"

The boy nodded.

"Good. I'm going to give you some instructions now, and I want to be sure you understand them. Listen carefully, and don't be afraid to ask a question if anything seems unclear to you.

"First and foremost, you must avoid the light of the sun. Direct sunlight will be fatal to you. Eventually you'll be

140

able to endure small exposures, but that's some distance down the road. For the time being, stay out of the sun. You'll die horribly if you don't. I've seen it happen to others.

"I'm going to take you to a place where you can rest in the dark. Do not leave it! You'll be safe there, and no one will disturb you. Do you understand so far?"

The young eyes were both fearful and intrigued, like the eyes of a volunteer soldier about to enter battle for the first time.

"I have to stay out of the sun or it'll kill me," the boy said. "I have to stay put."

"Precisely. You'll be unconscious for some of the time, but not all of it. While you're conscious, do *nothing*.

"This will be difficult for you, because you will probably experience a sensation similar to a desperate thirst. It will spur you to go outside, perhaps in search of water; but you must stay where you are and endure it. Besides, water won't quench this thirst. It'll only make you sick. This is the thirst for blood.

"I'll come back to see you tomorrow night, and I'll bring blood for you. Then we'll see if you're strong enough to move at night. If not, I'll take care of you until you are. Any questions?"

The boy's lips moved fitfully, fighting a question that struggled to get out. After a moment or two, he yielded to it.

"Sir, will I be able to . . . I mean, *when . . . how* do I turn myself into a bat?"

The Master laughed thunderously and gave the boy's shoulders a friendly squeeze.

"My dear friend!" he cried. "I hate to disappoint you, but this is reality, not the late-night horror movie. Put away your superstitions! Forget your folklore.

"You'll never have the power to become a bat, a wolf, or a green mist streaming under a closed door. You'll never look into a mirror and not see your reflection. Holy water won't burn you, crosses won't scare you, and you won't have to wait for an invitation to enter someone's home. You won't want to drink water anymore, but if you do, it won't hurt you. You won't have to sleep in a coffin; any dark place will do. And a stake through the heart won't kill you, provided it's removed before long—although by all means it's to be avoided."

"But I thought—"

"You have a lot to learn, my boy. I'll teach you. But the night is fading, and we have several miles to walk. Get up now, and come with me. And for the time being, remember this: Only the sun can kill you now."

Three

The old man was psychic.

He never used that word. It was, however, familiar to him. He understood what it meant when he heard other people use it. In these Godless times, men and women closed their hearts to wonder and in their confusion sought refuge in jargon. For them it would have been unthinkable to believe in second sight but eminently fashionable to believe in precognition, clairvoyance, ESP.

As the years stretched into decades, the old man gradually fell away from his charge to preach the Word. You could not preach to the deaf. You could not show miracles to the blind.

He had another charge. A lesser one, perhaps, in the total scheme of things, but it was the mission that God had given him. For its fulfillment he had been endowed, from birth, with a knowledge of hidden things. Second sight, they'd called it when he was a child. Now they would call it by other names, if they knew he had it. But the old man pursued his mission alone, sharing his burden with no one. He never explained himself. He never tried to warn worldly persons of their peril. They would not have understood a word of it—not even if he showed them the scars where Esperanza had clawed and bitten him.

Sometimes he would touch himself there, and let his fingers see the signs that God had written in his flesh. For he had been spared only to carry out his mission.

Wrapped in rags bound with twine, he carried a Spanish sword. The blade was of the best Toledo steel, and it was ancient. When it was forged, half of Spain still lay under the enemies of the Christian faith, the Moors. Against them it saw a hundred battles and was victorious in every one. It traveled to the New World and helped to cast down pagan idols that stank of human sacrifice. Finally, in a nameless corner of the jungle, it slew a creature that was an abomination in the sight of God. This was in truth a holy deed. Never again was the sword used to hew the flesh of men; for no man lived who was not made in the image of the Lord and the habitation of an immortal soul.

For centuries thereafter it lay in a blessed crypt beneath the Cathedral of San Salvador, until in 1931 a Roman priest of unique understanding was moved by God to give it to the only man who could put it to its proper use. That man had carried it with him ever since, and now he was white and gaunt with age. But his holy mission lent him strength.

He could no longer count the years he'd followed his quarry, hungry, penniless, his clothes in tatters. He lived on charity, going on foot while God's enemy rode first-class in luxurious private railroad cars, proud cruise ships, gleaming silver airplanes. The old man's quest was slow and laborious, and at the end of it his death awaited him, but the charge was laid on him and no other, and unquestioningly he toiled to achieve it.

No matter where his quarry fled, God led him unerringly on the trail. He was like the salmon that crosses the boundless ocean to find the little brook where it was spawned.

Now he came to Millboro.

He was reminded of the arrival of Mary and Joseph in Bethlehem, when there was no room for them at the inn.

Millboro's zoning laws excluded boarding houses, cheap hotels, rental rooms, and any other refuge for the poor. The old man hiked alone down the endless length of Main Street, studying the new homes and the recently constructed public buildings, foreseeing the day when they would swallow up the last green remnants of the township's farmlands. A police car pulled up next to him and stopped.

"Are you looking for someplace in particular, sir? Maybe I can help you."

The old man knew how he looked to the policeman.

"Thank you, officer, but I'm just passing through."

"Where to?"

"Leffertsville." The old man knew the geography of the area, having spent some time poring over a road map. The map had told him that an institution for the insane was located in the middle of this township. It would be natural for the policeman to suspect him of being an inmate on the loose.

"Why don't I give you a lift, then?" said the officer.

The old man smiled. "Thanks, but I walk for my health. And I'm in no hurry."

The policeman seemed to be on the point of asking to see the old man's papers. If it came to that, the old man knew he might be arrested for vagrancy. He had no papers. In the eyes of the law, he was nothing but a tramp.

He had been stopped for vagrancy many times before, but so far he had never been jailed for more than one night. He didn't think this town, however, would take the presence of a tramp in stride.

"On second thought, officer, I'd be grateful for a ride," he said. Let them roust the vagrant out of town and be done with it. "At my age, a little bit of hiking goes a long way."

It was a beautiful sunny afternoon, the summer's heat was still some weeks away, and the policeman was in a charitable mood. He chauffeured the old man out of town and dropped him off in Leffertsville.

He spent the rest of the day asking discreet questions, and by sundown he was ready to return to Millboro. Now that he knew that the township wasn't all fair lawns and affluence, he could select a destination.

He thumbed a ride from a bearded man in a pickup truck and was spared a second encounter with the Millboro police. The man took him down a U.S. highway and let him out at the appropriate exit, and he walked the rest of the way alone, under the stars.

He could walk all day without having to stop for rest, his long legs eating up the miles. He could sleep outdoors in bad weather, and often had to; yet it had been forty years since he'd last required the services of a physician. When he could, he cleaned himself thoroughly, shampooing his shock of white hair and the long white beard that gave him the look of a patriarch. From time to time the Salvation Army reclothed him and refilled his backpack with spare clothes and other necessities. He regularly thanked God for General Booth's Army.

Tonight he set a brisk pace for Alabama Road. During the day he'd learned that this was where he had to be if he wanted to stay in Millboro for any length of time. Even if he couldn't find a family to take him in, there were derelict buildings in that neighborhood that would be palaces compared to some of the shelters he had known.

"But you wanna stay away from there," said a man he met in Leffertsville; "it's all niggers."

The old man let it go without remarking that he had, in his time, enjoyed the hospitality of the Uixac Indians, whose fondness for brigandage led to their virtual extinction by 1960. His trust was in God. If any harm could come to him on Alabama Road, he would have seen a sign of it by now.

Even in the darkness, the contrast between this neighborhood and the rest of Millboro was dramatic. Here the streets were barely paved, and traversed with potholes filled with stagnant water. Whole blocks of buildings lay untenanted, their windows boarded or broken, squatting like dark beggars along the road. Sidewalks were a rarity. The hulks of worn-out cars lay rusting in backyards. Men sat on porch steps, talking softly and drinking beer from cans. He wondered if they would see as much of each other if they lived on half-acre lots in expensive developments, or know one another half as well. He had seen enough of affluence in his travels to distrust it.

Heads turned as he walked past, but no one tried to stop him. These people were not so poor that they'd fail to take notice of a tramp in their midst. In fact the old man didn't consider them poor at all. They weren't hungry, they weren't thirsty, they had roofs over their heads and clothes on their backs, and they didn't have to worry about warlords, revolutionaries, or death squads suddenly appearing in their neighborhood.

Materially, the old man was poorer by far than the least of them. For that alone they'd notice him—but he was white, too. He was out of place here, as much as he was out of place in the wealthy white sections of the township.

146

Even so, he felt certain that God had directed him here for a good purpose.

Three men stood on a street corner, smoking cigars and enjoying the balmy night. The old man approached them and excused himself, interrupting their conversation. They stared at him, not knowing what to make of him. Overhead, moths danced around the streetlamp.

"Gentlemen, I've come a long way and I'm tired. I wonder if you could tell me of a place nearby where I could spend the night without inconveniencing anybody. Anything with a roof will do."

"Who the hell are you, man?"

"Just a homeless wanderer."

"From where?" demanded the youngest of the three, striking a jaunty pose with the cigar clamped between his teeth.

"From Vermont, originally. But that was a long, long time ago. I'm not really *from* anywhere."

"So what you doin' *here*, then?"

"Looking for a place to rest awhile. Someplace where people won't be afraid of me because I'm poor."

That didn't sit well with the tallest of the men. "Who says *we're* poor?"

"I didn't say that. I say *I'm* poor. You can see that."

The third man looked him over carefully: his backpack, his secondhand clothes, and the long ragged parcel he carried under his arm.

"If you make a left here," the third man said, "and go down two and a half blocks, you'll find a little deserted house on the left-hand side of the street. You'll know it 'cause the houses on either side of it, they're in even worse shape. This little house, nobody's been livin' there for two-three years, but it don't look so bad. I don't think it'll be hurtin' anything if you stay there awhile."

"Yeah," the youngest man said, "that place be just fine. You won't be botherin' nobody there."

"Thank you very much, gentlemen." The old man bowed slightly. "The Lord will bless you for being gracious to a poor man."

He turned to leave them, but the tall man called him back. "Hey! Just a minute. You a preacher?"

"I am. But I don't have a church."

"What's your name, Reverend?" The tall man made a slight joke of the title, but in fact the old man was entitled to it.

"Benejah Thornall," he said. "You can call me Ben."

He left them feeling a little guilty about sending a man of the cloth to spend the night in a derelict building.

Thornall woke with sunlight on his face; it streamed in through a broken window. For a little while he basked in its warmth, his head cushioned on his backpack, old newspapers protecting him from the dusty wooden floor. He was so used to sleeping on floors and bare ground that he was sometimes more comfortable there than on a mattress.

He knew the enemy of God was in Millboro, living in some disguise among its prosperous citizens. Their senses dulled by affluence, their minds by rationalism, they would never suspect their danger. The enemy would take their blood with impunity.

In his last fifty years of hunting, Thornall had not seen his quarry face-to-face. But he knew the face had never changed—unless its owner had taken steps to change it. He frequently changed his name.

But Thornall had seen—and killed—others of the kind. Those had been good deeds, although they were not his mission.

This vampire was not like those others. The ones Thornall had killed were mindless things, protected only by superstition or obstinate unbelief. This one, however, protected itself. It kept moving, never staying long enough

148

in one place to put itself in jeopardy. In life it had been a man of science and an adventurer; in the unclean semblance of life that possessed its body now, these qualities seemed to guide it and inspire it.

Thornall was not deceived by this. He knew that the man's soul had fled the body altogether, or else was held prisoner by the evil that had overcome the flesh. That which animated the undead body now was not a human soul.

He prayed for strength and guidance, and for the achievement of his quest. He knew what he would have to do to destroy the vampire. He'd done it before. The body must be immobilized so that the sun could overtake it. Without the cleansing of the heavenly fire, there was no end to the evil. Thornall knew because he once severed the hand of a vampire and kept it sheltered in the dark; he had observed with revulsion how the clumsy fingers continued to twitch and tremble, to grasp the air and let it go again, night after night until he ended it by putting it out in the sun.

He concluded his prayer with thanks for the sunbeams that the Lord had sent to dance soothingly on his face.

Four

Bruce woke in utter darkness.

It wasn't the first time he'd wakened in a strange place. Only a month ago he'd gotten so ripped at a party that he couldn't recall staggering out to a car with a few of the guys and going to another party somewhere else. That was the time he woke up in a bed with a guy and a chick whose names he didn't know and never learned, in a cruddy rented room just outside Asbury Park.

So he didn't panic when he couldn't see and couldn't remember where he was. He lay still and tried to assess the situation calmly.

The silence told him he was alone. His sore bones told him he was lying on cement, with some cloth bunched under his head for a pillow.

He didn't think he was hung over, but he sure as hell didn't feel healthy. His thoughts kept dissolving into incoherent jumbles. His head felt like it was stuffed with sawdust, loosely packed so that it sloshed around whenever he stirred. His hands and feet felt like they were connected to his brain by remote-control hookups.

But more than anything else, he was thirsty.

He sat up. His head lost contact with his body and imploded. He sat for a measureless infinity before thirst pricked him to grope in the darkness. He had a vision of a marble fountain bubbling and spurting and brimming, not with water but with blood, sparkling red with life-giving bubbles of oxygen in it.

His fingers found and closed on splintery wood, and he maneuvered slowly to his feet. The vision dominated him, shutting out all thought. Had he been able to call it anything, however, he would not have called it a vision. It was reality. His whole being centered on attaining the fountain and quenching his thirst in it. It was waiting for him just beyond the darkness.

Wood opposed him, kept him from his goal. He blundered into it and tore his fingers trying to fling it aside. He wasn't hurt, but he whimpered in frustration. He could hear the blood burbling in its marble basin, he could smell it.

By chance his hand found a knob and remembered, without conscious direction, how to cope with it. Bruce stepped back and pulled the door open.

Whips of fire lashed across his eyes and skin before he could slam it shut again. The life-giving fountain vanished from his mind. He sobbed and leaned against the wooden door, safe in the dark again.

Now his memory began to show him strange scenes that gradually became familiar. He watched passively, like a sedated patient watching television. He saw the revel in the clearing, and the coven submitting to him, and then a huge old man with silver hair blocking his path when he tried to leave. He saw it all so clearly, up to the point where the old man cut his neck so he could suck his blood. After that the video became a garbled mess. But he heard the old man telling him, over and over again, that the sun would kill him, that he had to stay put until the old man came to see him again.

He remembered everything the old man told him. It was all happening just as the old man had said it would. And Bruce understood.

He was becoming a vampire. The old man had left him in a safe, dark place where the sun couldn't get at him and would come back for him later, to take care of him, help him. And the thirst that tormented him was the thirst for blood. He would have to resist it and stay where he was.

He couldn't remember his own name, nor the names of his family and friends.

Strong hands raised him from the hard floor.

"Can you see? Would you like me to give you some light? I have your flashlight with me."

Bruce tried to see. It wasn't as dark as it had been before. He recognized the old man by his size and shape and could make out a little of the whiteness of his hair. But that was all.

"I can't see much," he said.

"But you can see a little?"

151

"Yeah . . . a little."

"Excellent!" He saw the teeth in the old man's smile. "In point of fact, it's after midnight and the moon has set. That you can see anything at all is a sign that the transformation is proceeding very well. Otherwise it'd seem as black as a crypt in here to you. Do you remember me?"

Bruce nodded. "Tell me what you remember," the old man said. Bruce replied, "I remember it all," and described his memories. The old man grinned.

"Good! Very good. But can you remember anything that happened *before* our encounter?"

Bruce had been trying to do that, off and on, between fainting spells. All he got was a confused mess of faces to which he could give no names, names to which he could give no faces, and isolated incidents that refused to fit in any context.

"Can you remember your own name? Who are you?"

It hadn't occurred to Bruce that he had ever had a name. Now he groped for one, unsuccessfully, like a man groping in murky water for a lost pearl. He had a feeling that this lapse ought to frighten him, but it didn't. It was more like being unable to remember the word for a common and familiar item held in front of him. He shook his head.

The old man seemed disappointed, but not overly so.

"Let it pass for now," he said. "I'm sure it'll come back to you later. I have only my own experience as a guide, and it may differ from yours. But I can tell you that when my transformation was complete, I remembered everything. My mind was not the least bit impaired. The same should happen to you before very long. For the time being, however, let's see to your more immediate physical needs."

He produced a paper bag, and from it he pulled a large white rabbit. "This is for you," he said. "I broke its neck just a few minutes ago, so it's nice and fresh."

"I thought vampires were supposed to drink human blood," Bruce objected.

"Any fresh blood will do, in a pinch. You're still in the process of becoming a vampire, my boy, and there's plenty of your own human blood in your system yet. I've never tried to subsist for any length of time on animal blood alone, so I don't know what would happen if I did. The craving for human blood is so strong that I'm sure it reflects an actual physiological need. Be that as it may, my first few meals were animals, so I imagine animals will suffice for you."

He took a knife and smoothly cut the rabbit's throat. When the blood began to well out of the wound, Bruce became dizzy with desire. His hands trembled as he reached for the animal's body. The old man gave it to him. "Drink all you want, my boy," he said.

Bruce clamped his mouth to the open wound. He felt no revulsion whatsoever. The blood was better than water, better than wine, warm and smooth as life itself. He felt stronger and more alert with every swallow.

When the body was drained, he wiped his lips on the silky white fur and set it aside.

"That was delicious!" he said. He felt like standing up, but when he tried, his legs were rubbery and he had to sit back down.

"Take it easy. You won't have your full strength until the transformation is complete."

"Will I be as strong as you?"

"You'll be stronger than you ever would have been as a mortal human being. And you'll continue to grow stronger year by year. You won't age. Still, it'll be many years before you're as strong as I am now."

They sat together for some time, the old man patiently answering Bruce's questions. Bruce found himself growing sluggish, and he lay back down.

"Rest as much as you can," the vampire said. "I have to be going. Day is not far off. Stay here until I come back for you."

Bruce was unconscious before the Master could rise to his feet.

He woke knowing his own name and quite a bit more, but the knowledge was nothing compared to the feeling of exultation that overtook him as he contemplated his new status.

Furthermore, he could see.

He was in a little room with brick walls, resting inside an empty wooden enclosure that was like a low stall. Had he been older, he might have recognized it as an empty coal bin. Overhead stretched dusty wooden beams. The rabbit lay beside him, white fur stiff with dark blood. The room was closed by a stout wooden door with a rusty knob.

He yearned for blood. Remembering the savor of the rabbit's blood, he licked his lips. The yearning became a craving and engendered wild images of him battening on naked girls. Strangely, what excited him about these visions was not the beauty of the girls but the sweet taste of their blood. He found it just as satisfactory to imagine himself quaffing a man's blood, or a child's, or a fat old woman's.

The closed door tempted him. By some process that he neither understood nor questioned, he knew that the sun had set outside and the night had just begun. It called to him, a siren song of blood. He rose up and felt strong.

Only the sun could kill him, and the sun had set. He opened the door and found himself in a larger cellar. It was pitch dark, but he could see well enough to make his way without difficulty. Stone steps and a pair of rusty steel doors brought him outside.

The night was glorious. Overhead the stars gleamed like torches, and the moon was like a silver galleon under full sail. The air pulsated with life: the chatter of insects, the calls of night birds, the distant hum of wheels on asphalt, the song of the wind in the trees, the rustle of the paws of small, blood-bearing animals in the dead leaves all around. But he wasn't interested in animals just now.

Intoxicated by his freedom and his new strength and vigor, he fled through the trees in quest of his first taste of human blood.

VI. AT THE MALL

One

Chris called to say he wouldn't be home for supper; he had to meet an author who had just flown in from Nebraska. As usual, he was all apologies, but it was wasted. It was getting to the point where Dorothy didn't care anymore.

Could you divorce a husband because he gave everything he had to his job and had nothing left over for you? He wasn't cheating on her. He wasn't beating on her. He wasn't abusing her verbally. She would have to ask a lawyer whether benign neglect was grounds for dissolving a marriage.

She ate alone, mechanically shoveling food into her mouth without enjoying it. Maybe it really was time to see a lawyer. Or at least a marriage counselor. She'd suggested that to Chris several times this year, to no avail. "The only thing wrong with our marriage," he always said, "is that I'm at a stage in my career where I have to spend a lot of time at work. There's no way around it. There's nothing a marriage counselor can say to change it."

She could think of half a dozen men with whom she might have an affair, but the thought of climbing naked into a bed with any one of them made her skin crawl. Mark Lewin, who lived down the street, would be happy to oblige her;

but for all his good looks, Mark was a creep. You could pick up a disease from a man like that. And the others were as dull as unbuttered toast. What the hell, she could bang the mayor if she wanted to: Ron Leib had a reputation as a cocksman. But she didn't want to. If she was starved for sex, she was even hungrier for love.

If only things could be the way they used to be. . . . When she and Chris were first married, they used to get away to the shore on weekends, go to movies, play cards with friends. In the words of the old cliché, they laughed a lot. But that was all before they became successful enough to buy a house in Millboro.

Maybe she ought to write a book. Shit, she had a husband in the publishing business, he should be able to find a buyer for it. And writing would certainly fill the empty hours. She hadn't tried to write any fiction since her college days; but at this juncture in her life, it might be a good idea to see if she could write a novel. There was just this problem of what to write about. . . .

To stave off cabin fever, she decided to take a ride out to the Millboro Mall. Maybe she could buy a couple of paperbacks and find some inspiration in them.

She knew women who filled the abysses in their lives by compulsively shopping. They spent money as fast as their husbands could earn it. Dorothy considered shopping for its own sake to be a mental disorder on a par with anorexia or bulimia, drinking or gambling: self-destructive idiocy as a last gesture of rebellion. Also an indirect way to punish neglectful husbands. Anyway, it was a cornball thing to go to the mall just for something to do. But damn it, there were people there. Talking to a bookstore clerk was better than talking to nobody.

The Millboro Mall was always crowded. The township was such a decentralized sprawl that the mall was the natural destination when one had nothing in particular to do, nowhere in particular to go. Dorothy parked at the far end of the lot, where a fringe of trees still stood, relics of the large wooded tracts that the township would no longer have by the year 2000. She was in no hurry, and a brisk walk to the bookstore would do her good.

The mall was enclosed. Air-conditioned in the summer, heated in the winter, always brightly lit. Complete stabilization of the environment. But then you could say that about the moon.

Shoppers milled like cattle preparing to stampede. Dorothy saw no one that she knew. Two thirds of the township seemed to be here tonight, and all of them strangers. She made a point of walking slowly to the bookstores, and other customers swept past her on either side.

Dorothy favored meaty nonfiction: history, popular science, investigative journalism. When it came to fiction, her tastes were less clearly defined. But if she wanted to write a novel, she'd better pick a genre and bone up on it.

She used to like science fiction—the old-fashioned kind, with plot and character and fantastic settings—but there was no hope there. According to Chris, every jerk who harbored delusions of writing but couldn't put two articulate sentences back-to-back turned immediately to science fiction. If other editors felt that way, it'd be foolish to buck their prejudices.

Gothic romance, forget it. Dorothy didn't want to write anything that might wind up being offered free with the purchase of a box of sanitary napkins. And as for serious fiction—Christ, there was enough to be serious about already without trying to add to it fictionally.

She browsed, daunted by the blatant trivialities described on the book jackets. Slash 'em, fuck 'em, rob 'em, spy on 'em—popular literature was getting to be as bad as prime-time TV. She finally settled for a mystery by Lawrence Sanders, a chiller by Stephen King, and a historical novel by Louis L'Amour, this one set in the Middle Ages instead of the Old West. *Learn to write like one of these guys,* she told herself, *and you can't go wrong.* She paid for the books and stepped back out into the mindless flow of shoppers.

Now she wanted to get home and ready, so she didn't stop to browse the windows. But she did have to stop when a pair of goons blocked her path and leered at her.

High school kids, one in a black leather jacket, the other in denim. Tight jeans and acne. Leatherjacket wore his dark hair long and stringy; the other had his hair shaved close to the scalp, like a Manhattan queer's. They stood and stripped her with their eyes while she maneuvered around them. They didn't speak.

She trembled as she hurried past them, fighting a compulsion to look back and see if they were following her. She lost the fight and turned her head, but they had disappeared in the crowd.

Her hands were shaking so badly that she almost dropped her books. She swore at herself. Why get so upset over a couple of creeps? The mall was full of louts like those two. They had no more manners than hyenas, but they weren't doing any harm. Just a pair of schmucks eyeballing inaccessible women. A minor annoyance.

A security guard seemed to materialize out of nowhere. "You all right, ma'am?" he asked.

She nodded, pissed off at herself for overreacting. "Thanks, I'm fine." The guard nodded back and withdrew. *I must look a sight,* she thought, *for a guard to bother to take notice.* She took a deep breath to compose herself before going on.

As she exited the mall, she wondered where justifiable uneasiness left off and paranoia began. It wasn't so easy to tell anymore. For a moment her heart went out to Chris, working in New York City, where any stranger you met on the sidewalk might be fixing to pull a knife on you. But her sympathy was short-lived: Chris was too preoccupied with his work to notice things like that. He wouldn't worry about being mugged until someone actually jumped him.

Maybe she could write up the encounter in her next *Tales from the Developments*. "Suburban matron panics because a couple of kids look at her cross-eyed." So much for the pioneer spirit. Shit, the Monmouth Battlefield was only a few miles south of here. What would Molly Pitcher do if two underage lechers tried to stare her down? Probably knock their heads together with her trusty cannon swab.

Dorothy drank in the fresh air and walked briskly down the aisle between two rows of parked cars. Now that the incident was over, she could laugh at herself.

It was a big parking lot and it took her some time to walk to the end of it. Her car sat all alone under the shadow of the trees, waiting for her. She reached into her purse and fumbled for her keys.

A white hand came down and clamped itself on the handle of her car door just as she was about to thrust the key into the lock.

In a moment of panic she thought the two louts from the mall must have followed her. She'd been writing a column in her head, and she hadn't noticed anyone approaching the car.

But it wasn't either of them. It was another boy, a much bigger boy, blond and athletic. He towered over her. He would have been a good-looking kid, clean-cut and wholesome, a regular all-American farm boy, except for the way he showed his teeth at her. His eyes were in shadow.

She heard her voice rising to a squeak as she confronted him. "What do you think you're doing? Get your hand off my car! Get away from me!"

He made no reply but to show his teeth some more. Dorothy turned abruptly and tried to run away. A hand seized her shoulder and yanked her back.

She screamed. He clapped a hand over her mouth. His

palm was as cold and hard as ice. The fingers of his other hand dug painfully into her shoulder. She swung her purse at the side of his head and connected, but to no effect.

He started to drag her toward the trees. He made no sound. She couldn't shake her mouth free. His grip on her jaws was like iron. She dropped her purse, balled her hand into a fist, and battered him in the ribs with all her strength, again and again. He paid no attention to it. She tried to drive a knee into his groin, but he was dragging her and she couldn't keep her feet. She dropped her books and tried to hook fingers into his eyes, but her arm wouldn't reach up and around his shoulder.

Now she felt earth under her feet instead of asphalt. He was taking her into the trees, and once he got her there, all hope was lost. She thrashed, and then went suddenly limp.

The tactic worked; when she fell, he lost his grip. She screamed before she hit the ground. *"Help! Somebody help!"* But he was hauling her back up before she could roll and try to run. He jerked her from the ground as easily as if she were a baby.

Suddenly she was looking into his face, and for the first time she could see his eyes. They were pale and lifeless, blind eyes that rolled unseeing in their sockets like a pair of colored marbles. They made her fear worse than rape. They were eyes that no longer saw things from a human perspective.

He spun her around, and in doing so, lost his footing and fell on top of her. The ground slammed into the back of her head and sent her spinning into a black void.

The Schuylerville Nursing Home was all that was left of Schuylerville.

Other regions of the township clung to their old names: Evansville and Williamston, Macks Corner and Shining Valley. The housing developments aped this custom, so that speakers would get up at town meetings and proudly identify themselves as residents of Thoreau Manor or Royal Oaks II. But no one ever introduced himself as a man from Schuylerville. The name hadn't appeared on a map in twenty years.

Like the other villages and small farming communities, Schuylerville was incorporated into Millboro Township in 1934. Like the others, it fell headlong into the abyss of the Depression.

There are still one or two local historians who know of Schuylerville and can speculate as to why it embraced oblivion.

They can tell of a farmer named Charles Dexter, who slew his wife and four small children with an axe, then blasted away his throat and lower jaw with a heavy shotgun. They can rummage through their notes and produce yellowed, musty newspaper clippings that tell as much of the tale as will ever be known: how Dexter and the local bank fell into a bitter feud instead of trying to work things out; how the farm was lost; how the bank's officer and the sheriff's deputy found Dexter sprawled hideously on his front porch, blocking the door; and of the shambles within the house.

Other farmers lost their lands and went away. Those who stayed, despaired. By the time World War II kicked the national economy back into gear, Schuylerville was finished.

In 1944 a Dr. R. M. Wishingham came up from Freehold to purchase the mansion of the De Wet family, a clan that had been rich and envied since before the Revolution and was now forgotten utterly. He painted it white and had the roof redone with red clay tiles, and it looked like a villa by the sea. Tall pines sheltered it from the sun. At the time there were few who could afford to consign their elderly to such a resting place, but Dr. Wishingham was an optimist. By the time the first American troops landed in Korea, the Schuylerville Nursing Home had a six-month waiting list and Dr. Wishingham was a wealthy man. In 1956 he retired to Florida and let a paid director run the home. In 1958 he came up for a visit and was murdered by one of the residents, an old woman who mistook him for her long-dead husband and stabbed him with a pair of scissors in payment for old injustices. The woman died of a heart attack immediately after dispatching Wishingham; she fell dead across her victim's body. It did not help matters, afterward, when some of the more difficult inmates insisted that their late sister was still on the premises, padding silently about the halls with her scissors clutched in both hands. In 1960 the home was closed by order of the state.

Now it stood in ruin among the pines. From a distance it still looked like a substantial building, but that was illusion. The home was an empty shell, with holes in the roof and holes in the floors, chimneys crumbling brick by brick, mildewed wallpaper peeling in long scabrous strips, abandoned to the spiders, wasps, and rats. Termites bored in the beams, bats roosted in the attic. Nettles and saplings overran the yard. Up close you could smell the rot—except that no one ever ventured close.

It would have been demolished, only that would have cost the township money and no one cared enough to push for it. The home could not be seen from Dutch Mill Road and had near neighbors who didn't know of its existence. Dr. Wishingham's daughter owned the property; she lived in

Florida and paid the taxes by mail. She had never seen the building. And so it sat and moldered.

Dorothy thought she heard voices arguing in raspy whispers, but she woke in dark and silence.

For a fleeting moment she thought she was at home in bed, waking from a bad dream. But her body was sore all over, and she was sick with a fever. It was a dry fever. It made her feel like her head was stuffed with ashes. She tried to remember what had happened to her, but the effort produced only a kaleidoscopic reel of disconnected images: stars wheeling slowly overhead; Chris fondling her bare breast; a car's headlights; an open mouth with white teeth; two dogs fighting. It was as if her mind were a box full of unrelated odds and ends, and trying to think was like holding the box upside down and shaking it.

Over the confusion, over the fever and the aches and pains, over it all lay a consuming thirst. She saw a vision of a running brook, clear and cold, and she was strangely sickened by it. Her guts crept like snakes coming out of hibernation. She rolled onto her side and retched, bitterly.

I am Dorothy Matthiesen was her first coherent thought.

For some incalculable time it was the only thought that would come to her. Thirst prevented her from lapsing into a coma, but it also set up a noisy interference pattern in her brain. Gradually some of her other senses began to reassert themselves. It might have taken hours, even days. She had no way to count the time.

Her joints felt stiff and swollen. Her back ached from lying on stone or cement. Muscles danced in small, painful spasms.

Her second rational thought was a realization that she was not at her home. She was not in any place that she knew. *Where am I? How did I get here?* She didn't know and didn't remember.

165

She rediscovered her eyes. Wherever she was, it was dark, and yet some dim light filtered into it. Paying a price in pain, she moved her head and saw bright cracks splitting the shadows here and there. *Boarded-up windows in a basement. I'm in somebody's cellar.*

Now her eyes took in the flat cement floor, the heavy beams marching overhead, the boards across the windows. This was nobody's basement that she knew. It was vast and empty, like a plundered tomb.

Suddenly she remembered the boy with the blond hair and his attack on her: his clutching hands, strong as steel clamps, his snarling mouth, crazy eyes. She remembered falling down with him on top of her, his hard bones digging into the soft places of her body, his hellish strength, and the way he moved, fierce and supple as a shark. Her own scream echoed in her mind's ear.

Her memory stopped abruptly there, like a broken tape.

Had he raped her? She felt her clothes. Her top was buttoned, her jeans zipped shut.

Probably he'd meant to rape her but hadn't been able to get started. Maybe somebody came and scared him off. No way he would've taken her without messing up her clothes; and even if he had, he wasn't going to take the time to dress her up again, was he? Anyway, she didn't *feel* like she'd been raped. Just assaulted. She groped around for her handbag, couldn't find it. Mugged, she thought. Mugged and robbed right in the middle of Millboro, like it was the South Bronx. *A damaging blow to the prestige of the township.* This last almost made her smile.

Who scared the punk away, and who brought her to this empty cellar? And left her stretched out on the bare floor?

This was neither a hospital nor a police station nor a private home. Fear shot into her. She sat up.

Pain erupted inside her skull and sent her head skittering like a marble on a plate, and her vision dissolved in a galaxy of burning red and purple dots. Nausea rumbled like a subway train in her lower abdomen. She almost fell back down, but she stiffened her nerveless arms and sat rigidly until the pain passed and her head was clear again. Tears flowed from her eyes, streaking channels through the dust on her cheeks.

He'll come back.

She tried to get up. Her back screeched painful protest, her knees buckled, her head swam. Her hands found a wooden post and clung to it. She used it as an anchor as she pulled herself to her feet, then leaned against it, head throbbing like an overtaxed heart. But the uproar in her body took the edge off her panic.

Who *will come back? Whoever brought me here and left me.* She didn't know who that was. She'd been unconscious. But it made sense to be afraid. Anyone who meant well would've brought her to a hospital, or at least to police headquarters. Some inhabited place. Not here.

All I have to do is get out before he comes back. I'm in a basement, so there must be a way up. A flight of stairs. Find it.

She looked around, but the cellar was so big that the far walls were swallowed in darkness and she couldn't see them. The ceiling was close to her head; she could touch it without fully extending her arms.

It was empty, but it stank. Somewhere water was trapped, foul and dank. Mold grew on the wooden beams and added a mildew taint to the air. Insects chewed and tunneled in the rotting oak; their excretions and their dead bodies gave off a faint stench of wormy meal. All of these were blended, along with other odors that Dorothy couldn't name. Fresh air trickled in through the cracks in the boarded windows, but only enough to make the atmosphere endurable.

When she stood still and held her breath, she could hear small stirrings in the murk. Overhead the wood creaked as gravity strove with infinite patience to pull down the massive pile. Here in the darkness, water dripped intermittently, and faint rustling noises could be heard in the darkest places. Dorothy remembered having heard voices when she was first coming to, but she heard no voices now.

She had always had a dread of empty buildings. That was where the ghosts walked, that was where the monsters lurked. She couldn't pass a deserted house without feeling a bit of the old cold grue on her skin. To be in one, under any circumstances, was to be avoided. Under these circumstances it nearly paralyzed her brain.

Steady, steady, damn it! There's nothing here to hurt you. She got a grip on herself and proceeded to search for the steps, wishing she still had her purse so she could light a match.

She found the stairs in deeper darkness; the door at the top must be closed. The stairs looked solid enough from where she stood, but there was no telling whether one or more of the steps was rotten and apt to give way when she put her weight on it.

And maybe the door up there was locked. Maybe it'd be better to try to find something to stand on, pry the boards off one of the windows, and climb out.

The truth was that she was afraid to mount those stairs. She feared the undefined menace of that black tunnel that rose above her. She thought of every horror movie she had ever seen, and all the times she cringed when one of the characters ventured alone into a dark place to open a door that should have been left closed.

But if you want out, the quickest way is up those stairs and through the door. She put a hand on the dusty banister and tugged on it. Satisfied that it would support her, she began her slow ascent.

In the middle of the stairwell the darkness was absolute. On either side she could reach out and touch clammy brick walls. They smelled mossy, like the sides of a well. She wanted to hurry up the stairs and get it over with, but that was too dangerous.

Unable to see, she thrust her face into a mat of cobwebs. Her hands leaped to tear the clinging stuff away, and she

168

almost toppled backward. She slipped, grabbed the banister with both hands, and bashed a knee against a stair.

"Fucking shit!" Her knee was on fire, and her heart was trying to climb up her windpipe. With one hand she clung to the banister; with the other she clawed the cobwebs from her skin. She didn't care if she raked her face off doing it: it'd be better than having a spider drop down her shirtfront or fall into her mouth.

She knelt on the stair and panted until the mist cleared from her mind. *Thank God I can't see what I'm walking into,* she thought, *or I'd never have gotten this far.*

But it wasn't much farther before the stairs came to an end and she stood upon a landing, groping for a doorknob. She found one and gave it a twist.

The light hit her like a truck.

It slammed her against the wall of the stairwell and pinned her there. It jabbed like spears. And it was worse than painful. She felt like an escaping prisoner skewered by a searchlight. She turned into the blind wall and pressed her face to the bricks, shielding her eyes with her hands, sobbing.

Her sore knee, the one she hurt on the stairs, flared up when it knocked against the wall. The sudden sharp pain of it shocked her into silence.

She clung there like a pilgrim at the Wailing Wall, momentarily insane, eyes screwed shut, breathless. *God, I'm going to lose it.* . . . Rationality struggled back to the surface and reminded her that the way out was through the door. When her heartbeat slowed, she cautiously opened her eyes.

She saw bare brick. There was something comforting about its flat mundaneness.

It came to her that whatever lay beyond the door, her back was to it. She felt as if a bull's-eye were pinned between her shoulder blades. Acid gnawed at the inner wall of her stomach. Dorothy pushed herself from the wall and turned to face the doorway. It felt like letting go of a lifeline.

She stood looking into a bare room with boarded windows

through which a gray light seeped. The floor wore a thick pelt of dust. There were shoe prints in it.

Want to hang around to find out who made them? No? Better get a move on, then. She stepped into the room.

It might have been a butler's pantry, once upon a time. The walls had empty shelves on them, and there were little screwholes showing where cabinets and other fixtures used to be. It was a small room. Beyond it was a murky hallway. Dorothy placed her feet carefully, not wanting to make the floorboards creak. If she followed the footprints, she reasoned, they ought to lead her to a way out of the building.

She paused to peer down the length of the hall. It was narrow, with what appeared to be an ascending staircase at the end of it, on the right. There were closets behind it, all closed, and a blank plaster wall on the left, pierced by three doorways. Plaster had fallen from the high ceiling, showing the wooden laths like gray stripes and strewing white piles on the floor. Rusty stains ran down the walls. Decay thickened the air. It was a long hall, and its length daunted her.

I must be getting claustrophobic. It's only an empty hallway.

The undefined need she'd felt in the cellar—she could only think of it as a kind of thirst—reasserted itself then with rising urgency. It ran so deep that she couldn't trawl for it with words. It was not like anything she had ever known before. It was more basic than the hunger that came after the first eight hours of a fast, or the desire that quickened after the first few minutes of making love. It was alien, unnameable. Unsatisfied, it prodded her down the hall.

She would have run, but the silence that lay on the house was so oppressive that she feared to challenge it. She walked as quietly as she could. Fallen plaster crunched softly under her shoes. She looked into the yawning doorways as she passed them and saw only empty rooms that offered no clues as to their former use. The house had been stripped bare.

An old woman stood at the foot of the staircase.

"*Jesus!*" Dorothy's heart nearly stopped. She clutched her chest and gasped. "I'm sorry, I didn't know there was anybody here! I didn't hear you coming."

The woman made no answer. She stood motionlessly, with her yellowish white hair in an uncombed tangle. She wore a shapeless black dress and heavy black shoes that had given no warning of her approach. She must have been standing there all along, just out of sight, and only stepped into view when she heard Dorothy coming. Was the upper floor of this ruin inhabited, then? Or had the lady lived here once, and come back to visit or inspect it? Was she alone? She stood so still that Dorothy wondered if she were blind. And maybe deaf as well.

"I didn't mean to trespass, ma'am. My name is Dorothy Matthiesen, I was just on my way out. I . . ."

Dorothy fell silent. The old woman showed no sign that she had heard her, or even seen her. Dorothy had a feeling that she could break into a sailor's hornpipe dance without the old woman realizing she was there. She seemed to be in some kind of trance.

She can't be here alone. Dorothy was on the point of calling out, then bit it back. *Let's just get out of here, okay?*

There was room for her to sidle past the woman. She didn't want to meet whoever was with her. She backed up a step so she would maneuver around the woman without disturbing her.

—And found herself, instead, leaning forward, with her hands coming up slowly and her fingers tensed to seize, and the blood pounding in her head like loud machinery, and her mouth filling with saliva.

But the old woman grinned toothlessly and turned hot lunatic eyes on her, and flung back a knotted brown hand to stab her with a pair of scissors.

* * *

171

Dorothy heard her own scream still echoing up the stairwell. She ignored it, staring at the empty space in front of her where the old woman had been and was no longer, and the unbroken sheen of dust upon the floor where the old woman's bulky shoes hadn't even scuffed it.

Her mind boiled into chaos. She sobbed once as her feet uprooted themselves from the floor and she bolted past the place at the foot of the stairs.

Some instinct guided her to a warped oak door that would no longer fit its frame. She hurled it aside and stampeded across a rotting porch, down some broken steps, and onto the root-shattered remnants of a sidewalk.

The sun fell on her like a titan's hammer, and red pain burned away her vision before she could clamp her eyelids shut. She pressed her hands over them and spun in a blind circle, screaming. She couldn't hear it for the roaring in her ears. Her skin felt bathed in fire.

There was no escape. She had run headlong into an open furnace and was caught in it. She reeled, tried to run a few steps, stumbled, and fell backward into a roasting darkness.

Three

After leaving his safe cellar behind, and while the night was new, Bruce had passed swiftly through the woods, marveling at his newfound ability to avoid obstacles in the dark, and had come out on an unfamiliar stretch of road. He hiked briskly, without any sensation of fatigue.

After being cooped up in the coal cellar, he was surprised not to get any pleasure from the fresh air. He stopped to study himself. He'd practically run all this way and he wasn't even breathing hard, he hadn't broken into a sweat. In fact he wasn't breathing at all. This discovery was a mild shock. He made a conscious effort to suck air into his lungs. The appropriate muscles responded, the air came in, he let it out.

He was a vampire now, he remembered. Blood and darkness were his only needs. He would have to ask the old man whether he needed air, too.

Meanwhile his thirst gave him no rest. He yearned to meet someone whose blood he could savor, but Millboro residents never walked when they could drive. Several cars passed him. He tried to thumb a ride, but with a state psychiatric hospital set up in the middle of their township, Millboro residents never picked up hitchhikers, either.

Bruce tried to plan. He had enough awareness to know that he couldn't just walk up to a crowd of people and grab somebody. There was still a great deal he didn't know about being a vampire, so he'd have to be careful.

He struck Main Street and headed south. Half an hour's striding took him to Schoolhouse Road; from there he knew the way to the Millboro Mall. He turned his steps in that direction.

He'd spent a good part of his life hanging around the mall with his friends and disciples. You couldn't hang out on the streets of the developments; there was just no action. The township had Main Street, but that was just another county road following its planned course past developments, law offices, doctors' and dentists' offices, and farms.

The mall was the only place to go. It sprawled over half a dozen acres, and unless you wanted to sell crack from a stand, everybody was too busy to hassle you. You could meet drug contacts in the alleys between the stores or in the rest rooms, browse and shoplift in the stores, or just hang around the concourse, eyeballing the chicks and bullshitting with your friends.

173

In fact, there was a chance Bruce could run into some of his friends tonight. He imagined the meeting as he walked.

"Hey, Bruce, where you been, man?"

"Out in the woods all this time. I met a dude who turned me on to being a vampire."

"Yeah, sure."

"You don't believe me? Here, go ahead, try to cut my hand!"

Bruce laughed at himself. He doubted he was ready to let anybody try to chop up his hand. And as satisfying as it'd be to brag about it, he was sure it'd be better to keep his new life-style a secret. (*"Hey, man, you wanna talk alternative life-styles . . . !"*) The more he thought about it, the more it seemed to him that his old life would have to be abandoned. He couldn't go back home and lock himself in his room all day, every day. Couldn't go back to school—not unless they made it a night school. And if he couldn't do any of those things, he'd also have to give up his friends. No more parties, no more hanging around the mall. No more Sabbaths.

It suddenly dawned on him that except for the big old man—whose name he didn't even know—he was all alone in the world. He'd have to avoid his friends, not seek them out.

The thought brought neither bitterness nor regret. He accepted it as part of his new life, a price he was willing to pay.

He examined his feelings. He found that his parents no longer disappointed him. They were what they were. They toiled on a treadmill that had lost its power to enslave him. It used to piss him off that his old lady had so much time for niggers' kids and none for him. If he opened his mouth, she would throw other people's poverty at him. "You don't know how well off you are, Bruce. Today I met a boy your age who has a deformed foot because he was so malnourished as a child. He's missed so much time from school, he can hardly write his own name. *He* didn't have the advantages you take for granted. . . ." And blah-blah-blah. God-damn, that used to frost him. And the old man, hauling his ass off to Manhattan every day and dragging it home in the evening, too pooped to do anything but sit in front of the TV set and pontificate about his son's friends. "They're such *lowlifes*, Bruce. When are you gonna wake up and realize you don't need them, they'll only drag you down to their level?" The old fake. He wanted his kid to hobnob with Student Council types and bookworms.

His teachers no longer filled him with contempt. What a drag it used to be to sit in school all day, listening to a bunch of windbags who didn't know what the fuck they were talking about. If they were so smart, they wouldn't be teachers. Shit, every couple years they threatened to go out on strike because they earned so little. And they hardly deserved even that. All you had to do to get an A was turn in your home-work on time, raise your hand in class, ask the right questions, give the right answers. Nothing to it. Just a matter of jumping through the hoops. Bruce had learned the tricks long ago, and despised the teachers for not knowing that he knew they were tricks. Or maybe they did know, and just didn't give a fuck.

He saw things so clearly now. He understood things he hadn't been able to understand before.

Like Jeanne Burke, the only chick in the whole school who ever shot him down. Bruce had always been able to get pretty much what he wanted from the chicks, but not from her. He discovered her in junior high, fell desperately in love with her when they were freshmen, and just as desperately hated her by the time they were sophomores. When he finally found the nerve to ask her out, he was floored when she said no—and right in front of all his friends.

"But why not?" he hadn't been able to keep from asking. Why the hell not? He was the sharpest-looking guy in their class, and for the past few months he'd made a point

175

of sitting close to her in class, in the cafeteria, in the library, so he could show off his stuff where she could see it.

"Do you really want to know, Bruce?"

"Yeah, I really want to know."

She told him. "Because you're a selfish, smug, immature *jerk*," she said. "You think you're God's gift to this school, or maybe to the universe. Maybe you think you've impressed me, but you're wrong. I wouldn't go out with you if my life depended on it. Don't ask me again."

Since the face-off had taken place in the hall between periods, it was all over the school by lunchtime and it took Bruce months to live it down. He was crushed. He took countermeasures. He paid a couple of dummies to beat up Jeanne's boyfriend; he had someone plant pot in her locker; he tried to start disgusting rumors about her. Nothing worked. Everybody thought she shat rose petals, and nobody would believe anything bad about her. He used to fantasize about getting her alone in the woods and raping her, brutalizing her until he broke her mind and she became his slave. But they were bitter dreams because he knew they could never come true.

And now, just like that, he was over it. The thought of her no longer drove him up the wall. Yet now the old dreams—and newer, darker dreams—*could* come true. If he wanted.

What the hell, it was *all* behind him now. None of it could bug him anymore. All those people had lost their power over him.

All he wanted from them now—from any of them—was their blood.

The mall was lit up like a flying saucer.

How he would have enjoyed going inside and mingling like a piranha in a school of goldfish—but that was a temp-

176

tation he resisted. His folks and friends would be wondering where he was. What if somebody he knew saw him now?

He didn't know how he'd handle it, so it was best to steer clear of it.

Bruce knew the mall, though, like he knew his own back-yard—shit, better. He never spent any time at home. Here, in the midst of all this bustle, there were isolated spots where you could do damn well whatever you pleased. Parents and teachers would shit their pants if they knew half the things that went on. No one had ever been killed here, but Bruce knew where you could go to buy drugs, get high, have sex, or beat somebody up without interruption. He ought to be able to make his first kill here.

The best hunting ground, he ultimately decided, was the perimeter of the parking lot. There was cover close by, and once you dragged someone out of the lot, you were out of the lights. Now that he could see in the dark, he might as well take advantage of it.

There weren't many cars parked this far from the stores, which was good. He could take cover and wait for someone to come walking up alone. If he moved fast, no one would see him.

He found a place to stand among the trees and waited. As a mortal, it used to drive him up the wall if he had to spend any amount of time just waiting. Now it didn't bug him at all. Why should it? He was going to live forever. He found he could stand perfectly still, as still as stone, for as long as it suited him, with no discomfort. He was sure he could stand that way for hours and never feel the need to shift his weight, or fidget.

Nor did he get bored. There was so much to hear in the night that he'd never heard before. He overheard the con-versations of people coming out of the stores, hundreds of yards away, every word they spoke. Above him, in the trees, around him, in the underbrush, a hundred different kinds

177

of insects wove a tapestry for his ears. Every call was clear and distinct.

A woman came walking alone, straight toward the nearest car. He saw her closely when she was still far off. She was small enough not to give him any trouble, and young and pretty. Time was Bruce would have fantasized about fucking her. Now he didn't. He could be objective about her good looks, as if she were a flower. What turned him on was the thought of her blood in his mouth. He salivated almost uncontrollably. Some of it got loose and rolled down his chin.

He maneuvered silently amid the shadows so that he could get around the car and come up on her blind side when she stopped to unlock the door. He could see it was locked. He planned as he moved. He would grab her, silence her with a hand over her mouth, and pull her into the trees before anyone could notice.

She didn't hear him until he was practically on top of her. It was a kick, better than anything he'd ever done before. When he seized the handle of her car door, she spun around and turned into jelly at the sight of him. He relished it.

She tried to make a fuss, but he stopped her mouth with one hand and started to drag her off with the other. She struggled like a cat in a noose. His strength was glorious. When she scratched him, punched him, kicked him, he felt the impact but no pain. But his impatience for her blood was a shock. He wanted to throw her down to the asphalt and do it right there, under the lamps of the parking lot. Pulling her back to the safety of the trees took all the willpower he possessed. It was like trying to hold off the orgasm in the middle of the sex act.

He couldn't help it. As she writhed against him, he thought he could smell the blood in her veins. Accidentally he scratched her neck, breaking the skin. He drooled on her. They were off the asphalt now, and onto the ground.

178

She struggled harder, then went suddenly limp on him and slid out of his grasp.

She got off one thin scream before he yanked her back up. He yanked too hard and lost his balance. He spun as he fell, so that he landed on top of her.

She was out; she must've hit her head. The scent of her blood set up a crazy drumming in his skull. Like a lover, he pressed his mouth to the scratch on her neck and ran his tongue over it. The taste of blood was sweeter and more intense than any sex he had ever known.

And then, suddenly, he was in midair, flying away from her, and his consciousness exploded into chaos.

He found himself looking up at the old vampire. Nearby, the woman lay unconscious.

When he sat up, his head lolled heavily to his chest, and he couldn't raise it. Nothing hurt, but he was alarmed because he couldn't pick up his head. When he lay back down, it bounced against the earth. He couldn't keep it from doing that.

"What happened?" His speech came out garbled, barely intelligible. The big old man squatted down beside him.

"I told you not to leave the shelter, my boy."

"But I . . . how did you . . . ?"

"I got there just as you were leaving, and I followed you," the old vampire explained. "You were preoccupied with other things, and you never noticed me."

Bruce was ashamed. He should have heard something. He shouldn't have let himself get so carried away by his quest for blood.

"My head . . ."

"I broke your neck."

"But why?"

"My dear young man, you were too impulsive. I have

179

my own security to consider. I can't have an inexperienced vampire running around like a rogue tiger.

"In the old days I would have been protected by a mass of superstition. People believed in vampires then, but their beliefs were erroneous. Either they would remain passive in their fear, and take no measures to defend themselves, or else they would go running out to the cemeteries to hunt the vampires there—and of course no well-informed vampire would hide himself in a coffin, where they'd look for him, unless he was new to it and had not yet outgrown the superstitions he'd believed in as a mortal. But the same archaic beliefs which protected vampires could also be their undoing. I know because I began my new life in a primitive country where the peasants believed in vampires. And sometimes they would succeed in destroying one.

"But here and now, vampires are B-movie fare. No one in this township believes in them. This absolute unbelief is a much surer protection than any superstition. And we must take care to do nothing to shake it. If we force these people to believe in vampires, they have dangerous weapons they can turn against us. It would be sheer hubris for any vampire to pit himself against today's technology. So you see why I can't let you run free. You would make mistakes that might threaten *my* position."

Bruce's head swam. He had only gotten a little taste of the woman's blood, and to have it snatched from him so abruptly, so far short of satiation, was worse than having a broken neck. He tried to shake his head but could only make it wobble.

"You've created a serious problem for me," the vampire said, "and I'll be hard put to rectify the situation. Well, difficulties exist to be overcome. I'm sure I'll learn some valuable lessons from this." He reached into his pocket and came out with something that Bruce couldn't see. He lifted Bruce's head from the ground. "Open your mouth, please— that's it. Now cough. Expectorate."

Bruce tried to obey. He was on the old guy's shit list now; he'd better behave himself. He felt something razor-sharp being inserted into his mouth and felt it scrape the inside of his cheek. For some minutes the old man kept at it.

"What're you doing?" Bruce asked when his mouth had been released and his head lowered back to the ground.

"Taking samples. I'm a doctor."

Bruce tried to explain himself. "I felt so *good,*" he said, mangling the words. "So strong. I had to get out and get some blood. I had to have it. I couldn't wait. I'm sorry."

The old vampire gave him a smile and patted his shoulder.

"I know, my boy, I know. I understand. Some of the blame must go to me, for not foreseeing this and taking steps to prevent it. But the immediate problem is to dispose of this woman in some way that will guarantee my safety."

"What about me?"

"First things first. You created the problem, my dear fellow, so you'll have to be patient."

The vampire got up and flung the woman over his shoulder as if she were a sack of rags. Bruce wanted to get up, too, but the best he could do was to struggle to a sitting position, where his head lolled every which way. His arms and legs could only flounder helplessly. He sank back down.

"I thought you said I couldn't be killed by anything but the sun!"

"I said it and it's true, my boy. However, a broken neck is a broken neck. Your body has sustained a tremendous shock. You're too new to the vampire's condition to cope with it effectively. Were I to suffer a similar injury, I would survive it. You won't, without my help."

"But . . ."

"Your body is still in the process of completing its transformation," the vampire said. "You must be patient. And that means you must wait here patiently until I return for you. I have to do something about this woman first, and the night is waning. Stay here.''

Carrying the woman, he walked off noiselessly into the trees and was lost to Bruce's sight.

Bruce tried to crawl away, but he was so clumsy that he soon gave it up and resigned himself to wait. He lay on his back, looking up at the stars and watching the Christmas-tree lights of aircraft that passed sporadically overhead.

The sky began to lighten with the dawn.

VII.   MISSING PERSONS

One

The day passed in silence at the Schuylerville Nursing Home. That evening Dorothy became aware that she was peering up at the stars, surprised to see so many shining over Millboro. She was lying on her back in some bushes, with dead leaves in her hair. A minute or two went by before she remembered how she'd come to be there.

She sat up suddenly. Her head spun a little, but it was nothing like her first awakening in the cellar.

She remembered feeling as if someone had doused her with a bucketful of napalm. She was all right now. Her skin felt cool and normal, and the lancing pain in her eyes had passed away. She was free of the undefined thirst that had afflicted her during the day. She was tracking well enough to realize that she'd better be getting away from here while she still had all her faculties.

She stood up. Small thorns clung to her clothes, but the brambles were too weak to keep her down. She turned.

And saw a huge white building like a decaying mansion in a William Faulkner novel, tucked in among the dense pines that had grown up around it, swaddled in their shadows. The windows were boarded shut; the front door gaped like the jaws of a skull. It smelled of rotting wood and accumulated dust and mold.

She had no idea what it was, no memory of how she came to be inside it, and no clue as to where it was. It was dark now, and as silent as a picture on a postcard. *Having a wonderful time, wherever I am.* Hadn't there been an old woman inside it? Hadn't she seen . . . ? But that had to have been a hallucination. *I may be all right now,* she thought, *but something sure as hell was wrong with me while I was blundering around in there. Hallucinations, nausea, eyes popping out of my head when the light hit them, and that horrible convulsion when I ran outside.* She wondered if she'd been given some kind of drug to keep her knocked out until whoever had put her there could come back for her.

That thought was enough to get her moving out of the thicket, away from the house.

There seemed to be a kind of overgrown gravel path that twisted among the trees; considering its neglected state, she was surprised she could make it out well enough to follow it. She didn't know where it would take her, but what else was she to do? As long as it took her away from the house, it was going in the right direction—she hoped.

The path took her out to a paved road. She could see fields and the lights of houses. An airplane droned overhead, red and green lights winking like knowing eyes. Civilization.

She didn't know whether she was still in Millboro Township or someplace on the other side of the world, but for the moment she didn't care. All that mattered was to be on a road that led somewhere, hopefully to safety. She began to jog.

Detective Sergeant Musante phoned Van Wyck at home. "You might be interested in this, Chief. Henderson picked up a woman running down Dutch Mill Road a little while ago. She's here now. Looks like a possible rape and abduction. She wants to tell you about it."

There hadn't been a rape in Millboro since Van Wyck was a kid in school. "I'll be right there," he said, and hung up. He left without bothering to change into his uniform. He seldom wore it, anyway.

Musante had moved the woman to the chief's office, to keep her out of sight of any reporters who might happen to drop in. She sat calmly drinking coffee when Van Wyck arrived, not in the least hysterical. Musante stood beside her.

"This is Mrs. Matthiesen, Chief. She's from over in Thoreau Manor. Chaucer Drive. Chief Van Wyck, ma'am."

Van Wyck took her in with a glance. There was a bruise on her forehead, her hair and clothes were tousled, but otherwise she seemed to be all right. He liked the way she smiled at him when Musante introduced them. Sometimes the only witness to a crime was the victim, and too often the victim was too upset to be of any value as a witness. Mrs. Matthiesen looked like she could help.

"Mrs. Matthiesen was at the Schuylerville Nursing Home," Musante said. "Somebody took her there and left her in the cellar. Henderson and Peters are on their way back there to take a look. They find anybody, they'll bring 'em in."

Van Wyck nodded. He took another look at the victim. "Are you hurt, ma'am? We can get you medical attention right away, if necessary."

Dorothy shook her head. "I'm all right. I guess I ought to see a doctor, but first I want to tell you my story."

"Is there a Mr. Matthiesen? Has he been contacted?"

Her smile turned brittle and slipped off her face. Musante answered for her. "I called Mr. Matthiesen at his office, Chief. He works in Manhattan. He'll get here as soon as he can."

Van Wyck's instinct told him there was something more to that, but for the time being he put it on the back burner.

185

He pulled up a chair and sat down, close enough to the woman to reassure her, but not so close as to crowd her. She really was a nice-looking little woman, he thought. And she had guts. So many in Millboro went to pieces when you tried to question them.

"Sergeant Musante will be taping this conversation, ma'am," he explained. "Later we'll play the tape and use it to prepare a written statement, which you'll be asked to sign after you read it, make any corrections necessary, and approve it. Do you understand?"

"Just like on 'Kojaak,' " Dorothy managed to joke. Both policemen had heard jokes like this before, but they chuckled politely to make her feel at ease, and it worked. Dorothy felt safe and secure in the police chief's office, and relaxed in the company of these men.

She began her story. "Last night I went to Dalton's in the Millboro Mall to buy some books. I parked way in the back of the parking lot; I can show you exactly where. When I came back to my car, I was attacked." She described the big blond kid, and her struggle with him, up to the moment when she hit her head on something and lost consciousness.

"That was *last* night, ma'am?" Musante said.

Dorothy nodded emphatically. "I wonder if Chris ever noticed that I didn't come home last night, and wasn't there when he got up this morning."

Musante was burning to make a sympathetic comment, but he kept himself on a tight rein. Van Wyck appreciated his restraint. Musante was a family man: he couldn't fathom Mr. Matthiesen's failure to call the police about his missing wife.

"We'll ask him about that when we see him," Van Wyck said.

"I hope you put him under a strong light and slap him around some," Dorothy said. "Can you believe it? I was missing overnight, and all the next day . . . and when the *police* call *him,* and not the other way around, there he is at his fucking *desk* in his fucking office, like nothing had happened! He should disappear, see how *he* likes it!''

She was deeply hurt, yet trying to be brave about it. Bad enough to have an experience like the one she had. And to top it off, her husband didn't seem to give a shit. Van Wyck was moved. He sat close enough so that he could touch her if he wanted to, and he did want to. But it wasn't the kind of gesture a police chief made under the circumstances. He caught her eye instead and she didn't look away. She seemed grateful for the human contact.

''Could we have the description again, ma'am, of the individual who attacked you? If you can, try to remember what he was wearing. We'd also like you to try to estimate his height and weight. Every factual detail you can provide helps us and helps the case. We want to arrest the right person, and we want the charge to stick.''

Dorothy spent several minutes refining the description of her attacker. Her memory was clear, and it proved to be a lot easier to talk about the assault than to brood on Chris's indifference.

Van Wyck said, ''I don't mean to offend you by this next question. And I don't mean it as a stupid question, either. A lawyer is dead certain to ask it later.

''You say you were knocked unconscious when your assailant fell on top of you. At that point, you hadn't actually been raped yet. Now, do you have *any* recollection of what happened next? Anything at all?''

Dorothy shook her head. She wanted to be honest with these men, to help them all she could. She felt very strongly that they were here to help her. The chief especially seemed considerate of her feelings. She didn't want to tell him anything she wouldn't swear to on a Bible, in a court of law.

''I was out like a light,'' she said. ''I honestly don't think he raped me, but I suppose a doctor can verify that. I don't remember anything until I came to and I was in the basement of that old abandoned nursing home.''

"You don't remember how you got there?" Musante asked.

"No. I woke up in the cellar and I didn't know where I was. I never heard of that place, Sergeant, until the patrolman who picked me up told me what it was. I don't know what time it was when I came to, but there was sunlight coming through the cracks in the boards over the windows. And boy, did I feel *peculiar.*"

She told them the rest of it, in as much detail as she could provide, even including the old lady she'd hallucinated by the stairs. "You can understand why I need to see a doctor," she added.

They questioned her until she ran out of answers.

"Would you be up to going back to the mall, now, and showing us the spot where the attack took place?" asked Van Wyck. "Then we can have you examined by a doctor."

"I'll be happy to, Chief."

"If Mr. Matthiesen should call—" Musante started to say, but Dorothy cut him off.

"Let him cool his shit-kicking heels a while," she said. "The longer, the better."

The blond boy was still there.

Patrolman Ingersoll's flashlight beam landed on a pair of Nike running shoes protruding from some bushes a few yards from the edge of the parking lot, and Musante saw them and said, "Uh-oh. Over here, Chief."

Van Wyck brought his light and played it over the corpse. The boy lay on his back, neck crooked at an angle that could only be possible if it were badly broken. He was big and blond and he wore clothes matching Dorothy's description, so there was no doubt who he was—which was good, because the body was in stunningly bad condition. When Musante saw the face, he had to go off by himself and empty his glass stomach.

"Mrs. Matthiesen, I think we've found the party who assaulted you," Van Wyck said. "You'll have to identify him as such. But you'd better brace yourself. It's not nice. Ingersoll, get us an ambulance and contact the M.E."

Dorothy had been waiting by her car, which was still parked where she'd left it, still locked. By some miracle her purse, keys, and paperbacks still lay where they'd fallen. She picked them up and put them in her car while the police explored the area.

The chief's words froze her. An irrational fear flitted like a bat through her mind: the boy was dead, she was going to be charged with murder. But that was ridiculous. What was Van Wyck talking about? How could the kid still be here? And why was the detective sergeant down on his knees over there, retching?

The chief was waiting for her. She advanced slowly to where he was standing with the flashlight. The patrolman hurried past her on his way back to the squad car and the radio, face drawn. She came up to Van Wyck and followed the flashlight beam downward with her eyes.

The boy's lips were drawn back from his teeth in a grimace that made his face look like a Kabuki mask. His lips were black. His eyes were sunken out of sight. His skin was mottled filthily, and thrust between his teeth was his bloated, blackened tongue, like an obscenely swollen maggot that had gotten trapped trying to crawl out of his throat.

Dorothy screamed and shied away. Some reflex flung her into Van Wyck, and he held her while she gasped and quivered. He could not help noticing how snugly she fitted into his embrace. But it was a fleeting impression, quickly banished by the business at hand.

"It's all right, Mrs. Matthiesen, don't be afraid." As an unexpected revelation, it came to him that he liked this woman very much. "You're safe with us," he told her gently, and held her until she stopped trembling.

"Do you recognize him?"

She nodded against his chest. "That's him. He's the one . . . but I don't get it. He's dead."

Van Wyck couldn't explain it for her. She drew back from him, and he let her go. She looked up at him.

"Thanks for being patient with me," she said. "I'm sorry. I don't usually fall apart like that."

"Mrs. Matthiesen, this isn't exactly a Sunday drive in the park for any of us. Don't apologize. Are you all right now?"

"As long as I don't have to look at him again." She shuddered. "God! What happened to him?"

"Jesus, who knows? Maybe the medical examiner can tell us. But you're sure it's the man who assaulted you?"

"Absolutely."

When the crime scene unit was on its way, Van Wyck left Musante in charge and drove Dorothy to the county hospital. She seemed fully recovered by the time they got there, for which he admired her; half of what this woman had suffered would've turned his ex-wife, Helen, into a gibbering basket case.

A doctor was waiting. While Dorothy told him everything that had happened to her, and described all the symptoms she'd had while at the nursing home, he gave her a thorough examination and found no injuries that required treatment. He took blood and urine samples, and smears from her vaginal cavity.

"From what you've told me, and from what I can see," he said, "I don't think you were raped. But we'll know for sure when we look at some of these slides under a microscope. If you were molested, we'll find traces of semen." She'd already told him that she hadn't had sex with her husband recently (*Recently?* her mind screamed), nor with anybody else. "And if you were given any drug, or infected in any way, we'll see what's what when we analyze the samples. You can get dressed now," he added.

She reached for her clothes. "But what does it *sound* like, Doctor?" she asked. "I never felt so—so goddamned *strange!*—in all my life. It was like I was on LSD or something. I thought I was going to die."

"You don't want me to guess, Mrs. Matthiesen. I could be wrong, and that would do more harm than good. Let me get the test results first, then we'll see. Meanwhile, you seem perfectly healthy to me."

She couldn't get anything more out of him, except a prescription for a mild sedative in case she had trouble sleeping. When she emerged into the hall outside the emergency room, Chris was waiting for her.

When she saw him standing next to the police chief, she was actually disappointed he was there. Next to Van Wyck he seemed a pallid, insubstantial shadow of a man. The sum of all his parts was zero. At the moment she couldn't even be angry with him. She felt nothing for him. It was as if he weren't there.

He opened his arms and ran to her, and hugged her, and it felt like being hugged by a politician. She stood patiently in his embrace, enduring it and not returning it.

He held her at arm's length and stared at her.

"Dotty, are you all right?"

"Oh, fuck off, Chris," she said. He let his hands fall from her shoulders and groped ineffectually for something to say. She ignored him and turned to Van Wyck.

"The doctor says I can go home now, Chief. He's available if you want to talk to him. But I want to thank you and your men for all you've done for me. I don't know how I would've gotten through this without you."

"I'll have an officer bring your car home from the mall," Van Wyck said. He had a feeling that the husband had

191

intruded somehow, and he knew for sure that there was a scene in the making between the Matthiesens. He wanted to get clear before he was written into it. "And I'll be getting back to you with some more questions, probably sometime tomorrow."

"Thanks again," Dorothy said, "for everything."

"You're welcome, ma'am." He nodded. "And now, if you'll excuse me, I'd better corral the doctor before he gets called away."

He made his escape and left Dorothy alone with the shambles of her marriage.

Two

Dorothy's attacker turned out to be a Millboro High School junior named Bruce Randall.

The coroner's preliminary report didn't do much to explain his death.

True, his neck was broken. He had been hit hard on the back of the neck with some heavy instrument that didn't tear the skin, sustaining a sharp fracture of one of his cervical vertebrae; but it couldn't be said for sure that the blow had killed him. It looked more like he had aggravated the injury during the course of some wild struggle or convulsion. Pain and shock should have immobilized him, but they hadn't. Some worse pain had made him thrash violently until the spinal cord was ruptured, presumably causing death.

So far, so good; but then there was the preternaturally swift decomposition of the body to consider. Here the medical examiner was at a loss.

The rapidity of decay was awesome. Only when the body

was shoved into one of the morgue's refrigerated drawers was the process arrested. The brain was already a putrid, viscous mass when they cut into the skull. The other organs had fared better, but they were still much farther gone than they had any right to be.

Worse, whatever agent had caused the decay had deteriorated with the body. It refused to turn up in any of the chemical analyses the technicians could employ. They were still working on it, but with diminishing hope.

"Just like the guy we found in the woods out by Dutchman's Bog a couple of weeks ago," Musante was quick to point out. "Volden, I think his name was."

Bruce had been missing since the weekend, but his parents hadn't contacted the police.

For one thing, the boy frequently flew the nest on weekends without bothering to tell his parents where he was. Bruce looked like a good kid, but a search of his room tarnished that image. He had a nickel bag of pot and half a dozen vials of assorted uppers and downers stashed in his desk drawer, as well as condoms, a pellet gun his parents hadn't known about, and a nice collection of switchblades. His closet contained stacks of dirty magazines devoted to sadism and masochism, and his bookshelves featured titles like *The Satanic Bible*, *To Serve Dark Gods*, and *Pleasure in Pain*. His record albums were similarly unwholesome in their orientation.

All of it came as a complete surprise to the parents, who had made a point of respecting Bruce's privacy and never going uninvited into his room. There was a lock on the door and Bruce had had the only key. The coroner had found it in his pocket.

They were a respectable couple. Mark Randall commuted to Manhattan, where he worked as an investment counselor. Esther Randall was in the personnel department of the county's Bureau of Social Services. In her spare time she worked as a volunteer with disadvantaged children. Her husband had no spare time to speak of. Bruce got good grades in school, and they were proud of him. He had already applied for early admission at Michigan State University, and they'd felt sure he would be accepted.

How could this have happened to them?

"Where do you figure they thought he was, all this time?" Musante said, as he and Van Wyck drove away from the Randalls' house. "Hey, if my kid was gone all weekend and I didn't know where the fuck he was, I wouldn't wait till Monday to call the police. But these fuckin' people, it's fuckin' *Thursday* now. . . . Their kid was layin' there dead and they never called us."

And Christopher Matthiesen's wife was missing when he came home from work, and all through the night, and the next day, and he never contacted the police, either. Van Wyck pondered it. Were people that afraid of the police, or were they afraid of something else? What were they afraid of?

"I'll tell you something else," Musante went on. "It scares me, the way some of these people are out of touch with their kids. Like that Randall kid coulda been another Jack the Ripper, and *they* wouldn't a had no idea. It makes you wonder, it really does. What do these kids get up to while their parents make money and dick around and don't know what's going on under their own roof? And all of a sudden the kid attacks a lady in a parking lot, and even more all of a sudden, he's dead. Do you ever wonder what's going on that we don't even hear about, Chief?"

"That's a rhetorical question, Randy." Van Wyck didn't try to answer it. *Who knows what evil lurks in the hearts of men? Not me.* He was worrying about his own kids, out of reach down in Philadelphia with Helen and her dippy lawyer husband.

"They don't even know who his friends are," Musante

194

complained. "He spends whole weekends with these people, they know these people are bad news, and they still can't name one single fuckin' name. That's sick."

Bruce's teachers were able to fill in some of the gaps left by Bruce's parents. In fact the school staff had known him better than his parents had.

"I wanted a conference with his mother and his father," said the guidance counselor, "but they could never seem to fit it into their schedule." He rubbed the bottom of his nose compulsively, uneasy in the presence of policemen.

"His parents say he got good grades. Was he a discipline problem?" Van Wyck asked.

"Oh, no—he was too smart for that. Way too smart. Too much so for his own good, if you ask some of his teachers. A lot of them felt there was something not very nice behind that bright facade."

The counselor produced written reports. Van Wyck didn't look at them. "Why did you want a conference with the parents?"

"Mostly because his teachers didn't like the crowd he was running with. Run some of those names by your juvenile officer. I'm sure he knows them."

The counselor listed Bruce's friends. Van Wyck recognized a few of the names. Crazy, antisocial kids. The kind people moved to Millboro to get away from.

"They wouldn't have accepted a kid like Bruce," said the counselor, "unless they felt he was really one of them. He didn't look the part, he didn't act like a delinquent while he was in school—but of course a lot of us felt that where there's smoke, there's fire. We were kind of afraid he was getting away with things. Things we didn't know about."

Van Wyck remembered the treasures Bruce had hidden in his room, and nodded. The boy had gotten away with plenty. He wondered just how much.

However, that was something Bruce's teachers didn't know for a fact. All they had was a deeply rooted mistrust of Bruce's bright-boy act, and the knowledge that his best friends were out-and-out delinquents: vandals, drug users and dealers, shoplifters, harassers of the elderly, drinkers, statutory rapists—and probably much worse, if the full truth could ever be known.

"You know what I couldn't help thinking?" Bruce's English teacher confided in Van Wyck. "I'm a Sherlock Holmes fanatic, and I secretly thought of Randall as a teenage Moriarity—safe behind a pretense of respectability, controlling a network of criminals. All those punks he hung around with, I imagined he was the brains behind them all." She shook her head. "I know it was far-fetched, but what can I say? I have an active imagination."

Van Wyck and Musante returned to headquarters.

"You know what I can't figure?" Musante said. "Why a smart, careful kid like Bruce suddenly decides to jump a woman in a public place. It doesn't fit with what they say about him. You'd think he wouldn't ever take a risk like that."

Van Wyck had a gut feeling that it was never going to fit.

Three

Dorothy lay in bed alone, wondering what the hell she was going to do, where the hell she was going to go, now that her marriage had been removed as the keystone of her life.

So much was dependent on it, things you wouldn't have thought, at first, to have anything to do with being married. Basic things, like where you lived, how much money you had on tap at any given time, even what you ate, what you wore, what you did with your free time. What kind of job you could realistically hope to get. It was all tied up with marriage. For almost seven years the person she used to be had drifted steadily away from her, borne on the current of time. The distance was too great now. No way of picking up where she'd left off. It was like having to get off the bus in a strange city.

Everything would have to change. *Everything*. It wasn't even a question of starting over. It was more like boarding an immigrant ship heading for an unknown country, and she would have to do it alone. Get a divorce. Get a full-time job. Find another place to live. Be lonely. Get back into the rigmarole of dating and sex and courtship. Try to make new friends. The tasks piled up in front of her like a jumbled pyramid, blotting out the pleasing vista she had once had of a comfortable, secure future.

But what else could she do?

"You never tried to find out where I was," she said to Chris, when they got home from the hospital. "You went off to work as if I didn't exist. Business as usual."

Chris could look genuinely anguished when he tried, but it didn't faze her anymore. He reached out for her and she backed away.

"I thought you were mad at me," he said. "I thought you'd decided you needed some space for a while. I did call from work, several times. Whenever I had a spare minute. You never answered. I was afraid to call your mother, or any of our friends. For God's sake, Dot, I thought you'd left me!"

"Without a word? Without a note? Jesus Christ, you could have called the police just *once!* Just in case I was splattered across Route 9 or something. Drop dead, Chris."

"I was *going* to call the cops. I wanted to. But put yourself in my shoes. I was afraid you'd left me. That wouldn't be

197

a police matter. Don't you understand? I didn't know what to do!''

She wouldn't listen to him. She wouldn't let him touch her. She locked herself in the bedroom and made him sleep on the couch.

She didn't expect to be able to sleep, but within minutes of her turning out the light, exhaustion fell on her like a lead blanket, as sudden and dreamless as death.

She woke with a headache that was like a set of poorly meshed gears grinding in her skull. It was complemented by a sense of extreme vulnerability—almost a low-level panic state.

Morning light came sizzling in through the inadequate shades on the two bedroom windows. The room was filled with glaring, searing sunlight.

Dorothy tore a blanket from the bed and rushed it to the nearest window, squinting and averting her face from the terrible light. Somehow she was able to get it mounted to the curtain rod so that it hung down over the window. It helped. With some of the light shut out, she was able to secure the blanket so it wouldn't fall, then snatch up the last blanket and fix it over the other window.

The effort drained her. The gears inside her head ground torturously. She reeled back to bed and lay down with her head sandwiched between two pillows, and faded out.

She faded in and out the whole day long. It destroyed her sense of time. Torment had no beginning, no end.

There were moments when she was harrowed by thirst, moments that went on and on until she faded out again. Occasionally in the chaos of her mind the thought of water took form, along with a muddled realization that she could easily get it from a tap if she wanted it and drink her fill.

But that would mean opening the bedroom door and leaving her safe island of darkness to plunge into a killing surf of light. Anyway, the thought of water made her sick. In its own way it was as bad as light.

The sun followed its path across the sky and eventually stopped launching its bolts directly at Dorothy's bedroom windows. As the room became darker her pain lessened. Wrung out, she slept away the entire afternoon.

She woke to the sound of Chris pounding on the bedroom door and shouting.

"Goddamn it, Dorothy, will you answer me? I'm gonna call an ambulance if you don't!"

The room was night-dark now. Dorothy sat up. She was tired, but her headache was gone as if it had never been. Almost automatically she groped for the bedlamp and pressed the switch. The light that jumped into the room was as harmless as it had ever been.

"Dotty, open up!"

Chris was unshaven, and his clothes were rumpled from sleeping in them. She was too tired to dodge him when he seized her shoulders.

"I haven't heard a peep out of you all day," he said. "Are you sick, or what?"

Another man, she thought, might have broken into the room after several hours of unresponsive silence. For all Chris knew, she could have taken an overdose of sleeping pills and been slowly dying.

How did he get to be like this? Whatever happened to "you and me against the world"?

"Let me out, Chris. I want something to eat."

He dropped his hands and stepped aside, then followed her to the kitchen.

"I was here all day, Dotty. I didn't go in to work today." He made it sound like a major sacrifice, worthy of praise. *Hey, boss, I need the day off. Just one day. My wife was assaulted and she disappeared for twenty-four hours. I'll be back tomorrow, though—no sense going off the deep end.*

She stood at the sink and drank two glasses of cold water. Vaguely she remembered being sickened by the thought of water hours ago, but that symptom had passed. She hoped so.

"Honey, I want to help."

"You've forgotten how, Chris."

He had to fish for a minute before he could come up with a reply to that. Dorothy opened the refrigerator and started to make herself a boiled-ham sandwich.

"All right," he said, holding up his hand. "I see where you're coming from. And maybe you're right. Maybe I've lost the knack of being a husband. But I don't want it to be that way. If you think it'll do any good, I'll go into marriage counseling with you."

She came closer to pitying him. He was an empty man; all of his feelings had slowly leaked out, somewhere along the way, without his even knowing that he'd lost them.

"It's too late for that," she said. "Counseling won't work unless you care enough to make it work, and you don't care. Once I'm gone, it'll be like I was never here. You'll just keep on working. You won't miss me."

She watched him try to drum up some emotion about it, and she was glad when he finally gave it up and left her alone to eat her sandwich.

VIII. A VISION

One

There were signs—visions sent by God—and there were bad dreams raised up by the sinner's own timorous soul, emanations of guilt and fear and weakness; and sometimes it was hard to tell one from the other.

Thornall saw a dark hulking shape with gleaming eyes bending over him as he lay on his bed of newspapers, reaching for him; and he heard a heart—his own or the demon's, he wasn't sure which—pounding like a drum.

He opened his eyes to see an old woman standing over him, and a young man behind her.

"You all right, mister? I knocked and knocked, and you never budged an inch. I was afraid you was dead."

Thornall sat up stiffly. After waking to the warmth of the sun on his face, he'd fallen back to sleep. Now his bones ached, and the sun has risen so that it no longer shone directly through the window. *Getting old,* he thought. *Too old.* It wouldn't be long before he came, at last, to the end of his strength. There was a limit to what mortal flesh could endure, and he knew he was approaching it.

He decided that the vision he had had must have been a nightmare.

He looked up at the woman. Her hair was white, her skin

201

like parchment. *Mixed blood*, he thought: Negro and Indian. A healthy, vigorous woman in her seventies who still had all her wits about her. The eyes told him that much.

"You'll have to pardon me, ma'am, for not getting up to greet you more properly," he said. "I guess I was more tired-out than I thought."

"Old man like you," she said, "oughtn't to be sleepin' on the floor like that."

"I'm used to it. I don't mind."

"That don't make it right. I hear you're a preacher. Is that true?"

Thornall nodded. "I don't have a congregation," he said, "and I surely don't have a church to call my own; but I was called to the Lord when I was young and I've served Him all my life. I used to be a missionary, a long, long time ago." He smiled to show he was feeling better. "My name's Benejah Thornall."

"Emma Plews." The woman introduced herself with a small old-fashioned curtsey. "And this is my grandson, Toby Hicks." The young man nodded, keeping a careful eye on him.

"Reverend," she said, "you can't stay here. These old houses, they ain't healthy. Why don't you come over to my place and let me fix you up a nice breakfast? It's just down the street a little ways. Toby, help the reverend up."

The young man was strong, and lifted Thornall easily.

"If you'll forgive me for saying so, Reverend, you look more like a tramp than a preacher," he said.

"Toby!" cried the grandmother, but Thornall raised a hand to quiet her.

"It's all right, Mrs. Plews. A tramp is what I am, and have been for more years than I care to count. It's the path the Lord has chosen for me, and I don't complain. But I still appreciate a good breakfast when I can get it."

* * *

202

Toby kept his mouth shut while his gramma filled the old man with bacon, pancakes, and milk.

He looked harmless enough, but you couldn't tell about somebody you found sacked out in an old deserted house. There were homeless men all over, these days, and a lot of them were mental patients thrown out of the hospitals because there was no room for them and they weren't so crazy that the hospitals had to keep them. Or so the doctors hoped, when they turned them loose.

This one claimed he used to be a missionary somewhere in South America. It could well be true, but he could also be just a loony old fart who only thought he'd been a missionary. He was full of talk about God; crazy people often were. Toby remembered a guy in his platoon who insisted that God talked to him every night, person-to-person. What God told him, he wouldn't say. The army hadn't lost much time discharging *him*.

Later, when the old man was resting on the porch and Gramma was doing the dishes, Toby tried to reason with her.

"He could be some kind of a nut, y'know. I'm not saying he's dangerous, but for all we know, he could be. Why take the chance?"

Gramma let her hands rest in the hot soapy water and gave him a look that was like a kick in the pants.

"Boy, you better pray the Lord'll keep you young forever, 'cause it'll take that long for you to get some sense. You think it's right for an old man to be sleepin' in a pile of newspapers in some old ruin of a house?"

"Of course not, Gramma!"

"Your momma tried to bring you up so's you had some Christian charity."

"I'm not uncharitable," Toby said. "Gramma, you watch the news on TV. You listen to the radio. You know there's lots of homeless old men wandering around right

203

now, and some of them are crazy. They were in institutions, and they got turned out because the government cut the budgets.''

''If they got turned out once,'' Gramma said, ''then there ain't no sense in sendin' 'em back there, is it? This poor old man got no place to stay, Toby. He's tired, and he don't look too good. It won't hurt to let him stay here with us for a while. We got room for him. Anyhow, *I* like him!''

Toby gave up the argument for the time being.

Reverend Simms from the Zion church a few blocks away came by that afternoon to talk to the old man. When he left, Toby followed and caught up with him a little way down the street.

''Reverend, I hope you talked some sense into Gramma,'' he said. ''She wants to *keep* that old guy, like you'd take in a stray dog that you found.''

Simms, whose Indian blood showed in his slanted eyes, shrugged and grinned. ''Toby, you know nobody ever talked your Gramma out of doing anything she set her heart on doing. Besides, I don't see the harm in it.''

''What did you think of him?'' Toby asked.

''Oh, I think he's just what he says he is—an old missionary without a home.''

''You think he's for real?''

''Sure. We got along just fine. I asked him a few questions, to test him, like, and he had all the answers. He surely was a minister at one time, although I'm unfamiliar with the church in which he was ordained. And he surely knows all about Central America. I'm convinced he was a missionary there, just like he says. I don't think you have anything to worry about.''

''I still never heard of a minister bumming around like some kind of hobo,'' Toby said.

Simms gave him a syrupy smile that was a lot harder than

it looked. "I'm surprised at you, brother. You never heard of a man named Paul?"

Toby thanked Simms, not feeling particularly thankful, and turned to walk home. He wasn't buying the comparison of this scruffy old white man to any of the Apostles. St. Paul preached wherever he went, and founded churches, and was recognized as an important man and treated as such. He didn't bed down in deserted houses.

He had half a mind to phone the police chief and see what he thought of it. Van Wyck wanted to know if any strange characters turned up in the neighborhood; the old tramp could certainly be called that. True, the chief was trying to solve a murder, and there was no way the old geezer could've had anything to do with that. And Gramma would be madder than a hornet in a jar if the police showed up and plucked the guest from her porch.

The old man was still there, resting after his long talk with Simms. Emma Plews' wicker rocking chair was more comfort than he'd known in quite a while. His breakfast sat well with him, and the sun warmed his legs. At his feet snoozed the family dog, a flop-eared red hound who was going gray around the muzzle.

Thornall saw Toby coming up the street and knew he'd chased after Reverend Simms to see if he could find an ally. He knew the young man didn't trust him. *Lord have mercy,* he thought, *it's that kind of a world.* The stranger at one's gates was to be kept out, lest he rob or murder you. Thornall had never been robbed, but he'd met more than a few individuals who needed no special inducement to commit murder. From these the Lord had kept him safe, but they found other victims. In the poorest flophouses you found men who'd gladly slit your throat to rob a nickel from your pocket. On the meanest streets there were children who would kill an unconscious drunk just to see the color of his blood. Thornall didn't blame the grandson for wanting to send him on his way. There were too many men these days who carried the mark of Cain.

He took his eyes off Toby for a moment, distracted by a blue jay screaming in a nearby tree.

When he looked again, the young man was coming up the walk with a bright sword in his hand.

Two

On Whittier Avenue, the builder started you out with linoleum on the basement floor and inexpensive paneling on the walls and let you do the rest.

Blanche remembered when a basement was the place where you stored the stuff that was too dirty to be kept upstairs, but living in Royal Oaks II made her feel like a time traveler who'd gotten lost in the future. Here a basement was another floor of the house and was treated accordingly. True, it was still the place for the husband's workbench (if you could still find anybody who knew a ball-peen hammer from a ball-point pen) and the wife's washing machine and drier (although many of the women still took their clothes to the coin laundry, just as they'd done in Brooklyn and Queens and Jersey City); but even those traditional basement facilities were passing out of ken.

Now the basement was a showplace, like the rest of the house. You installed a false ceiling as soon as you had your furniture off the moving van, and put up better paneling as soon as you could afford it. In many homes the basement was the teenagers' living room, where they could entertain in style and still keep out of their parents' hair. You might set up a guest bedroom down there, or a den, or an office

206

for the family paperwork, or a nice little bar for political get-togethers. Some homes had pool tables down there—the *real* kind with the slate tops, not the plywood tops that soon warped and caused the balls to follow paths as tortuous as the moves in a Dungeons and Dragons game. Others boasted Ping-Pong tables, home video nooks, stereo systems, wine racks, home fitness centers, or any combination thereof. The more, the better—especially if it was more than they had next door.

Blanche wished her house could feature such amenities, but here the basement belonged to the Master. The door to it locked from the inside, and he had the only key.

Blanche stared at the blank door and wondered what he was doing down there.

He was peering through a microscope at the samples that he'd taken of Bruce Randall's blood, saliva, and inner-cheek tissue, looking for some tangible sign of vampirism. Unfortunately, it was the kind of microscope one might find in any respectable high school biology lab, and so far it had yielded only negative evidence. Non-data, the Master liked to call it. Maybe later he could get a sample from the woman Bruce attacked. Her case might make a very interesting study.

The microscope was ideal for spotting such signs of invasive organisms as roundworm eggs, trypanosomes, amoebae, and whatnot. Bruce's samples revealed nothing like that. The best the Master could do was to make an inference: If indeed there was a vampire organism, it would be something on the order of a virus—too small to be seen with anything but the best equipment.

When the Master had learned his laboratory science, there had been no such thing as an electron microscope, let alone a gas chromatograph; but he kept up with the scientific journals, so he knew what was available—to mortal scientists.

If only he had the right equipment, he was sure he could take giant steps forward in his research. His nomadic lifestyle, however, had always made that impossible. He had to get by with less. He was still wedded to the kind of basic apparatus he used to lug through the jungles of Guatemala.

He pulled up from his fruitless examination, leaned back in his chair, and closed his eyes.

The windows of his basement were painted an opaque green—black, he felt, would have attracted attention—and shielded by plywood. No ray of sunlight could penetrate his refuge.

The builders had put up a partition that divided the basement in two. The part closest to the stairs was his laboratory; another locked door separated it from the room in which he took his rest.

His entire scientific inventory was accommodated by a single workbench: microscope and slides, racks of test tubes, a Bunsen burner with its tank of propane gas, tripod, crucible, specimen jars. (It wasn't the quality of the equipment that mattered, ran his motto, but the quality of the mind that made use of the equipment. Besides, much of his research was in the nature of observations made in the field rather than the laboratory.) Overhead lamps provided all the light he needed, which was little. A living scientist would have found the room uncomfortably murky.

On portable steel shelves around the walls were arranged his books and pamphlets, a library that would have raised a few eyebrows among any scientific faculty. It would come as a shock to serious scholars to discover how many other serious scholars had soberly researched the subject of vampirism and written articles, monographs, and even books about it—some of them published out of their authors' own pockets, and not a few under pseudonyms. A prominent Japanese physicist: *My Encounter with a Vampire.* The French dramatist, DeSautels: *The Un-Dead.* Bishop Lorenzo Colcha: *A True Account of a Vampire in the Sicilian Town of Lumenti.* Here were writings that had, in many cases, demolished their authors' reputations. In the canon of twentieth-century dogma, belief in vampires could only be described as heresy.

These writings were difficult to obtain, but for the Master they were a necessity. He paid agents handsomely to track them down for him, and by circuitous routes they reached him. His agents were hired by other agents, and the complexity of his affairs was crucial to his privacy.

The farther room of the basement was where he spent his dormant hours, lying on silk sheets with his eyes open, unseeing, while his mind wandered trails too thorny for conscious memory. A natural rhythm caused this torpor to fall upon him with the rising of the sun; only by stressful exertions could he resist it. During this dormant period he did not dream, as far as he knew; nor did he think. He often pondered the nature and the function of this state of nonbeing, but he was in no position to explore it.

Into this private chamber Blanche never came. In an emergency she could only hammer on the basement door until she roused him. Sometimes he would entrust her with the key to his laboratory, but she had never even seen the key to this last door.

Had she been privileged to enter here, she would not have felt so easy in her partnership with the vampire.

The air within the room, which had no escape and was not necessary to the Master's survival, was curdled thickly with an odor that would have inspired images of death in the mind of any living human being. It was the odor that the Master fought by washing thoroughly with strong soap and dousing himself with dollops of cheap after-shave. It had no power to disgust him, but he could smell it, and he could easily imagine its effect upon the living. Unless he smothered it in soap and after-shave he could never pose convincingly as human.

The chamber was furnished in silk and antique wood,

obtained at no little cost, but because of the odor that clung to it, not one of those items could ever be resold.

Three

"What's the matter, Reverend? You look like you've seen a ghost."

Thornall blinked. The grandson's hands were empty now. He stood at the foot of the porch steps staring up at him. The dog woke and thumped its tail on the floorboards.

The vision—as his visions often did—had taken him completely by surprise; it made his heart race and drove the warmth from his body. He tried to conceal his shock, but from the way the young man stared at him, he knew it showed all too plainly.

He had recognized the sword. It was the Spanish sword, *his* sword, which now reposed in its thick wrappings in a corner of Mrs. Plews' kitchen. Why had he seen it in her grandson's hand? Why had the Lord shown him such a thing?

There was no time to pore over it just now. The grandson already had his doubts about him, so this was not the time to try to confide in him. Maybe later.

"I'm sorry, Mr. Hicks," Thornall said. "I must have been daydreaming. You startled me when you came up the walk just now."

Toby, thinking the old guy really must be nuts to get such a jolt out of a little thing like that, muttered an apology for sneaking up on him.

"Not at all," said Thornall. He ventured a smile and didn't get one back. "I'd appreciate it, though, if you sat with me for a little while. Your grandmother is cleaning house, and I could use the company.''

Toby took the chair next to the rocker, not liking it, and liking it even less when Thornall said, ''You're not very happy about my being here, are you, Mr. Hicks?''

''Gramma lets her generosity run away with her sometimes,'' Toby said, unable to put his thought more tactfully. ''If the truth be known, Reverend, I think she ought to be more careful. There's a psychiatric hospital just a few miles from here, and the patients are always going AWOL. You see a strange face around, you never know who it might be.''

''You have a right to feel that way, Mr. Hicks. But if you check with the hospital, I'm sure you'll find out that I'm not one of their patients.''

''I already know that. Your clothes tell me that. They wouldn't let you wear those clothes in any hospital I ever heard of. But I still can't figure out how a white minister winds up crashing in an old house in the black section of Millboro. Where did you come from, and why did you come here?''

''My last stop was the Salvation Army shelter, down in Freehold, Mr. Hicks. Before that, I spent some days in Philadelphia. As to why I'm here,'' Thornall said, pausing for a moment before he continued, ''I go where the Lord leads me, as I've done all my life. Why he led me here, I can't tell you. But I promise you I'm harmless, and I have faith that I'm here for some good purpose.''

There he goes again, Toby thought, *talking like God took him by the hand and marched him right up Alabama Road.*

''You're worried about your grandmother,'' Thornall said. ''You're afraid I'll steal from her, or bring some other kind of trouble to her.''

''A man's a fool if he doesn't think about things like that, Reverend. They aren't exactly what you'd call wild improbabilities.''

211

"I wish you weren't right about that, Mr. Hicks, but I know you are. Tell me, though—do I look like a thief?"

"No," said Toby, slowly. "I wouldn't figure you for a rip-off artist. You're too poor."

"A religious fanatic, then, perhaps?" Thornall pointed to his temple and twirled his finger to make the crazy sign.

"If you were, you wouldn't know it."

Thornall laughed, enjoying the sharpness of the parry. "I can see you weren't raised to be a fool, Mr. Hicks. Well, if you really are that uneasy about me, I'd rather arrange to stay somewhere else. Reverend Simms has offered to put me up. Maybe I'd better accept his offer."

"I think that'd be a good idea."

"Well, I don't!"

Gramma stood in the doorway, arms folded on her chest, and Toby cringed, wondering how much she'd overheard.

"Tolbert Dale Hicks, you better see a doctor about your memory. You keep forgettin' this is *my* house! If I want the reverend to stay awhile, he stays. And I don't want to hear no buts about it."

Toby knew when he was licked, and said nothing, but the old reverend tried to play the peacemaker.

"Now Mrs. Plews," he said, "don't be so angry. You should be thankful you have a grandson who cares so much about your safety. It's obvious to me that he loves you very much."

Gramma melted like a silly girl being asked for a dance by the handsomest male teacher in her school. Toby found it acutely embarrassing.

"Reverend," she said, "you got a godly turn of phrase and that's a fact!"

"Thanks, ma'am. Still, I'd hate to be the cause of any strife in this happy home. I think I'd better stay with Reverend Simms."

"You'll do no such thing! Look at you, Reverend: you're a tired old man. You been hungry too long, and it's sapped your strength. You need proper feedin' and lookin' after, and you ain't gonna get it from Reverend Simms. Not like you can get it here. You just set back and let me take care of you awhile, and pay no mind to Toby. He'll soon come to his senses—if he knows what's good for him!''

Toby held up his hands in surrender. ''Gramma, I used to think old Sergeant Davis was the meanest dude I ever met. But next to you, he was jelly.''

Over supper, Toby decided that maybe Thornall wasn't the worst thing that could happen to this house.

The old man said a truly beautiful grace that brought tears to Gramma's eyes, and praised her pork and greens to the skies so that she glowed. And he had a wealth of stories from his missionary days—so many that he couldn't possibly have made them up. Whatever Thornall was now, Toby no longer doubted that he'd been a missionary.

He was also interested in Toby's army stories. Toby knew he was being buttered up, but it still felt good. Shit, none of his friends wanted to hear those stories anymore, which was a bummer, because Toby still enjoyed telling them.

They continued swapping yarns after Gramma shooed them out to the porch while she cleaned up the kitchen. Toby told him about the time he'd been shot at while on patrol and had to dive out of the jeep and hug the ground until the sniping stopped.

''The worst part of it,'' he said, ''was that we didn't know if it was really over, or if the sniper was just waiting for us to get up so he could have a better shot. I'll bet we stayed down for two whole hours after he gave up and went away.''

''You never got a chance to shoot back?''

''Never saw the guy.''

''Suppose you had,'' said Thornall. ''Would you have shot him?''

213

"Well, hell, Reverend—he was shooting at *me!* I was kinda mad about that, y'know? Hey, we were supposed to be at *peace* with those people. I wasn't hurting him, why'd he want to start shooting at me for? You bet I would've shot back, if I could see him. Let *him* crawl around in the dirt awhile!"

"But not necessarily kill him?"

Toby had had some time to think about the incident, and knew more or less where he stood.

"I don't guess I would've seriously tried to kill him, man. But I did want to give him a taste of his own medicine.

"See, he could've shot up the jeep all he wanted, and he didn't. And he wouldn't be a sniper if he wasn't a damn good shot, so maybe he could've killed us while we were still in the jeep, if he really wanted to. So I think maybe he just wanted to scare us, show us who was boss. *That's* what I would've given a month's pay to do to him! But kill him? I guess not. It was peacetime, after all."

"And if it had been wartime?"

"Then I'd have to try to get him," Toby said, "before he got me. But damn it, Reverend, it *wasn't* wartime. We weren't in South Korea to fight anybody. Just to watch over the demilitarized zone and make sure it stayed demilitarized."

Thornall nodded approvingly. The young man understood the difference between duty and personal inclination. Not everybody did.

IX. SECRETS

One

Van Wyck was surprised not to find Chris Matthiesen at home when he went to see Mrs. Matthiesen that evening.

"He went out," she told him. "I'm afraid we had a fight."

She wore a blue terry cloth robe and pink slippers, and hadn't bothered to put on any makeup. Her pale brown hair was confined in a loose ponytail by an orange rubber band. She hadn't been out of bed for very long, Van Wyck supposed.

"I know I'm a mess," she said, "but I just don't have the energy to do anything about it. If you want to talk, you'll have to take me as I am."

Van Wyck fought a sudden, irrational urge to take her into his arms. There was something about this woman that reached into his heart and raked up coals that he thought had burned out years ago. He would have to be careful.

His ex-wife, Helen, would rather face a firing squad than be seen without her panoply of makeup, clothes, and expensively styled hair. Helen could shock you, the way her looks went down the tubes when she wasn't feeling up to par. It was so easy for a woman like that to slip from glamour girl to hag . . . and yet Dorothy Matthiesen, who in the past few days had seen more rough traveling than Helen had seen in all her life, was still easy on the eyes. His eyes, at any rate.

She startled him by asking, "Are you married, Chief?"

He shook his head. "Divorced."

She'd been on the point of saying something that his answer persuaded her not to say, and she'd forgotten what it was. But she smiled at him sympathetically, and in a way that somehow put them on the same side of a high wall that wasn't easily climbed.

"Come into the living room. We can talk there."

There was an easy chair that probably belonged to her husband, and he didn't feel like sitting in it. Instead he took one end of the couch; she balanced him at the other, with only a couple of feet of golden yellow cushion between them.

"How do you feel, Mrs. Matthiesen?" he asked. "Any better?"

She shrugged. The baggy robe gave away a hint of delicately rounded shoulders.

"I feel like hell, if you really want to know," she said. "I get dizzy if I stay on my feet for more than a few minutes. My appetite is off. And I've been drinking like a fish since I got up a few hours ago. Water, that is. Still, I'm a lot better than I was."

She looked frail and tired. Why wasn't her husband here to take care of her? *If she was my wife,* Van Wyck caught himself thinking, and made himself stop.

"I'm waiting to hear more from the doctor," she went on. "I hope he calls soon. I'd like to know what's wrong with me. Somebody must've drugged me. Whatever it was, I feel like it must've damn near killed me."

She offered it as a simple observation, without any hint of self-pity, rekindling Van Wyck's admiration of her courage. The lady was really hanging in there. Under the same circumstances, Helen would've been hysterical . . . but he doubted these comparisons were conducive to good police

216

work. He was here to help the woman, not get a crush on her.

"We've identified the boy who attacked you," he said.

"Who was he?"

"A high school junior named Bruce. Bruce Randall." Van Wyck gave her the address and asked her if she knew the family. She shook her head sadly.

"Sometimes I feel like I don't know anyone in the whole damned town," she said. "We moved here five years ago, and it still feels like it was just yesterday. I wanted to become part of the community—only there's no community to belong to."

That was something that had crossed his own mind more than once. But he said, "You never met any of the Randalls before Bruce assaulted you the other night?"

"Not that I can recall. I don't think I know anybody from their development, Triangle Mountain." She paused to make a grimace. "Can you believe this town? There isn't a mountain within a hundred miles of here. And if somebody lives in another development, he might as well be living in another county."

Painfully true, Van Wyck thought. Meanwhile, there seemed to be no prior connection between Dorothy and Bruce, no personal motive for the attack. Dorothy had been a random victim, nothing more. The first name drawn out of fate's hat.

But that was only the beginning of the story.

"We had the Schuylerville Nursing Home under surveillance last night and all day today," he said. "Nobody showed up. Of course, somebody could've come and gone before we got there."

He could see her shudder under her robe at the mention of the nursing home. The experience had left a shadow on her. He wanted to free her from it and didn't know how.

Why did it matter so much? Millboro was full of people who had problems they couldn't solve without his help.

217

Normally he didn't get cranked up about them. Okay, this wasn't some strident harpy from Brooklyn calling the cops because the neighbor's kid ran across her nice green lawn and gave her the finger when she tried to tell him off . . . but he didn't think it was the incident itself that got him cranking. It had more to do with the way he felt about Dorothy Matthiesen.

Again she startled him with a question.

"You really *care*, don't you? About what happened to me, I mean. You care personally."

Was she reading his mind? There were veterans on the force who could do that, but those were men he'd known for years, his closest friends. He didn't think he was all that transparent.

"I'm sorry," he said lamely. "This case upsets me. You'll have to pardon me, Mrs. Matthiesen."

"Pardon you for caring? Hell, no, Chief. It feels good for a change. For the first time since this thing started, I feel like I've got somebody in my corner. And I'm glad it's you."

But it was more than just being in her corner: an undeniable degree of physical attraction; an honest admiration of her character; a sense of being tuned to the same wavelength—there was enough here to get him into trouble, if he let it. With an effort Van Wyck wrenched the talk back to business.

"We had the detective squad take a look around the Schuylerville Nursing Home today," he told her. He remembered the dead rabbit in the cellar, but decided not to tell her about it just yet. *(Am I drawn to her because she's in danger? Is that part of it, too?)* "We found your footprints, and those other prints you mentioned, but no evidence to indicate who brought you there. I don't suppose you've remembered anything more since last night?"

"I went straight to bed and fell asleep right away," she said. "And then I was sick all day. I can't remember anything beyond what I told you last night. Great, huh? I'm a real big help."

"You're doing fine. A lot of crime victims can't tell us anything at all."

She gave him a slightly crooked smile. "Want a beer, Chief? I know policemen aren't supposed to drink on duty, but I feel like a beer just now and I wish you'd have one with me. For the companionship."

He almost blurted out an ill-considered crack about what her husband's duties were in the companionship department, but he called it back in time. He wished Chris Matthiesen would get home from wherever the hell he was and act like a normal husband. Then he could relax and have a beer and not feel like he was opening the door to temptation or something.

But he knew she wouldn't buy it if he suddenly went stiff and formal on her. So he said, "Thanks, Mrs. Matthiesen, I believe I will," and resigned himself to enjoying the way her body would move under that soft robe when she got up from the couch. It'd make him feel guilty, but he'd still enjoy it.

"Please, don't call me Mrs. Matthiesen anymore. My name's Dorothy. I want us to be friends, if it's possible."

"Dorothy, are you always so *direct* with people?"

She laughed nervously, with a blush rising to her cheek. "Oh, Lord, no!" she cried. "Usually I'm the other way around. I must be getting good vibes from you. Isn't it funny? You look like a man who could clean up Dodge City any day of the week, and I'm not the least bit scared of you. Do I have to keep calling you Chief?"

It was Van Wyck's turn for a nervous laugh. "No, you'd better call me Ed from now on," he said. So now they were Ed and Dorothy. It had a nice ring to it. *Matthiesen, you asshole, will you get back here and take care of your wife?* Jesus, Millboro was full of neglected wives who'd been lonely too long. Any cop could tell you that.

"Let me get our beers," she said. When she left the room, she drained it of a tension that was the more perilous because it had somehow become pleasurable. But she brought it back with her, and supercharged it when their hands touched as she gave him a bottle of Heineken.

"Yuppie beer," she said, "but still good."

"I know. Thanks." He tried not to react when she sat in the middle of the couch instead of at the far end. She truly didn't seem to do it consciously.

Van Wyck ended the night sitting at his kitchen table, alone, chewing on a liverwurst sandwich and trying to unwind so he could go to bed.

He tried to convince himself that he missed Helen, but he knew it was a lie. He'd only married her because she looked great in a bikini; it was an ego trip to be seen with her, and he was too damn young to know any better. That was all she'd had to offer. He didn't miss her spending sprees, her rotten lousy cooking, or her pop psychology approach to sex and child rearing. He missed her like he missed his patrolman's salary.

He missed the kids, but that was something else again. The kids had nothing to do with the way he'd responded to Dorothy Matthiesen.

He recognized the truth that he was a lonely man who got through life by devoting himself to his work and settling for casual friendships that cost little in terms of emotional involvement and didn't take time away from his job. He sometimes thought he was a good police chief because he literally had nothing better to do.

He'd sat and listened as Dorothy told him the story of her life, highlighted by the decline and fall of her marriage: things a police chief didn't need to hear, but which he wanted to hear because they came from her. He'd sat and reminded himself that she was a married woman, that she was too young for him, anyway, and that the way he was beginning to feel about her was based on fantasy—none of which kept him from telling her about *his* failed marriage, and his sense of powerlessness as his children were raised by Helen (who'd never shown any interest in them whatsoever until the day she asked the court for custody) and that dipshit she met in Philadelphia, and all the rest of it. Things no citizen needed to know about her police chief. But she'd listened to them all, and time passed by in big chunks, and fuckin' Chris never showed up, and it was all he could do not to kiss her as she let him out her front door.

It was one thing for a politician to spread his joy around. Hell, it hadn't hurt Ron Leib when he came up for reelection. The mayor could be as randy as an alley cat, but a police chief was expected to be virtuous. Van Wyck learned that much when his divorce came up and there were mutters about replacing him with somebody who kept his private life in better order. It never got past the whispering stage, but the whispers had been bad enough. It took months for them to die away.

He imagined Dorothy sitting across the table, having a sandwich with him before they went to bed. He could see it as clearly as if she were really there, and had been there for years. *It shouldn't be so easy,* he thought.

She'd given him a few back issues of *Tales from the Developments* to take home with him. One of them lay on the table beside his sandwich, and a stray paragraph seemed to leap at him from the page.

Why is it that the same people who sit glued to their TV sets when "Dallas" or "Dynasty" is on, lapping it up when the characters trash each other's marriages, cheat each other in their business dealings, and lie and plot and scheme for the sake of lying and plotting and scheming, are the first ones to hoot and holler when somebody in real life does the same damned shoddy things?

Lady, he thought, *you got that right.*

Two

No one named Winslow Emerson had ever been graduated from Trinity Physicians College. In fact, no one surnamed Emerson had ever earned a degree there.

Interesting; but what did it mean? Felix sat back and wondered.

He knew a thing or two about aliases. If your real name was John Smith, you didn't start calling yourself Myron Papadapoulos. You picked something with a familiar link to your own name, like John Smithson or Joe Smith, so you could answer to it readily. Felix liked to read the FBI bulletins in the post office lobby, and from them he'd learned that most criminals who adopted aliases didn't like to tax their memories. But a few picked up new names that were so unusual that they must have been easy to remember. Like James Earl Ray, the man who assassinated Martin Luther King; he'd called himself Eric Starvo Galt. It might be harder to respond instantly to a moniker like that if someone unexpectedly called it out, but it'd certainly stick to the memory. But "Winslow Emerson"? What kind of alias was that?

Of course it didn't have to be an alias. It just sure as hell wasn't the name of any doctor who'd ever come out of Trinity Physicians College. Harvard had sent Felix a complete list of Trinity's graduates, and Winslow Emerson wasn't on it.

But had he read it carefully enough? It wouldn't hurt to

go over it again. Felix took a can of beer out of the refrigerator and sat down to peruse the list once more.

That was how he found W. Emerson *Taylor*, Class of 1894.

Felix chewed that one over for a while, finally hypothesizing that the man across the street must have been named *for* Dr. W. Emerson Taylor. The surnames were different, but so what? Possibly this Dr. Taylor was Emerson's maternal grandfather. That'd explain his knowledge of Trinity Physicians College, and his choice of it as his phony alma mater. If you wanted to pose as a doctor, what better way than to claim you'd attended your grandpa's medical school, knowing that it had gone out of business so long ago that it couldn't easily be checked without a computer?

The motive for the masquerade, however, was still as obscure as ever. Felix now had a lot more information than when he'd started, and the damned thing was still a mystery. It was like solving a cryptogram that translated into nonsense, a code within a code.

What next? He supposed he could write again to the AMA, and to the Harvard Medical School Library, asking for information on this Dr. Taylor. The only reason not to was that it probably wouldn't help solve the puzzle. On the other hand, his curiosity was piqued, and it would only cost him a few minutes' work and a few cents' postage to pursue that line of inquiry while he tried to think of something more productive. He went to his typewriter and wrote the letters.

But that was delving—probably idly—into the past, and the mystery was in the present. Maybe he ought to check with the real estate people and see what they had on Emerson. It was Colonial Realty that had sold the house to Emerson, Felix recalled. *Same broker who sold my house to Elroy.*

Elroy had closed the deal for Felix's house with an agent named Kasko—probably short for Kaskowicz or something, Felix had always thought. Diane ("Call me Di!")

Kasko. She'd earned a nice commission on it and still had friendly feelings for Felix and his son, so she didn't mind dropping in at lunchtime the next day to see what Felix wanted.

"It's so nice of you to remember me!" she told him at the door. She wore a three-hundred-dollar suit and a sixty-dollar haircut. Her nails were manicured, her handshake soft and warm—feminine in a contrived sort of way, Felix thought. He put on his best manners for her.

"There's little chance I'd forget *you*, Mrs. Kasko. Please come in."

She entered the foyer and peered into the living room. "I love the way you've done this house, Mr. Frick! So tasteful! Your furnishings are so much nicer than Mr. and Mrs. Blasingame's were. And you keep it so clean!" She was already trying to calculate how much she'd make if Felix decided to sell it, he perceived. He motioned her toward the living room.

"Make yourself at home, Mrs. Kasko. I'll bring us some coffee."

"Call me Di," she reminded him as he went out to the kitchen.

She praised her cup of Maxwell House instant as if it were espresso from the Waldorf, asked how Elroy and his wife were doing, commented glowingly on the current state of the real estate market in Millboro, and adroitly covered up her disappointment when she finally realized that Felix hadn't asked her here to sell his house for him.

"Actually," he said, "I was wondering if you could obtain a few little items of information for me—confidentially, I must add. Just between the two of us."

"Oh!" She licked her lips thoughtfully. "Well! What kind of information?"

"Nothing that'll put you to a lot of trouble," Felix said. "But I have to have your promise not to discuss it with anyone. It'd be kind of embarrassing for me if this got out."

"Mr. Frick, I can't agree to help you unless you tell me what you want. But you can trust me to keep it under my hat, whatever it is."

Felix doubted that, but he was prepared to accept a small calculated risk.

"It's about that house across the street from me, Number Forty-three. Dr. Emerson's house." Di craned her neck to look out the window. She was tall enough to see the house without getting up from the sofa, and she nodded to show she understood what Felix meant. "What about it?" she asked. "Are you interested in buying it?"

Felix had anticipated that. "Well . . . Elroy has been talking about it. Only talking, mind you. But I promised him I'd ask a few little questions for him first. He's by no means sure about it, and at this point in time, he wouldn't want anybody knowing he was interested. But he trusts you to be discreet."

"Naturally. Real estate can be a delicate business, sometimes."

"Did you sell that house to the Emersons, Di, or was it another agent?"

"It was Fran Metzger, she handled it."

"Do you think you could look up that transaction for me?" Felix asked.

"Sure; but why don't you just ask Fran?"

"Oh, I'm more comfortable with you. And so is Elroy. If it ever comes down to making an offer . . . ."

"Of course!" Di smiled warmly at him. Felix smiled back, reading her mind. *These real estate bitches,* he thought. *They'll steal the teeth out of each other's mouths if they get half a chance.*

Having set the hook, he proceeded to reel her in.

"Elroy believes that the more you know about a person, the better off you'll be when you do business with him—especially if he doesn't know you know it, if you catch my drift."

"Perfectly. It sounds like your son knows what he's talking about."

"You can say that again. Anyway, we'd like to know a little more about Dr. Emerson before we approach him. *If* we approach him. Naturally, we'd be grateful to anyone who helped us accomplish this."

"I don't see any problem there, Mr. Frick."

"I'm glad, Di."

"You want me to talk to Fran and see what I can find out about the doctor?"

"Yes, if you could. Just a few little things—like where he came from, how he financed the deal, what kind of mortgage he got. Anything at all."

"I could dip into the files for you." Di smiled again, showing her capped teeth. "Not to tell tales out of school, but Fran Metzger isn't the most trusting person in the world. If I ask her too many questions, she'll jump to the conclusion that I'm trying to cut in on some business that ought to go to her. I'm afraid real estate is a very competitive field, these days."

"Just a little peek would do it," Felix said. "Elroy just wants a few items that'll help him down the road toward a decision. If you could get back to me sometime during the next few days, I'd really appreciate it."

"I think I can manage that for you."

She phoned two nights later.

"Mr. Frick? I've had a look at Fran's file on the Emerson transaction."

"Good, good! Let me get a pen and paper," Felix said. He kept a notepad near his living room phone. "Okay, shoot."

"There's really not much to it," she began, "although you may be surprised to know that the mortgage is in *Mrs.* Emerson's name, not the doctor's. In fact, he kept his name out of the transaction altogether. It's because of his health, Fran says. Apparently he's not a well man, and I imagine there might've been a problem if he'd been included in the financial arrangements. Bankers aren't heartless, but you don't want people who owe you money dropping dead on you."

"I understand." The old and the sick were second-class citizens; Felix already knew that. It was why his home had to be in Elroy's name. "Where are they from, Di? The Emersons."

"Some little place in upstate New York called Morainville; that was the address given. Do you want the exact address?"

"Yes, please." Felix wrote it down.

Di continued. "There's a thirty-year mortgage on the house. Don't ask me how they swung that; you'd think they'd both be too old to get that. But it seems Mrs. Emerson has some kind of trust fund—an inheritance or something, I guess—administered by a lawyer in Boston, a J.R. Hanratty. So the mortgage can be paid off that way if Mrs. Emerson dies."

"And the bank?"

"The mortgage is held by the Battleground Savings and Loan, in Freehold. It seems Mr. Hanratty set that up, too, with help from one of the local law firms, Fitch and Swazy. All Mrs. Emerson had to do was come in and sign the papers."

Felix made sure he had it all on paper before he asked, "Anything else?"

"Not much. Dr. Emerson is retired, which you probably know already. Place of birth, Boston, Massachusetts. Under Mrs. Emerson's occupation it says housewife, but I gathered from Fran that she used to work for the doctor as his nurse, back when he was still in practice.

"It must have been quite a practice: they seem to have a lot of money socked away. It's a hundred-and-seventy-thousand-dollar home, Mr. Frick, and they only had to put twenty thousand down. I don't know how they got away with less than forty."

Felix did a quick calculation. The Emersons were obligated for five thousand a year, not counting interest. All in all, they'd managed to swing a sweet deal. So sweet as to add to Felix's suspicions. Di gave him the rest of the financial data, and he took it down.

"That's about it," she said. "Fran only had to show them the house once, and they decided right then and there to take it. Easiest sale she ever made, she says."

"At those terms," Felix said, "I'm not surprised."

"Fran really didn't have much contact with them. The lawyers and bankers handled it pretty much among themselves."

Felix thanked her, promised to let her know what Elroy finally decided, and hung up the phone.

He sat and pondered the data, wondering what it meant.

Three

Now that she had actually decided to euthanatize her marriage, Dorothy found herself dawdling over it.

Her first excuse was to wait and see what the doctor said. The doctor said she was fine, not a thing wrong with her. No problem. Well, what he really said was that they couldn't *find* anything. No recognized toxic substances had turned up in her blood or urine. So either she hadn't been drugged or poisoned the night she was attacked, or else she'd been given something that broke down rapidly once it was in her system, and was impossible to trace.

But that didn't mean her physiology was back to normal. Hell, no. *We got some major problems here, Doc.* ("Well, Mrs. Matthiesen, there's absolutely *nothing* in the tests to indicate . . .") Like the way her skin seemed to crawl, sometimes, when she went outside. And the headache she invariably developed after fifteen or twenty minutes in the sun. ("You understand, don't you, that the victim of an unprovoked assault will sometimes manifest physical symptoms that, although they seem real enough, actually have no physiological basis . . .") And the thirst that no amount of water, wine, or beer seemed to satisfy.

What the doctor meant was that it was all in her head, and you didn't have to be Perry Mason to know that you didn't walk into divorce court at a time when your husband could prove, with testimony from your doctor, that your mind was full of imaginary ailments. ("Your Honor, everything was hunky-dory until my wife was assaulted. Since then, she's been as crazy as a March hare. . . .") When you lived in Millboro, where they had a nice big booby hatch right in the middle of the township, you tried to avoid giving the impression that you belonged inside the walls.

Hence Dorothy didn't tell her doctor, let alone her future ex-husband, about some of the things that actually *were* all in her head. They didn't show, and as long as she kept quiet about them, no one would realize they were there. She could have her very own collection of secret quirks.

Why do I cringe at the sight of a sunbeam dancing on the carpet? Why do I crave rare meat, when it always used to be I'd get queasy at the sight of an underdone steak?

And don't forget the dreams! Hey, I've got a regular nonstop Sam Peckinpah film festival running inside my head all night. Bodies flying every which way, exit wounds as big as footballs, squashed skulls, blades hissing through the air to sheer off arms and legs . . . and blood. Lakes and seas and oceans of blood. And I wake up thirsty, and I drink water until my bladder's fit to burst, and I don't dare scream because then I'd have to come up with some kind of explanation, *ha ha.*

But that's small stuff, folks, because—are you ready for this?—I can see and hear things that I could never see or hear before. That's right, voices in the night. Like private conversations overheard at impossible distances. And I'm telling you I can see in the dark like a fucking cat! Well, maybe not quite that well, but a hell of a lot better than I ever could before. I can get around the house at midnight, with all the shades down and all the curtains drawn, and never bump into anything. Not because I know where everything is, but because I can see it. It's not microscopic or X-ray vision, nothing outlandish like that. Just your plain old everyday night vision that suddenly gets to be almost as good as your daytime vision, for no apparent reason.

Oh, yeah, it'll all sound so great at my commitment hearing. . . .

Her other excuse was that there was no real urgency to get the ball rolling on a divorce. Her feelings for Chris were as dead as the Babylonian national debt. Since she no longer cared when he came home from work, or whether he came home at all, his absence had lost the power to trouble her. He was just a man who got his mail at the house where she lived.

She supposed she ought to feel guilty about living off his labor, but she didn't. For one thing, it'd stop cold as soon as she got a divorce. For another, *he* wasn't complaining, was he? And the situation wasn't her fault. She was the one who'd done all the suffering, not Chris. Hadn't she tried everything she could think of to rekindle his interest in their marriage? He was the one who'd stopped caring first. He was the one who hadn't even made a single *phone call*, for God's sake. Never mind his excuses, his supposed good intentions, his alleged confusion. If they gave a Nobel prize for apathy, Chris would win it hands down. Dorothy didn't waste any sympathy on him.

The only awkward part of it was the sleeping arrangements. Whatever the man's faults, it wasn't fair to expect him to sleep on the couch till doomsday. It didn't do the couch any good, either. But to share the bed with him . . . it just wasn't possible. She knew because she'd tried it.

It had been months since Chris had initiated any love-making, so sex wasn't the issue. Might as well sleep with a mannequin. But Dorothy found she couldn't sleep when he was in the bed with her. Chris worked his balls off all day and corked off as soon as his head touched the pillow. Dorothy would lie there, as far away from him as she could be without falling out of bed, listening to him breathe and feeling—as the Victorians liked to say—decidedly queer. It was not repulsion. It was more like a sense of being in the wrong place.

So she set up a spare bed in the basement and did her sleeping there. The floor was linoleumed, the walls were paneled, and there was a soundproof ceiling overhead, so it wasn't a matter of sleeping in the cellar. But even down here she could hear the springs creak when Chris stirred in the queen-size bed upstairs.

Ed Van Wyck had done a good job of keeping her adventure out of the papers, and no one seemed to know about it. None of her friends, indeed, seemed aware that she had had any kind of difficulty at all. When she got a phone call, she only had to say she didn't feel like going out to the pool or the tennis courts just then, and that was that. No questions asked.

The fact was that she no longer liked to go out during the day. Why not, she couldn't imagine. If it was really sunny she would get an urge to draw the curtains or retreat to the basement. This posed a problem because she didn't want to turn into a goddamn hermit, after all. She knew she had to get her life back in gear—unless she wanted to go around the bend altogether.

Getting back to work on *Tales from the Developments* would be a start. Attending public meetings, too, filled in those gaping holes of time. And Millboro offered a plethora of meetings. Council, planning board, zoning board, school board, local utilities authority, regional sewerage authority, recreation commission; you could go to a meeting every night, if it took your fancy.

And there was plenty going on. With the primary-election campaign heating up, there were some marvelously vicious exchanges at the council meetings. Politics slopped over into the planning and zoning board sessions, too, livening them up considerably. They even managed to drag it into discussions of the township's water and sewer services, and politics touched off some nifty set-tos at recreation commission powwows. As far as *Tales* was concerned, the only difficulty lay in choosing what to make fun of.

Heck, there was fat Marc Kaminsky, running all alone as an Independent Democrat because none of the established factions would touch him with a ten-foot pole. He was running because he'd let his Swim Club membership lapse and now he couldn't get a renewal; naturally, he accused the parties in power of doling out Swim Club memberships as rewards for political loyalty. There were just enough assholes in Millboro to believe this and feed Marc's illusion that he could win an election one of these days.

Then you had Stan Bosman and Dick Birnbaum, Richie Phelps' hand-picked stooges. Phelps was a man to watch, Dorothy thought. Elected to the council as Ron Leib's personal protégé, and then to the chairmanship of the regular Democratic executive committee, he was just about strong enough now to push Leib and Council President Tom Thurlow out of the driver's seat. But he wouldn't be able to do it with Bosman and Birnbaum, whom people were already calling the Bobbsey Twins because they couldn't tell them apart. A pair of dumpy little guys with moustaches, they never said boo unless Phelps held up a cue card first.

Finally you had Levi Grossman and Sol Puka carrying the banner for the John F. Kennedy Club, the major faction of Democrats opposed to Leib, Thurlow, and Phelps. Levi was a very intelligent financial manager with the personality of a strand of overcooked linguine. Sol was a good guy, but for Christ's sake, how could you win an election with a name like Puka? The last time he ran, Richie Phelps bought a bunch of airsickness bags and had them printed up with the legend, "Don't make me Puka!" Very classy.

Dorothy was sitting in the back row, watching Marc Kaminsky hog the floor mike during the public portion of the council meeting, when Felix Frick took the seat next to her.

"Not very edifying, is it?" he said. She hadn't noticed him until he spoke.

"Hi, Felix. You gonna spring anything on 'em tonight?"

He shook his head and said, "I'm getting too old to listen to this. What say we go up the road for an ice cream cone?"

Dorothy grinned spontaneously for the first time since the night she was attacked.

There was a Baskin-Robbins ice cream parlor at a mini-mall on Main Street, next to a building that had used to house the township offices until the new municipal complex had been built a couple years ago. Dorothy and Felix bought their ice cream cones and retired to a bench outside the store.

"So what's your next big exposé?" she asked.

Felix took a bite of his lime sherbet and said, "Mm! I'm afraid I'm not at liberty to say."

"You're a tease, Felix."

"I've been called worse."

"You ought to dig up something really major," Dorothy said, "and write a book about it. I'm serious. That's what I'd do, if I had your investigative skills."

"My dear, nobody wants to read about the trivial pettifogging that goes on in a silly township that they never heard of."

233

She had a sudden urge to confide in Felix, although she hardly knew him. *Shit, the doctors don't know what's wrong with me, the police can't figure out what happened—why not Felix?*

"I wouldn't say everything that goes on in Millboro is trivial," she said. "There've been two unexplained deaths here in just a few weeks."

"Indeed there have—plus an abduction." He looked shrewdly at her. *"Your* abduction," he added.

She gulped for words. He nibbled at his ice cream cone.

"Nobody's supposed to know about that, Felix!"

"Can't keep that kind of a secret in a town this size."

"But how did *you* find out?"

He wasn't about to tell her that he paid a patrolman for keeping him current with the gossip around police headquarters.

"Mrs. Matthiesen, I have nothing to do all day but find things out. I keep my ear to the ground. Just because something doesn't appear in the papers doesn't mean it never happened. But I don't mean to imply that I know everything. All I know is that you were attacked outside the Millboro Mall some nights ago and were missing for twenty-four hours. Your attacker was the boy whose body was found near the mall parking lot, but your abductor is unknown. And that's all I've heard about it. It was enough to arouse my curiosity, though. I was hoping you'd tell me the rest."

Dorothy couldn't answer. Felix wasn't supposed to know, *nobody* was supposed to know. Were the policemen blabbing about it? Her ice cream turned into a pile of slush in the pit of her stomach.

"I can appreciate that it must be a shock to you, hearing me speak about this," Felix said. "But I'm genuinely interested, and I want to help. At least I'd like to know how a resident of this township can be assaulted in a public place, disappear for twenty-four hours, and the police still not have a clue after a week's investigation. Futhermore, I'd like to know how come a Millboro High School junior, with no prior police record, can suddenly attack a woman and just as suddenly be found dead, and how the police department can be so utterly at sea over it. And I'm assuming that you, too, would like to know the answers to those questions."

If she had ever thought of him as a cranky old man who idled away his golden years quibbling with public officials over absurd minutiae, it seemed a hundred years ago now.

"You wanted me to look into this before you even knew you wanted it," he said. "You said I should investigate something really major. Well, this is certainly something that's worthy of investigation. And besides, you'll feel better if you can talk about it with someone who doesn't have to worry about losing his job if he happens to step on a few toes."

They went to Felix's house. In a way it was a small betrayal of Van Wyck, and Dorothy felt guilty about it. On the other hand, she could hardly be expected to go through an acute personal crisis with only the police chief to confide in. Van Wyck cared, but whether he cared or not, it was his job to listen to her. That, too, was unfair, in a way. But Felix was right: as police chief, Van Wyck had official responsibilities that were bound to limit what he could do for her.

She wasn't trying to convince herself that Felix was interested because his heart bled for her. He comforted her with his Wise Old Teacher act, but he had no emotional investment in her. Somehow that made it easier to trust him—as one would trust a doctor.

After she left him, Felix had to admit that he couldn't blame the police for not knowing what to do with this one. It was a confusing case.

They were dealing with two parties: the boy who had attacked Dorothy, and whoever had transported her miles away to the Schuylerville Nursing Home. Was there any connection between them? Felix thought they must have been working together, but he knew there was no logical basis for that conclusion. Maybe the police had some information that made it even more confusing. If so, he would have to find out.

The boy's death had been in the papers, but the condition of the body hadn't. Having heard Dorothy's description of it, Felix wasn't surprised that the police had suppressed the details. When confronted by facts beyond its understanding, the official mind never chose to publicize its ignorance.

For once Felix had a suspicion that he'd bought a puzzle he'd never be able to solve.

X. AN INCIDENT IN SHINING VALLEY

One

The Master was intrigued by the name: Shining Valley.

It wasn't a valley, and the only thing that shone there was the chrome on the residents' cars, but it was still intriguing.

For one thing, it wasn't a development. It was an enclave of semirural affluence that had built up gradually as farmers sold their land piecemeal, builders put up houses one at a time, and professional people bought them. There were more doctors, lawyers, and accountants in Shining Valley than there were in any of the "prestige developments" that blew their own horns so lustily.

For another, it was somewhat off the beaten track. Its only major road was Ford's Lane, a country road that didn't connect directly to any of the state highways or centralized business districts in the area. That kept traffic down to a minimum. And from what Blanche had gleaned in conversation with her neighbors, nobody in Royal Oaks II was particularly well acquainted with anyone from Shining Valley.

"They're kind of aloof up there in the valley," said Nancy Kruzek when Blanche asked her about it. "They aren't really into politics. Mostly they like to sit back and count their money, and contribute enough to the candidates to make sure nobody messes with their zoning between elections. Most of 'em aren't from the city, and they tend to be snobbish about it.''

Tucked into the northeastern sector of the township, Shining Valley went its own way.

These were the factors that persuaded the Master to choose it as the site for his new experiment.

"Aren't you afraid someone will notice us, driving all around here two nights in a row?'' Blanche asked.

"From what you've told me,'' said the Master, "I doubt it. Oh, it'd be different if they had problems with burglary or vandalism, but the local criminal element doesn't seem to have discovered this neighborhood as yet. I'm sure they feel quite secure.''

Blanche drove. The Master sat beside her and observed through the windshield, learning what he could of the geography and economics of the area.

"I don't like going up the same streets two nights back-to-back,'' Blanche said. "What if somebody calls the cops?''

"Have I ever done anything which resulted in our getting rousted by the police?''

"No,'' she grumbled, putting it down more to luck than to any foresight on the Master's part.

"Some of these people own large dogs,'' he said. "I can smell them.'' He had the side window down.

"All the more reason to be careful, I say.''

"Blanche, I'm not afraid of dogs.''

"If they get one whiff of you, they're going to bark and carry on to high heaven.''

The Master sighed and nodded, conceding the point. Human beings, with their dull senses, could be fooled by a bit of after-shave, but not dogs. There was something about the vampire scent that drove dogs into a frenzy, and cats didn't like it, either.

"I'm right, aren't I? Admit it for once."

"If there are too many dogs," he said, "I'll just have to call it off, that's all. I admit you're right."

That pleased her enough to silence her for the time being.

When he had learned all he could by car, and by sending Blanche to the library to peruse the telephone cross-directory, he set about reconnoitering the area on foot.

He understood Millboro well enough to know that a pedestrian was cause for comment wherever he might appear, so he was careful to avoid the streets and sidewalks, and to confine his activities to the darkest part of the night. As quiet and as agile as he was, it was easy for him to slip from backyard to backyard, keeping to the shadows and becoming as motionless as a boulder whenever he saw need. Long ago he'd reasoned that this facility for stealth lay at the root of the legend of the vampire's power to dissolve himself into a green mist. A mist could not have passed through Shining Valley more quietly.

When he stood still and sniffed the air, he could smell the life of the neighborhood: the smoldering charcoal and burnt grease left in the barbecue pits, the alcoholic tang of spilled drinks on the patios, the acrid mix of chemical fertilizers in the lawns. He couldn't smell the good soil that he knew lay beneath it all, where it had supported farms here for generations. Now he smelled the chlorine in the water of the swimming pools, inground and aboveground, and the various insecticides and herbicides that were sprayed on shrubs and lawns. And lawn mower exhaust fumes. Even the semi-sweet whiff of polyethylene radiating from newly purchased lawn furniture.

With a little bad luck, he thought, *I could poison myself with tainted blood here.* Small wonder they all expected to develop cancer, before they reached their seventies. They lived amid a witches' brew of chemicals.

239

Even in the chaos of odors that filled the air, the Master could still smell dogs. The people of Whittier Avenue favored toy dogs and poodles, but this was Doberman pinscher country. The big dogs barked and howled when he passed, but they were all indoors, and although most of the houses still had some lights on, the dogs' owners told their pets to shut up and remained glued to their television screens.

The Master could hardly blame them for that. Television was profoundly fascinating, and in countless ways. Just this afternoon he'd told Blanche to go ahead and buy a VCR. He loved high technology and was old enough not to take it for granted. It challenged him, but he was afraid it only dulled the minds of the living. It had certainly atrophied their senses. What smug idiocy, to ignore their dogs when they sounded the alarm.

As he explored the neighborhood, the early risers began to put out their lights and go to bed. The night was moonless, overcast with clouds that would drop their rain elsewhere. Inside an expensively refurbished farmhouse, a man and a woman argued noisily. Televisions chattered. High overhead, jet engines shrieked.

And much closer, a big dog had gotten loose and was racing toward him.

He could stand his ground and kill the dog easily enough, but that was only to be considered as a last resort. The dog might just as easily dance out of his reach, barking and yapping until it had drawn a crowd. The Master didn't want that. In Millboro it wasn't proper to appear in a strange neighborhood, miles from your own development, without a car.

The dog was only a few lots away now. With a speed that would not have seemed possible for his bulky frame, the Master crossed the yard he was in and tried the back door of the nearest garage. It was unlocked, and he let himself in without a sound. There were lights on in the house, but the garage itself was dark.

He watched through the window as the Doberman came bursting through the hedge, graceful as a gazelle on its long, slender legs, deadly as a wolf in the white menace of its fangs. The Master appreciated animals for their beauty, but he couldn't own any. No dog would abide the scent of undead flesh. Insects seemed to like it, though, and when a cloud of insects gathered around a vampire, bats would sometimes move in for an easy meal.

The dog pranced nervously around the yard, sporadically barking. It knew its quarry had taken shelter in the garage, and it knew it couldn't follow it. It whined in frustration, then finally loped away.

The garage light came on.

"And who the hell are you?"

The man stood in the doorway with a bunch of keys dangling from his fingers, angered to find an intruder in his garage but also confused. Fat, elderly men don't break into garages. The homeowner wasn't sure how to react.

"I'm so sorry to trespass," the Master said. "But there was a Doberman on the loose, and all I could do was run for shelter. He seems to be gone now, but I'm sure you heard him barking. He followed me right up to this door."

"I heard him, all right. But you haven't answered my question, sir. And since this is my property, and I know I've never seen you before, I'll repeat it. Who are you?"

The Master put a smile on his face and introduced himself by a false name. "You must forgive me," he added. "When I saw that dog coming for me, I just panicked and ran up your driveway, and then around behind your garage. Thank God I didn't have a heart attack; as you can see, I'm too old and fat for that much exercise."

Calling attention to his apparent weaknesses did much to

calm the property owner. In a culture where prosperous white adults could expect to be victimized by teenagers, blacks, and drug addicts, a fat old white man with a weak heart could hardly pose a threat.

"Well, I'm sorry you had a scare, sir," the man said. "I'd ask you in for a drink, but as I happen to be on my way out, I'll just invite you to leave. Maybe we'll meet again under more conventional circumstances."

"I hope so," the Master said. "You have no idea how embarrassing it is to be caught in such an undignified position, Mr. . . . I'm sorry, I don't know your name."

"Norm Rubin."

Rubin came up alongside the car to usher the stranger out of his garage. The Master let him approach, then seized him from behind and applied pressure to the carotid arteries. Unconsciousness followed swiftly.

The Master preferred to cut his victims rather than bite them, but he bit Rubin on the back of the neck, under the man's modishly long hair, and fed briefly.

He gathered from the house and the car that Rubin was a successful professional man, like most of the inhabitants of Shining Valley. It could be reasonably inferred that Rubin was intelligent and capable. The Master wanted to see how such a man would adapt to a sudden transformation to the vampire state. By feeding on him mouth-to-wound, the Master could again test his theory that the transformation was effected by intimate vampire-to-victim contact, implying the transmission of a vampire organism.

He didn't want to leave the man in the garage or carry him back into the house, in case he was married. Mrs. Rubin might find him and call a doctor, maybe even take him to a hospital. That would give Rubin an opportunity to describe his encounter in the garage, and that would never do. It would be better to leave him someplace where the sun would quickly destroy him if he panicked, or else force him to stay put until he understood the change that had come over him.

Could he understand it? Could he become as successful in his new life as he'd been in his old one? What effect did the transformation have on the subject's intellectual faculties?

The Master slung the body over his shoulder and ventured out of the garage.

Several lots over he spied what he was looking for. He hustled to it quickly and silently, opened the prefab aluminum toolshed, and stowed Rubin inside. There he applied his medical knowledge to ensure that the man would remain unconscious throughout the night.

He would have to tell Blanche to keep a sharp eye on the newspapers these next few days.

Two

"There's a man in my toolshed."

"There's a man in your toolshed?" said Dispatcher Ballantine, who wasn't sure she'd heard it right. But she'd been taking police calls long enough to recognize the brittleness of a voice on the brink of losing control. Keep 'em calm was the cardinal rule. "May I have your address, ma'am? We'll send an officer right away."

"Four-fourteen Redcoat Hill Road. That's off Ford's Lane. Please hurry. I've been watching the shed all this time, and he hasn't budged."

It sounded like another bird had flown the booby hatch, this one coming to light in Marge McNally's backyard, Ballantine thought. Rounding up patients gone AWOL from the state psychiatric hospital was almost a daily problem of

243

police work in Millboro. When were they going to get some fuckin' security at that place? They had some pretty dangerous characters under treatment there. Ballantine remembered the flap last fall when one of the escaped patients, a black belt in karate, beat the living shit out of a patrolman who'd made the mistake of not knowing who the guy was when he'd stopped to question him. Then—as now, it seemed—they never called the police when one of the crazies turned up missing. They were supposed to, damn it; if Arnie Woods had known there was a mad karate expert on the loose, he never would've tried to tackle the guy alone. But the hospital didn't like to broadcast its mistakes and clung tenaciously to the excuse that any missing patient could always turn up under a bed or inside a broom closet in one of the hospital's many facilities. Can't spread the alarm till we rule *that* out, can we?

But Marge McNally had one more thing to say. "I *think* it's Mr. Rubin from down the street. I didn't get a real good look, but I *think* it's him."

"An officer will be on his way, ma'am," said Ballantine. She was glad it'd be left up to the officer to ask what Mr. Rubin could be doing in his neighbor's toolshed in the middle of a weekday morning. "Meanwhile, stay calm and call back immediately if the man comes out of the shed."

Patrolman Lou Sforza, who hated the nickname "Schwartz" but couldn't seem to shed it, knew a sticky situation when he saw one. And he remembered Arnie Woods' face when they found him after the wild karate man was finished with it. Arnie looked like a plateful of mashed strawberry pie.

"I went to open the door," Mrs. McNally said, "and he *attacked* me! Let out the most godawful shriek you ever heard. I think he's gone crazy."

Sforza approached the prefab metal toolshed and thought

244

he heard someone sobbing uncontrollably inside it. He retreated back to the house.

"Are you sure it's this neighbor of yours, this Rubin?"

"I'm pretty sure."

"Did he say anything to you?"

"Officer, he didn't even sound human! The noise he made was like an animal."

That does it, Sforza thought. He radioed back to headquarters for help, and plenty of it.

By the time Van Wyck arrived on the scene, the man was still in the toolshed, Sergeant Rossovich and four patrolmen having failed to get him out.

"Chief, the guy must be messed up on angel dust or something," the sergeant reported. "Every time we touch the door, he screams bloody murder and bangs around inside something fierce. He might hurt himself. Then again, he might hurt us—if we get too close."

A mindless howl went up from the toolshed. Rossovich shuddered.

At least they'd confirmed the ID. The man in the shed was indeed Norman Rubin, a thirty-eight-year-old attorney who was a junior partner with a big law firm in Long Branch. Mrs. Rubin had gone out to play bridge last night and come home at midnight to find the house empty. She assumed her husband was tied up with something in his work that had come up unexpectedly and urgently. Sometimes he had to hop a plane and handle something out of state. But when she called his office in the morning, they hadn't known where he was, either. She was about to call the police when the police called her.

She was here now, standing next to Mrs. McNally and all but wringing her hands. "She insists her husband doesn't do any drugs," Rossovich said. "Of course, she has no idea why he's acting up like this."

Van Wyck paid the women his respects. In spite of the presence of the police, they were both on the verge of becoming hysterical.

"Don't you hurt him!" Mrs. Rubin cried.

"Ma'am, we don't want to harm a hair on his head," Van Wyck said. "That's why I'm here to supervise this operation personally."

"You can't just let him stay in my toolshed!" Mrs. McNally said, as if that were a viable option the police were seriously considering. "He's been in there for *hours!*"

It was going on noon. "We'll get him out of there as gently as possible," Van Wyck said, and went back to his men.

"It's football time," he told them. They stared at him. "There's six of us and only one of him. If we do some old-fashioned gang tackling, nobody should get hurt. But first we've got to get this shed open."

"Chief, there's tools in there," Rossovich said. "He might charge out of there with a trowel and stick it in somebody's chest."

"He won't be able to, if we all move together." Van Wyck paused to take a closer look at the shed. "Okay. The door opens inward. I'll kick it open. We'll have a man on either side of the door. You two, Sterns and Simpson. When he comes out, jump on him from behind. You know how, you both played high school ball."

"Yeah, but I played for fuckin' Millboro!" Simpson complained. "We never tackled anybody while I was there." He got a laugh. The Millboro Mounties had been the doormats of their conference since LBJ was in the White House.

"I'll try to stop him head-on," Van Wyck said. "Rossovich, you back me up. You two, Kelly and Sforza, over there. You hit from the sides. Be quick, in case Sterns and Simpson miss him when he pops out. I want a nice big pile-up. That'll be safest for everybody."

He positioned his men. Inside the shed, Norman Rubin

246

moaned and gibbered. From the way he sounded, he was completely out of his gourd. It might mean he was too far gone to wield a weapon, or pose any threat whatsoever, but it wasn't much of a morale booster to stand around listening to him.

When the men were ready, Van Wyck took a deep breath, then launched a straight-on thrust kick at the flimsy aluminum door.

It flew open with no resistance. Rubin hadn't locked it, hadn't tried to prop it shut. Nor did he come flying out in a berserk rage. He only screeched.

He was on the floor, curled up in a fetal position and screaming his lungs out. He didn't put up a fight when Van Wyck went in and slapped handcuffs on his wrists. But he wouldn't stop screaming, and they couldn't talk to him.

"We'll carry him out and put him in your car," Van Wyck said to Rossovich. "But first let's see if his wife can get him to shut up for a minute."

Mrs. Rubin wasn't easily convinced to approach her husband. "I can see him just fine from here," she said.

"He might snap out of it if he hears your voice, ma'am," Van Wyck said. But she was too afraid to try. He had Mrs. McNally take her into the house.

"Let's get him down to headquarters, guys. But be careful. He might start struggling any minute."

He started struggling as soon as they got him out of the shed, thrashing, writhing, and kicking. It took all four patrolmen to wrestle him back to the squad car and pile him into the backseat. Once inside the car, he threw himself to the floor between the seats and wedged himself in like a lizard. He kept on screaming.

"Have a doctor waiting at the station. We're gonna have to dope him up before we can find out what's the matter with him," Van Wyck said. "Get a move on. Mrs. Rubin'll ride with me."

* * *

247

Bobbie Rubin stared straight ahead, oblivious to the car's passage through some of the more scenic portions of the township. Considering what she was going through, Van Wyck thought she was bearing up pretty well. She calmed down a little once he'd assured her that they weren't looking to hold her husband on any criminal charges.

"We just want to help him, Mrs. Rubin. This is just protective custody until he's quiet enough to be sent home or to a hospital, whatever's best. We really have no choice; right now, he could be dangerous to himself or others."

She nodded stiffly, a woman in her mid-thirties who had suddenly aged twenty years or more.

"I can't understand it," she said. "Norman is so calm, so low-key. I've never seen him lose his temper. I just don't understand what's happening to him."

Van Wyck questioned her gently, obtaining a string of facts that led nowhere.

Rubin had gone to his office yesterday as usual, put in a full day's work without incident, including an appearance in court, and left for home—according to his secretary—at the usual time. Mrs. Rubin had eaten alone, left him a cold supper in the refrigerator, and gone out to her bridge club. She had played better than usual and stayed late, getting back home well after ten. Norman hadn't been there, but she hadn't worried about him. His work was like that, sometimes, she explained: Things came up without notice. She had gone to bed expecting him to come home later, or else phone her in the morning from another city.

She hadn't noticed any irregularities in his behavior lately. No strange changes of mood, no unexplained absences, no signs of stress, nothing. Same old Norman. She strongly rejected the suggestion that he might be on drugs.

"Norm only *drinks* to be sociable," she told Van Wyck. "Actually, he's a health nut. He jogs. He doesn't smoke. He's as straight as a ruler. He has nothing but contempt

248

for anyone who takes drugs. Some lawyers he knows, they've dabbled with cocaine. Norm says they're snorting away their careers.''

"Maybe it's some weird kind of food poisoning, then," Van Wyck said. "Something like that. We'll know more after a doctor's seen him.''

But while Van Wyck was taking his time driving back to the station, giving Mrs. Rubin a chance to recover her nerve and himself a chance to question her, Norman Rubin was turning police headquarters into a madhouse.

They had to sit on him before Dr. Simonsen could inject him with a sedative. Simonsen, who had rushed over from the psychiatric hospital, gave him a good hearty dose, then stood back and stared in mild amazement as the drug showed not the slightest sign of taking effect.

"I can't give him any more," the doctor said during a brief lull between Rubin's screaming fits. "I gave him the maximum safe dose.''

"Are you sure?" said Rossovich.

"I gave him enough to stop a racehorse in its tracks!" the doctor snapped.

"Holy shit!" one of the patrolmen exclaimed. "Look at his face!''

They held Rubin so that the doctor could get a good look at him. Rossovich got a good look, too, and turned away with an expression that Dispatcher Ballantine would later describe as "haunted—like he went to put flowers on a grave and somebody came up out of it.''

Rubin's face had taken on a dreadful shininess that reminded the doctor of wax fruit, with a purplish, grapey tinge around the eyes, nostrils, and lips. His screams had died down into choking sobs. There were brown lesions on his cheeks and forehead: rotten spots.

"What's happening to him, Doc?''

"He's going limp on us, Doctor," said one of the officers who were holding Rubin. "Guess that shot you gave him finally got to him." But to Simonsen it looked as if the patient was dying.

Why, why had he allowed his name to be put on the police emergency list? *Good P.R. for the hospital, Sy* . . . He felt Rubin's wrist for a pulse. It was weak and getting weaker. The man's skin was cold. Simonsen pulled up an eyelid with his thumb and saw the white of the eye suffused with blood, the pupil shrunken to a pinprick. Suddenly he noticed there were blisters on Rubin's lips. Where the hell had *those* come from? For a moment he was struck by the conviction that he had, after all, overdosed the patient. He dismissed the thought as unproductive.

"What the fuck, is he *dyin'* on us?" Rossovich said.

Simonsen was damned if he knew. He felt like a premed student being called upon to do brain surgery. He felt Rubin's forehead. The brown lesions seemed to smear when he touched them, and his fingers came away moist and evil-smelling.

Simonsen had the policemen cart his patient to a holding cell and laid him on a cot, covered him with blankets. It did no good. Rubin continued to fade. Simonsen tried heart massage and mouth-to-mouth resuscitation, and he was about ready to risk a shot of adrenaline when the patient died.

That was about thirty seconds before Van Wyck entered the lobby with Rubin's wife.

Later, in the privacy of Van Wyck's office, Simonsen was able to ventilate a little.

"I swear I've never seen anything like it," he said. "I can hardly wait till they do the autopsy. Whatever killed that man, it was something completely outside my experience." He added a bitter smile. "And where I work, Chief, a doctor experiences almost everything."

"You don't have a clue, Doctor?"

"Not a blessed one. Of course, it'd help if we knew where he was, what he was doing, before you brought him in. They say he was holed up in somebody's toolshed, but I mean before that. I suspect it'd make a pretty wild story."

"What makes you say that?"

Simonsen glared at him. "You didn't notice the bite mark on the back of his neck?"

"Bite mark?"

"Yes! A *human* bite mark, plain as day. Take a look, you'll see it. Somebody bit him on the back of the neck, and quite hard, by the look of it."

"Maybe that wound up killing him . . ." Van Wyck started to say, but Simonsen shook his head vehemently.

"Human bites do tend to be dirty, Chief, but this is ridiculous. You can pick up any number of diseases or infections from a human bite, but nothing that'll kill you like *that*."

"I thought he could've been poisoned, Doctor."

"Could be. But by what, I don't know."

"Some kind of drug, maybe?"

Simonsen laughed disgustedly. "I work in a drug abuse facility, Chief. Believe me, *no* drug I've ever seen or heard of produces effects like what I saw today. You can stake your badge on it."

They were interrupted by a knock on the door.

"Chief, Sergeant Rossovich says you gotta see this."

Van Wyck went, followed by Simonsen. Before he was halfway to the holding cell, he knew what he was about to see. His stomach pitched and rolled, set in motion by the smell of ripe carrion.

Rossovich was standing there with his hands on his hips, looking down at the thing on the cot and shaking his head.

"If the M.E. doesn't get a move on," he said, "he ain't gonna have nothin' left to autopsy."

Norman Rubin, attorney-at-law, who less than twenty-four hours ago had been arguing a case in civil court, and who had begun this day as a screaming lunatic hiding in a neighbor's toolshed, was now a limp, blue-brown, stinking corpse. The buttons of his shirt had popped, revealing a black belly swollen with the gases of decomposition. His lips and gums were black now, too. Black as tar. Van Wyck turned to Simonsen, who threw up his hands.

"Don't look at me, *I* can't explain it!" he said. "Christ, I see it and I can't believe it. It's like a special effect in a science fiction movie."

"You mean a horror movie," said Rossovich.

"Seeing this, though, I don't feel so bad," said Simonsen, as if to himself. "There was nothing in the sedative I gave him that could cause . . . *this*. No way they can get me for malpractice on this one." He turned to Van Wyck. "Chief, if you've got a police photographer on hand, I suggest you get some pictures. Everything that's happened here today has got to be documented thoroughly. No one's going to believe it, otherwise."

Van Wyck glared at Rossovich, who should have seen to the pictures already. The sergeant mumbled an apology and scurried off to find Patrolman Frankel and his camera. Another officer came in to announce that the coroner's meat wagon had been held up in traffic, but it'd be here in fifteen or twenty minutes. Van Wyck glanced at the corpse again and was glad Bobbie Rubin hadn't seen it. She was closeted away with a policewoman, waiting for a car to take her to her family doctor.

"I've got another suggestion for you, Chief," Simonsen said. "Once this gentleman is removed from here, have this cell thoroughly disinfected, and incinerate the bedding and the mattress from this cot. I don't know what we're dealing with here, but I sure as hell wouldn't take any chances."

Van Wyck nodded, not trusting himself to speak.

He was afraid. He followed the news; he understood how old innocuous germs could mutate into new and strange organisms, simmer for a while in some out-of-the-way place like the jungles of Africa or the air-conditioning ducts of a big hotel, and suddenly burst upon the world. Look at AIDS. Legionnaire's Disease. But he was also remembering a story his grandpa told him when he was a boy. *One morning a ship appeared in the harbor. This was in Norway, where they knew all about ships, so they could tell from far away that this ship was in trouble. Some volunteers went out in a boat to see if they could help, but when they boarded the strange ship, they found everybody dead. Captain and crew, all the passengers—with a dead helmsman lashed to the wheel. They towed the ship into port to see if the harbormaster could solve the mystery. And that was how the Black Death came to Norway, kiddo. The plague. Killed half the folks in Europe before it was finished. They hadda run carts through the streets twice a day just to collect the bodies, there were so many. . . .*

"Are you all right, Chief?"

"Fine," Van Wyck said. "Just fine."

XI. A DEATH IN THE FAMILY

One

"Morainville Town Clerk's office, Miss Moresby speaking."

"Hi. My name's Felix Frick. I'm a reporter with the *Central Jersey News*. You won't have heard of us up there."

"I can't say I have," said Miss Moresby.

"Well, no reason you should've," Felix said, in the comfort of his own living room. "Actually, I'm calling about a former resident of your town. Residents, rather: Dr. and Mrs. Winslow Emerson."

"What's this about?"

"It is part of a *very* dreary exercise in local politics down here, Miss Moresby. Let's just say that Dr. Emerson has gotten himself involved in politics, and I need to ask a few questions about his background. Is he really from Morainville?"

"Let me check for you. The name doesn't ring a bell." She put Felix on hold for a few minutes, then came back to him. "Dr. Emerson lived here, sir, but not for very long. Only about a year and a half. I can give you our tax assessor if you'd like to know more."

"Yes, please."

From the tax assessor Felix learned that the Emersons had lived in a farmhouse located just outside the town. "They're just an entry in the records, mister. Nobody knew 'em. They kept to themselves, and they weren't here two years before they sold the place and moved away."

Felix got in touch with the Morainville realtor who had handled the Emersons' transactions. As in Millboro, contact with the Emersons themselves had been minimal. They were on hand to sign the final documents; otherwise, everything else was left to bankers and lawyers. In fact, the name of attorney J.R. Hanratty came up again, the Boston lawyer who administered Blanche Emerson's trust fund.

He then called Fitch and Swazy, the Freehold firm that had closed the deal on the Emersons' house on Whittier Avenue; but they, too, could only cite J.R. Hanratty as the prime mover in the transaction. All roads seemed to lead to Boston, Felix thought.

A call to the Massachusetts State Bar Association confirmed that James R. Hanratty was a member in good standing. Indeed, he was in excellent standing: He was a former member of the U.S. Attorney's office and the District Attorney's staff in Boston. He had been in private practice for the past twelve years, however, and was semi-retired.

Still, thought Felix, *here's a tie-in with the almighty* government, *for cryin' out loud!* Or was he jumping to conclusions? Anyway, it was food for thought.

Meanwhile, he was receiving some interesting mail.

Having traced his own roots back to the sixteenth century (he was descended from a line of prosperous wool merchants in Hamburg, thank you), Felix well knew how to obtain old census data, passenger lists of immigrant ships, and all the rest. He'd put his talents to use since hearing from the AMA and the Harvard Medical School Library, soon locating the young Dr. Winslow Emerson Taylor in Cambridge, Massachusetts, at the turn of the century.

This original Dr. Taylor, the one who had been graduated from Trinity Physicians College in 1894, had interned at City Hospital in Boston and established a private general practice in Cambridge by 1906. The Cambridge Historical Society graciously—and promptly—supplied the rest of the story.

The routine of private practice hadn't suited Taylor. In 1908 he sold his practice and went to Cuba, where he pursued an interest in parasitology; in subsequent years, he published several papers on the subject. He returned to Cambridge for a little while, served as a medical officer with General Pershing's army in France in 1918, and went on to do some highly acclaimed yellow fever research in the Canal Zone after the war. He returned in 1922 to lecture briefly at Harvard, and in the spring of 1923, he departed to study the endemic parasites of rural Guatemala.

He was last seen in Guatemala City in June of 1925, where he delivered a lecture on encephalitis. Days later, he went back to his work in the interior and was never heard from again.

He had never married, and was presumed dead with no known heirs.

"Sonofabitch!" Felix muttered.

There must have been survivors: brothers, sisters, cousins, whatever. A little genealogical research would clear that up. Heck, Dr. Taylor had been a respected scientist in his time. Some relative, shortly after his disappearance, might have named a son for him to keep his memory alive. And if so, that son might be the Millboro man who was currently posing as a retired physican—*why,* God alone knew. Emerson seemed a little young to have been born at the time of Taylor's greatest prominence, but that was a trivial point.

But there was no such person. Not from the Boston metropolitan area, at any rate.

Felix tried not to let it throw him. *Ours is a nomadic society,* he reflected; *families scattered from sea to shining sea.* Massachusetts would have no record of a baby born in California. Millboro's Dr. Emerson could have been born anywhere.

It wouldn't be impossible to track him down, but such a search could take years. *At my age,* Felix thought, *you can't exactly throw the years around like confetti anymore.* And the whole effort would come to naught, he realized, if it turned out that "Dr. Winslow Emerson" was just an alias after all.

That landed him back with the questions that had stumped him from the beginning, and he might have remained in the dark forever, if it hadn't been for the six o'clock news on Channel 2.

It was a story about a local newspaper editor in some little one-horse town in Kansas, and the federal prosecutors' ongoing efforts to throw his ass in jail. The man was in the soup because he'd exposed one of his community's ordinary citizens as a former Chicago mobster who'd turned state's evidence some years ago and been given a new identity to protect him from his estranged friends and colleagues. Naturally, the ex-gangster had been given a full pardon in return for his cooperation with the authorities. With his new name, new personal history, and new location—all provided by the U.S. Department of Justice—he'd been reasonably secure from retribution.

—Until the editor of the weekly newspaper in his new hometown plastered the story across his front page. "It had to be done," he told the TV reporter on the scene. "Pardon or no pardon, this man is a dangerous criminal. For a price, he'd gun down his own mother. The people of this community had a right to know. Personally, I don't see where the Justice Department gets off, placing a known killer in our midst."

Then followed a brief explanation of the government's program of protecting members of organized crime who turned on their masters, and some puerile editorializing by the glamorous airhead they had as anchorwoman. Felix wished they'd taken the time to reveal *how* the local newspaperman had pierced the former hit man's new identity, but this was TV news, and TV news was to journalism as TV dinner was to haute cuisine. It was all over in ninety seconds.

He thought immediately of Emerson. *Why not?* The man's lawyer had high-powered government connections. Why not set him up as a retired doctor somewhere? He wasn't trying to defraud anyone; the Dr. Emerson routine was simply a disguise. Camouflage. He wasn't in Millboro to practice quackery; he was here to hide from the Mob. And probably the Dr. Taylor who had disappeared in Guatemala was an admired ancestor of his. Partially adopting that identity would be a way of keeping in touch with who he really was. He wouldn't have to sever himself completely from his past.

Sure. Then again, maybe he's a top-drawer KGB defector, or the Lost Dauphin of France, or a spy for the Klingons. Grow up, Felix. There wasn't a scrap of evidence that even hinted that the man had anything to do with crime, organized or otherwise. He was a fat old man with a dowdy wife and bogus medical credentials. And he liked to do business through his lawyer. That was where the facts began and ended.

He also kept late hours, claimed to be suffering from a degenerative nervous condition, and had a kind of funny smell under all that $1.98 after-shave he wore.

And there was nothing to *dis*prove the theory that he was a mobster who'd gone underground. If the facts didn't support it, at least they didn't militate against it.

What we need here, gentlemen, is more data. No tickee, no shirtee; and we don't have the tickee.

I wonder if he's got his diplomas on display in his living room. Hanging phony sheepskins on the wall would lend realism to the masquerade. It'd also be the kind of nice touch one would expect the government to provide—although Felix knew there were lots of places where you could get a fake diploma printed up. You could find them on the boardwalk at Seaside. There was no law against it. *What the hell, I can go to some little booth on the boardwalk and have 'em make up a diploma from anywhere I want, in any subject I like. University of Khartoum, bachelor's degree in ufology, magna cum laude. A fake diploma proves nothing.* But it would indicate, he supposed, more than a casual interest in putting on a convincing show.

Asking unobtrusive questions around the neighborhood, he soon ascertained that *nobody* on Whittier Avenue had ever been inside the Emersons' house.

True, Millboro's prestige developments were inhabited almost exclusively by city people for whom privacy used to mean being alone in the bathroom when you had to take a crap; having finally obtained their own homes in the suburbs, they were apt to be persnickety about their property rights. But at the same time they were proud of their castles and could seldom pass up a chance to show them off. They vied with one another to see who could flaunt the greenest, most uniform lawn and called in landscapers to help them go one up on the yard next door. Intimacy was rare, but there was always a great deal of casual visiting. How else could you show off your new living room set? How else could you find out what the competition was doing? The visits were the only way of keeping score, and it struck Felix as kind of odd that the Emersons weren't in the game.

All right, maybe they were just too old to waste their time on a lot of yuppie one-upmanship. Maybe they couldn't afford it—although Felix knew a number of families that went into hock so they could keep up with their neighbors.

All he knew was that when people went over to the Emersons', Blanche met them at the door and didn't let them in. Not *impolitely*, mind you; no one could complain about her manners. She just never asked you in.

And the old man himself never came to the door. The

popular belief was that he was slightly deaf and couldn't hear the doorbell. Several neighbors had gone to that door when they knew Blanche wasn't home, but the doctor was; he'd never answered them.

He was never known to answer the phone, either.

I don't know what the heck he is, Felix admitted to himself. *But if he ever was a doctor, I'm the Queen of Sheba.*

Two

Dorothy was walking down the main concourse at the Mill-boro Mall, amid shops and shoppers, when the dead blond boy stepped out from behind a pillar and blocked her way. Before she could dodge him, he seized her wrist. His grip was like chilled steel. She couldn't bear to look at his face.

She screamed. A security guard stood only a few yards away, but he pretended to look right through her. She struggled. A well-dressed woman with her arms around a box from Alexander's stared at her, then hurried on her way.

The boy started to drag her off. She tried to dig her heels into the floor but could get no purchase on its smoothly polished surface. When she fell, he dragged her more easily. The floor was slippery; it negated her efforts to resist.

She screamed and pleaded for help, but the shoppers only gave her a wide berth and continued on their business. One man actually had to jump to avoid her flailing ankles. Even in her panic, she noted the opened-grave smell that clung to the dead boy.

Through his legs she saw a black space between two shops. She cried for help but the shoppers only scurried past, like ants in a tunnel in the dirt.

Suddenly she was sitting upright on the sofa, staring at a curtained window in her living room.

"Hello, is Chief Van Wyck in?"

"Who's calling, please?"

"Dorothy Matthiesen."

"I'll see if his line is free."

She drummed her fingers on the kitchen table while she waited for the dispatcher to put her through to Van Wyck. She almost hung up. *He's a busy man. Why am I bothering him?* Around her the house loomed large and empty. It made her feel small and vulnerable.

"Mrs. Matthiesen?" She recognized the police chief's voice. Her stomach did a little loop. "Hi," was all she could say at first.

"Is everything all right?" he asked.

"Uh . . . I just called to see if you had anything more on . . . on my case."

"Well, we've been working on it. But I—are you sure you're all right?"

"As a matter of fact, no." It just came out. She couldn't call it back. "I'm not all right. To tell the truth, I've been feeling pretty lousy all day."

"I'll come over."

It was exactly what she wanted. He'd known it. But she hadn't been going to *ask* him to come. *Jesus Christ, you don't call the police because you had a bad dream. You're supposed to call your husband.* . . . Only the marriage was dead, and calling Chris would have been no more helpful than dialing the weather. *Still* . . .

He brushed aside her weak protest. "I was just about to knock off for the day, anyhow," he said. "I'd like to see you, if it's okay with you."

Chris would be working late again tonight. *I'm about to have an affair,* she thought. She hustled it out of her mind, covered it up like a housewife hanging a picture over a stain on the wall.

"It's okay," she told him. "Thanks."

As he turned on to Chaucer Drive, he almost decided to bag it.

Since he'd realized his attraction to her, he'd tried to keep his distance from Dorothy. The way she kept creeping into his thoughts, he judged it was a wise decision. He didn't need the temptation. The woman's marriage was on the rocks, she was planning a divorce, and the last thing Van Wyck needed was for his name to come up in a divorce hearing.

But he needed her. Trying to deny it was like trying to stay awake after twenty hours on the job without a rest.

She called me, he thought. She was a person involved in an active police investigation, the victim of a crime, and she had a right to be kept informed on the investigation's progress. He was going to see her on legitimate police business. It wasn't like there was anything that could force him into an improper relationship with her. If he couldn't handle this correctly, he had no business being a police chief anyway.

He parked at the curb, noticing that her husband's car wasn't in the driveway and that the front lawn was beginning to look a little scruffy. In a few days, neighbors would be calling to complain about it—as if the police could compel people to manicure their lawns. (Well, they could, in Cannon Creek; but that was another township.) *What a bunch of pricks,* Van Wyck thought. For two cents he'd quit this fucking job and relocate to the city, where a cop had honest crimes to deal with. Fuck Millboro. It wasn't the nice country town it used to be when he was growing up.

He rang the doorbell, feeling like a kid on his first date. How many gossip-hungry neighbors were peering out their windows at him? He should have come in uniform, he thought, and in an official car.

She was smiling when she opened the door to him.

"Hi! You really shouldn't have come all the way out here, but I have to admit I felt a lot better as soon as you said you would."

He'd seen her bruised and dirty following her escape from the nursing home, and wan and listless in her robe, and was drawn to her each time. Now he was seeing her scrubbed and fresh, in brushed denims and a pale blue top, with her arms bare, her hair combed and fluffed around her neck and shoulders—and he suddenly had doubts about his ability to resist her. Doubts? Holy Christ, he was like a toy car on the edge of a highly polished table top. One little push and he'd be gone.

"I'm glad," he managed to say without stuttering. God, did she have any idea how hard it was for him to keep his hands off her?

"Come in and sit with me," she said, and led him into her living room. *What am I about to do?* "I tidied up the place when you said you were coming. Tidied myself up a bit, too. Can I get you a beer?"

"Sure. Thanks."

She went to the kitchen, and he sat at one end of the couch. It was bad enough he was drinking Chris Matthiesen's beer and getting the hots for his wife; it was more than he could do to sit in the guy's easy chair. Why wasn't the stupid bastard ever home? It was like the guy was saying, *Take my wife . . . please.*

Dorothy brought him a bottle of Heineken and joined him on the couch, discreetly out of reach, for which he felt thankful. The cold beer helped, too.

"So . . . do you have any news for me?" she asked.

He shrugged. "Not really. We've been keeping an eye on the nursing home, but nobody's been seen since you left it, as far as we can tell.

"I can't go into this in detail, but we have reason to believe that some pretty nasty people had been getting together there." Van Wyck decided not to tell her about the dead rabbit detectives had found in the root cellar. It'd only scare her, and it wouldn't help. "Kids, probably; but still nasty. So far we don't know who they are, but we're working on it. We're taking this case very, very seriously."

"The boy . . . ?"

He knew which boy she meant, and told her what he could.

"He was a unique kind of individual," Van Wyck said. "Good grades in school, good manners, nice personal appearance—and he knew every rotten punk in town. A lot of his friends were regular delinquents. We're working on them, but so far we haven't been able to get anything out of any of them. But the damnedest thing is the fact that he had no record, himself. Never got in trouble at school, never got arrested, never got caught stepping out of line. I think he must've been out of his mind when he attacked you. That wasn't his style."

She looked down at the shiny surface of the coffee table, saw a fuzzy reflection of her face in it, and said, "He was out of his mind, all right. Have they done an autopsy?"

"Yeah. He was hit from behind, and it broke his neck. He seems to have made the injury worse, trying to crawl away."

"So whoever did that," she said, "picked me up and carried me off to that abandoned nursing home. I wonder what would've happened if I was still there when they came back for me."

She shuddered, and he ached to put his arms around her.

She went on. "The doctors say I wasn't drugged and I'm not sick. I went back once for further tests and they couldn't find anything wrong with me." She looked up at him, intensely. "They're full of shit, you know. I haven't been right since it happened.

"I haven't been sleeping well. Lately I've been catching up on my sleep by taking naps during the day. Only I get nightmares, so it isn't really all that restful. I had a doozy this afternoon. That's when I called you.

"I suppose I could see a shrink. He'll tell me that I've been under a lot of stress, which I know already, and prescribe some kind of sleeping pills. He'll be clever and sympathetic and seventy-five bucks an hour richer every time he sees me—and I still won't know what really happened to me, will I?"

Van Wyck returned her look and said, "No, I guess you won't. But that's what we're trying to find out. And I won't let up until we do." He sipped some more of his beer and wished he could tell her something that would make it all right again.

She startled him when she asked, "Can we go out to dinner, Ed? I've been cooped up all alone here, and I'm starving." She smiled. *You can feel safe in a public place,* she thought; *safe from temptation, and worse.* "I know it's not in the normal line of police duty, but can we do it anyway? Dutch treat, of course."

"I don't see why not," Van Wyck said. In fact there were whole boatloads of reasons why not, but he didn't feel like seeing them. Mostly he just saw her.

Van Wyck took her a ways out of town, to a place near Sandy Hook where you could see the boats coming in after a day's fishing. The sun was low; it made Raritan Bay shine like a burnished copper shield.

Dorothy had never personally known a policeman before. Up until now she'd hardly given the police a second thought. Which was strange, she thought, living in a society that was frankly preoccupied with the subject. How many cop shows were there on TV just now? How many had there been? Christ, *hundreds.* Maybe thousands, if you counted the crook,

266

lawyer, and courtroom series in which the cops got second billing. Then there were the movies, and maybe a million books in print focusing on cops and their work, fiction and nonfiction. Yet Dorothy hadn't watched many cop shows on the tube, hadn't seen too many cop movies, and seldom read anything on the subject.

She grew up in a small town where the policeman was the friendly man in blue who visited the classroom to give safety tips and the police force was the jolly bunch of guys who played baseball against the firemen every Fourth of July at the town picnic. The few times police officers had pulled her over for one thing or another, they'd been impeccably polite and nonthreatening. Unlike many of her acquaintances, she didn't get edgy when she saw a police car in her rearview mirror. And as for the gory and/or disillusioning police stories you saw on the TV news every single time you turned it on—well, that was New York news, what did you expect?

Dorothy's attitude toward cops hadn't changed materially since she was ten years old. And the Millboro cops, Van Wyck's men, had been just super: From the moment the patrol car picked her up on Dutch Mill Road, they couldn't have shown her more consideration. And this at a time when her husband's utter lack of concern was impossible to deny. *Without them, this thing might have knocked me off my pins.*

Under all the circumstances, Ed Van Wyck would've had to be some kind of ogre for her *not* to like him. And he was a long, long way from being an ogre.

C'mon, Dot, what kind of a game are you playing here? She knew women who bounced from man to man without ever having to land on the hard ground floor of self-sufficiency. *Am I one of them? Am I trying to use this big cop as a safety net, because I know I'm through with Chris? Say it ain't so!*

"You're nice to spend all this extra time on me," she said, after they'd ordered.

"Right now it's my time to spend," he answered.

He'd been trying to play it close to the vest from the moment he appeared at her door, but sometimes his guard slipped and she thought she saw through it. It was so easy to misjudge a man . . . but he was there, wasn't he?

"If you went out to dinner with everybody in this township who needed help from the police," she said, "you'd weigh four hundred pounds."

"You asked me."

"Only because I thought you'd like me to." She couldn't be wrong about that, could she? Was there any way she could possibly be misinterpreting the way she caught him looking at her when he thought she couldn't see? "Anyway," she added, "I really wanted to be with you for a while."

He laughed the kind of laugh that covers uneasiness. "You don't mince words," he said.

"You can waste *years* dropping subtle hints." If Chris had taught her nothing else, he'd taught her that. Chris hadn't taken a hint for years, and now it was too late. "You *are* here because you want to be with me, aren't you? Please, let me know if I've got it wrong."

"Dorothy, you ought to take up poker. Or else I ought to give it up. No, you don't have it wrong. And since we're not dropping subtle hints, and since you can see right through me, okay, yes. I like you so much, it scares me."

He wasn't just using a figure of speech. His ice blue eyes hardened when he said it.

He continued, "I'm not kidding. I have good reasons for wanting to keep my personal life as uncomplicated as can be. Since my divorce, I've gotten pretty good at it. Now I'm afraid I'm losing my touch."

"What are you scared of, Ed?"

"Scared I'll get myself involved in something that'll cost me more than I can afford to pay."

"I'm not sure what you mean."

"Dorothy, suburban police chiefs aren't supposed to have private dinner dates with taxpayers' wives."

Their appetizers arrived. As they ate, he told her about the flap over his divorce: councilmen getting inquiring phone calls from upright citizens worried about the moral climate of the township; rumors buzzing around headquarters about the chief getting fired; the mayor sticking his nose into it, calling Van Wyck at home and asking all kinds of highly personal questions.

"Those self-righteous sons of bitches!" Dorothy interrupted. Van Wyck looked at her and laughed.

"You're really mad, aren't you?" he said.

"You're goddamned right I'm mad. Those sanctimonious, hypocritical shitheads! As if it was any of their business!"

"It wasn't, but they made it their business, and there wasn't much I could do about it. Only smart thing I did was decide not to contest the divorce. I think they really would've canned me if it'd been a messy one."

Dorothy seethed, and she was still seething when her entree was placed in front of her. She wanted to defend the man and was frustrated because it was far too late for that. He worked *hard* for Millboro, he gave them a damned fine police force they could all be proud of, and what did he get for it? Celibacy lectures from Ron Leib!

And he'd told her about the divorce. Just another case of two people who shouldn't have been married in the first place going sour on each other. He hadn't cheated on Helen, hadn't abused he. She got him on mental cruelty, big deal. Ed fell out of love with her and was honest enough to admit it. And for that they'd considered taking his badge away? Bad enough he'd lost his kids.

"I hate the way they treated you," Dorothy said. "I can't tell you how much I hate it."

He was smiling now, when he wasn't shoveling fried shrimp into his mouth. "I believe you," he said between

269

mouthfuls. "And it makes me feel good. Better than I've felt about it since it happened."

She reached across the narrow table and squeezed his hand; hers was too small to cover it. "I hate the thought of them kicking you when you were down, Ed. But if they ever try to do it again, they'll have to kick me, too."

Van Wyck surrendered to fate.

They parked on a scenic drive overlooking the bay and watched the red rays of the sunset tint the distant Verrazano-Narrows Bridge. The twin towers of the World Trade Center were like a concrete mirage. White sails dappled the blue water.

Dorothy snuggled up to him and he put his arm around her, loving the way she fit against his body. *It's been too long,* he thought. *Too goddamn long.* When it was dark, they kissed.

"I'd better take you home now," he said, not long afterward. "I need some time to think about this. It's happening so fast, I have to be sure it's real."

His caution scared her. "If you back out on me," she said, "I guarantee I *won't* understand."

He grinned. "Lady, when I kissed you, I kissed that idea good-bye! I won't back out."

But he was right about things happening too fast, and on the way back to Millboro, they retreated in their talk to the relatively safe ground of the investigation.

"They still don't know why that kid's body decayed so suddenly, do they?" Dorothy said. "I never heard of anything like it."

"Medical examiner's working overtime on it, but they're still stumped." Van Wyck wasn't sure he ought to tell her that now they had three bodies in the morgue to stump the coroner: three cases of absurdly accelerated decomposition, and all three from Millboro.

The M.E. was trying to keep it out of the papers for as
270

long as possible, and all Van Wyck knew was that they were afraid there was some kind of germ on the loose and had sent tissue samples down to the Federal Center for Disease Control in Atlanta to see if the government doctors could get a handle on it. So far the feds were stumped, too.

The germ theory made chilling sense to Van Wyck. It seemed to explain why a slick operator like Bruce Randall would jump a woman in a parking lot, and why a sane, successful lawyer like Norm Rubin would barricade himself in a neighbor's backyard toolshed. It might even explain what Arthur Volden, who hadn't known a living soul in Millboro, had been doing in the middle of the woods off Alabama Road. Syphilis, rabies—what the hell, there were lots of germs that drove you nuts before they killed you.

Only thing wrong with the theory was that they couldn't fuckin' prove it. But until proof was found, one way or the other, the last thing anybody wanted was banner headlines about a lethal germ making the rounds in Millboro.

So Van Wyck didn't tell Dorothy about the death and decay of Mr. Rubin at police headquarters and the rotten dreams he'd been having since he'd witnessed it. Humdingers: putrid hands reaching for him from the grave, rotting faces looming up in front of him. By order of the medical examiner, he couldn't even tell the mayor what he'd seen.

Not that the mayor didn't know . . .

Three

Dorothy answered the phone on two rings, hoping it'd be Ed, disappointed when it only turned out to be Nancy Kruzek.

"Hi, Nancy, what's up?"

"I haven't seen much of you lately, Dot. Is everything all right?"

Warning bells began to clang. "Everything's fine," Dorothy said.

"Dot, why didn't you tell me you were *attacked?*"

Oh, shit. Dorothy hadn't expected to be able to keep it a secret forever, but Jesus . . . Were some of the cops shooting off their mouths about it? Was Felix? Would it turn up in the newspapers next?

"Who told you about that, Nancy?"

"Relax, will you? I haven't been gossiping. Actually, Walt told me."

"Walt?" How on earth had Nancy's husband found out?

"Yeah. He had to work late yesterday, and he happened to run into Chris in a steak house. Chris told Walt and I haven't told a soul, cross my heart. I just called to see how you were."

"I'm fine." So Chris told Walt—who was just a neighbor, an acquaintance, a guy who sometimes took the same bus into the city. Hardly a confidant. *Hey, Walt, didja hear my wife got jumped by some guy? No shit, right there in the Millboro Mall parking lot. And she's been spooky ever since, a real head case. Howdya like that?* How could he just *blab* about it to the first familiar face he met? Dorothy no longer had a clue as to how her husband's mind worked.

"You're sure?" Nancy persisted. "I mean, you've been keeping so much to yourself lately, I thought maybe you could use a friendly shoulder to cry on. . . ."

No thanks, Nance, I've been crying on Ed Van Wyck's shoulder lately, and the two of us have got a good thing going—which is good, because I've decided to divorce Chris. Now *that* would give good ol' Nance something to gossip about. For a moment Dorothy titillated herself by imagining Nancy's reaction to such a bombshell, but it was an easy temptation to resist.

"Nancy, I appreciate your calling, but it was a truly lousy

experience and I'd rather not talk about it. And if anybody else brings it up, I'll know they got it from you."

"My lips are sealed," Nancy said. "Trust me."

Nancy came back from a trip to the A&P later that afternoon and spotted Blanche Emerson watering the little round bed of pansies that grew around her front yard lamppost. She honked as she passed, and Blanche waved. Nancy parked her car and invited Blanche over for a drink. The sun hadn't dipped below the yardarm yet, but the day was getting to be quite a hot one for the time of year, and an iced vodka gimlet suddenly seemed like an excellent idea.

She hadn't intended to talk about Dorothy, but by the second gimlet that, too, seemed like a good idea. Blanche was a doctor's wife, after all. She might be able to help.

Blanche listened sympathetically and with great interest, the ideal audience. Nancy was inspired to tell her not only what she knew, but what she thought.

"*She* says she's fine, but Walt gathered from Chris that she's still pretty shaken by it. Bad enough she got attacked and hauled off to some dirty old building in the middle of nowhere, but then they made her go back and look at the body. The kid who actually attacked her was found dead. It must've really unnerved her, because she's been shut up in her house ever since. Moved out of her bedroom, too. She set up a bed in the rec room—they have a nice finished basement—and sleeps there. Won't hardly say a word to Chris.

"But then I always suspected they might be having problems in that marriage. Of course, Dot's the type to keep it all bottled up inside, but I *know* she's unhappy with the hours Chris has to spend on the job. He's a hotshot editor with one of the big publishing houses in Manhattan, and he's on his way up, so he can't slack off. He and Dot have been kind of drifting apart. I noticed it months ago."

Blanche broke in to ask for another drink. Nancy decided to have one, too.

"Now Dot's been to the hospital," Nancy went on, "and I gather they did absolutely nothing for her. *Physically* they can't find anything wrong with her, so naturally they tell her there's nothing wrong with her. She wasn't raped, so everything's just peachy keen—right? Men can be so *obtuse,* don't you think? They should have sent her for counseling, right away."

"Maybe she wouldn't go," Blanche said.

"She needs some convincing, then. We can't sit by and let this experience turn her into a hermit. *I* can't, anyway. But she won't listen to me unless it's something to do with politics, and Chris obviously isn't in tune to what's happening with her. Maybe you should talk to her, Blanche."

"Oh, she doesn't know me. She'd resent an outsider butting in."

"You're probably right. I wish there was something I could do for her, though."

Their talk flowed into other channels, and Blanche finally said she had to go home to fix supper.

Nancy would have been surprised, had anyone put it to her later, at how much information she had given Blanche about her friend.

"Well, well," the Master said, after Blanche had finished her report. "So the little lady made it home from the temporary refuge which I found for her. I was wondering about that. Very interesting."

"You should've killed her," Blanche said. "If you take my advice, you'll kill her now. She might wind up going to see a psychiatrist, and that could lead to some sessions of clinical hypnosis. There's no telling what they might dredge up out of her memory. What if some hypnotist gets her to remember *you?*"

274

"Tut-tut, Blanche. She was quite unconscious at the time. We have nothing to worry about on that account. Rest assured that I'm in control of this. I've been planning to follow up on it. Meanwhile, the young lady is no threat to us."

"Sez you. It'd be a lot safer just to make her disappear—this time for good."

The Master wasn't thinking along those lines. Here was an individual who had had blood contact with a vampire and survived. What could be learned from her? Maybe her contact with Randall had been too minimal to result in any transmission of the vampire organism. Maybe her immune system had somehow fought it off. Possibly it might be lying dormant in her body, to become active at some future time. *And maybe the entire premise is wrong.*

Well, if there really was no vampire germ, he might as well find out now. It would be disappointing to see his theory go up in flames, but not a crushing blow. He would just have to continue his research along some other line.

He smiled as he thought of the frustrations of a mortal scientist. There were those who simply couldn't bring themselves to look at data that destroyed a cherished theory. Others would accept the data, but only in the way the citizens of Rome had been forced to accept the Goths. The Master had been working on his germ theory for forty years, and now he was calmly contemplating the possibility that the work had all been wasted. But he was a vampire; he had four hundred years at his disposal, or four thousand. To be free from the certainty of death, he reflected, lent true objectivity to one's science.

Four

Dorothy felt a pleasing tingle of anticipation as she made the turn into Van Wyck's driveway.

She wouldn't have been overly surprised to discover that Van Wyck was the kind of old-fashioned male who didn't invite a woman into his home until he'd married her. But she was sure that was a prejudice; deep down inside, she expected police chiefs to be puritanical. And it gave her an insight into his problem. Ed was no prude. Still, he couldn't entirely suppress his uneasiness when they were together—as if he expected, any minute, some concerned citizen to jump out of the woodwork and brand him with a scarlet letter.

She knew he wouldn't have asked her to come here unless he was seriously committed to their relationship. *That's how the phone-in psychiatrist on the radio would say it,* she thought.

He came out to meet her, took her hands, and said, "Here you are."

The house was set back about fifty yards from the road, with an old hedge screening it from passing cars. There was a good acre and a half of property here, but new houses were already encroaching on it.

It wasn't what Dorothy had come to think of as a Millboro house. It was old and had stood in the same place for so long that now it belonged there, like the ancient oak in the front yard that stretched its boughs toward the porch. Dorothy knew nothing about architecture, but she was sure they weren't building houses like this one anymore. This one had been put up by *people*—and with loving care, because they'd planned to live in it for several generations—and not by a cabal of faceless builders looking to unload a hundred others just like it on the next wave of yuppies from the big city.

Dorothy looked past Van Wyck to the roomy front porch. *God, he has a glider!* she almost said aloud.

"I can't believe it. Ed, it's beautiful!"

"Glad you like it."

"Can we sit in the glider and drink lemonade?"

He laughed at that, shedding his awkwardness; he was on his home turf now. "I don't know if I've got any lemons on hand, but I'm sure I can come up with a reasonable substitute. Come on!"

They wound up drinking cold seltzer flavored with reconstituted lemon juice, but it tasted enough like real lemonade. They sat on the glider and rocked it gently back and forth. Dorothy loved it.

"I feel like I've just landed in the nice part of a Ray Bradbury story," she said, "or a Norman Rockwell painting. Damn it, who ever decided that housing developments was the way to go?"

"Money," said Van Wyck. "The farmers get tired of farming, the builders buy up the land, and they sell as many houses as they can. I had to sell off a couple acres to settle with Helen. That was only three years ago, but that land's all built up already."

"I'm going to divorce Chris." *There, I've said it.* "But I'm not looking to make money on it."

"Helen wants to be buried with golden screws on her coffin." He paused and looked at her intently. "Are things really bad for you?"

"They've been bad for a long time," Dorothy said, "and they won't get better."

I know he wants me to spend the night with him. And I know I want to. But he has to say so. If he doesn't—if he winds up sending me back home—there's just no future in this thing.

Her worries turned out to be groundless.

Chris got home almost two hours earlier than he'd expected. He dropped his briefcase to the floor, shed his jacket, and headed to the kitchen for a beer.

Dorothy was out again. This time she'd left a note to tell him she'd be back when she damned well pleased, and if he wanted anything for supper, he could damned well fix it himself.

Damn it to hell, you bust your ass ten or twelve hours a day (not counting the commute!) trying to build a good life, a good career—and you get treated like Heinrich Himmler for it. Policemen stare at you as if they'd caught you trying to sell your wife to the white slavers—as if their own wives weren't sitting around while they put in their famous policemen's hours. Fate hits you with a fuckin' conundrum and you're supposed to have all the answers.

He had to keep reminding himself that it hadn't been his fault. Suppose he'd been home that night. Dotty still might've gone to the mall without him. Hey, he could've been taking a nap, watching a ball game on the tube, fertilizing the lawn . . . and she *still* would have been attacked. And she *still* would have been abducted. What earthly good would it have done to call the cops? *Yessir, Mr. Matthiesen, we'll get on it right away, sir! Why, we'll send a car right over to the Whatsisname Nursing Home, just in case your wife was taken there. Hot damn, it'll be the first place we look!*

No, goddamn it, no way it was his fault. But the way Dot was carrying on, you'd think it was. Not talking to him, not eating with him, moving out of their bedroom. What the fuck did she want from him?

He took his beer out back to the patio and stretched out on a lawn chair to drink it.

All right, so I work a shitload of hours and I'm not home an awful lot; and when I am home, I'm so fuckin' tired that I just vegetate. Since when was hard, conscientious work a crime? Goddamn woman; does she want us to live on Social Security in our old age? "Whatta

we got for supper tonight, hon—*Mighty Dog or Puss 'n' Boots?''*
Was that what she wanted? She'd never said so.

Chris was sustained by a vision of retirement to a luxury
condo in Florida, deep-sea fishing every day, parties every
night. *Isn't that worth sacrificing for?* He wanted to make a pile.
Why couldn't she understand that? He was doing it for her.

True, he hadn't been what you'd call a million laughs
lately. He admitted that their sex life had suffered. *Suffered?
You're an editor, man, wouldn't you say* expired *was more accurate?*
All right, their love life had gone down the tubes. But anyone could see that that was only temporary. Just while he
was toiling to establish himself in his field.

Where was she now? Probably at some bullshit meeting,
listening to a bunch of politicians flap their jaws. *See? I'm
here, she could be here, too, if she wanted. She could be sitting right
here with me, having a beer and watching the stars come out. She's as
much to blame as I am.*

It hurt to have his wife distancing herself from him, but
what could he do about it? She wanted space, fine, he gave
her space. He couldn't force her to be with him. Damn it,
it wasn't as if he'd been running around with other women,
blowing his paycheck at the track, whooping it up with the
boys. *See? I've tried to be a good husband. And look at the thanks I
get.*

He had another beer, stripped down to his underwear,
and went to bed.

There were lights on in the house, but everything was
quiet and still.

The Master flitted through the Matthiesens' backyard as
silently as fog, cautiously approaching the house to peer
through the windows. From what he could see, it was difficult to believe there was anybody home.

But there must be, he reasoned. There was a sliding-glass

door leading out to the patio, and it was open. They wouldn't go out without closing it.

The open door tempted him. Wasn't it a virtual invitation to come in? Oh, there was nothing to the old bit of folklore that said you had to invite a vampire to come in before he could cross your threshold. The Master had entered many houses uninvited. Even so, it was amusing to note another instance where the old wives' tales were paralleled by real life.

If the Matthiesens were out, there was nothing to be risked by going in and having a look around. He'd hear them coming back; he could make an escape quite easily. And they wouldn't hear him. For all he knew, there was useful data to be collected inside the house. He'd never have a better opportunity to see.

Satisfied that none of the neighbors were watching, he slipped noiselessly across the patio and into the Matthiesens' dining room.

According to Nancy Kruzek, Dorothy Matthiesen had been practically a hermit since her encounter with Randall. The Master wondered if that could mean that a *partial* transformation had occurred: a low-level infection that she was still trying to fight off. But he warned himself not to twist the facts to fit the theory. Maybe the woman was suffering from simple psychological trauma.

That was what he had come here to investigate.

There was nothing about the house to indicate that one of the occupants had contracted vampirism. The refrigerator was full of ordinary grocery items; there was no smell of blood or raw meat in the air. But then, it was hardly likely that the woman would advertise such a condition by doing anything eccentric.

You never knew with new-made vampires, though. . . .

He heard the sound of breathing. He followed it to a bedroom and peeked around the doorframe. A man lay sound asleep, alone on a queen-size bed. His arms and legs were bare. In the subdued light that trickled into the room, the Master could still make out the blue tracery of veins on the man's left wrist. How easy it would be to take a knife and slash that wrist, one slash clean to the bone, and drink the hot sweet blood! The Master smiled and shook his head; one never outgrew the temptation. He backed off, still smiling, and found the entrance to the basement. He went down the stairs and saw a small foldaway bed set up in the darkness.

Had she found that sunlight oppressed her? Did she feel a need to hide from her husband?

The Master turned and went silently back up the stairs.

Chris woke from a dream in which his secretary marched abruptly into his office and pointed a gun at his face.

He woke with his heart fluttering and beads of sweat tickling him under his T-shirt. For a very brief moment he was desperate to know why Toni would want to shoot him. It was one of those dreams that was stomach-clenchingly real, and it took him a few more seconds to put it behind him.

He used to grab Dotty whenever he had a nightmare and be comforted back to sleep by her warmth and the rhythm of her breathing—*but that was then, this is now,* he thought. He grabbed his pillow instead, and was blindsided by a sudden flare-up of loneliness and loss.

Maybe I have *been putting in too many goddamn hours on the job,* he thought. He didn't know what he could do about it, but for the first time he was aware of it as a problem. It came to him like a voice from a burning bush. *I'm not happy. What good does it do me to earn any amount of money, if I have to feel like this? It feels like hell.* He wanted his wife, he wanted their good times back. When was the last time they'd dropped in on a real friend—someone who didn't care if you spilled a little beer on his rug? When was the last time they'd gone to the park and thrown the old frisbee around? Simple things:

staying up late to watch a grade-D creature feature on the tube; chasing each other through the surf at Sandy Hook; hopping into the car and taking off for some oddly named rathole in the Pine Barrens just because neither of them had ever been there before. Making love in the middle of a Saturday afternoon. Simple little things. You'd think you could do without them, but you couldn't. Not for long.

And now she wasn't here. He looked at the clock on his nightstand and cursed.

He sat up. The bedroom door was open; the lights were still on in the living room, the hall. Waste of electricity. He got up to turn them out. *Might as well have a drink while I'm at it.* There was a bottle of Scotch in the kitchen. He could stay up till Dot came home from wherever the hell she was and try to have a talk with her. The whisky would be good company while he waited.

He stepped into the hall and happened to notice that the basement door was ajar. She must have come home, after all, and gone straight downstairs.

The lights and the whisky could wait. The important thing was to go down there and sit on her bed and tell her how much he missed her. He smiled crookedly to himself. *She'll tell me to piss up a rope. And I'll deserve it.* But if he waited until the next time they were both awake and in the house together, it might be too late. Lady Macbeth was right: The longer you hemmed and hawed over something, the better the chance you'd chicken out.

It was dark down there. She was probably asleep already. He felt his way down the stairs, moving as quietly as he could.

The Master waited for him.

He knew just where to hit, and how hard, to render the man unconscious. He caught him before he hit the floor and effortlessly held him while he pondered what to do.

He could, of course, leave the husband collapsed on the floor and simply make his exit. The man would think he'd fallen down the stairs in the dark. At worst, he'd assume a burglar had hit him.

He could feel the blood coursing through the man's veins. He could almost taste it.

The Master drew his pocket knife and made a neat incision on the back of the man's neck, where the hair would fall over the cut and hide it from casual examination. He licked the blade clean before he closed the knife, then pressed his lips to the wound. He had to suck on it to make the blood come freely. Peace and contentment filled him with each swallow. There was really nothing better than this close contact with the victim; it made him feel like a nursing babe.

When the flow ceased, it was all he could do to resist the temptation to enlarge the wound and continue feeding. There had been a time when the least taste of blood would send him into a frenzy of delight, and he would feed to repletion; but he'd learned to be satisfied with less, realizing that he couldn't hope to survive unless he could control his appetite. He knew of vampires who battened on their prey even as the sun rose and were destroyed with their victims in their grasp. Blood is sweet, and in the first discovery of its sweetness, a vampire might easily neglect his own safety. But the Master had been lucky enough to survive that phase of his development.

He left the man in a heap at the foot of the stairs. Before he went on his way, he made sure his fingerprints were to be found nowhere in the house. He could see them plainly, and wherever he saw them, he removed them.

Five

Not having heard from Felix, Diane Kasko was in a lather to know whether Felix's son had decided to buy the Emersons' house. The old man was a dear, but he'd left her hanging.

He couldn't have wanted all that information about the house and its owners unless something really was afoot. *We aren't talking about idle curiosity here.* Mr. Frick had pumped her for a lot of inside dope—and she'd had to *steal* a peek at Fran Metzger's paperwork, if the truth be known—and now he wasn't saying a word. Di felt like a guest who goes upstairs to powder her nose and comes back down to find the party dissolved, the house empty.

Maybe the Emersons' really was about to be put up for sale. She tried to pump Fran—subtly, because a rep doesn't make the Million Dollar Club by allowing other reps to cut her out of a deal. It was like trying to pump water out of Death Valley. She had to drop it before Fran smelled a rat.

No, the only thing to do was to get on the horn and discreetly sound out the Emersons themselves. And she'd have to do it at home: too many ultrasensitive ears at the office.

"Hello . . . Mrs. Emerson?"

"Yes?"

"Hi! This is Di Kasko calling from Colonial Realty. How are you doing?"

"Fine, thanks. What's this about?"

"Well . . ." Di paused for a moment. She knew she was butting in and not particularly welcome; Mrs. Emerson's guarded tone told her that much. Still, you couldn't afford to be thin-skinned in the real estate business. You couldn't begin to count the deals that would never have been closed if some hungry rep hadn't butted in. "Well," she said, "I just thought you might be contemplating a move in the near future, and if you are, I want to help.''

''A move? Why would you think that?''

''Oh, in this business you have to keep your ear to the ground!'' Di tittered: a light, musical little laugh she'd been practicing for years. It helped to put the customer at ease.

''Why don't you talk to my husband?'' Mrs. Emerson said. ''Hold on a minute and I'll get him.''

Di held. Although the wife's name was on the deed, she wasn't surprised to have to wait for the husband before she could talk business—especially when the husband was a doctor. Di knew more than one doctor who spent more time on his real estate investments than he did on his patients. For some of them, medicine was just a way of raising enough capital to get seriously into real estate.

Anyway, she preferred to negotiate with men. They were more susceptible to her charm.

She waited for what seemed a long time, until a man's deep voice came on the line and said, ''Yes? This is Dr. Emerson.'' She reintroduced herself, putting that little extra something into her tone that was supposed to make a man think she was dying to meet him, and not necessarily for business reasons.

''What can I do for you, Mrs. Kasko?''

There was something about his voice that made it hard to tell whether he was likely to warm up to her, but she continued on the expectation that he would.

''Please, call me Di! Business is so much easier to conduct on a *friendly* basis.''

''Very true, Di. Now to what do I owe the pleasure of this call?''

That was better. The old man had beautiful manners, even if his wife sounded like a middle-class cow.

''I was just thinking, Doctor, that you might be entertaining plans which Colonial Realty might help bring off profitably for you.''

285

"Ah . . . you're wondering if we're planning to buy another house, perhaps—or sell this one."

"That's the general idea," Di said.

"Well . . . I won't admit it hasn't crossed my mind," said Emerson. "But I must say I'm surprised to be hearing from you. You must have a crystal ball."

Di tittered, enjoying the banter. "Oh, nothing like that! But it *is* my job to keep on top of things. . . ."

"You seem to be doing it superbly. I'm impressed."

"You're very kind, Doctor."

"I mean it, though—I *am* impressed. I haven't really discussed my plans with too many people. I'm amazed you've gotten wind of this already."

So it was true: He *was* thinking of selling, he'd been in touch with Elroy Frick. And here she was, first in line. She'd have to take Felix out to dinner after the deal was closed. Fran would be livid.

"I have my sources," she said.

"I'm sure you do. And very accurate sources they are. May I ask who it was who brought this to your attention?"

"Actually, I promised not to tell. . . ."

"I'd keep it to myself. And of course I'd be obliged to you, Di. I'd owe you a favor."

And you'd be ticked off at me if I didn't tell, Di thought. Really, though, it was only a matter of playing one side against the other. How could it be right to funnel information to the Fricks and hold out on the Emersons?

"Well, it'd have to be our little secret, Doctor. I did promise. . . ."

"Naturally. But I assure you I'll respect your confidence, Di."

"I'm sure you will, Doctor. Otherwise my lips would remain sealed. But seeing how it's just between the two of us, the person who gave me the tip was a neighbor of yours. Felix Frick."

"Felix Frick?"

"Yes! Elroy Frick's father. He lives right across the street from you."

"Yes, of course . . . I had forgotten. But I'm afraid I don't know him personally. It doesn't matter, though, does it?"

Di conceded that it didn't. They talked a little longer, as friendly as could be, and Dr. Emerson promised to let her know as soon as he needed a realtor. By the time she hung up, she was very pleased with herself.

"What was that all about?" Blanche said.

"It seems Mr. Frick has been playing games with our friendly realtor," the Master said. "Apparently he told her we're planning to sell this house—to his son."

"Is he out of his mind?"

"I doubt it. More likely he told her that in hopes she could tell him a thing or two about *us.*" The Master shook his head. "I'm afraid Mr. Frick has been trying to invade our privacy. And the business ethics at Colonial Realty leave something to be desired."

Blanche was slow to understand. "But why call the realtor?" she wondered. The Master explained it patiently.

"This isn't funny," she said. "First he tries to spy on us with binoculars, then he tries to poke into our private business. I wonder what that woman told him. I wonder what *else* he's up to!"

"Precisely the point, my dear—what else indeed? Mr. Frick, as we know from the newspaper accounts of his accomplishments, is not what you might call a harmless busybody. There's no telling how deeply he's delved into our affairs."

Blanche suddenly had to sit down. She feared the past, nor was she comforted by the passage of the years. How many doddering old men had been dragged back to Israel to be hanged for crimes they'd committed fifty years ago?

287

Sometimes it seemed to her that the longer she went without being brought to account for the murders she'd committed as a young nurse at the hospital, the more certain it was that the day of reckoning would come. It was like a dice game: The longer you kept throwing the dice, the surer you were to crap out.

The Master pondered the problem. There was nothing the real estate agent could have told Frick that would genuinely pose a threat; every trail he could follow would only bring him to a dead end. Nor would Frick gain much by attempting to investigate his medical credentials. He might discover that there was no official record of a medical doctor named Winslow Emerson, but beyond that he would be unable to go. Surely there was no cause for alarm.

But how much *did* Frick know? And what did he suspect?

The Master sighed. The threat lay not in any possibility that Frick would uncover the truth. If the truth stared him in the face, he would turn away from it.

No, the real menace was the continued flow of questions. If Frick kept at it, eventually he would inspire someone else to raise questions, too. That was what had to be prevented.

Besides, the whole thing was upsetting Blanche. She was inclined to be a worrier, and Frick had given her a lot to worry about. She could hardly be an effective servant if Frick destroyed her morale.

"It seems," the Master said, "that we can indulge Mr. Frick no longer."

Six

Dorothy stayed at Van Wyck's house the next day while he went off to work.

They'd been at it like bunnies all night—only natural, she thought, for two people who'd been deprived of sex for longer than either of them wanted to remember. Under the circumstances they probably would have slept together regardless of the future of their relationship. Unless you have a real vocation for it, you couldn't remain celibate forever.

It was the future she was thinking of now.

If they stayed together, she'd have to deal with the demands his job placed on him. She had heard stories about policemen's hours, but they couldn't be any worse than the hours Chris was putting in at his editor's desk. The thing about Chris, though, was that he didn't *care* enough to do his job efficiently. Nothing else mattered to him, anyway. He really didn't seem to mind that his marriage had disintegrated.

"You're not a workaholic, Ed, are you?" she asked him over breakfast.

"I don't think I am," he said.

She didn't think so, either. His house was too lovingly maintained. Workaholics don't care about their personal living conditions. *But God help me if I've got a thing for men who put in crazy hours.* . . .

"I know you can't be a police chief and count on working nine to five," she said. "But you have slow days, too, don't you? And you work right here in town, so there's no commute. Once I get my divorce, I could drop in on you at the station. We could get together for lunch or supper. We wouldn't be out of touch with each other. . . ."

"That's true."

Neither of them said anything about moving in together, or marriage. She was, after all, still married to another man.

But some things didn't need to be said in order to be heard.

She got to know him better by getting to know his house. He had pictures of his kids in his living room, but none of Helen. His bookcases were full; some of them, in fact, were double-stacked with paperbacks. *A good mix,* she thought: mysteries, westerns, sci-fi, even fantasy—his copy of *The Hobbit* was limp with long use. He had the whole rainbow of John D. MacDonald's Travis McGee thrillers, too. Obviously he was a man who knew how to read himself out of the daily grind.

He had nonfiction, too: psychology and history, home and car repair, popular science. Books on fishing, boating, and chess. Studies of famous crimes. Old college textbooks. Biographies of explorers, generals, literary figures. *He must read himself to sleep every night,* Dorothy thought.

The living room was scrupulously neat, but lived-in. There was good-quality furniture here that had served two or three generations of Van Wycks. Nothing that looked like it had been acquired solely to impress the neighbors. An old fieldstone hearth bespoke comfort against the cold nights of winter. Over it was a marble mantelpiece with a collection of china cats on it, and on the wall were various plaques and commendations he'd earned for his police work.

She ventured outside. She found she could endure the sun and appreciate the beauties of the day. But it didn't last long, after all. In a few minutes her skin began to itch, and a faint nausea crept into her stomach. She felt fatigued, suddenly, and went back inside.

The couch beckoned, and she took a nap.

She had supper waiting for him when he came home, having found frozen bluefish in the freezer. She did it up with rice and bits of celery, with fresh green peppers, carrot slices, and radishes on the side. He loved it.

"I don't get much home cooking," he said. "It's the one thing I never learned how to do for myself. I can prepare my own taxes, but I can't prepare a decent supper."

"You're lucky I came along, then," Dorothy said, beaming because it was so good to be appreciated for a change. She was proud of her culinary abilities—and married to a man who probably wouldn't notice if she shredded the telephone directory and served it up as salad.

Van Wyck told her about his day. A patient escaped from the psychiatric hospital, but was picked up before he got too far. An officer named Collins passed the test to become the township's first female detective. A drunken driver—a local businessman who'd had a liquid lunch—ran into a utility pole on Main Street and had to be taken to the hospital with a concussion.

The investigation of Bruce Randall and his friends was still sucking wind.

Chris was always too tired to talk about his work when he came home—or so he said.

"Ed, I'd better be getting back," she said when they finished eating. "I'd almost like to see just how long it'd take before Chris noticed I was gone, but I'd just hate it if he suddenly decided to report me as a missing person." There was nothing like a bite in the ass from reality to break up an idyll, but there would be more happy times. She'd see to it. "You call me tomorrow," she added.

He took her hand. "Why don't you see if he's home? If he's working late again, you could stay a little longer."

Dorothy phoned home and got no answer.

"That does it," she said, hanging up after a dozen rings. "He doesn't give a damn what I do, or where I am. Right now he's sitting at his desk, drooling over a manuscript or something."

Van Wyck took her into his arms. "Stay here another night," he said. "What sense does it make to go back there and sleep alone?"

It made no sense at all, and Dorothy saw that. "I ought to go back and get some things," she said.

"We'll go together. I'll drive."

They didn't waste time, but when they got there, Chris's car was in the garage. He must've just gotten home. Dorothy decided to go in alone while Van Wyck waited for her. She'd stay for only as long as it took her to pack a bag.

The front door was unlocked. As soon as she touched it, she felt a compulsion to turn around and have Van Wyck drive her away. She stood on the front steps with the door-knob in her grasp, suddenly shaking like a first-time sky diver freezing at the airplane's hatch. She could no more have gone into her own house than she could have brought herself to jump out of a plane. She let her hand drop from the knob. Abruptly she turned and fled back down the side-walk, dumping herself back into the passenger seat of Van Wyck's car and slamming the door noisily behind her.

"What's the matter, Dorothy? Jesus, you're as white as a sheet!"

She had the chills. She hugged herself tightly, but couldn't stop the trembling. "I can't go in there," she said.

Van Wyck knew blind fear when he saw it. He felt it, too. As if by instinct, his hand went to the radio and patched in a call to headquarters.

"Send a car to One-oh-one Chaucer Drive," he told the dispatcher.

"What's the trouble, Chief?"

"That's what I've got to find out. Just send the car. Out." He returned the speaker to its bracket and pulled Dorothy into his arms. Her teeth were chattering. *She's scared shitless*, he thought, and her fear was contagious. He could already feel it seeping into his stomach.

"What're you afraid of? What is it?"

She stared at him, eyes blank with confusion. "I don't know! I just can't go in there, that's all."

"Did you hear something?" He knew she couldn't have

seen anything; she hadn't opened the door. "Smell something?"

She shook her head again. "Nothing. I'm sorry, I know I'm not making any sense."

"Dorothy, *something's* wrong here, and we're going to find out what it is. In a few minutes I'll have some backup. Then we'll see."

Dorothy turned her head and stared at the house. There was nothing to see. *Only the curtains are drawn across all the windows.* The house was blind. *Do I do that?* She couldn't remember leaving the curtains drawn for Van Wyck's visit the day before yesterday. Or doing it before she left to see him yesterday.

Two officers arrived in a squad car, Romano and McLane. Van Wyck introduced them.

"This is Mrs. Matthiesen, and that's her house." The officers' eyes followed his pointing finger. "I'm going to go in with Mrs. Matthiesen. You two back me up."

"What's going on, Chief?"

"I don't know yet." He turned to Dorothy. "Ready?"

How could she tell him that she'd *never* be ready? Not for this. It was as if she had suddenly developed a full-blown phobia of her own house. A mindless, all-consuming fear of something that really couldn't hurt her. Like an aunt she had, who flipped out whenever she had to travel over a bridge. Stark, unreasoning terror.

But there were three cops here, and if she didn't get on with it, there might soon be more. And the neighbors had to be watching from their windows. So she nodded, and Van Wyck took her arm and guided her up the sidewalk, the two officers following close behind.

She stood in front of the door. She hadn't felt like this since she was six years old, when her big sister's dumb boyfriend dragged her kicking and screaming into the spookhouse on the Asbury Park boardwalk. She honestly didn't remember anything beyond that point. Only that she knew there were monsters, and she was going inside to meet them.

Eyes screwed shut, she opened the door and stepped into the foyer. Van Wyck came in beside her; his men waited on the steps. She opened her eyes.

All the lights were off, and all the windows were shut, shaded, and curtained, so it was dark inside. But that was all. No bodies sprawled messily upon the floor, no bloody handprints on the walls, no shattered furniture. Everything neat and normal. Yet she wasn't comforted. Her fear clung to her like a heavy woolen sweater drenched in a winter rain.

Van Wyck squeezed her elbow, letting her know he was there. She took a step toward the living room. Fear dried the saliva in her mouth; her voice cracked when she tried to raise it.

"Chris? Is anybody here?"

Cloth rustled, and a spring made a muffled groan as the easy chair tipped slowly erect, then froze with a soft thump. Chris came out from behind it.

He looks like hell, Van Wyck thought. Like he'd spent the night in the gutter, having visions. It was a relief, though, to find him still in one piece.

But Dorothy stared at him and saw nothing that she knew. Her eyes registered it as a man, her man, but her mind perceived it as a shape of darkness, a darkness that swallowed up the room, lit only by two unwholesome lamps: his eyes. They were lit with a light she'd seen before—and knew with a sickening intimacy—burning in the eyes of the boy who'd attacked her outside the mall.

He came at her like a rabid dog bolting from a cage. She didn't even have time to scream, and her reaction made her fall backward.

Van Wyck tried to stop him, but he was hit hard and thrown against the wall.

Dazed, he came back and tried to pull the man away from

Dorothy. One of Chris's arms hit him like a beam and threw him into the wall again. Fear exploded in his brain. *No one's that strong!*

His hand didn't wait for an order to leap for his gun. Without having the time to put it into words, his policeman's mind understood what he was seeing and acted accordingly.

Leg shot! his mind screamed. *Knock his pins out!*

Chris had just bent over and seized one of Dorothy's ankles when Van Wyck's gun went off. It was a Police Special, with plenty of stopping power, and Van Wyck made a point of staying in practice with it—and he missed. The bullet cracked into the opposite wall of the foyer.

By now Romano and McLane were in the doorway, and their guns were out, too.

Matthiesen yanked at his wife's ankle. She screamed and writhed. Her shoe came off in his hands. He straightened up a little.

He's going to kill her right in front of me, Van Wyck thought. He had one more shot, and he took it. He tried to bring up his left hand for a steadier, two-handed shooter's grip, but his palms were sweaty and they slipped, deflecting his aim just as the gun went off.

The bullet hit Matthiesen like a crack-back block and threw him forward, stumbling, then crashing face-first to the carpeted floor. Van Wyck had never shot a man before, but he knew what the bullet would do. It would start to deform and tumble as soon as it hit, and on its way out it would tear off chunks of Matthiesen's heart and lungs and carry them out through an exit wound as big as a softball, and shower the foyer with at least a quart of blood.

Matthiesen fell. He should have been dead before he hit the floor, but he wasn't. His arms and legs moved. He looked as if he were trying to swim, maybe do an Australian crawl to the family room. There was a spot of blood in the middle of his back the size of a silver dollar.

McLane and Romano charged past Van Wyck and stood over Matthiesen, guns drawn. The body continued to move. The gurgling sounds they heard were Matthiesen trying to say something through a mouthful of carpet.

"Get an ambulance," Van Wyck said. McLane ran out to make the call on the squad car's radio.

Dorothy sat on the floor, staring at her husband as he groveled on the rug. Her ears still rang with the sound of the shots. She saw Van Wyck's lips move but couldn't make out the words. And the thick fear began to seep from her mind, like infected matter oozing from a wound.

She watched Van Wyck and the other patrolman gingerly turn Chris onto his back, and heard the chief clearly when he said, "Dear Christ!"

He was looking at the exit wound in Matthiesen's chest. He could have thrust his fist into it. He saw splintered white ribs and shredded flesh, and a lump of red meat that looked like raw sirloin but that he recognized as Matthiesen's heart. A big piece of it was gone. What remained was motionless. It wasn't beating—and yet Matthiesen's arms and legs continued to move sluggishly.

There was blood, but the heart wasn't pumping it. It puddled lifelessly in the cavity of the wound.

"He's not dead, Chief," Romano said.

McLane came back in to report that an ambulance was on its way.

Dorothy continued to stare at what remained of her husband as Van Wyck helped her to her feet. She didn't feel his touch. She felt as though she had somehow been locked out of her body. Van Wyck led her to the living room couch and made her sit down.

She couldn't measure the time it took for the ambulance to arrive. She sat passively as the white-clad paramedics came in and loaded Chris onto a stretcher. She surprised herself by getting up and trying to follow, like a mourner following the bier, as they wheeled the stretcher out of the house. They'd had to strap Chris in; he was still moving. They had seen enough trauma to know that what they were seeing now was not possible, but they followed the routine of their job nevertheless—too engrossed in it to notice the way Dorothy stopped, trembling, at the doorway. She watched the stretcher roll away, unable to follow it out into the sunlight.

Thanks to daylight savings time, it wouldn't be dark yet for another hour. Dorothy saw neighbors peering intently from their windows or standing in their front yards to watch the show. What could she tell them?

A beam from the sinking sun fell softly onto Chris's face. He screamed.

XII. A LITTLE REVENGE

One

The man screamed all the way to the hospital. By the time the ambulance got there, he had already begun to rot. But still he screamed.

The two EMT's who rode with him in the back of the ambulance were almost incoherent when they delivered their report. The physician in charge was inclined not to believe it. He changed his mind when he saw the patient.

Hadn't they tried to sedate him?

One EMT laughed, not merrily. The other said, "We doped him good, but he wouldn't shut up."

"I swear," said the EMT who'd laughed, "his goddamn *heart* was blown away, and we still had to strap him in. He wouldn't stop moving."

"The way his skin started to turn brown—"

"The smell—!"

Everything they said was true, and the attending surgeon knew he was working on a twitching, screaming corpse. A young nurse gagged on its graveyard smell. The anesthetist threw up his hands and cursed. And then, almost two hours after the patient's heart was turned into hamburger by the policeman's bullet, the wriggling and the screaming stopped and the emergency surgical team heaved a collective sigh.

299

What they had on the table in front of them now was silent and still, as well behaved a corpse as any pathologist could ask for.

Only it smelled as if it had been dead for three days, and looked worse.

In visions, the Lord showed Thornall his enemy several times a day: a bulky figure that drank blood and trapped souls in undead, unclean bodies. Thornall saw him move silently among the trees, among the houses, hunting human prey.

And he was powerless to respond.

Thornall had no strength in his limbs. He could only sit in the sun on Emma Plews' front porch, praying silently for one last day and night of strength, and not receiving it.

Had God deserted him? *No! I was brought here to fulfill my mission.* He would have to find a way.

He lacked the strength in his arms to wield the sword. He doubted he could even lift it. It was clear, then, that he would have to find someone else to strike the blow. And it seemed equally clear that this would fall to Emma's grandson, Toby. Thornall had been shown a vision of the young man carrying the sword.

But how could that be brought to pass? *Toby, you must listen to me. The Lord has a mission for you, son. He wants you to take up this sword and kill a vampire.* Thornall grunted to himself as he imagined Toby's response. You didn't need second sight to know what it would be. The boy would be on the phone to the insane asylum before you could say Jack Robinson. *Send somebody down here right away, Doctor. We got a crazy old man who wants me to kill a vampire for Jesus.*

Thornall sat in the sun and prayed—not for strength, but for the right words to speak to Toby.

* * *

300

They met in the county prosecutor's office: Van Wyck, McLane and Romano, the chief prosecutor, and the county medical examiner. *And if it doesn't go well,* Van Wyck thought, *I can kiss my badge good-bye. Shit, I'll be lucky if I can stay out of jail.*

Fortunately, Romano and McLane had seen enough to back his story to the hilt.

"The man was out of his mind, sir," Romano told the prosecutor. "I saw it—he nearly threw the chief here through the wall. And he was half the chief's size!"

"We can't test the mental state of a dead man," said the prosecutor.

"But there's evidence that the officer is right," the M.E. said. "I have Mrs. Matthiesen's statement. Plus we have the testimony of the emergency medical technicians, and Dr. Barker from the county hospital. The only thing we know for certain in this case, Fred, is that we don't know what the hell we're dealing with."

The prosecutor scowled. The coroner's people had had Matthiesen's body for going on twenty hours now, and they still couldn't give him a straight answer to any of his questions.

"Let me have it again," the prosecutor said. "Chief, *why* did you feel you had to shoot the guy?"

Van Wyck felt sweat on his palms. "Because he was going to kill Mrs. Matthiesen if I didn't, Mr. O'Brien."

"You're absolutely sure of that?"

"You weren't there, sir. You didn't see him. He came at her like he was shot from a cannon. If she hadn't fallen down, he would've had her. I tried to stop him without using lethal force, but he was way too strong for me."

"Did he *say* anything?"

"He just growled, sir."

O'Brien indicated a thick file on his desk. "There's been some pretty funny stuff going on in Millboro these last few weeks, Chief."

"You have my reports," Van Wyck said. *Thank God my ass is covered there.* "You know I requested assistance from the county detectives. They've been working on these incidents, too."

"And the deceased's wife, Dorothy Matthiesen—she was involved in one of these capers?"

They reviewed the attack on Dorothy, and her abduction. Then it got nasty.

"You got something going with the little lady, Chief?" O'Brien sneered when he said it. Van Wyck growled inside. The prosecutor had a reputation as a lady's man that'd make Ron Leib look like a hermit monk.

It wasn't going to be easy, but it was too late to pussyfoot around the truth. Van Wyck took a deep breath, then plunged into it.

"Sir, Mrs. Matthiesen and I have become good friends. If you want to know are we romantically involved, the answer's yes. It wasn't something either of us expected or planned, but it did turn out that way.

"When Mrs. Matthiesen was abducted, she was missing from her home for approximately twenty-four hours. Mr. Matthiesen never reported it. She says he never called any of her friends or relatives to ask if she was there. The marriage had been going badly, and that was sort of the straw that broke the camel's back. She told me she was going to file for a divorce."

"Did Mr. Matthiesen know you were having an affair with his wife?"

For dragging this up in front of the two patrolmen, Van Wyck would have gladly decked O'Brien. But for the time being he could only answer the little prick's questions.

"I doubt it, sir. I don't see how he could have known. Mrs. Matthiesen and I haven't seen all that much of each other, and Mr. Matthiesen was always in Manhattan. He only came home to sleep."

The coroner interrupted. "Fred, I don't see how this helps us."

"I'm just wondering," O'Brien said, "whether Mr. Matthiesen lost his cool because Chief Van Wyck was making it with his wife. That'd explain why he attacked her."

"It *wouldn't* explain why he continued to yell and carry on after half his heart was shot away."

"It might explain why the chief shot him, though."

Van Wyck felt his temper start bucking like a bronco, and he held it down with an effort.

"Mr. O'Brien, I resent that insinuation. You have statements from Mrs. Matthiesen and from officers Romano and McLane corroborating my account of Mr. Matthiesen's behavior. I'm no doctor, but from the medical aspect of this story, it ought to be quite clear that Mr. Matthiesen was suffering from some condition that turned him into some kind of berserk animal. If you've read the report, you know the same thing happened to Norman Rubin."

"He's right," said the M.E. "Plus you've got Randall, the juvenile who attacked Mrs. Matthiesen outside the shopping mall, and Volden, the corpse that was found in the woods. We don't know what happened to Volden, but Rubin and Randall both displayed irrational and violent behavior just before they died."

"And you can't tell us what caused it!" snapped the prosecutor.

"I'm a medical examiner, not a seer. We tested those cadavers for umpteen toxins and never found a trace of one. We're testing for biological causes, too. The problem there is that some microorganisms die when their host dies. They can deteriorate, which makes them very difficult to detect. But I might as well be talking gibberish. I can't begin to account for what happened to those people."

The prosecutor fumed. "There'll still have to be a hearing on this shooting," he said.

"As of this morning, sir, I've suspended myself from active duty until that hearing can be held," Van Wyck said.

"Is a hearing really necessary?" the M.E. said. "It sounds like an open-and-shut case to me."

"Thanks, Doctor. I know I did nothing wrong. But I don't want there to be any doubt about it."

At the same time, Dorothy was on the phone with the mayor. She was almost shouting.

"Damn it, it isn't fair, Mr. Mayor! Chris attacked me. He would've killed me if Chief Van Wyck hadn't shot him. It had to be done! There was nothing else he *could* have done—unless you think he should've stood there and watched my husband murder me."

"Now, Mrs. Matthiesen—"

"Jesus, he had two patrolmen with him! *They* saw it. *I* saw it. Chris threw the chief out of the way like he was a rag doll. He could've killed all four of us. And for *this* Chief Van Wyck is suspended? For saving my life?"

Ron Leib sighed. This was one of those times when being mayor was more trouble than it was worth. "Mrs. Matthiesen, the chief has *voluntarily* suspended himself . . ."

"I know! That's why I'm asking *you* to reinstate him!"

"I'll have to discuss it with our township attorney. I'm not sure what we can or can't do, Mrs. Matthiesen. This hasn't happened before."

For a guy who has his own law firm and is in his second term as mayor, you don't seem to know much. "What do you mean, you're not sure?" Dorothy said.

Leib sighed again. In point of fact, he did have the power to reinstate Van Wyck, pending the county prosecutor's investigation, which was required by law. But he'd been hoping not to get involved in this mess, whatever it was. He sure as hell didn't want to rush in to reinstate Van Wyck, when for all he knew, something might come out tomorrow that'd force him to turn around and suspend the man again. He could just hear himself: *Chief, we're behind you a hundred and ten percent!* And then the stage whisper from the prosecutor's office, and the sick, sick feeling in the pit of your stomach as you turn to the audience . . . *Er, sorry, Chief, I'm afraid I'll have to ask you to hand over your badge, after all.* God, Democrats had been doing this Cain-and-Abel shtick ever since McGovern dumped Eagleton. It was like there was a curse on the whole damned party. . . .

"Mr. Leib," said Dorothy, "there's a council meeting tomorrow night. Do you want me to go there and tell everybody how you wouldn't stand by your police chief after he saved my life? You don't want that."

No shit, Leib agreed silently. There was a pause.

What the hell, he thought. *This isn't one of those wonderful cases from the big city, where the white cop shoots the black teenager and you've got a mob outside your office howling for the cop's balls on a platter. All we've got here is the deceased's widow calling the cop a hero.* And if there was anything more to it, the county prosecutor would find out. Let Fred O'Brien play the heavy.

"Mrs. Matthiesen, I'll get in touch with Chief Van Wyck as soon as I can and tell him to put himself back on active duty—okay? But the final determination will have to be made by the county prosecutor. That's the law. Whatever he decides, it'll be out of my hands then. All right?"

"Fine," Dorothy said. "Thanks, Mr. Mayor."

"Don't mention it. By the way," he added, "I think I know you. You're a friend of Nancy Kruzek's, right? And you put out that funny little sheet once or twice a month, what's its name—*Tales from the Developments?* Very funny. A takeoff on the old horror comic, *Tales from the Crypt.* I'm sure we've met a couple of times." *And a very tasty-looking little lady she is,* he thought, *if my memory serves me well.*

"That's right, Mr. Leib. I didn't think you'd remember me."

305

Oh, I never forget a pretty face or a shapely pair of boobs, he almost said, but caught it before it could slip out. Now was not the time for such gallantries. He filed the attractive new widow—as he'd seen her at poolside, in a swimsuit—in his libido's Maybe Later drawer and went to look up Ed Van Wyck's home phone number.

Van Wyck put down the phone and grinned wryly to himself. Dorothy must've given Leib a real earful. Ron wasn't the kind of mayor who liked to make decisions that might be second-guessed somewhere down the road.

He didn't grin for long, though. As his old man would have said, he was more than halfway up the wrong mountain now. You don't strike up an affair with a citizen who comes to you for help—as if suburban police chiefs were restricted to some special, secret way of meeting women. But oh, did it complicate things to have shot the woman's husband! *Thank God I had the presence of mind to call for backup— and witnesses—before I set foot in that house.* With Romano and McLane backing him, there wouldn't be much the prosecutor could do to him.

But what nobody seemed able to do was to raise a wall of rationality around the horror they had seen. No one would ever know how he'd felt when Chris Matthiesen flung him aside like a styrofoam dummy. Van Wyck had played high school football, he knew what it was like to get hit hard and knocked for a loop. This was worse. His whole body, from head to heel, ached from being smashed against the wall. He might as well have tried to stop a charging bull.

And of course that was *nothing* compared to what Dorothy had had to go through.

Now, when he had nothing on hand to occupy him, he saw Matthiesen's eyes, as they were when he burst out of the living room, and as they were when Van Wyck and Romano rolled him onto his back. Half his heart shot away, gone, and the eyes still glared crazily from their sockets. Wide open.

(Like Norman Rubin's eyes, when four strong cops held him down so the doctor could give him a sedative.)

Jesus God, thought Van Wyck, *what is going* on *here?*

And there were no fucking explanations. Nobody had even made a stab at one. What was the coroner *doing* with all those bodies he had in the morgue?

Meanwhile, Van Wyck decided he'd be damned if he'd stop seeing Dorothy just because that little prick O'Brien wanted to be the moral arbiter of the universe. But they would have to be careful about being seen together.

Two

It was one of those rare nights when Felix didn't feel like hauling himself off to a public meeting and instead turned to the pages of *TV Guide* for inspiration. What he found there made him wonder if it was worthwhile to keep his television set. The big networks offered a brand-new made-for-TV melodrama about a couple of homos dying of AIDS, and a new sitcom featuring idealistic young teachers and crusty-but-benign old administrators in an inner-city high school full of swaggering teenage louts with hearts of gold and IQ's that just wouldn't quit. The concept went beyond being laughable. Since the offerings of the local stations were no better, and the educational channel offered nothing but a bunch of foreigners caterwauling at the Met, Felix turned for solace to his bookshelf.

That was when his doorbell rang.

He wasn't expecting anyone, and it was seldom that any of the neighbors dropped in unannounced. *But bring 'em on,* he thought as he crossed the living room to answer it. *I'm prepared; the cleaning woman was here this afternoon.*

"Good evening, Mr. Frick."

Impelled by an instinct, Felix tried to slam the door shut; but Dr. Emerson already had his hand on it, and it wouldn't budge. Beside him stood his wife with a face like granite.

The doctor was smiling, and the smile on his face was so fixed, so lifeless, that Felix stepped back from the doorway. At the sight of that smile some inner voice barked out an order to man battle stations; his pulse rate suddenly soared, and adrenaline began to seep into his system.

When he stepped back, the Emersons crossed the threshold after him. Mrs. Emerson turned to close the door.

What have I let into my house? Felix fled across the room to his desk. When his hands touched the wood, he regained command of himself and was able to speak to them with some authority in his voice.

"I've been expecting you," Felix said, "and I've got a little something for you."

Casually, although his heart was bouncing like a car with no brakes tearing down a rocky hill, he slid open the top drawer of the desk and brought out his gun. He'd bought it long ago, when his Jersey City neighborhood began to deteriorate, and kept it all these years without ever telling a soul that he had it. It was only a .22 target pistol, but it'd put a hole in anyone. As he'd explained to the gun-store clerk when he'd bought it, "I'm not looking to kill anybody. I don't expect I'll ever pull the trigger. But when somebody points a real gun at you, it's the thought that counts, not the caliber."

He pointed it at Emerson. Emerson's wife shied back half a step, but the doctor only smiled his rigid smile.

"That won't help you, Mr. Frick."

'It sure as hell won't help *you,*" said Felix. "Why don't

you get out, and save yourself a painful and possibly lethal experience?''

"When I leave here, Mr. Frick, you will no longer be among the living." Emerson turned to his wife. "Get behind me, Blanche." She lost no time in obeying. She dropped way behind him, almost back to the door, and shifted off to the side, out of the way of any bullets that might pass through his body. *Almost as if she's done this before,* thought Felix.

"I mean it, Doctor. I'll shoot."

"We'll see."

Emerson advanced a step, still smiling. Felix's hand was trembling. He gripped the gun with both hands and was able to hold it steady.

"Doctor, there's a couple of German soldiers who could tell you what a big mistake you're making—if they weren't dead."

"I don't doubt it," Emerson said.

He came another step closer. Felix knew he was dead if he allowed the man to reach him. He squeezed the trigger.

His ears rung and he could hear nothing, but he could see that Emerson was still on his feet, still smiling, and still coming forward. *Jesus H. Christ, I missed him!* He fired again, and when that didn't stop Emerson, he keep on firing until the gun was out of bullets and the doctor was gently but firmly prying it out of his hand.

Felix saw powder burns on Emerson's jacket, and holes in the cloth where the bullets went through. He saw no blood.

"How the hell," he wondered, "did you know to wear a bulletproof vest?" For the moment he was too astonished even to be afraid.

By way of an answer, Emerson opened his jacket, unbuttoned his white dress shirt, and rolled up his undershirt, displaying a bare expanse of pallid, doughy flesh. There were four small holes in it, and dark blotches where the pow-

309

der had burned through his clothes. The holes in the skin were bloodless.

Felix's first thought was, *How the holy hell did I manage to miss him twice?*

Before he could have a second thought, he fainted.

"Kill him and get it over with, and let's get out of here!" Blanche said. "Why does it always have to be a big production number?"

The Master was tying the old man's wrists to a towel rack in the wall over the bathtub, using strips he'd shredded from the towel. Blanche stood in the bathroom doorway, folding her arms to keep them still. The Master had never seen her so nervous before. *She's getting old. Better start looking for a new servant.*

Satisfied the old man wouldn't be able to escape, he turned to answer Blanche.

"I want him to tell us exactly how much he knows about us and how he obtained the information. Killing him outright would hardly accomplish that, my dear."

"If his phone should ring right now—"

"If his phone rings, it won't be answered."

"And if someone should come to the door?"

"Stop dithering and get my bag," the Master said.

When he had his bag, he listened to Frick's heartbeat with a stethoscope. "The old gent's made of pretty stern stuff," he told Blanche. "We don't have to worry about him having a heart attack before I can finish questioning him." He put the stethoscope away and revived Felix with a whiff of ammonia salts.

Felix didn't remember passing out, but he knew he must have. The last thing he remembered was staring at the holes in Emerson's paunch. Now he was tied to the towel rack.

with his feet in the bathtub and Emerson sitting on the edge, regarding him with those clayball eyes of his.

"Welcome back, Mr. Frick."

"Drop dead."

For some reason this struck Emerson as funny, and he laughed. Felix looked past him and saw Mrs. Emerson fidgeting in the doorway.

Emerson was holding a scalpel. He held it so Felix could see it, but he didn't actually brandish it.

"As you can appreciate, Mr. Frick, you're in an exceedingly weak position. The only choice left to you is to decide how much you want to suffer. Believe me, I can make you suffer. But I can also grant you a relatively painless death. It all depends on how much you're willing to cooperate."

Felix knew he ought to be scared. But it was like that time the German StG-III burst out from behind a ruined church and came barreling up the street at him, its machine guns spraying chunks of cobblestone all around his ankles, its big tank-destroyer gun pointed at him like the finger of God. Somehow the sight of it had turned his mind into a survival computer. He spotted an open doorway and dove into it, rolling and coming up against the far wall ready to dive again. And the StG-III went right on past, hunting for bigger game.

His mind computed now, and the sum of the equation was death. His number was up. There was no getting out of this one, unlike the experience with the assault gun. He wouldn't be around later to collapse on jelly knees and puke his guts out with relief. This was absolutely the end of the road.

It angered him.

"What do you mean, 'cooperate'?"

"Tell me what you know about me," said Emerson, "and how you came to know it."

Felix's eyes kept straying to the powder burns on the man's shirt and jacket. "What I don't know about you is probably a lot more interesting,'' he said. "Like, why aren't you stretched out on my living room floor, bleeding to death? You were hit by four bullets.''

"Indeed I was. I told you the gun wouldn't help you.''

"I can't believe you aren't hurt.'' Felix shook his head. The whole thing was too much like a dream. He knew it was real, but it was too bizarre to *feel* like reality. "I don't get it. Do you know some kind of karate that I never heard of?''

Blanche Emerson stamped her feet on the tiled floor. "Will you get *on* with it?'' she cried.

"Get me a glass,'' Emerson told her, without looking back at her. She stormed off in a huff. "Mr. Frick, what do you *think* I am?''

Felix didn't know what he thought anymore. The events of the past few minutes had shot to hell every theory he had ever had. "What am I supposed to think of anyone who doesn't bleed when you shoot him at point-blank range?''

"Well, what *did* you think?''

"I thought maybe you might be a big-time criminal who'd been set up with a new identity after turning state's evidence against the other gangsters,'' Felix said. He was almost embarrassed to say it. In light of what was happening now, it was palpably absurd.

Blanche came in with one of Felix's glasses from the dish drainer. Emerson stood up and bared Felix's left arm, rolling the shirtsleeve up to the elbow. He seized the arm in a grip that was too strong even to twitch against. Felix didn't feel the scalpel slice his skin, didn't realize he'd been cut until a moment or two later, when Emerson stepped back with half a glassful of blood in his hand and Felix saw the bright red ribbon snaking down his bare arm and falling off to spatter dark drops on the white porcelain of the tub. That was when he felt the first stirrings of uncontrolled fear, and the computer in his mind began to break down. He shook, and his stomach crumpled in against itself.

Emerson held up the glass of blood and smiled.

"Salud," he said, toasting Felix with the glass; then he raised it to his colorless lips and drank the blood.

Felix clamped his eyes shut and turned his head away. Nausea blossomed in his bowels, and if he hadn't been tied to the towel rack, he would have fallen.

"Now what do you think I am, Mr. Frick?"

Felix kept his eyes shut. His heart was racing now, and he prayed silently for it to stall on him. He heard Emerson's stiff trousers rustle as he sat down. He felt the blood oozing warmly down his arm.

"How did you know I wasn't just the retired physician that I said I was?" Emerson asked.

It was a lot easier, Felix discovered, to keep talking. Hell, it wasn't like he'd been captured by the SS and was telling them where all his buddies were hiding out. He was in this all alone. And as long as he kept talking, he might keep his sanity, too. He had no other means of distracting himself from sinking headfirst into the horrors that had welled up around him.

He explained how Emerson's vagueness and avoidance of jargon, when they had discussed Felix's ear at the Kruzeks' backyard barbecue, had made him doubt his standing as a physician. That, plus Emerson's obesity. "I never saw a really fat doctor," Felix said. "I've known doctors who smoked, and doctors who drank, and doctors who played around with drugs; but I'd never met a three-hundred-pound doctor."

"It used to be a bit more common," was all Emerson would say to that, but he seemed to find it amusing.

Felix described his search through the medical records, his discovery that Trinity Physicians College had closed its doors in 1918, his puzzlement at finding the name of Winslow Emerson Taylor among the graduating class of 1894.

"When I read that Dr. Taylor went down to Central America in 1923," he said, "and never came back, and was finally presumed dead, it really threw me. You couldn't be him. He didn't marry, he had no children, no brothers or sisters, so you probably weren't a descendant who'd been named for him. I couldn't understand the connection between him and you. And I couldn't imagine what anybody had to gain by claiming to be an obscure doctor who'd disappeared so long ago."

"So you called the real estate agency," Emerson prodded.

Felix told the rest of it and answered questions until Emerson seemed satisfied.

"It seems I'll have to take better care to cover my tracks," he said, more to himself than to either Blanche or Felix. "It never occurred to me how easy the present computer technology makes it to backtrack through the past. Nor did it ever occur to me that a private citizen would take it upon himself to investigate me. Why did you do that, Mr. Frick?"

Felix tried to shrug, but his arms were getting numb. "I like to know things that other people don't know," he said. He was feeling light-headed now—*probably from loss of blood,* he thought. "I like to uncover things that people try to hide. Mostly I do it in the public interest, to keep the town fathers honest. They'll cheat whenever they think they can get away with it. But I'm retired, my son's as rich as Croesus, I have all the money that I need. It's just my way of keeping busy."

"What would you have done," Emerson asked, with an appearance of genuine interest, "if you'd found out that I really was an ex-gangster placed under cover by the government?"

"I don't know." *God, I need to lie down!* "Kept it to myself, I guess. I don't have the strength to cross swords with the federal government."

Emerson nodded. *When's he going to kill me?* Felix wondered. *When's he going to get it over with?*

314

"Mr. Frick, I admire you and your work. Honestly, you're not a man to be trifled with."

"Forgive me for saying so, Dr. Emerson, but under the circumstances, that compliment isn't worth a condom with a hole in it."

"Of course not. I understand. Still, it doesn't seem appropriate to snuff you out like a candle. You deserve better." Emerson stood up, moving as fluidly as an Olympic gymnast. Not at all like a fat old man who'd been perched on the edge of a bathtub for a while. He looked Felix in the eye. This time Felix didn't look away, and he was proud of it. He had never wanted to meet death like a coward.

"Mr. Frick, would you like to know what I really am?"

Felix sighed. What the holy hell did it matter now? And yet it did.

"Yes," he said softly, "I would like to know."

"I can't believe that."

"Really, Mr. Frick! What reason could I possibly have for lying to you *now?*"

Felix couldn't think of one. He couldn't think of much of anything just now. He had no feeling in his hands and feet, and the rest of his body was wrapped in a dull, debilitating ache.

"You saw me absorb four bullets without blinking an eye," Emerson said. "I showed you where they entered my body. You do believe what you see with your own eyes, don't you?"

Felix nodded wearily. He'd never had hallucinations before; he doubted he'd had one tonight. *Just because a guy can take a bullet easier than Rocky Marciano could take a punch, did that make him a vampire?* It sure as hell didn't make him an ordinary human being, though, did it?

"Before you die, Mr. Frick, you're going to believe in

the truth of what I say. It would be a shame for you to die in ignorance.''

He reopened the cut on Felix's arm and pressed his cold mouth to it. His lips felt like damp clay. Felix's head whirled; he was too weak to scream. Besides, he felt as if he were drifting into a bad dream. None of it was real.

Far, far away, Blanche Emerson lodged an ineffective protest. ''Is this absolutely necessary? Have you lost your mind?'' She sounded as if she were calling from the Kruzeks' backyard.

After a time that Felix was unable to measure, Emerson stepped away from him, licking his lips.

''There!'' Felix had to strain to hear him. ''Within twenty-four hours, Mr. Frick, you will be on your way to becoming a vampire. Exposure to the sun will destroy you. In a few minutes, you'll lose consciousness. When you regain it, you will no longer be here. I'll stow you someplace where you'll be safe long enough to realize the truth of what I've told you. In your weakened condition, the sun ought to finish you off quickly. But not before you learn to believe in vampires.''

The last thing Felix saw was the vampire's awkward smile, and his own blood on the yellowed teeth.

Blanche sat rigidly, hands clamped to the steering wheel, having her say.

''This time you've gone too far. It's bad enough we had to kill the man, after he's made inquiries about you all over creation! How many times did he mention your name? He wrote letters, he made phone calls—and now he disappears. Your name's going to come up again, you can bet on it!''

The Master hardly thought so. A search of Felix's desk had turned up all his correspondence with the AMA, the libraries, and the rest. He would burn it later. It would be a long time before anyone found any evidence linking him

316

to Frick in any meaningful way, and by then he and Blanche would be long gone. Even if the local authorities tried to trace him through his business dealings and his lawyers, they'd come up dry at the end. Over the years, the Master had become adept at burying his money aboveground.

Blanche went on. "And to top it off, you have to make this grandstand play! You can't just kill him and bury him, that's too simple and reasonable. Have you thought about what could happen if the sun *doesn't* finish him off? What if he's able to get to someone and tell his story?"

The Master didn't see how Felix could accomplish that, but he obliged Blanche with an answer.

"In the unlikely event that he does get an opportunity to tell some third party what happened to him, whatever he says will be put down as the insane ravings of a dying man. Nothing he could say would touch off a vampire hunt throughout Millboro Township, Blanche. The worst that could happen: a confused and embarrassed policeman will stop by to ask us a few hurried questions."

"Famous last words!"

"Shut up, Blanche."

He almost never told her to shut up, but when he did, she shut up.

The Master carried Felix a good distance into the woods and left him lying there under a small tarpaulin. The tarp ought to protect him just long enough for him to change his mind about vampires.

Blanche picked him up when he came out from among the trees. She was still simmering.

The Master let her simmer. She would not speak to him again until he gave her permission.

Three

Felix didn't know where he was. He knew only that the sun was hunting him, and that when it found him, it would kill him. He huddled under the tarpaulin, knowing the sun was up there looking for him, soaring like a hawk, turning its cruel red eye earthward.

The sun's rays tried to sear him through the canvas. Instinctively he burrowed in the dead leaves. Beneath them the earth was moist and cool, a comfort to him. Water seeped through his clothes to soothe his skin.

Clouds advanced across the sky and shed their load of rain. More importantly, they masked the sun. It was as if a fallen tree had been lifted from the tarpaulin.

Suddenly Felix remembered somebody telling him that the sun would kill him; and then, in a jumble of disconnected pieces, he remembered all the rest. He fit the pieces together and understood their meaning.

Emerson was a vampire. *Emerson drank my blood, so now I'm a vampire, too. That's why the sun will kill me, get it?*

Vividly he remembered the puncture wounds in Emerson's skin where the bullets had gone in: little bloodless holes. And he had a sharp, clear picture of Emerson sipping blood from a glass *(my blood!)*, and later sucking it directly from his veins.

It was then that Felix became aware that he didn't have a heartbeat.

You learn to listen for your heartbeat when you get to be my age. You can't help wondering when the old ticker's gonna crap out on you. So you like to hear it pounding away, thumpty-thump, nice and regular. What a lovely sound. Like a new mother lying awake at night, listening to her baby breathing in the cradle.

He could hear the rain tapping softly on the canvas, and worms and insects creeping through the humus, but he couldn't hear his heartbeat. Couldn't feel it. He searched his wrists for a pulse and couldn't find that, either.

Well, Emerson was right; Felix believed him now.

"I'm dead," he said aloud. "I mean *undead*." That was the term they used in all the monster movies. Undead. *My heart's not beating.* What a fool he'd been. Everybody knows you can't kill a vampire by plugging him with a .22. *He drank my blood. I saw him do it.* So much for the old mob-informer-in-hiding theory.

I can't be dead. I think, therefore I am. Only the guy who said that obviously never woke up to find his heart not beating. *It was Descartes; Descartes said that.* Descartes had never had to watch helplessly while a vampire swigged his blood, either. It might have changed his perspective.

Now I'll have to drink blood, too. The thought of it excited him; it was like getting turned on by a dirty book. And it brought on a thirst that was more acute than any longing he had ever known.

But it was a perverse longing, and it disgusted him. It was like wanting to molest a child. He rebelled against it, but it wouldn't go away.

I want to do it—but I'll be goddamned if I will! Rage filled him. He crammed a handful of muddy leaf mold into his mouth and bit down on it. He could barely taste it; it was like chewing on paper. It helped a little, though.

He remembered that time the Luftwaffe had come over and bombed the Allied line, and how he had cringed in a hole in the ground, scared so badly that he pissed himself. And hadn't that made him mad! He couldn't reach the German planes, but he had cursed them until his teeth were sore from grinding his jaws together, and he had pounded the earth until his fist was bruised and bleeding. He felt that way now.

How many others had that bloated bastard done this to? How many victims, Mr. Vampire? Felix doubted he was the first, and he sure as hell wasn't going to be the last. Not unless Emerson was stopped somehow. Unmasked. Exposed.

Didn't know it was going to rain, did you, fat boy? You should've listened to the weather report. With something like glee, Felix reasoned that the rain had upset the vampire's plans. He wasn't supposed to make it through the day, but now it looked as though he would.

And that makes it a brand-new ball game, he thought.

The rain fell equally on the hundred-and-fifty-thousand-dollar ticky-tacky in Triangle Mountain, on the derelict buildings scattered around Alabama Road, and on the tastefully renovated farmhouses of Shining Valley. It rained on other places besides Millboro, too.

In the pathology department at the county hospital, where there were no windows, nobody knew it was raining. And only a very few knew that the corpse of Christopher Charles Matthiesen, if taken out of refrigeration for an hour or so, still twitched its blackened fingers.

Dr. Albert Hassan, the chief medical examiner, swore his deputies to secrecy and continued his vain exploration of the body. The three assistants he'd chosen to work with him on this kept looking to him for answers, as they ran test after test and came up empty every time. No toxic substances present in the tissues. Nothing growing in the petri dishes but the old familiar bugs you found in every human body. No words of wisdom coming up from Atlanta, where the federal doctors were every bit as bamboozled as the locals.

It was enough to drive you to drink. It wasn't as if the corpse got up and danced a polka every fifteen minutes, but it might as well have been.

Chances are, Hassan thought, *a layman wouldn't even see it.* You had to watch intently for extended periods of time. If you were diligent, and your concentration didn't lag, you would see a finger or a toe move an eighth of an inch. His assistants were logging the movements, and the pattern was clear: the deceased's hands were trying to clench themselves into fists. That they were not quite succeeding seemed totally irrelevant.

They hadn't figured out yet just what the toes were trying to do.

Meanwhile the internal organs were decaying into mush, the body fat was turning into soapy, hideous, evil-smelling adiposere, and the skin was blackening by the hour. Refrigeration arrested the process, but as soon as you took the corpse out of its drawer, the rot picked up where it had left off. If they ever got around to releasing the body for burial, it'd have to be cremated. Hassan and his assistants had to cremate their paper coveralls after every exposure to it. He insisted on their wearing masks, too, and got no arguments. Whatever was running loose in Christopher Matthiesen's body, no one wanted any part of it.

And the tiny movements grew tinier and less frequent every day. *Soon they'll stop for good,* the coroner thought, *and that'll be that.*

Lying in his bed, listening to the rain drumming on the windowpanes, Thornall saw an old man wandering confusedly through the woods. The vision lasted several minutes, then faded like a dream. What could it mean?

Toby looked in on him.

"You feel all right, Reverend?"

"It must be the weather," Thornall said. His legs felt chilly. He had little time left. "Toby, you know that parcel I have, the one that's wrapped in cloth? Would you bring it to me, please?"

Toby went to the kitchen to get it. Thornall prayed for the power to persuade him. They had the house to themselves just now, Mrs. Plews having gone down the street to the church, where her sisterhood was meeting this afternoon.

Toby returned with the parcel. Thornall asked him to move the chair closer to the bed and sit with him a while.

"I have something to tell you," he said, "but first I want you to unwrap my parcel."

Toby wished Gramma was home; the old man didn't look well at all. He might need a trip to the hospital.

Well, she'd get back soon enough. He could always run over to the church if he needed her in a hurry. Meanwhile he could keep the old man company.

The parcel was wrapped in heavy burlap held in place by twine. It had been a long time since the knots had been untied, and Toby couldn't do much with them. Thornall said it was all right to cut them, so he did.

He hadn't thought much about it, but now that he was about to open it, he wondered what was in the parcel. It was heavy, but not as heavy as the M16 he'd carried in the army. But it was about the length of the rifle. It had sat there in the kitchen for days, and he'd never given a thought to it.

The burlap fell away, and he sat staring at a sword.

Dorothy got off the phone with Chris's boss feeling kind of spacy, as if she and he had been talking about two entirely different Chris Matthiesens.

No, said Eric Biggers, he hadn't noticed anything at all strange in Chris's behavior, his last day at work. Certainly he hadn't mentioned feeling sick, and he hadn't looked sick. How could he be dead?

Dorothy didn't tell him that Chris had been shot by a police officer. Nor did she mention that he'd come after her like a human barracuda, with eyes that weren't human. She didn't know what kind of eyes they were.

Mr. Biggers didn't know the circumstances of Chris's

death, so there was nothing to color his recollections of Chris's final days at the office: poring over manuscripts, handing off the unsolicited to whoever wanted to read them (there were always secretaries and receptionists who dreamed of discovering the next Judith Krantz in the slush pile), going to staff meetings, taking phone calls from authors and their agents. He worked late without complaint, as a custom, and never let on that there might be anything askew in his personal life. Never a peep about that.

Fucking businessmen, Dorothy thought. All of them acting out a fantasy that nothing mattered but their jobs. *My marriage? Forget my marriage! How many widgets did we sell today?*

"He was so happy to be doing what he was doing," Biggers said. "You could see it in his face. It was like all he ever wanted was to bury his nose in a manuscript. We'll miss him."

Sure you will, Dorothy thought. *You weren't the one he tried to kill. And you weren't here when they carted him off, kicking and screaming, with half his chest blown away. And now you'll have to find some other sucker who's willing to sign his life away for a lousy paycheck.*

She said good-bye and hung up the phone. Around her, the stillness of the house could be felt as something palpable.

XIII.   THE HOUR OF THE WOLF

One

Toby was waiting for him in the rain, and when he neared the curb, Toby hustled through a muddy patch and threw himself into the passenger seat.

"Drive," he said. "I don't want him to see us talking together."

Van Wyck cruised slowly down Alabama Road, remembering the phone call that had brought him here.

"Chief, you remember asking me to let you know if any peculiar characters showed up around here? Well, I've got one for you. An old tramp who says he came here to kill a vampire. I wouldn't take him seriously, except he's got this big motherfuckin' sword. . . . "

The words set off some kind of psychic Mayday that was like a distress signal from an alien space vessel. You couldn't translate the words, but you knew a cry of terror when you heard it. Van Wyck told Toby to stay put, he'd be there right away.

Now he listened to the story of how Ben Thornall had come to stay at Toby's grandmother's house.

"Tell me more about this sword," he said, after Toby had finished the first part of his tale.

"He *says* he got it from some old cathedral down in South America somewhere. A priest gave it to him. It's supposed to be a special holy sword come all they way down from the

Middle Ages. He had it all wrapped up in burlap. I'm telling you, Chief, that sucker's sharp as a razor. And heavy, too. You could chop off somebody's head without half trying.''

"And he's going to kill a vampire with it?" said Van Wyck, feeling as if he'd been suddenly thrust into the middle of a Hammer Film, and the old man at Mrs. Plews' house would turn out to be Peter Cushing.

Toby grinned, but not with good humor. "I told you he was peculiar. He says he's already killed half a dozen vampires with it. But they don't hardly count, he says, because he's looking for one vampire in particular, and that's the one he's got to kill.''

Van Wyck looked back to those golden days a couple of million years ago when he could have easily dismissed all this as the ravings of a demented old man. But that was before he looked deeply into the hole in Chris Matthiesen's chest and saw the inert shred of meat, all that was left of Matthiesen's heart—not beating, not doing anything. Just lying there oozing blood. And Matthiesen screaming when they carried him out to the ambulance.

And Norman Rubin falling into rot within minutes of his death.

Van Wyck had seen these things, and they still sounded crazy when he tried to put them into words. *He* sounded crazy.

Toby continued. "He's got quite a story, man. Must've been cooking inside his head for years. If they gave prizes for this kind of thing, he'd win hands down. See, he's been given this mission by God. . ."

As he summed it up for Van Wyck, Toby wondered how he'd been able to listen to it without interrupting Thornall to tell him he was nuts. The rich detail of the fantasy had overwhelmed him. The old man had gone on for close on two hours before his strength gave out and he had to take a nap; yet that was only a skimpy outline of the saga, he'd

326

cautioned Toby. It boggled the mind to imagine the fecundity of the psychosis that could produce such a harvest of delusion. Toby knew he could never tell it like the old man told it—not unless he wanted to follow the old guy 'round the bend. He gave Van Wyck the bare skeleton of it, fleshed out with a profusion of skeptical comments that— he realized uncomfortably as he neared the end of it—he put in to reassure himself that he was in no danger of believing it.

But he wished Van Wyck would laugh or something.

"I hope you weren't expecting me to take him into custody," Van Wyck said, a few long, silent moments after Toby came to the end of the story. "I've got enough troubles just now."

"I was thinking maybe you could get a doctor from the bughouse to come by," Toby said. "The reverend ought to be in a hospital, but Gramma doesn't want to hear it. She might listen, though, if a doctor and a policeman talk to her."

"Do you think he might be dangerous?"

"Jesus, who knows? Right now I think he might be too sick to get out of bed."

"I'd better see for myself."

Thornall was awake when they returned; he invited them into his room. Van Wyck was in civilian clothes, but Toby felt guilty about deceiving the old man, so he didn't try.

"This is Mr. Van Wyck, Ben. He's a friend of the family, but he's also the chief of police around here. I told him what you told me. I really felt I had to."

Thornall was disappointed, but not surprised. How could he have expected a young man raised on television and computers to believe him? Toby's generation was hard put to believe in God, let alone vampires.

Van Wyck looked down at the old man in the bed and thought, *Jesus, he looks like an Old Testament prophet.* You

327

couldn't be a cop in Millboro for long without running into any number of persons who were certifiably insane and had the papers to prove it. Every other week another one escaped from the state psychiatric hospital. Almost all of them were picked up by police before they reached the township's border. Van Wyck had seen the face of madness. He wasn't sure he was looking at it now. He wished he were.

"I don't want to scare you, sir," he said. "I didn't come here to arrest you. On the other hand, I'm not comfortable with the idea of people strolling around the township carrying swords."

Thornall saw something in the police chief's eyes that he'd seen before, in the troubled eyes of priests and scholars and *alcaldes* who had seen things that upset their faith, their learning, and their law.

"I'm not afraid, Mr. Van Wyck," he said. "In fact, I believe that this is a meeting that was meant to be. We can help each other."

Van Wyck didn't like the sensation produced by that remark. It was like going to the doctor for a simple checkup, having him order you into his office, open a file you didn't know he had, look you grimly in the eye, and say, "I've been expecting you."

"May I suggest something to you, Chief?" said the old man. "Just hear me out, then tell me if I'm right or wrong."

Van Wyck nodded, as Thornall knew he would. They always nodded, once events had pressed them hard enough.

"You've had some inexplicable deaths in this town," Thornall said. "Not only inexplicable, but bizarre and even horrible. Sane people suddenly become insane. And when they die, their bodies begin to decay immediately. Drastically. And you don't know why."

Van Wyck took his time replying. The deaths had been reported in the papers, there was no reason this old man shouldn't know about them. But the details had been successfully suppressed. Not a word had been printed about

328

the condition of the bodies; keeping *that* out of the papers was the one thing all the authorities agreed on. And the local journalists weren't aggressive enough to dig deeper, thank God.

"How do you know about that, Mr. Thornall?" he asked. "You couldn't have read it in the papers."

"I know because I've seen it before, Mr. Van Wyck. More times than I care to count, and in more places than I like to remember.

"Maybe you think it isn't possible for me to know about these things unless I was in some way involved in them. Maybe even responsible for them. But Toby and his grandmother can tell you I haven't set foot from this house since the day they brought me here, haven't received any visitors, telephone calls, or letters in the mail. And I'm sure some of these deaths antedate my arrival in your town. I can easily vouch for my whereabouts on any date you'd care to name, with statements you can easily check for accuracy. Nevertheless, I know who has caused these deaths. Millboro is only the latest of his many hunting grounds. I came here hoping to make it his last."

"Mr. Thornall," Toby said, "you can't *prove* what you're going to try to tell the chief."

"On the contrary. It would be very easy to prove."

"Prove what?" said Van Wyck, although he already knew what Thornall was going to say.

"That you have a vampire in your midst, Mr. Van Wyck."

It was time, thought Toby, for the chief to call the funny farm and have them send their wagon. For two cents, he'd say so. But Van Wyck was acting like a man who knew something Toby didn't know, and Toby felt the skin prickle under his clothes—as bad a case of gooseflesh as he'd ever had on a night patrol along the DMZ.

"Mr. Thornall," said Van Wyck, "if the mayor and

council knew I was even listening to this, I'd be out of a job so fast it'd make your head spin."

"But you *are* listening, aren't you? Because things have happened here that no one can explain."

"That doesn't mean I have to start organizing a posse to round up Bela Lugosi."

"Of course not. But you've had experiences that have forced you to open up your mind somewhat. You've seen things that make you doubt your own sanity."

"I never doubt my own sanity," said Van Wyck. "I know what I saw. And if I saw it, it happened."

"Tell me what you saw."

The conversation was sliding into a mode of unreality that made it relatively easy to share confidential police information with an old man who was quite possibly off his rocker. It never occurred to Van Wyck *not* to tell Thornall what he'd seen.

He described his encounter with Chris Matthiesen. "I was sure I killed him," he concluded, "but when they took him away in the ambulance, he was still moving around—and screaming."

"He screamed because he was exposed to sunlight," Thornall said. "But that's not the only thing you've seen, is it?"

"No." Van Wyck told him about Norman Rubin and the two previous cases, Randall and Volden. Toby had heard about these incidents, but the details were news to him. Hearing them now, he remembered finding Volden's body in the woods and almost rejecting, later, what Van Wyck had told him about the autopsy.

Holy shit, he thought, *you mean it fuckin' happened* again? *And Van Wyck* saw *it happen?* It made him think of his old platoon sergeant, who had fought in Nam and learned hard lessons there. *"Boy, when you are sure you seein' things, one of them things gonna turn out to be real, and it gonna kill your ass."* But Van Wyck wasn't saying that he'd seen a vampire.

330

"All of these things, Mr. Van Wyck, are the work of a vampire," Thornall said. "I know because I've hunted him for over fifty years. His victims cannot be numbered! Wherever he goes, he sows death and worse than death. And it will go on and on and on, until this creature is destroyed."

Van Wyck struggled against the rising conviction that this was all beginning to make sense. *But Christ,* he thought, *the answer's more impossible than the questions.* He most emphatically did not want to believe in vampires; didn't even want to entertain the notion . . . although as a boy he had believed in them. He remembered that stage in life where the movies and the lurid comic books were all too real. And the boy that still lived within him, at the core of his adult persona, still believed. He fought for his adulthood.

"How am I supposed to arrest somebody who can turn himself into a bat?" he growled.

Thornall shook his white head, rumpling the pillow. "That's just folklore, my son. I know these creatures. I know their powers and their limitations. They are fiends in human form, but to the human form they're chained. They aren't phantoms, but real, solid, tangible *things* of unclean flesh and blood. To exist, they must consume blood and avoid the rays of the sun. The rest is superstition.

"Some of them fear holy objects. But this vampire, the one who is battening on your community, can walk brazenly into a church, sit in the front pew, and take communion. He has been seen to do this. He doesn't fear God. A mirror will reflect his image as easily as it reflects your own. He can cross running water as easily as you do.

"And vampires are *strong*. You've seen that for yourself. They can't be killed, except by sunlight—although you may immobilize one by cutting off its head or physically destroying its heart. You've seen that, too."

With an effort, Van Wyck kept his voice down to a normal speaking tone. "Are you telling me that Christopher Matthiesen, the man I shot, was a *vampire?* That I couldn't kill him because he was already dead?'' *Guess what, Dorothy* . . .

"I thought you could kill 'em with a stake through the heart!" Toby said.

"You can't. I know. I've tried," said Thornall. "You can only immobilize them that way. If you remove the stake, the vampire will eventually rise again. If the stake remains in his heart, however, he'll eventually succumb to starvation. They can't exist without blood. But the only sure way is to let the sun destroy them."

The whole thing was getting crazier by the minute, Toby thought. "If that's true," he said, "then how come you carry around a special sword?"

Thornall caught his eye and held it.

"With that sword, Mr. Hicks, I will dismember the vampire. And then I will place the pieces under the sun and watch them decay into nothingness. Or would, if I had the strength."

"Let me see the sword," Van Wyck said.

One of Van Wyck's patrolmen was into military relics. Van Wyck had gone over there once to see his collection. The guy had American swords dating all the way back to the Revolution, plus a sampling of foreign blades: a Japanese samurai sword from the eighteenth century, an old cossack colonel's saber, a German officer's dress sword from World War I, an ornate Italian sword that had belonged to some general from the Napoleonic era. "They're all the real McCoy, Chief," Officer Bockman had said. "I don't buy a weapon unless it's fully authenticated. Too easy to get stuck with a replica, otherwise."

Van Wyck had handled Bockman's swords, tentatively cutting the air, imagining the shock of steel against bone. The memory came back like déjà vu as his fingers closed around the hilt of Thornall's weapon.

It was a heavy sonofabitch—had to be close to fifty ounces. Heavier than Babe Ruth's bat, and scalpel-sharp. The handle was long enough so you could grip it with both hands in case your arm got tired, and it wouldn't be long before that happened. This was not a sword designed for pretty exhibitions of one's fencing skill. No playing Zorro with this baby. You'd hoist it up and you'd slam it down, and whatever was in your way would be gone, one way or another.

The blade was long and straight, with a fine point. Time had darkened it, except along the cutting edge, which glimmered like moonlight on dark water.

Handling some of Bockman's weapons, Van Wyck had experienced a sensation that hadn't been altogether pleasant, as if some faint psychic charge of battle still lingered in the blade. "I feel that way, too," Bockman had said, unsmiling. "You can always tell if a weapon has really been there."

Well, this weapon had been there. Times without number.

"How old is it?" Van Wyck asked.

"They told me it was forged in Spain over six hundred years ago, during the long crusade to drive the Moors out of the country," Thornall said. "Before it was given to me, it had reposed in a crypt since the year 1600. It came to the New World with Cortez's expedition."

Van Wyck's imagination conjured up holy war in Spain, pitched battles on the steps of Aztec pyramids, screams and slaughter, blood thick in the air like mist, men's flesh carved like meat. . . . The spell was strong. It almost seemed to darken the room around him.

There was an engraved inscription on the blade, but he couldn't read it. "What's this say?" he asked Thornall.

"It's Latin. It means 'Divine Love Forged Me.' "

Somehow that made it worse.

* * *

Hating the way it sounded when he said it, Van Wyck asked, "So who is this vampire who's supposedly settled down in Millboro?" There was no way to make it sound sane.

Thornall looked like death and said, "God help me, I don't know. I can't tell you his name. He uses many names. He has papers to prove he's any number of different individuals. I haven't found out what name he's using here, nor where he's living.

"I've never gotten close enough to see him face-to-face. Only the ruin he scatters in his path. To tell you what he looks like would be to risk confusing him with an innocent man. But I would know him if I saw him. I would know him instantly."

And that was all the old man could say before falling into an exhausted slumber.

"Well?" said Toby. "What're you going to do? Is the man crazy or what?"

They had gone out onto the porch and were watching the rain drip from the eaves. Thornall slept.

Van Wyck shrugged. It wasn't a cold day, but there was a chill working itself into his bones.

"I don't have the authority to have him committed, if that's what you're thinking," he said. "He hasn't broken any laws. I can't take him in for vagrancy as long as your Gramma is giving him a room."

"What about the sword? Can't you get him for carrying a concealed weapon?"

"It was in a package, for all intents and purposes. He's allowed to transport it as long as it's packaged properly, so that it can't endanger public safety. I don't think we have a municipal ordinance that applies to swords."

"No danger, huh?" Toby said. He didn't like the way

he was getting excited over this, but he couldn't control it. "You heard what he said, man—he's gonna kill a vampire with it! Chop him up in little pieces, lay 'em out in the sun to dry."

"He hasn't threatened any specific individual."

Toby knew, in spite of all his resistance to it, that he was inching closer and closer to buying Thornall's line of madness. The expression on Van Wyck's face was no comfort to him.

"Goddamn it, Chief, you can't *believe* him!"

Van Wyck turned to him slowly and said, "I know I can't. And heaven help me if I have to."

Two

His face was the face of one who has passed through darkness without knowing where or when he entered it, or where he was when he came out. Dorothy cupped his face in her hands and said, "Ed, what's wrong?"

"I don't know."

But she knew he wouldn't have asked her to come to him so soon without a pressing need. Not with the prosecutor theorizing that he'd shot Chris to lop off a corner of a love triangle.

So she came when he called, and parked her car in his garage so that no one would see it.

"Come and sit in the living room," he said. "There's something I have to talk to you about."

His hands were cold.

They sat on his couch. It took him some moments to organize his thoughts before he could begin.

"I'm going to tell you something you probably won't

335

believe," he said, "I'm not sure I believe it, either. But I need to know what you think."

He told her about an old man on Alabama Road who carried an ancient sword and claimed he had come to Millboro to kill a vampire. It was long in the telling. He correlated it with things he had seen for himself in recent weeks, up to and including his encounter with Chris. He didn't waste time editorializing about it. He simply laid it out for her, with the strain showing in his face and hands. Dorothy listened without interrupting.

Only at the end did he venture from the path of a simple narrative.

"I'm trained to think in terms of solid evidence," he said "Points that can be proved in court beyond a reasonable doubt. Arguments that can stand up when a lawyer tries to knock them down. Anything less is just no good to me. Physical evidence corroborated by eyewitness testimony, and testimony corroborated by the evidence: that's what I have to try to get when I investigate something. I can't make an arrest based on opinions and speculations. I have to have facts.

"The fact is that people have been dying in this township in a way that nobody, not even the medical examiner, can explain. Another fact is that now I've got a man who says *he* can explain it. In fact, he *describes* what's happened very well—even though none of the details have been released to the public. But he says it's part of a pattern that he's seen before. Finally, it's also a fact that he couldn't have been physically present at any of these incidents. I spent most of this afternoon confirming that."

Van Wyck rubbed his hands together, rubbed his face, and then continued.

"If a perfect stranger came up to me and described, in detail, a nightmare that I had when I was ten years old, and which I never told anyone about; and if he said he knew about it because he used telepathy to read my mind . . .

should I believe him? How else could he know about my nightmare?

"If a murder is committed, we always keep some of the details from the press. We have to: it's our only way of checking whether a witness is bullshitting us or telling the truth. So when somebody comes forth with all this information that we never released to the public, we have to accept him as a reliable witness. Someone who knows what he's talking about. Do you see what I'm getting at?"

He was so tense that Dorothy was afraid to touch him. He startled her by suddenly laughing bitterly.

"Can you see me going up to the prosecutor and saying, 'Hey, Freddie, I know what's been causing all those funny deaths in Millboro—we got a vampire on our hands!' Jesus Christ, how long do you think I'd last?"

"Ed," she said as gently as she could, "there's no such things as vampires."

"Yeah. I know. Only I don't know how Thornall can describe things which he couldn't have seen or read about. I don't know how you can find a fresh tuna fish sandwich in the stomach of a rotting cadaver."

He's going nuts, thought Dorothy. *The strain has gotten to be too much for him, he's having a breakdown. For God's sake, what do you do when somebody's about to crack in front of you?*

She was frightened now, and she didn't know what to say.

Felix walked in the woods.

The sky was overcast, although the rain had stopped. It was dark. He could appreciate how dark it was, and yet he had little difficulty seeing—further proof of Emerson's contentions. But it wasn't needed. Whenever he had doubts, Felix had only to pause and try to discern a heartbeat. His heart remained inert, even when he ran.

He could feel the damp, but it didn't bother him. If he

337

rapped his fist on a tree, it didn't hurt his knuckles. He walked on and on with no hint of fatigue.

I'm dead. I ought to be huffin' and puffin' like a broken engine. I'm soaked to the skin, I ought to be shivering and sneezing and coughing. I lay on the ground all day, I ought to be as sore as a boil. But I'm having none of those little discomforts because I'm dead.

He had at times fantasized about his own death, imagining Elroy and his highfalutin doctor wife feeling guilty at the funeral, a whole gaggle of crooked politicians heaving sighs of relief when they read his obituary in the paper. He'd always loved that scene in *Tom Sawyer,* in which the boys eavesdrop on their memorial service and hear themselves praised to the skies by the same adults who used to scold them as good-for-nothing varmints.

Well, now I can crash my own services if I've got a mind to. Might be worth it, to see the look on Elroy's face. He'd hide somewhere and listen to the eulogy, then come swaggering down the aisle. He could have a ball—until the sun got him.

Even through the clouds, the rain, the treetops, and the heavy canvas—through all these he'd felt it beating down on him. A heavy boot that would crush him like a bug on the sidewalk. *No more backyard siestas for you, ace.* Knowing it was up there, that searing ball of fire, had almost flushed him out from under his canvas. Just knowing it was there. There was a lot to be said for being dead (or undead), and beyond all worldly pains and cares, but the menace of the sun made it all a joke. Like winning the lottery on the day they started World War III.

Yet worse than the sun, in a way, was the black longing that he recognized as the thirst for blood. Next to this, quitting cigarettes had been a picnic. Unbidden, his mind kept filling with obscene pictures, all of them focused on the slaking of that thirst. In his imagination he gulped down gallons of it, dark blood gushing from severed necks and wrists, each vision more intense than an adolescent boy's most vivid wet dream. They filled him with a hideous delight, and at

338

the same time revolted him more than anything he had ever known in his life.

The worst of it was the dreadful suspicion that he had had these foul yearnings all along, tucked away in some slimy hole in his unconscious. What if they'd come out while he'd been teaching? *Is this what I am? Is this me?* A Gilles de Rais, a John Wayne Geczi, psychopathic monster masquerading as a teacher and a gentleman?

His only comfort was the absence of a heartbeat.

I'm not me anymore. Felix Frick is dead. What we have here, class, is a vampire. A thing that walks around in my body, with a little piece of my mind, my soul, held prisoner inside. I can't block out these disgusting cravings because they're not mine.

He could only fight them. *I can't help what I've become, but I sure as hell can remember what I used to be.* Remembering, he felt a craving for revenge that was every bit as deep and strong as this new craving for blood. Emerson had destroyed him, violated him, ruined him; but it was still a debt he thought he could repay, if the sun didn't get him first.

And, he thought, *if I can find my way out of these friggin' woods.*

Thornall saw the old man shamble out of the woods and stand staring up at a huge decaying ruin that had once been a great house. Thornall saw it clearly: the sagging verandah, the boarded windows, weathered and splintering planks, rusted nails, the broken door. He saw many other things besides. The old man vacillated for some time, then trod resolutely up the yielding, shifting steps and disappeared into the house

Thornall woke with a gasp, to find himself sitting upright in his bed, the room pitch dark around him. His heart threw itself against the prison bars of his ribcage, and there was pain. For a moment he was convinced he was going to die right there, but in a little while the pain subsided.

More importantly, he suddenly understood it all. The meaning of the vision was clear. Ignoring what it did to his pulse rate, he swung himself out of bed and marched upstairs to Toby's room, turning on lights as he passed. He yanked open the door and turned on Toby's light.

Toby flung a forearm over his eyes and groaned. "What the fuck—" He sat up and squinted angrily at Thornall. "Reverend! What do you think you're doing, man?"

Thornall advanced to the bed and leaned over. "There's no time!" he whispered harshly. His heart's erratic beating told him there was less time than that. "I've got to see the police chief—now!"

"What? Are you crazy? It's the middle of the night!"

Thornall marshaled some of his precious strength and gripped the younger man's arm. "Call him! Call him now!"

Toby looked into Thornall's eyes. It was like looking into a pair of black caverns from which distorted screams issued. He was suddenly wide awake, and scared—honest-to-Christ, wet-your-pants scared. Whether he was scared of the old man, or of the dense night that pressed in on the house from all sides, or something else again, he didn't know. For a moment he was a little kid again, waiting to hear some unnameable thing go bump behind his closet door.

"Hurry!" Thornall whispered.

Toby climbed out of bed, feeling the old man's eyes on him like a pair of bayonets. He slid his feet into his slippers and went tentatively down the stairs, Thornall closely following.

He was a little more in command of himself by the time they reached the living room, and turned to argue before picking up the phone.

"Man, do you know what time it is? I can't call the chief now; he'll be in bed. Anyhow, I don't have his number."

"Get him!" Thornall said.

"All right, all right." Shit, he had to do something or

hey'd wake Gramma. But the only thing to do was to dial
he number for police headquarters.

The chief wasn't in right now, the dispatcher informed
him, after he gave his name. "You'll have to wait until he
comes in this morning, Mr. Hicks."

He turned to Thornall. "See? He's not in." Thornall
gave him a look that instantly reminded him how scared he
was. "Get him, for the love of God!" Thornall said.

"Uh, it's kind of urgent," he told the dispatcher. Jesus,
how could he explain this? He was asking them to get Van
Wyck out of bed, and he didn't know what to say. "Can
you call him at home and ask him to call me back?"

"Sir, it's after one in the morning. Why don't I give you
Sergeant Niles, and he—"

"No!" said Toby. "It's got to be the chief." Van Wyck
had met Thornall, he might understand what Toby was up
against. "Look, Chief Van Wyck asked me to let him know
right away if I . . . I mean, I know it's late, but believe me,
he'll understand. He knows what this is about. Just call
him—please!"

"Mr. Hicks, it's almost one-thirty A.M.—"

"Damn it, I *know* what time it is! Just call him and have
him call me back. I'll be waiting." He hung up before they
could connect him with the sergeant.

Thornall flopped onto the couch, gray-faced and short of
breath, as if he'd just run through a minefield.

"Reverend, will you please tell me what this is all about?"
But Thornall seemed not to have heard him.

Felix knew the Schuylerville Nursing Home from Dotty
Matthiesen's description of it. But she hadn't said anything
about its being inhabited.

Lost in the woods, with his mouth full of rotten leaves to
take away the imagined taste of blood, he stumbled on it.
Now he stood marveling, because in spite of its obvious

341

state of decrepitude, there were lights in its windows and snatches of talk and music floating on the rain-sodden air. Yet the building was a ruin, fit only for the wrecker's ball.

And the lights were discolored, the words rambling and disconnected, the music out of tune. This soon after the rain, the odor of decay was ponderous. He smelled mold and mildew, rotting woods, the acrid tang that told of termites and beetle larvae chewing tunnels through the beams; it enveloped the house like a cloud. He saw the front door hanging askew on its rusted hinges, the gutters drooping from the eaves, loose boards dangling from fragile rusty nails. How could there be talk and music here, and lights in all the rooms?

Where the windows weren't boarded up, he saw vaguely human shapes flit back and forth. He saw stiff figures milling in the hall. He heard them talking.

" . . . so I sold them, every last one."

"You lying bastard shit."

"I feel fine, Doctor, it's just my digestion. . ."

" . . . and I don't know anymore, I don't know. . ."

The figures moved fitfully, aimlessly, like dust-motes dancing in a ray of sunlight. The music faded out and faded in. Someone sobbed. Someone laughed. And Felix was afraid—until he remembered what he had become. He laughed out loud at himself.

"You can't hurt *me!*" he cried at the building's ruined facade. And knowing that there was nothing in there that could hurt him, he decided to go inside. *Might as well join the party: the undead among the dead.*

When he placed his foot upon the step, the music stopped. When he reached the top step, the voices fell silent.

He peered through the open door into the hall. In a garish yellow light, like insects preserved in amber, the guests of the house stood frozen. Some last echo of their speech hung in the air, and in it Felix perceived that none of the guests had been speaking to one another; they were all, each nd every one, talking to themselves. Nor could they see ne another. That was clear from the way they stared hrough, stared past, each other. The hall was crowded, in he way that a shelf gets crowded with accumulated figu- ines, each one separate and self-contained.

They were old. Old in the sense of worn-out machinery, lead letters, expired licenses. They were frozen in confu- ion, in fear, in sadness and in loneliness; and more than a ew of them were insane.

All this Felix saw as he came to the top of the porch steps, out before he could bring up his other foot, the lights winked out and he found himself staring into any empty hall. Empty as a plundered tomb, he thought, which in a way it was.

Weren't vampires supposed to return to their graves be- fore daybreak? *Be glad to, ma'am, only I haven't got a grave.* He reached into his mouth and felt his teeth. No fangs, either. A sorry excuse for a vampire. But then he wasn't intending to make it his life's work.

He grimaced at his own choice of words.

Meanwhile, the night was waning. He'd wasted hours roaming around in the woods. There was a lot he had to do, but it would have to wait until tomorrow night. No sense starting something he couldn't finish.

He went into the house and stood in the hall, listening. He heard the voices again, but now they were only whis- pers. *Place is lousy with ghosts,* he thought. He had never be- lieved in them, and he supposed he should have been excited to find out they existed, after all, but he wasn't. They were just a part of the background, as innocuous as crickets chirping in the grass. They had no significance.

He passed among the whispers, looking for a place where he could stay until the sun had come and gone again.

Three

A rainy day was not the same as night, and the Master knew it.

He himself could function in a heavy rain, if need be, for several hours—but at a price. Within thirty minutes of getting back indoors, his skin would start to blister. Within an hour he would be weak and shaky, fit only to lie dormant in the darkness until he was recovered. That would take some forty-eight hours.

Ten or twenty minutes out in the open on a sunny day would produce the same effect.

He could survive these trials, he reasoned, because the vampire organism was so long and firmly established in every cell of his body. But a new-made vampire couldn't. He knew because he'd studied it firsthand.

He was surprised, however, when he returned to the spot where he'd left Frick and found only the canvas tarpaulin lying rumpled on the leaves. He examined the ground and saw that Frick had preserved himself by burrowing into the damp humus and staying under the tarpaulin. That, plus the rain, had saved him for the time being.

He wondered how long Frick would last. Immediately after the transformation, most—but not all—vampires entered a kind of panic phase. Their intelligence seemed temporarily reduced. This was when most of them got caught by the sun.

Evidently Frick was one of those uncommon individuals who'd been able to keep his wits about him. He'd waited for the sun to set and then wandered off in search of a more secure refuge. If he could find it, and control his thirst until he'd successfully obtained his first feeding, he might survive—for a little while. Millboro wasn't the hinterland of Guatemala. It was far too demanding an environment for an inexperienced vampire.

The Master wished Frick well, but doubted he would endure for very long.

They slept in the same bed, but they didn't attempt to make love. Van Wyck was too wound up for that, and Dorothy was still coming down from the scare he'd given her. It was a truly frightening thing, she reflected, when a person you love and respect suddenly starts coming out with totally irrational statements that he seems to believe. It was like he'd claimed to have been on board a flying saucer.

Only he *knew* that what he was saying was irrational, and that made the difference. He *didn't* run around the house hanging wreaths of garlic from the windows.

Chris turned into a vampire.

I'm sorry, I simply can't deal with that. I'm not going to try. She denied the whole damned thing and anesthetized her nerves with beer. *The truth doesn't always make you free,* she thought. *Sometimes it can make you crazy.*

Only it wasn't the truth, was it? Couldn't be.

They went to bed, and Van Wyck, lying there with his thoughts going around and around like a broken record, was still awake when the phone rang. He plucked it from his nightstand before it could jangle twice, but the one ring was enough to wake Dorothy.

She knew the phone didn't ring this late at night unless it rang with evil tidings. Some family catastrophe: a death, a highway accident, an arrest. For the moment she'd forgotten she was sharing a bed with a policeman, whose phone could reasonably be expected to ring in the middle of any given night. By the time she remembered, Van Wyck had hung up.

"Ed? What was that?"

He turned on his reading lamp and sat up to rub his eyes. With his hands still clasped to his face, he said, "Toby Hicks just called headquarters. He wants me to call him back."

"What time is it?"

Van Wyck rubbed his eyes again and peered at his alarm clock. "Just about quarter to two."

Afraid of the answer, but compelled to ask, Dorothy said, "What does he want?"

"He wouldn't tell the dispatcher. He only said he wanted me to call him right away." *He must be out of his fuckin' mind. Thornall must've died on him.*

Dorothy was thinking the same thing, but she held her peace as Van Wyck got Emma Plews' number from directory assistance and dialed it.

Hicks answered quickly enough to cut the first ring short.

"This is Chief Van Wyck. What's the matter, Mr. Hicks?"

"The reverend wants to see you, Chief. Right *now.*" Hicks was keeping his voice down, but it was easy to discern how upset he was. "If you wait till morning, it might be too late. He doesn't look too healthy just now."

So he wasn't dead yet, thought Van Wyck; but he must be sinking fast for Hicks to call at this hour.

"Have you called a doctor?" he asked.

"No, man! He doesn't want a doctor. He wants *you.*" Hicks dropped to a whisper. "Damn it, Chief, I was sound asleep in my room when he comes busting in and says I gotta call you. Scared the bejesus out of me. Look, the man won't tell me what it's all about, he just says he has to talk to you right away. *Do* something, all right? Before he drops dead on me."

"He won't say what he wants?"

"Will you just get over here, man!"

"All right."

"Hurry!" Hicks hung up, leaving Van Wyck listening to a dial tone.

"What does he want, Ed?" Dorothy asked.

"Oh, fuck, I don't know," Van Wyck said. He put the

phone back. It didn't take long to repeat the little bit Hicks had had to tell him. "I guess I'd better go," he added.

He got out of bed and started to dress. Dorothy was abruptly stricken with a dread of staying behind alone. She wasn't aware that it had anything to do with all their earlier talk of vampires. It was like a snake that slithered out from under the bed and threw cold coils around her ankles before she knew it was there.

"I'm going with you," she said.

"Dorothy, we can't—"

"I might be able to help, Ed. I can wait in the car if I'm not needed, but I won't wait here."

Van Wyck didn't argue the point. The truth was that he wanted company. He had a feeling he wasn't going to enjoy hearing what the old man so desperately wanted to say to him. And if Thornall did go ahead and die on them, Emma Plews might be glad of another woman in the house.

It was 2 A.M. when they went out the door; about the time, Van Wyck thought, when human biorhythms drop like oversold stocks and nothing you try to do can turn out right. He remembered a Bergman film he saw in college, *Hour of the Wolf*—an endless series of nightmarish, quasipsychotic imagery. It all came back to him with unwelcome vividness. Up until now he hadn't understood the meaning of the film. Now it was starting to come in loud and clear. His own hour of the wolf was close at hand.

Hicks met him on the sidewalk, fully dressed and wide awake.

"Gramma's still asleep, so let's keep it down." He didn't spare a glance for Van Wyck's car, didn't see Dorothy waiting in the passenger seat as Van Wyck got out. "Come on!" Dorothy stayed behind.

The downstairs lights were on. Hicks led the way through the living room to the spare bedroom. Thornall was back in bed, glassy-eyed and laboring to breathe. There were hollows around his eyes and under his cheekbones that Van Wyck hadn't seen that morning. His mouth hung open.

Van Wyck slid a chair to the bed and sat down close beside him. Thornall seemed to shake himself out of a trance then, but was too weak to sit up.

"Thank God you've come!" His voice was like the rustle of heavy boots through dry leaves. "I don't have much time."

"Take it easy, Mr. Thornall. We've got to get you to a doctor."

The old man's hand shot out, startling Van Wyck as badly as if it were a striking snake. The gnarled fingers dug into his wrists like talons. The eyes came alive.

"Listen to me!" he rasped. "There's a vampire not too far away. He's in a derelict building in the middle of a wooded area. A big house with pines around it, a mansion. Red clay tiles on the roof, a big verandah. It's been empty for years, and is falling into ruin. Do you know it?"

It was a clear enough description of the Schuylerville Nursing Home. Thornall must have been there, must have seen it—but when? Between his departure from the Salvation Army shelter and his appearance on Alabama Road was only a matter of hours. Twelve, at the most. And his movements during those hours hadn't been difficult to trace. It wasn't possible that he'd had time to make a detour into Schuylerville on foot. He must have visited the place some time ago.

Bullshit, said a voice in the back of Van Wyck's mind. Under his clothes, his skin began to crawl with gooseflesh.

"Do you know it?" Thornall said, squeezing the wrist until Van Wyck was ready to jump out of the chair.

"I know it," said Van Wyck. His mind was like a legislative chamber in which all order has temporarily broken down. *This isn't happening,* said the members of the majority party. But there was plenty of dissent. *Call a doctor!* cried

348

one voice. *Time to turn in your badge,* whispered another. There were other outbursts as well, ranging from *You're finished, Van Wyck!* to *Jesus Christ, I'm scared.* It was worse than the Township Council the week before the primaries.

"Go there!" said Thornall. "Go right now! You'll find one of them there. He's waiting for you. But he can't stay long. If you waste too much time, he won't be able to help you."

Help us? You mean we're not supposed to pry up the lid of his coffin and pound a stake though his heart? Van Wyck stifled an urge to giggle.

Thornall beckoned; Hicks came cautiously to his bedside, like an officer who knows his general will give him one last impossible order before dying from his wounds.

"Toby . . . you take my sword. You're young and strong; I'm too old to wield it anymore. God has ordained that you should strike the blow my labors have prepared."

Hicks looked to Van Wyck but found no help there.

Thornall removed his hand from Van Wyck's wrist and let it fall gently to the sheet. He sighed deeply and closed his eyes.

"He's still alive," Van Wyck said, straightening up after bending over to listen for the old man's heartbeat.

Toby felt suddenly rubber-kneed, and backed up to lean against the wall. He was glad the wall was there.

"What're we gonna do, man?"

Van Wyck shook his head and shrugged. Just a few days ago he'd called off the close watch on the abandoned nursing home. Now the patrols took a brief look once a day and once during the night. They wouldn't notice anything quieter than a torchlight orgy.

"Did you understand what he was talking about?" Toby said. *Fucker knows something he isn't gonna tell me!* It was the same kind of not-so-paranoid fear that sometimes hit the soldiers guarding the Korean border. *If they were getting ready to start a war, would they tell us? Or would they wait until some of us got our asses shot off first?*

Something of that fear communicated itself to Van Wyck, who didn't appreciate it. "What do you want from me?" he snapped. "The man wants us to run over to the Schuylerville Nursing Home to meet a vampire. What could be simpler than that? Meanwhile, he's dying."

Toby looked down at the bed. Some color had returned to Thornall's face, and he seemed to be sleeping peacefully. "I don't think he looks so bad, now," Toby said.

"Hm. He looks better."

"So what's next? Are you going to go to this place in Schuylerville?"

Van Wyck didn't want to go. Reason insisted that the old man couldn't possibly know what he was talking about, that the whole thing was just another big fat bubble of madness boiling to the surface of a senile mind—but then reason hadn't been scoring too many runs lately. Van Wyck had a sickening feeling that it would not turn out to be a wasted trip.

"I think I'd better," he said. Even as he said it, he tried to warn himself that he might be walking into a trap. But it was nothing that simple. Thornall had been in his room all day, weak and sick. What opportunity had he had to set a trap?

"I'm going with you," Toby said.

"Mr. Hicks, I can't bring a civilian—"

"Horse *shit!* If you think I'm gonna sit here wondering what the fuck is going on, you're crazy. No way. And you're gonna need some backup. Or would you rather call some of your men out to help you arrest a vampire?"

He had a point there. This wasn't the kind of thing you wanted to share with headquarters. Anyway, Van Wyck had the radio in his car. He could call for help when he got there, if it really looked like he needed any.

"All right, Mr. Hicks. But if you're coming with me, I hope you know how to obey orders."

Toby grinned. "Shit, Chief, I just spent four years of my life doing nothing *but* obeying orders!"

"Let's go, then." He turned to leave, but stopped when he saw Toby picking up the sword. "What's that for?"

The vampire, Toby almost said. But that was crazy, and he bit it back in time.

"I'd just as soon not leave this laying around the house while I'm not home," he said. "It'll be safer with us. Don't want the reverend waking up and chopping off Gramma's head because he thinks she's Dracula." Besides, the heavy weapon felt good to hold right now, in a way it had never felt before. It felt better than an M16.

Van Wyck nodded and led the way out of the room.

Four

Dorothy had heard of Alabama Road, but she'd never been there before. Now, sitting in Van Wyck's car in front of the Plews house, she found it difficult to believe she was still in Millboro.

It wasn't Appalachia, it wasn't the South Bronx—but it sure as hell was a long way from Triangle Mountain, Royal Oaks, or Thoreau Manor. She wondered how many of the families living in this neighborhood had Swim Club memberships. Had she *ever* seen a black family sipping Diet Pepsis at poolside? They'd seem as exotic as Tibetans. How many of them had contracts with Lawn Doctor, private tennis lessons, memberships in any of the popular Democratic Party clubs? She racked her brain, but could only come up with one black man she'd ever seen in public office here in

Millboro: old Charlie Baylor on the township water authority, who voted the way the mayor wanted him to vote and never made a peep. The rest was lily white: council, school board, zoning and planning boards, and the multitude of committees and commissions that had charge of everything from kids' soccer to the collection of the township's history. *And nine out of ten of us would be only too happy to march in a demonstration against apartheid in South Africa. Wouldn't it blow the white Afrikaners' minds if they could see how we've got things all sewn up in Millboro?*

Meanwhile, Ed was certainly taking his time in there. What were they doing—playing Scrabble? If the old man in there was dying, why didn't they send for an ambulance? The doctors at the county hospital would be furious if they let the old guy die before they got a chance to stick a bunch of tubes up his nose.

Finally Ed came out, followed by the man who'd been waiting for them when they got there. Van Wyck opened the door and dumped himself in behind the wheel. The other man opened the back door and carefully placed something on the floor before climbing into the backseat.

"Who's this?" he demanded, meaning her.

"This is Mrs. Matthiesen. I brought her along in case your grandmother needed someone," Van Wyck said. "Dorothy, this is Mr. Hicks."

"Will somebody please tell me what's happening?" she said. She heard a hint of a complaining whine in her voice; Hicks' brusqueness had gotten under her skin.

"We have to go someplace," Van Wyck said. "I'd like you to stay here. Reverend Thornall is sleeping now—he didn't die—but I'd like you to look in on him every few minutes, just in case. Mrs. Plews is asleep, too."

"And she'll be just as pleased as punch if she gets out of bed and finds a strange woman all alone in her house— sure!" Dorothy said. "what did that old man have to say to you, Ed? I'm not budging till you tell me."

Van Wyck didn't answer right away. Hicks said, "Lady, you don't want to know," but the remark was swallowed by the silence.

"We're going out to the Schuylerville Nursing Home to meet a vampire. Mr. Thornall told us we'd find one there. Don't ask me what it means because I don't know. But it might be dangerous, Dorothy."

Her experience at the nursing home came back to her like the crack of a whip, all in a flash. Here in the car, she could almost smell the place in all its mildewed emptiness. And she felt suddenly as if everything lay ahead of her like a steel track, from which deviation was impossible.

"If there's anything to be seen there," she said, "that has anything to do with what happened to me, I want to see it. I have to see it."

"Can't we just get going?" Hicks cried.

Van Wyck had the sensation of being swept helplessly along by an irresistible tide. He turned the key in the ignition.

He advanced as far up the overgrown driveway as the Escort could go. Ahead, the building loomed pallidly among the trees. He let the headlights linger on it for a moment, then shut them off and killed the engine.

No lights flickered in the darkness, and only the breeze stirred the undergrowth. If there was anybody here, he was hiding.

"Wild goose chase," Hicks muttered.

Van Wyck was rooting for him to be right, but at some deeper level of consciousness, where thoughts are experienced rather than articulated, he knew he wasn't. He couldn't see the house now, but its presence was still oppressive. He knew it was there. He felt like a blind man standing on the brink of a sinkhole.

Dorothy could see the building—not well, but she could

353

see it. And a reddish light glimmered within it, outlined by the main entrance. A dark figure crossed the red-lit space.

"Somebody's there," she said.

"I don't see anybody," Toby said.

"I do."

Toby gritted his teeth and said nothing more. *Fuck it, it's as dark as the inside of your hat out here. Lady, you can't see a thing. And thanks a fuckin' pantload, Chief, this is just what we needed on this expedition—some spaced-out woman who thinks she's seeing things. Don't know what we would've done without her.*

Van Wyck finally found his voice, but God, his mouth was dry. He had to lick his lips before he spoke.

"It doesn't look like anybody's here, but we can't count on that. I'm going to have a closer look. You two wait here."

"Is your name John Wayne?" Toby said. "I'm going with you, man. I want to be out in the open when the boogeymen jump out."

Dorothy added quickly, "That makes three of us. I didn't just come along for the ride, Ed."

Van Wyck sighed, ticked off at himself for being so relieved that they were coming with him, and even madder because he was afraid and couldn't see anything to be afraid of.

"I don't know about the police," Toby said, "But in the army you don't split up unless there's a damn good reason for it. We'd better stick together, Chief."

"All right," Van Wyck said. He felt absurdly grateful for the rationalization. "But that means *close* together, folks. We have to assume that this is a trap of some kind. First thing happens, we book it back to the car and radio for help. Is that clear?"

"Brother, you don't have to say that twice!"

The got out and gathered in front of the car. Van Wyck opened his holster but didn't draw his gun; another shooting was the last thing on the agenda. In his left hand he

354

carried a heavy-duty flashlight with a long barrel that left little to be desired as a bludgeon. He glanced at Hicks and saw that he was carrying the sword.

"Put that back," he said.

"No dice. We might need it. Don't sweat, it won't go off by accident."

Dorothy had been peering straight ahead, at the eldritch forms that were framed by the ruined doorway. Now she turned to Toby and saw the sword for the first time.

"Where on earth did you get *that?*"

"The reverend gave it to me."

"Can we get moving, please?" Van Wyck said.

With an armed man on either side of her, Dorothy advanced. The smell of the decaying building curdled in her nostrils. The beam of Van Wyck's flashlight speared the verandah steps, but she didn't need its help to see.

She'd never expected to come back here. Her memory hadn't dwelt on it; if anything, she'd been trying to push the episode into the background. She hadn't even gotten a good look at the place after finding her way out of the cellar.

But now, as it towered in front of her like a tsunami about to break, it was all she could do not to turn and run from it. Unconsciously her hands sought out the two men's hands and linked with them, but there was little comfort in that. She could hardly feel their grips.

"This is bad," she said to Van Wyck. "I feel just like I did when I couldn't open my front door until you came back up the sidewalk with me. Exactly the same feeling."

Toby squeezed her hand. He didn't know what she was talking about, specifically; but whatever it was, he was sure he felt it, too. His other hand squeezed the sword, which he carried upright like a torch. As heavy as he knew it was, his system was feeding on adrenaline and he felt like he could carry the damn thing up the steps of the Washington Monument if he had to. *You just show your face, Mr. Vampire, and I'll fuckin' chop you right in half. . . .*

Lord, he was thinking just like Thornall now. *We're all crazy, all three of us. We know there's no such thing as vampires . . .and here we are.*

Van Wyck squeezed Dorothy's hand, too, but said nothing. The last time she had a feeling like this, he wound up shooting somebody. He didn't believe in clairvoyance, but it was an observable fact that you disregarded certain premonitory feelings at your peril. Every cop knew that.

He wondered whether he'd be able to get through the next hour without shooting anybody. He wondered what had made Thornall send him here. Who was waiting for them inside that house? A bunch of Bruce Randall's satanist friends? Van Wyck imagined them crouching in the shadows, high on crack or speed, clutching switchblades or machetes as they waited for him to cross the threshold. Maybe they were tired of sacrificing animals. . . .

He didn't mention this thought to Dorothy. He didn't try to blot it out of his mind, either. Satanists he could deal with.

As they came closer to the house, the light in the hallway dimmed. Dorothy knew she was the only one who saw it. *I'm like one of those canaries*, she thought, *that miners used to take down into the mines with them*. The bird would keel over before the men could smell poisonous gases. As a warning system, it had worked out well for everybody but the canary.

Was that someone standing in the doorway, watching them?

No. It couldn't be there, or the men would have seen it, they would have said something. Van Wyck played his flashlight beam across the empty space. Nothing.

At the foot of the porch steps, they paused to listen.

The house was silent. Toby looked up and thought he detected a faint lightening of the sky, a fading of the stars. In a couple of hours the sun would be coming up. But down here, shadowed by the tall pines that hemmed in the house, it was still as dark as midnight.

"Wait here," Van Wyck said, almost under his breath. "I'm going up for a closer look."

Dorothy felt herself trembling and could hardly bear it when he released her hand and slowly mounted the verandah steps. If Hicks hadn't been holding her other hand, she would have unashamedly—and without having a choice in the matter—turned and fled. She clung to Hicks' hand as she would to a lifeline, and his grip on her was just as tight.

Toby felt her trembling and wished she'd stop, knowing she couldn't. She was staring at the house as if it were a gigantic bomb with a burning fuse. Goddamn, it was just an empty building. His neighborhood was full of empty houses, some of them in worse shape than this one. There was nothing in them but varmints and bugs, and tetanus germs festering on the points of rusty nails. Nothing to stare at. Damn woman was shaking like a leaf, and if she didn't stop soon, he'd be shaking, too.

The steps shifted under his weight, but Van Wyck got to the top without breaking through. He stood on the verandah and shone his light into the hall, playing it up and down from floor to ceiling.

The dust had had a chance to resettle since the detectives had been here, and the floor was gray with it—except for where a single set of men's footprints had exposed the naked wood. The prints led inward, into the dark. And you didn't have to be Daniel Boone to see that they were fresh.

Someone had been here, and had come alone. It perturbed Van Wyck that Thornall should have known that. Bound to his bed, he'd had no business knowing it. But for the moment that was a side issue. Whoever had left those footprints, was he still here?

"What the fuck's he *doing?*" Toby muttered though

clenched teeth. Van Wyck heard him and backed away from the doorway, stopping at the lip of the verandah.

He gestured to them to come up, keeping his hand held out for Dorothy. She reached for it and borrowed some of his strength to help her up the steps. Her feet didn't want to go; she felt like she was plodding through deep mud. Hicks came up with her.

"Look!" Van Wyck whispered. He led them closer to the entrance and shone his light on the prints.

"He's in the cellar," Dorothy said.

"How do you know that?" Toby snapped.

"I know," was all she could say. *I know it the way you know there's bad news in the mail before you open the mailbox.* Nobody knows how you know things like that.

"We'll follow the prints," Van Wyck said.

No police officer drags civilians into a potentially hazardous situation, but Van Wyck was stuck with these civilians. To order them to wait on the porch, or to go back to the car, would be a waste of breath.

He supposed they could all go back to the car and sit tight while he sent for help. The moment he radioed headquarters, however, the adventure would become an official police action requiring written reports. Van Wyck didn't think any of it would look too good on paper, no matter how he phrased it. He sure as hell didn't want to try to explain what he was doing at the Schuylerville Nursing Home in the wee hours of the night, in the company of a man armed with a sword and a woman whose husband he'd shot just a couple of days earlier.

Besides, to take the civilians back to the car and call for backup would be to admit that he was taking Thornall seriously . . . and he couldn't do that yet. It wasn't an admission he chose consciously not to make. It went deeper than that.

The footprints led straight to the cellar door. Van Wyck stopped well short of it.

He's down there, Toby thought, *waiting for us, just like the reverend said.* Up until this moment he'd been able to cling to a thread of rationality. Now it slipped though his fingers. Thornall had been telling the truth all along. *And because I'm a damned fool, here I am.*

Dorothy shivered. *What if it's Chris waiting for me down there? With that mangled hole in his chest and that ungodly glint in his eyes?* She looked at the footprints and knew there was no way they'd find the cellar empty.

"Get close to the wall and don't move," Van Wyck whispered. He ushered them into position and let go of Dorothy's hand.

He approached the door. It was slightly ajar. He positioned himself so that he'd be a poor target in case there was anybody parked at the foot of the stairs with a gun, then hooked his fingertips around the edge of the door. He turned off his flashlight, then slowly pulled the door open.

The darkness was profound. It seemed to creep out from the stairwell like a fog. With it came a cloying smell of damp stone, and a silence that was almost tangible. Van Wyck's right hand crept to the butt of his Police Special. He felt the blood rushing through his veins like flood waters though storm sewers. He strained his ears but heard nothing but the muffled thud of his heart against his chest. After a few hard beats, he broke the silence:

"This is Chief Van Wyck, Millboro Police! Whoever's down there, you'd better come up—and take it slow!"

His voice boomed in the stairwell, then left a deeper silence behind it. It took all he had to leave his gun in the holster, but his fingers curled around the butt, and his left thumb groped for, found, and adhered to the button of the flashlight. His eyes stared vainly into the murk.

He nearly jumped when he heard the dull clatter of a latch, and the soft creak of a door on its hinges. His guts

359

shrank when he heard, far below, soft footsteps on the cement floor.

A familiar, reedy voice said, "Don't shoot, Chief! I'm glad you're here."

Five

Dorothy knew that voice, but at first it didn't register. At the sound of it, her mind went falling-down drunk with relief. It wasn't Chris's voice. He wasn't here. He wasn't coming back.

Someone was climbing the steps, slowly.

"You want to use your light, Chief? I think'll you'll be less tense if you can see me."

Now Van Wyck knew the voice, and his grip on his gun relaxed. He flicked on the light and probed the darkness until the beam fell on the speaker's face.

It was a strong spotlight, police issue. You could blind a man with it. But the man on the stairs made no effort to shield his eyes. He didn't even blink. Van Wyck almost dropped the light.

"Mr. Frick! What in God's name are *you* doing here?"

"I'll explain it all. It's rather a complicated story."

Dorothy's ears rang with disbelief. She recognized Felix's voice now. Why did she still feel as if it were the Frankenstein monster coming up the stairs?

And then he was at the top, with the light on his face; she knew his face, but it was changed.

Toby stared. *Another* screwy old man? And from the cut of his clothes, a very well-to-do old man. The clothes were dirty, stained with mud and pasted with clumps of leaf mold, but you could tell they weren't Salvation Army clothes. His face and hands were filthy, too, as if he'd crawled on his belly though a swamp to get here.

The reverend at least *looked* normal, but this dude was *gone*. Gone so far out, he'd never come back. A one-way ticket to the end of the fuckin' line. In the army Toby had seen men bombed out on every kind of drug you could think of, and this was worse. At least when you were fucked up on drugs somebody could look into your eyes and see *something,* even if it was only chemically induced psychosis. Looking into this old man's eyes was like peering down the empty stairwell there: nothing. You saw *nothing.*

And he stank of muck and mold. And something else. Something worse.

When Van Wyck held out a hand to help him up the last few steps, Felix almost took it. But as he reached for it, he could almost smell the blood that circulated through the living flesh; he could almost taste it. A bright flame of obscene anticipation shot up from the depths of his undead psyche. He smothered it with self-disgust. He halted on the steps and warned them.

"Don't anybody touch me. It's not safe."

"Mr. Frick—" Van Wyck tried to say.

"I'm not joking!"

They all gave back a step or two, and for the moment Felix was satisfied. He tried not to smile. The muscles of his face responded sluggishly. *Just like Emerson,* he thought.

"Please . . . there's a reason for it. I just hope to God you'll believe me when I tell you what it is."

He came out of the stairwell and stood in front of them. He looked at Dorothy, and she turned away. *She knows,* he thought. *She knows already. But how?*

"Let's talk outside," he said. "We have a lot to talk about."

He made them go first, then followed at what he judged to be a safe distance. But even from yards away their blood drew him, tempted him. If he hadn't heard them when

361

they got out of the car, and had time to prepare himself to resist the temptation, he knew he would not have been able to carry out what he planned to do. *Had* to do.

It was better on the verandah, but still not good enough. "This is an evil place," he said. "More evil than any of you can possibly imagine. I understand it was, at one time, a nursing home. Believe me, there was precious little nursing here! It's best we have our talk out in the open."

He stopped them between the house and the car, made them stand a few paces from him, and began to tell his tale.

"Mr. Frick, that can't be true," Van Wyck interrupted, after Felix had told most of it. "Look, you could've been drugged, or infected with some kind of exotic disease. You can't *literally* be a vampire."

Felix had expected disbelief. But he was used to having to prove his point, and he knew that there were many things people didn't believe because they most vehemently didn't want to believe.

"Suppose you're right, Chief—although I assure you, you're not. Let's say I'm drugged or sick, or both. I'm still telling you that Dr. Emerson and his wife broke into my home and assaulted me, and then dumped me in the middle of the woods. I'm telling you the man drank my blood. And I'm willing to testify to all of this in front of a judge and a jury. I'll swear out a complaint. I want the Emersons arrested."

And that's all well and good, thought Van Wyck. What was not so well and good was the thought of Felix on the witness stand, telling the court how he'd shot Emerson at point-blank range and didn't hurt him *("Yessir, he showed me the holes where the bullets went in!")*, turning to the jurors and telling them he had been a vampire ever since, that Emerson had made him one. Somehow Van Wyck didn't think

362

the defense would have much trouble impeaching the credibility of such a witness.

And this was not the Felix Frick of old. Van Wyck had seen him in action at many public meetings and had spoken with him any number of times. Whatever had really happened to him, it had changed him profoundly. Would a jury believe him, seeing that faraway, nobody-home look in his eyes? *Can I?*

He tried to put it tactfully. "Mr. Frick, I can arrest the Emersons on those charges. But I can't arrest them for being vampires. And the moment that word comes out in court, the case against them will go out the window."

"Chief," Toby said softly, "ask him if he knows the reverend."

Van Wyck hadn't gotten around to that yet. Now that Hicks brought it up, it hit hard. Thornall had told them they would find a vampire here, and at least they'd found a man who claimed to be a vampire.

"Do you know a man named Thornall, Mr. Frick? A tall old man with a white beard, indigent. A tramp."

"The Reverend Benejah Thornall," Toby added.

Felix shook his head. "Never heard of him. For God's sake, Chief, is this any time to be bringing in side issues?"

"You've never met anyone who answers that description?"

"I would certainly tell you if I had. What on earth does this person have to do with it?" Felix hadn't counted on the police chief being so obtuse. For the first time since sunset, he began to fear that nothing would come of his efforts to denounce the Emersons. *If I could turn into a bat and fly in circles around their ears, they still wouldn't believe me.*

Dorothy shivered. She'd listened to Felix's story without comment. She hadn't even asked herself, yet, whether she believed him.

But his eyes were like Chris's eyes, and the eyes of the boy who'd attacked her by the mall.

Toby looked up. The stars were nearly faded from the sky, which now had taken on a pearly hint of gray. He could make out individual trees in the background, and he could see both the house and the car. In another hour or less the sun would be coming up. He'd be glad to see it.

"I think we ought to take you home, Mr. Frick," said Van Wyck. "It's getting kind of damp and chilly out. Don't want you coming down with pneumonia."

Sure, Felix thought, *we'll just hop into the car, putt-putt away, and all live happily ever after.* Only he knew what would happen if he got into a confined space with a living human being. They'd believe him then, all right. Imagining it was almost like experiencing it. Some evil projectionist in his mind showed a film that made his head spin. *Is this what a pervert would feel, if some pretty child were to ask him for a body rub?*

He could never go back to human society. He knew that now, knew what would happen if he tried. He would never testify in court. How could he, unless they kept him safe in a steel cage? *(Bailiff, bring in the witness. Rumble, rumble, clankety-clank. Yes, Your Honor, I've got to stay in this cage. I'm not responsible for what I'll do if I get out. I have an uncontrollable thirst for blood. Believe me, you don't want me riding up in the elevator with the other witnesses. It could be messy, heh-heh. . . .)*

And they still wouldn't believe him. Even now, as he stood here in front of them and marshaled all his willpower to keep from springing ravenously at the nearest throat, they thought he was a daffy old fart who might catch cold if he stayed outside much longer. *How's about I slurp down a couple quarts of your blood, Chiefie? Then will you believe me?* Only then they'd just believe he sincerely *thought* he was a vampire. It wouldn't work.

But there was still a way to get at Emerson. . . .

"Tell me more about his Thornall guy," he said.

* * *

364

Ed and Felix batted their questions back and forth, and for Dorothy it began to take on the semblance of a never-ending tennis match. She soon lost track of the score.

They were still going on about it when Felix suddenly stiffened and fell silent, with his eyes locked on some distant point beyond. She turned and followed his gaze.

The red rim of the sun had just shown itself over the tops of the trees.

A shudder went through Felix that shook him like a shirt on a clothesline in a stiff breeze. *Oh, shit, he's bought it,* thought Van Wyck. *We stood around flapping our jaws, and now he's going to die on me.* "Well, Mr. Prosecutor, I guess I didn't realize . . ." Without thinking, he stepped forward to catch the old man before he crumpled to the ground—

And froze in tracks, because the mask that stared back at him was nothing human. It stopped him like the sudden opening of a chasm at his feet. It was far, far worse than anything he could have imagined.

The dead jaws gaped, and from them rushed, like a gout of waste from a ruptured sewer, an overwhelming reek of carrion.

Van Wyck fell, gagging.

"Don't touch me, you idiot! Don't anybody touch me! Stand back if you want to live!"

Dorothy couldn't move. Toby nearly yanked her off her feet when he pulled her back with him. He wanted to scream. He wanted to vomit, too. He shook from head to toe. An inner voice cried, desperately, *It's only a man, a puny old man!* But he was still within a hair of letting go of Dorothy and stampeding headlong into the woods.

Van Wyck tried to get up from his hands and knees. *I'm okay. I'm not hurt,* was all he could think at the moment.

Felix stared unblinkingly at the sun, trembling as violently as a man dying of the chills. He stank. He could smell it himself.

Van Wyck looked up at him and almost gagged again.

Frick's skin was burning: first an angry, lobstery red, then dull brown. The change was fast, but Van Wyck was in no condition to judge the time it took. It was like watching a pet-store chameleon change from brown to green—only a chameleon wouldn't sway drunkenly, rocking left to right, ankles loose, legs and body stiff, head wobbling to the left when the body lurched to the right, lips drawn up from the bare teeth in a rictus of inexpressible pain. Blisters erupted like bubbles of boiling water on the old man's face and hands, but they only endured for seconds, swelling to globularity and then collapsing. When the skin was nearly black, the blistering stopped.

A low sobbing groan oozed from his mouth. It seemed interminable. It quavered without changing pitch.

But it finally did stop, and then he fell.

The sun was above the tree line.

His mind a horrified blank, Toby released Dorothy and gingerly approached the fallen man. He stood over him as if in a trance.

Van Wyck got up and joined him, powerless but desperately needing to do *something*. He didn't know what.

Dorothy couldn't come any closer.

Felix's eyes had sunk deeply into their sockets, where they shone flatly like the surfaces of stagnant pools viewed from a high-flying airplane. He worked his jaws silently, as if he had to chew the words soft before he could get them out of his mouth.

"Well?" he slurred. "Now do you believe me?"

A sudden seizure snapped his body out in all directions and held it there, rigid and quivering. His mouth gaped, tongue black and swollen. A whispered scream blossomed in his throat, then withered with a gargle. The seizure released him abruptly, and he lay broken at their feet, corrupt of flesh and truly dead. A miasmic cloud rose from him.

Toby spun away and stumbled, and was drastically and messily sick before his hands and knees could hit the ground.

XIV. THE CITADEL
OF REASON

One

Blanche spent the morning packing her suitcase.

For twenty years and more she'd served the Master, and in that time she'd never seriously considered leaving him. She wasn't sure she wanted to leave him even now. But one had to do what one could to survive.

During those twenty-odd years, and without being consciously aware of it, she had rebuilt her life around certain observations and expectations, which gradually hardened into immutable articles of faith carved into the granite of her psyche. Blanche had been raised in a no-nonsense Christian household, a psychological heritage that she could repress but never escape. Fundamental to this was the axiom that unrepentant sinners are to be roasted in Hell for all eternity. It was this belief that bound her most firmly to the Master. For her only hope of escaping everlasting torment was to escape death itself—and this would be accomplished when the Master fulfilled his promise to grant her the gift of vampirehood. Without it she would inevitably die. And her father's devils—the old man had been a lay preacher with a gift for painting lurid word pictures of the pains of damnation—would howl with infernal glee when her soul fell into their eager talons.

She'd served the Master because he was superior to any living human being—stronger, more knowledgeable, infinitely more cunning. People were his prey, his meat on the hoof, his chattels. He overtopped them like a god. She wanted to be like him; any other ambition was contemptible.

And now he was behaving like a fool—an arrogant, shortsighted, sloppy, mortal fool.

Consequently that meddling old busybody, Frick, was still on the loose. When the Master had told her that last night, she had been nearly frantic.

"Find him! Find him and finish him off!" she cried. "He can ruin us!"

"My dear, Mr. Frick is one of us now, whether he likes it or not."

What criminal foolishness! How many times had he explained to her that the subject's basic personality and intellectual capacity *survive* the transformation?

Thus Felix Frick, vampire or not, would remain a prying, snooping, dangerous sonofabitch, and he might very well retain his determination to destroy the Master and herself. Hadn't he, before they'd done anything to deserve his enmity, taken it upon himself to strip away the Master's secrets? Now he had reason to be their enemy, and the Master's prediction that he would not live through the day had proved to be wrong. Wasn't there a lesson to be learned in that?

"You've got to go back and track him down," Blanche had said, and she could have screamed when the Master only laughed.

"Blanche, I may be a vampire, but I'm not a bloodhound. My education never included the art of tracking a quarry through the woods. I couldn't find him now if I wanted to. But you're worrying needlessly.

370

"Mr. Frick will only last for as long as he can find shelter from the sun. And even supposing he can do that, sooner or later he'll have to have human blood. Somehow I doubt he'll be very skillful in obtaining it."

Blanche had been too upset to pose specific objections, and the Master persisted in misunderstanding her—willfully, no doubt.

"Are you afraid he's going to turn up *here* some night while I'm out, and break your neck for you? Honestly, Blanche, his chances of accomplishing that are virtually nil. And if he does show up, you have his gun. Immobilize him with a bullet to the heart, and I'll do the rest when I come home."

She didn't know what Frick might do, or try to do. Maybe it wouldn't be anything as straightforward as a murderous visit to their house—returning the call they'd paid on him, as it were. According to Nancy Kruzek, the man was a glutton for publicity. Maybe he'd find a way to get to one of the newspapers and tell his story there.

"Really, Blanche!" the Master had said. "Do you think any paper would dare to print it? No one will believe it. No matter whom Mr. Frick tries to talk to, he won't find anyone who'll believe him. But that's actually beside the point. Mr. Frick knows nothing about being a vampire, and this is an exceedingly difficult environment in which to learn. I promise you he won't last long enough to threaten us."

That promise, Blanche reflected as she packed her bags, sprang up from arrogance and wishful thinking.

And selfishness. The Master, as usual, was only thinking of himself. He might be able to escape at a moment's notice, but she was getting too old for a life on the run. If things got too hot for him in this country, he could always retreat to one of those damned banana republics that he liked so much and live in a cave in the jungle. *She* couldn't.

They would undoubtedly have to flee Millboro soon. They'd lose the house and all the money they'd put into it.

All right, the Master didn't have to worry about money. He had heaps of money, deposited in banks in half a dozen different countries, discreetly invested through dummy corporations, generating more money all the time. A vampire could always get rich, he'd explained. Rob your victims, rob their houses. Over the years, it added up. But *she* couldn't get rich. On her own, she'd be lucky if she could eke out any kind of living at all. What could she put down on a résumé? "For the past two decades, I was the personal servant of a vampire . . ." And who knew what warrants might still be out on her? It was all computerized these days. Without the Master's protection, she'd always be looking over her shoulder. In his service she had committed a thousand crimes. How could she know what the authorities had on her?

He was resting now. Unless he had need to remain active, he became dormant during the daytime hours. It wasn't sleep as mortals knew it; he didn't dream. He was down there in the basement, behind a securely locked door, with the windows painted opaque green and shuttered with plywood to keep out the sunlight. He would stay there until the sun went down, and thus be of no help at all throughout the day.

She finished packing her bags and looked out the window.

What she saw made her sick to her stomach with dread.

Two

Toby crawled away from the spot where he had been sick and rested on his hands and knees, gulping in the damp dawn air.

His mind kept showing it, over and over again, like an

instant replay that couldn't be turned off: the old guy standing there, hale and hearty, and suddenly getting the shakes; Chief Van Wyck going down with his hands over his face; and finally Mr. Frick collapsing to the earth and turning into carrion as fast as white bread turning into burnt toast.

Now do you believe me?

Holy God, Mr. Frick, I believe you, I believe anything you say— Jesus help me if I don't. Just promise not to make me look at you every time I close my eyes from now on.

He heard Van Wyck say, "Let's get out of here," and was grateful to the chief for helping him back to his feet. In the minute or two it took him to pick up Thornall's sword and return to the backseat of the chief's car, a sanity-saving aura of unreality had already cloaked itself around the incident, and he was able to talk about it. But he did feel a little light-headed.

"What're we going to do?" he said.

For some moments the question floated on a lake of silence. Then Van Wyck sighed and said, "I'll have to think about it."

Dorothy sat and stared through the windshield at the house. Now that the sun was up, it was only a pile of rotting boards and mossy brick. Her fear of it was gone, leaving in its place a wordless void.

But she knew, without needing words for it, that Felix had told the truth. Any doubts she'd entertained had decayed with his body.

"I'll tell you what I *won't* do," said Van Wyck. "I'm not going to radio headquarters and tell them that I've seen a vampire."

He knew, Dorothy thought. *He knew what'd happen to him when the sun came up. He waited for it. Maybe he knew it was the only thing that'd convince us—if we saw it, from start to finish, with our own eyes.*

She found words, then.

373

"He was telling the truth," she said. "And the way he died proves it. It was the only way he could get us to believe him."

But Van Wyck was still thinking in terms of exotic diseases, chemical warfare experiments gone awry, genetic tampering—anything but that other. But Frick's statement was like a battering ram pounding rhythmically upon the door, and he doubted he could long keep it from breaking in.

"He must have *thought* he was telling the truth. . . ."

"Shit, man!" Toby's interruption was half a whisper, half a cry of panic. "Don't you believe your own eyes? You think the man was jiving us? You think some special effects artist did that to him? Holy fuck!" He shook his head. "The reverend was right. I thought he was crazy, but he was telling it like it is."

"Mr. Hicks . . ."

"God damn you, Chief, you *saw* it!"

"We all saw it," Dorothy said.

The door broke down.

He'd seen too much. The truth was a pillaging horde, and it overran his defenses. He suffered numbly as the citadel of reason was sacked.

"What are we going to *do*?" Toby said again. He reached over the seat and seized Van Wyck's shoulder.

Van Wyck felt like a suspect caving in after endless hours of interrogation. He spoke wearily, but also with a subtle feeling of relief.

"Obviously we have to settle with this Dr. Emerson. But we can't do that just yet. We have to find out more about him. And we can't use police resources. At the end, we're going to have to do something that falls a long way outside normal police procedures." He found he couldn't say *We'll have to kill him.*

"What more do we need to know?" Dorothy said. "Felix told us this man is a vampire. He wasn't lying."

374

"Felix also told us he investigated him at some length, on his own," Van Wyck said. "Before we do anything else, I'd like to have a look at any information he might've gathered.

"We've also got to do something about Felix. My men check this place once a day. They'll find him. And his neighbors might notice that he's missing. I think we'd better arrange it so I can report it before the patrol stumbles over it. Then I can be on firm legal ground when I search Felix's house."

They spent some minutes working up a cover story.

Toby, having been asked by Van Wyck to report any strangers in his neighborhood, called last night after seeing a man answering Felix's description prowling around his backyard. Van Wyck came over and questioned him, not realizing at first that the prowler had been Mr. Frick. The stranger had since vanished into the woods, but at first light Van Wyck, unable to get back to sleep, decided to have a look at the Schuylerville Nursing Home. Why not? He had reason to believe the place was being used for illegal activities. Now that the watch on it had been slackened, maybe it was being used again.

And there he'd found the body. He took a look inside the nursing home, found nothing, and returned to the corpse. Because what remained of the face looked familiar, he ventured to remove the wallet to check for identification. After learning that the deceased was a township resident, he radioed headquarters for detectives and an ambulance.

By the time they arrived, Toby had been dropped off at his grandmother's house and Dorothy was waiting at Van Wyck's; and Van Wyck was hoping the cover story would pass muster. It ought to, he supposed; his men were accustomed to taking his word for things.

Randy Musante took one look at Felix's remains and promptly lost his breakfast.

"Judas Priest!" he gasped. "How many times does that make, Chief?"

"Five."

Musante didn't look that way again until the EMTs zipped Felix into a body bag and were loading him onto the ambulance.

"What was his name again, Chief?"

"Felix Frick."

"Sounds familiar."

"It should. He got his name in the local papers often enough."

"Oh, yeah! He's the guy who gave the mayor hell about those tax sales. Now I remember. What the hell was he doing all the way out here?"

"God knows," Van Wyck said. "Soon as we can get a warrant, we'll search his place and see what we can find."

"He liked to dig into things," Musante recalled. "The mess his clothes were in, he must've liked to dig into things *literally*, too. Course, we can't forget the Matthiesen case. Somebody conked her out and brought her here. Maybe the same folks wasted Mr. Frick. Maybe he was digging into their business and they didn't appreciate it."

Van Wyck nodded. "Sounds good." Sometimes Musante, for all his glass stomach, was a hell of a detective; he'd noticed the state of Felix's clothing even as he was turning away to heave. "Let's check out the premises, meanwhile."

"You want the county crime lab?"

"Better not. We've had 'em out here once already, and it didn't help us. Let's let our boys handle it."

Every local police chief was aware of the county's budgetary problems. The mobile crime lab was a nice resource; no single municipality had a right to hog it. Van Wyck's reluctance to call for it again so soon wouldn't raise any eyebrows.

The police were at Frick's house.

Blanche watched them going in and out the front door. One of them was even poking around in the shrubbery. Her imagination went on fast forward, so that she could quite clearly see them trotting across the street to come knocking on her door.

Just as clearly, she saw herself snatching up the suitcases—right now, before the cops came—and hotfooting it out the door. Given her car and a few minutes' head start, they'd never catch her: there were too many roads leading out of the township, and not enough police cars to cover them. By sundown she could be safely on the back roads of Pennsylvania.

The vision was so real that she caught her feet trying to turn her from the window, her legs quaking as they were pulled along by the same yearning. But she refused to lose control. She clamped down hard on the windowsill and willed herself to stand firm. *Think* about this! Mustn't go off half-cocked.

What did it mean? Obviously they'd found Frick. But where had they found him, and under what circumstances? He might have been caught away from shelter by the rising sun, and withered by it; someone might've found the body and summoned the police. In that case, the crisis might not yet be at hand. Frick would be just another inexplicable death. Naturally they'd search his home for clues, but they wouldn't find anything that would point across the street; she and the Master had taken care of that, and thoroughly.

That was the most likely possibility. But unfortunately there were others.

For all she knew, Frick had succumbed to the bloodlust

and attacked someone. Worst of all, he might have been captured. And if his mind were clear enough, he could tell a tale that would put her and the Master in acute jeopardy. Even if the police didn't believe him, they'd want to question the Master. And even if he could fend them off with his answers, the margin of safety would have vanished.

Frustratingly too late, it occurred to her that they should have bought a police radio scanner.

Well, either the cops knew about the Master's role in Frick's downfall, or they didn't. Meanwhile, she had to get out of the house before they could question her. Let the Master handle the questions, after dark. It wouldn't be the first time.

She took the suitcase from the bed and went downstairs. All the downstairs windows were curtained: no risk from prying eyes. She paused to look around the living room.

Blanche had grown up in a drafty frame house with a leaky roof that had too many people under it; to her, this house on Whittier Avenue was an *Arabian Nights* palace. For most of her life she'd never dreamed of living in a place like this, let alone owning one. *This is* mine, she chanted to herself. *My name is on the deed. Blanche Milliken, homeowner. And homeowner in a prestige community, to boot.* Here it was easy to believe that the more desperate years of her existence had been only a nightmare. Here she never though about her father flaying her backside with his belt while bellowing passages of Scripture; the cruddy rented room, where the thin walls forced her to listen to the whore next door servicing her johns; all those sleazy motels along the Gulf of Mexico, where the air-conditioning never worked and the bedbugs never slept; bickering roommates, snooping landlords, other people's filthy babies yowling round the clock—here on Whittier Avenue, it was as if those other places had never been.

She just hoped it wouldn't kill her when she lost this house.

She slunk out through the garage door and locked it after her, loaded the suitcases in the trunk of the car, and drove past Frick's house unmolested.

Three

Van Wyck saw a car back out of the Emersons' driveway and watched it as it passed. A woman, probably Mrs. Emerson, was driving. She was alone.

Of course she's alone. Her husband is a vampire, he can't go tooling around in the middle of the day. He's holed up in a coffin somewhere. Van Wyck shook his head to rid it of what were, at the moment, unproductive thoughts.

Soon he'd call off the search and dismiss the men. They hadn't found anything to confirm Felix's story; but then, they hadn't heard Felix's story. Their chief hadn't told them.

Without attracting attention to himself, Van Wyck had managed to get a close look at the bathroom. If Emerson had tied Felix to the towel rack over the bathtub and bled him like a kosher slaughterman, no sign remained of it. The tiles were sparkling clean. A closer examination, assisted by crime-scene technology, might come up with blood in the cracks, microscopic particles of burnt gunpowder in the rug, scraps of hair and fiber that could be matched to the Emersons, but then Van Wyck would have to explain how he knew a crime had been committed here, and that was devoutly to be shunned.

Still, Musante was having a ball with evidence they'd turned up pertaining to some of Felix's other interests.

"Chief, he could've wrote a book with all the dirt he had!" The detective sergeant was sitting on Felix's couch, the coffee table in front of him strewn with thickly stuffed manila folders and heaps of loose paper. "Not that anyone'd want to read it—nothing here but stuff on Millboro. But goddamn, if you were a politician in this town, you couldn't blow a fart without Mr. Frick knowin' all about it."

"Maybe we oughta just hang onto it," said one of the detectives. "Show it to a few councilmen the next time they vote on the police department budget. We could all get raises."

"Just wrap it up and seal it," Van Wyck said. "We don't want to get involved with any of it until the prosecutor tells us that we can and has a court order to go with it."

It'd be a headache later on, but for the time being he was grateful to Felix for leaving so much political dirt behind. *It'll sure as hell keep everybody's wheels spinning while I go vampire hunting.*

Since sunrise, the little men in lab smocks and three-piece suits inside Van Wyck's head had been laboring to repair the breaches in their walls. *You don't really understand what you saw this morning,* they kept insisting. *You know there's no such thing as vampires. For Christ's sake, Van Wyck, what're you going to do? Bust into Dr. Emerson's house and pound a stake through his heart? You know you can't do that.*

In truth Van Wyck didn't know what he was going to do.

He only hoped Thornall could tell him.

When Thornall woke and found Toby sitting close beside the bed, he knew the young man's doubts had passed away.

"You saw?"

Toby nodded. "I saw it."

"And you believe?"

"Oh, hell . . . I don't know." Toby got up and went to look out the window. "I know what I saw. And I know

380

what I heard. And I'm pretty sure of what I have to do about it. But I still don't understand it. I just don't see how it can be real.''

''Sit by me and tell me about it.''

It was a deeply troubling tale. Never, in all the years he'd hunted them, had it occurred to Thornall that one of these soulless beings might be capable of sacrificing itself for the greater good. How could one of them desire anything but the blood of God's children? It had been Thornall's credo that all of them, each and every one, were nothing but demons in the flesh, despoilers of the soul, bond-slaves to the Prince of Hell. And acting on this faith, he had destroyed every one of them that had ever crossed his path.

Ah, Lord! Have I been no better than a Popish inquisitor, who persecutes the innocent in Thy name? Have I misconstrued my mission? If I have set my sword's edge against just one poor tormented soul who still craved the love of God, then I have sinned, and failed in my trust. And he knew, now, that it must have been so. Otherwise God would have sustained him and allowed his to be the hand that smote down the great vampire, the bloated enemy. *I am like Moses, who for his sin was denied passage into the Promised Land. And yet like Moses I am allowed a glimpse of it, a clear view from afar—and for this I must give thanks.*

''You all right, Reverend?''

Toby's question brought him back, and he sighed for the burden that was on his soul.

''What are we going to do, Reverend?''

''You have the sword.''

Surprisingly, Toby grinned. ''Yeah! I almost lost it, though, I was so freaked out. I'm surprised I didn't leave it lying there. I still can't remember it falling out of my hand. But don't worry, I still have it.''

''Good, my son. It may be that this sword is the only weapon which God has ordained for this battle, and the only one by which you might prevail. Now listen to me.

''This vampire, this monster, this fiend in human form,

381

is a great deceiver. He will promise you anything, he will blind you with his honeyed words—so you must be resolute. Remember that he's not a man but only the shell of one, possessed by by an unclean spirit. The man has long ago been lost. Take up the sword, and as soon as you come near him, strike. If you hesitate, he will destroy you.

"Remember that he has done murder—and much worse—a thousand times, and it would no more trouble him to murder you than it would to swat a fly. Your life will be at hazard. You were a soldier, my boy; you understand that. Kill or be killed."

Toby nodded. Basic training, combat training, the long months spent patrolling a supposedly demilitarized frontier, never knowing when a sniper was going to let fly at you—it hadn't been so long ago. Not even a year. He'd never killed anybody, and he was glad he hadn't; but a lot of U.S. government money and research had gone into making sure he knew how. And it was all still there, still close to the surface. There hadn't been much time to bury it.

"You must dismember him with the sword," Thornall said, "but even that won't be the end of him. Afterward, you must gather up the fragments and arrange so that they will lie exposed to the sun for a whole day. He's old. I've followed him for over fifty years. When I started, there was peach fuzz on my cheeks, my skin was smooth, my hair was black. You can see how much I've aged. But *he* has never changed. He is now as he was fifty years ago and will be fifty years from now unless you end it. In him the vampire spirit has a long-established stronghold, and nothing less than a full day's sun will suffice to burn it away.

"Above all, my son, don't listen to him! He was once a clever man, a doctor. I don't know how long he's been a vampire, but it's been at least six decades. That's how long he's had to sharpen his cunning. Without the help of God, no man could hope to challenge him."

Toby felt like he was trapped in quicksand, with the only way out through the bottom of the pit.

Dorothy started when Van Wyck unlocked his door.

She'd fallen into a doze on his living room couch. Exhausted as she was, she knew she wouldn't be able to stay awake for long, but she'd wanted to take her nap outside, in the sun.

It was the first time she'd wanted to be outside since the day she woke in the cellar of the nursing home. Little by little, too gradually for perception, she'd been shedding her phobia of sunlight. She remembered back several days when she couldn't feel safe unless she was indoors, preferably with the blinds down and the curtains drawn. At the time, she'd explained it to herself as a species of agoraphobia arising in reaction to the shock of Bruce Randall's attack on her. You go outside, you have a life-threatening, mind-blowing experience, and voilà: you don't want to go outside anymore. No mystery in it.

But that was before she saw Felix turn into carrion when the sun came up.

She stayed outside for as long as she could, exploring Van Wyck's vegetable garden, sitting on the back-porch steps and trying to think rational thoughts. The sun climbed higher. Her skin faintly tingled, like the tingle of a sunburn coming on, and she fell prey to a sensation of being covertly watched from the neighboring houses. It left her as soon as she went indoors to phone for current temperatures. The voice on the tape said it was seventy-one degrees outside, and she shook her head. *Feels more like eighty-one.*

Once inside, she kept finding excuses not to go back out. Sleep caught up to her in the living room.

A dream caught her, too.

She was a bride waiting to speak her vows, and in the

subterranean logic of dreams, it didn't seem strange that her wedding dress was stained and moldy, and that she was getting married in the cellar of the Schuylerville Nursing Home and not a church. Nor did she question the fact that Chris, her groom, had dirt and cobwebs on his tuxedo and a gaping hole in his chest. Bruce Randall, black-faced with corruption, with his head lolling uselessly over his shoulder, was the best man. And Felix, as she had last seen him, stood beside her like a father, to give her away.

They were waiting for the minister, only she knew it wouldn't be a minister. They heard him moving around upstairs, heavy feet thumping ponderously on the floor over their heads. At this point Dorothy wanted to scream and break loose, but in the way of such dreams she was powerless to move.

The cellar door rattled open. Van Wyck's key rattled in the lock. Dorothy woke with the scream rising in her throat. She swallowed it back.

"Are you all right?" Van Wyck said.

"I was asleep." She didn't want to talk about the dream. "You're back so soon."

"We've finished with Frick's house for the time being."

"Find anything?"

"Nothing that'll help." He sat down beside her and told her about the search. He looked beat, she thought. *Like he won't be able to get up from the couch.*

"Gotta go out to Alabama Road and see what Thornall has to say," he muttered. "I don't know what the fuck we're gonna do next. Maybe he'll know. He seems to be the only one who *does* know."

Dorothy's earlier cogitations returned to her. She had reached conclusions that had to be discussed, but she found it hard to begin.

"Ed . . . how did Felix become a vampire? Or whatever he was when he died."

384

"He said this Dr. Emerson drank his blood. Isn't that the way it's always done?"

"Whatever Felix was . . . would you say that boy who jumped me in the parking lot—was he the same thing? The same as Felix?"

"I guess I'd have to." *And the same as Norman Rubin, Arthur Volden, and your husband,* Van Wyck added silently. He'd seen the bodies. They were the same.

"So if Felix was a vampire," said Dorothy, "they were *all* vampires?"

"If he was, they were." For Christ's sake, hadn't half the men in the department seen Rubin die after they'd dragged him out into the sun?

"And they probably all became vampires in the same way," she said.

"I don't know, Dot. They must have, I guess."

"Ed . . . When the Randall boy attacked me . . . I mean, when I saw the doctor, he found a cut on my neck. A scratch. It was small, but it must have bled."

She went on, the words coming because they had to now; she couldn't have held them back.

"After I came home, I knew there was something wrong with me, even though nothing showed up in the blood and urine tests. I thought it was all in my mind. But I was afraid to go out, unless it was well after sundown. I could see in the dark. I thought I could hear things that I'd never heard before. I was thirsty all the time and I couldn't quench it, no matter how much I drank, no matter what.

"I thought I was having a mental breakdown—but I wasn't, was I? It was worse than that. Ed, that boy got some of my blood. That's what was wrong with me. I was turning into . . . one of them. Like the boy. Like Felix. Poor Chris, God help him—he was one. That's why I couldn't go into my own house that day. Because of Chris. I knew what he was, and I knew he was there. I didn't understand it then, but I think I do now. It was the same when we went looking

385

for Felix. I knew he was there. And it must be because . . . because I'm *tainted*. My blood . . . Bruce Randall drank it. . ."

She couldn't go on. Van Wyck had to hold her. She wept silently. He tried to soothe her.

"It's all right. Whatever happened, you're not like them, you're not the same. You can stand the sun." He kissed her hair.

She battled to regain control of herself and won, and looked up at him with red-rimmed eyes.

"I'm getting better," she said. "Somehow it didn't take. Randall must have been stopped before he could really do anything. My hearing is getting back to normal, and being in the sun doesn't bother me anywhere near as much as it did a few days ago." Then she pulled away from him a little, and added:

"Don't you see? I *know* Felix was telling the truth! We have to believe him. There's no choice anymore. We have to stop this before there are more like him . . . and the others."

Van Wyck wasn't sure he understood her—not intellectually, at any rate. But he believed her. She was speaking from experience. He helped her up from the couch.

"Let's go see the reverend," he said.

Four

There was so much more he had to tell the young man—needed desperately to tell him—but he didn't have the strength. The words formed in his mind but lacked the power to make their way out through his lips.

The woman who had served the vampire for the past two

decades: she was only mortal. He needed her to be his agent in the daylight hours, when he couldn't stir lest God smite him. She was a threat, but it would be a sin to slay her; losing her master, she might yet repent. Her soul might still be saved. It was vital to say so.

But Thornall slept.

Blanche sat in her car, flogging her brain as if it were a failing horse that were her only hope of safety.

She'd parked in the big lot outside the municipal complex, only fifty yards or so from the new police station. If they were looking for her, this was the last place they'd expect to find her. None of the cops going in and out the doors even bothered to glance in her direction.

The Master had been careless. Why had he done his hunting *here*, where he lived? Any time he wanted to feed, she would have happily chauffeured him anywhere. Millboro lay within easy reach of boroughs that were almost cities, sleazy boardwalk towns with high crime rates, isolated housing developments in otherwise rural townships. Why here?

Well, he wanted to do *experiments*, god damn him—like he was some kind of fucking anthropologist lording it over the natives of a South Sea island. He said he wanted to keep an eye on the results.

Some results.

She listed his mistakes. It was a long list. But the worst mistake of all, Blanche thought, had sprung from that idiotic experiment with that high school kid. Hell's bells, you couldn't control the damned brats when they were alive and placed under supervision at school. How on earth could you expect to control them if you turned them into vampires?

The Master's new pet got loose and attacked a woman—and instead of finishing her off, he let her get away, for the sake of his idiotic experiments. And then did the same damn fool thing when he met her husband. Real smart. The big genius. And he shrugged it off when Blanche learned that the township police chief had personally shot the husband. End of problem, according to the Master. Sure. And the moon is made of green cheese.

Now that same police chief was rummaging through Felix Frick's stuff, and as careful as she and the Master had been to remove anything that could link them to Frick, the way things were going, she wouldn't be surprised if it turned out that they'd *missed* something. Wouldn't that be swell?

The whole idea of successful vampirism, as Blanche had come to understand it, was that you didn't let your victims *live*. Survivors were a threat. Did he really need her to point that out to him?

She stopped short of wondering whether she really needed him. Her habit of servitude to him was too ingrained for that.

What was that woman's name, the one that got away? Nancy Kruzek knew her. Her name was . . .

Matthiesen. Dorothy Matthiesen.

"We have to chop him into pieces with the sword," Toby said, "and put the pieces out in the sun so they'll die."

That's great, Van Wyck thought. *Take a sword and chop a man to pieces. Just like in the Middle Ages. Maybe we can burn a few heretics while we're at it.*

Thornall was sleeping. Emma Plews, having no idea what had been going on, was down the street gossiping with a friend. It was going on three in the afternoon.

"I just wish we could get it over with," Toby said, "but I don't guess we can go marching up to his door in broad daylight, with the whole neighborhood watching. We'll have to wait till after people go to bed."

388

"Where *is* the sword, Toby?" Dorothy said.

"Under the reverend's bed. I put it there so Gramma wouldn't see it."

Van Wyck looked from Thornall to Toby and shook his head. "I'm sorry; I just don't see how we can do this. I'm a cop, not a butcher."

"We have to do it, Chief. But I'll do it alone if I have to. Just don't you throw my ass in jail afterward."

"You can't do it alone," Dorothy said. "None of us can. We're in this together."

"Dorothy—"

"I'm not looking forward to it, Ed. But I'm not staying behind, either."

"Mrs. Matthiesen, you've got guts. But this is no job for a woman."

She didn't mind Toby saying so, but he was wrong. "It's no job for a man, either," she said. "For anybody. I'm not going along as the token woman, though. You'll need me."

She explained why, and Toby accepted it.

"Hi, Nancy. It's Blanche."

"Hi, Blanche! What's up?"

"Oh, nothing. I'm stuck at this garage, having my car fixed, so I thought we could chat a little to pass the time."

Blanche was at a pay phone in a lobby of the public meeting hall. The hall wasn't in use today, and she stood scant risk of being interrupted.

They nattered idly for several minutes, until Blanche judged it was safe to get down to brass tacks.

"By the way, how's that friend of yours, the one you told me about? Mrs. Matthiesen."

"Dorothy? Gee, Blanche, I really don't know. I haven't seen her for days. I phoned once, but nobody answered. I think she's out of town. After what she's been through . . ."

"What? The attack?"

"You mean you haven't heard?"

"Heard what?"

"Holy shit, Blanche, Dotty's husband's dead!" Nancy lowered her voice. "Can you believe it—the *police* shot him!"

She went on to tell Blanche all about the shooting. And more.

"Paula Herbst—you don't know her, she lives across the street from the Matthiesens—saw it. Dot came home with Ed Van Wyck, he's our police chief, and then two more cops came along. They went inside, Dotty and the chief, and *Ka-boom!* Chris was shot. They had to call an ambulance. But Chris died before they could get him to the hospital.

"That's not all. Chief Von Wyck, he suspended himself right away; but Mayor Leib revoked it and put him back on duty. The way I hear it, Dotty says Chris *attacked* her, and he would've killed her if the chief hadn't shot him.

"Keep this under your hat, Blanche, but I happen to know there's more to it. Apparently the chief's been seeing quite a lot of Dorothy. Well, he's divorced, he's a good-looking guy, and Dotty's marriage, it was on the rocks—but still!"

Nancy went on for quite a bit. For all her protestations that she wasn't a gossip, once she started, she couldn't stop. Blanche was only able to terminate the conversation when she ran out of coins for the phone.

She walked slowly back to her car.

If only she had known this earlier. They'd been able to keep it out of the papers, although the whole township knew about the shooting; but this was the first Blanche had heard of the woman having an affair with the police chief.

The situation was even more dangerous than she'd realized. The Master, for once, didn't know his peril.

Well, leave it to good ol' Blanche to pick up the pieces—as usual. She'd gotten so that she would do it automatically.

Anyway, what else could she do? If they got him before he could make her a vampire, where did that leave her? After all her years of faithful service, what would she have to show for it?

Sighing, she turned and walked over to the tax assessor's office, to see if she could unobtrusively find out where the police chief lived.

Five

They left the Plews house before Toby's grandmother came home to ask what the police chief and a strange white woman were doing there. They took Van Wyck's car, so he could check in with headquarters every half hour or so to see if there was anything he ought to know about. He let it be known that he was dog-tired after his short night's sleep and needed to get away to rest and think. As long as he was in touch by radio, no one would think twice about him not being there in person.

They looked for a place where they could expose the pieces of Emerson's body to the sun without somebody stumbling over them and running for the nearest phone, once he'd finished puking.

Millboro was developing like mad, but it was a big township and it still had thousands of acres of untended woodland, swamp, and brush. Except for the blocks around Alabama Road, practically the entire northwestern corner of the township was taken up by Dutchman's Bog and the woods that grew within it and around it.

The bog had often featured in the news in recent years,

largely because of the statewide preoccupation with toxic dumping. It was an old story to Van Wyck, but new and sensational to the media.

Here and there, tucked out of sight, were pools of standing water that could burn the naked skin, small mountains of rusted metal drums, and places where poisons mingled in the earth, seeping down toward the layer of water-bearing rock that was the primary source of drinking water for all Millboro and beyond. Some of these sites had been in use since the 1930s. Trucks would come from as far away as Brooklyn, dump their loads in the dead of night, and move on. Over the years their comings and goings had worn many narrow tracks that weren't on the map. Van Wyck knew most of them.

There were other dump sites that weren't hot news and never would be. These were the spots where generations of township residents habitually deposited their trash, rather than pay a carter to take it away. Millboro had an efficient trash disposal system now: all you had to do was leave your garbage on the curb, and the township would take it away. Only a few of the older residents still followed the old rutted trails to the unofficial dumps. Here reposed vast collections of broken and empty bottles, weather-hardened blocks of newspapers and magazines, splintered furniture, threadbare tires, and used-up appliances made unrecognizable by rust and dirt. The council had passed laws against it, but woodland dumping was a township tradition that wouldn't quite die. The dumps were unsightly, but nobody saw them. The laws weren't worth the trouble to enforce. Van Wyck knew most of these sites, too.

"Let's not pick one that's still popular," Toby said. "There's one site a couple hundred yards off Bower Street; the Nature Study Club goes there every day, turning the junk over to look for snakes and salamanders. We want someplace nice and private."

"I know a place nobody uses anymore," said Van Wyck, and before five o'clock rolled around, they found it.

Police chief or not, he's got to come home sometime, Blanche thought.

She watched the house from one of the township's new miniparks across the street. It wasn't as close as she would have liked, but it was as close as she dared. One thing about Millboro, it was full of prying eyes. *They may not want to get involved, but they sure do like to watch.* Somebody was sure to make a fuss if a strange car parked on his street for any length of time, and somebody was sure to be watching if she tried to break into Van Wyck's house.

That would have to be left to the Master.

Having shot Mr. Matthiesen and bedded the man's wife, the police chief would have a personal interest in finding out why the woman had been abducted, and by whom, and why her husband had attacked her on sight. There had been too many unexplained deaths in his township recently, and he more than anybody else would be under pressure to find the explanation. If the hunt ever made its way to the Master's doorstep, it would be the police chief who led it.

The obvious solution was to kill the police chief. But even if the Master didn't want to go that far, it was still vital to find out how much the chief knew.

And if the Matthiesen woman ever remembered anything about being taken to that abandoned building in the woods, her policeman boyfriend would be the first to know. She had to go, too; Blanche had said so from the beginning. Not even the Master could afford to leave all those loose ends dangling. Loose ends had a way of tangling around your ankles when you least expected it.

Blanche watched Van Wyck's house for the time being because she couldn't think what else to do. If the chief came home soon, took a leisurely supper, and didn't go out again, it might mean that Frick's death had stymied him. But if he didn't come home at all, or came and dashed right back out again, it could mean he was busily following up some leads. Either way, the Master had to know.

Do you want to go down the chute with him? Get out while you can! You've packed your bags; you can go right now. Let Mr. Know-it-all Vampire try to solve his problems without you for a change.

But the truth was that Blanche had been with the Master for so long that she couldn't envision life without him.

And he made a promise to her, and after twenty years of slaving for him, she'd be damned—literally—if she couldn't find a way to make him keep it.

"What about his wife?" said Dorothy.

Van Wyck was maneuvering the car out of the woods and had nothing to say until they were back on the road.

"You saw her drive past while you were at Felix's," Dorothy said, "so she can't be . . . she can't be a vampire. Not if she goes out in the middle of the day."

"How can she live with him, then?" Toby said. "Why isn't she one, too?"

Van Wyck had been thinking about that, off and on, for hours.

"If Emerson can't go out in the sun," he said, "he might need someone who can. She could do a lot for him. Spy out the territory, gather information, run errands—maybe even protect him during the day. In her own way, she's probably as dangerous as he is."

"So what do we do about her, Chief?"

"Shit, Hicks, I don't know!" Chopping up some kind of monster was one thing. Killing a woman in cold blood was something else. But could he arrest her? And on what charges—aiding and abetting a vampire?

"Chief, if she's been working for him, she knows the score. He might not be able to live in Millboro without her.

e'd have to trust her, right? So all those people that he's illed, she's as much to blame as he is—even if she never illed anybody herself. You're a lawman. You know the guy who drives the getaway car's as guilty as the guy who pulls he trigger. Hey, there was a case down South a couple ears ago where the gunman copped a plea and the fuckin' *river* got the electric chair!"

"I know, I know. But let's cross that bridge when we ome to it, okay?"

It was not so much a suggestion as a cry from the heart.

Dorothy hadn't thought of Mrs. Emerson at all—not un- il Felix told how she'd stood by and watched while Emer- on drank his blood.

Watching the news on TV, she often asked herself, *How an such things be possible?* Two teenage girls set up a child prostitution ring so they can earn money to buy crack. Sci- ntists blithely invent a weapon to kill every man, woman, nd child in a major city. An anonymous stranger shoves a young musician into the path of a subway train.

Why boggle at a woman who chooses to serve a vampire?

And it had to be the woman's free choice. She had all the daylight hours in which to run away if she didn't choose to serve.

Dorothy had never understood human evil, and she didn't understand it now.

Six

Sunset.

The police chief still hadn't come home, and Blanche's back was sore from sitting in the car.

She wondered if it was safe to go back home. The Master would be getting up soon, and he would have to be told that the police had been at Frick's house. Maybe they were still there, spying on her house with the old snoop's binoculars. Maybe they were only waiting for her to return before they came across the street to pound on her door.

She almost missed it when Van Wyck's car came around a bend in the road, but he had to pause for oncoming traffic before he could make a left turn into his driveway, and that gave her a second chance to catch him.

Because of the damned hedge that grew there, she couldn't see Van Wyck's front door. But the car was right in front of her now, and she had the presence of mind to turn on her headlight, stamping the floor switch to activate the high beams.

The policeman had a woman with him.

Blanche had never seen Dorothy Matthiesen, and she didn't have an unobstructed view of this woman's face—but who else could it be? Van Wyck was divorced, Nancy said. Mrs. Matthiesen wasn't home; she'd been committing adultery with the chief—it had to be her.

The Escort turned into the driveway as Blanche started her engine.

For a long time the Master silently pondered the information. *At least he's thinking about it,* Blanche thought. She didn't interrupt him.

Finally he said, "It was to be expected that the police, once Mr. Frick's body was found, would want to search his home for evidence. I wish I knew where they found the body. Well, that might be in the newspapers tomorrow. Meanwhile, I don't see any real cause for alarm. We left nothing among Mr. Frick's belongings that could implicate us in his death. For all they know, he died of natural causes."

"With a nice fresh *cut* on his wrist?" Blanche said. "They won't miss that. And what'll they make of it?"

"They won't find it was the cause of death, my dear. As indeed it wasn't. However, you raise a good point. I ought to do an autopsy on the next person who fails to survive the transformation. I've been wanting to do that for years, but I've never had the facilities to make it a fruitful exercise."

"So it doesn't bother you that the police were right across the street from us today?"

"A miss is as good as a mile," the Master said. "It'll be just another death they can't explain. Still, if it makes you happy, I suppose I could ease up for a while. We don't want too many unexplained deaths in Millboro. As you've been good enough to point out, I can feed in other towns."

Now *he comes to that conclusion?* Blanche snorted.

"I guess it doesn't worry you that the police chief is carrying on with that Matthiesen woman, either."

The Master felt like going back down to his room in the basement and locking the door behind him. *She doesn't mind what I did to the woman's husband, but she can't stand the thought of the widow consoling herself with the affections of the policeman.* Not for the first time, he reconsidered his promise to her. There seemed to be a lot that could be said against loosing a prudish vampire upon the world.

"All right," he said, "I promise you that when the opportunity arises, I'll make an end of Mrs. Matthiesen. Will that satisfy you?"

"The police chief. . ."

"My dear woman! In one breath you're entreating me to lay off; in the next, you're proposing that I depopulate the town! Furthermore, killing the police chief wouldn't help at all. They'd just appoint another one—and *that* would be the one killing that they'd never close the books on."

It galled her when he was right, so much so that the next

question flew out of her mouth before she could think about it.

"When are you going to make me a vampire?"

He turned eyes on her that would have quailed a pirate but she had seen that look before and was no longer much fazed by it.

"I've been waiting for it for twenty years," she went on. "Meanwhile I'm getting old. My back is *killing* me. I could have a stroke. I could have a heart attack. These things come out of the blue; I could have one tomorrow. It's time you stopped stringing me along, Doctor. You owe me, and you know it."

"Blanche, now is not the time—"

"Damn you, it's *never* the time!"

He tried to placate her. It wasn't as if he'd never paused to give fair consideration to the matter. He had. As a physician, he knew her fears of strokes and heart attacks were groundless. Blanche was a strong woman, more so than others half her age. There were years of useful service left in her.

But if she were psychologically unfit . . . *She's losing her nerve. This hysterical fear of the police chief proves it.* If he'd told her once, he'd told her a thousand times: the wise vampire never attacks the local power structure. Kill off the peasants, but don't touch the police chief, the mayor, or the priest.

"Blanche, I've given you my word and I intend to keep it. But right now, as you yourself have been saying for weeks, we are at a delicate juncture in our career. If we really are in danger—and you're the one who says we are—then it would be folly to disrupt the arrangement which has served us so well for so many years. Don't you think it would be much wiser to wait until the immediate crisis has passed?"

He was right again. She knew it, and she didn't have an answer to it, but she wasn't about to cave in altogether.

"After you kill Mrs. Matthiesen," she said. "It has to be soon. I can't go on like this."

He believed her. Their partnership was at an end. She was approaching the limit of her reliability and would soon lose her usefulness to him. He would have to start looking for another servant.

"All right, Blanche," he said. "I'm agreeable to that. It's just that I've come to rely on your service, and I know I'll be lost without it. But in all justice, I see I have to give you what you ask."

If he could have felt regret, he would have regretted lying to her. She had lost her nerve, and simply could not be entrusted with the gift of vampirehood.

"Meanwhile," he added, "why don't you relax? Go out and have a few drinks. I was planning to stay home tonight, so I won't be needing you. I want to study some of my notes."

He got up and left her in possession of the living room, already planning how to dispose of her body when the time came.

Dorothy sat and tried to watch the six o'clock news while Van Wyck busied himself on the telephone, getting up-to-date on police matters and making sure this or that detail was taken care of. It was comfortably mundane: petty vandalism at the middle school, speeders on Beak Hill Road, a new radio set for car number twelve, a transmission job for thirteen, a retirement dinner for Sergeant Pezzuoli. Life goes on.

And my life will go on, too, she thought, *once I get done helping my friends chop a man into little bitty pieces. Not because he's an enemy soldier come over to conquer America, or a sex criminal caught red-handed in a day-care center, but because he's a vampire.* (She kept seeing images from old horror films. Bela Lugosi: *"I never drink . . . wine."* Christopher Lee writhing on a stake. And at the drive-in, *Blacula*. And on TV, *'Salem's Lot* crawling with the undead. Jejune imaginings, cheap thrills. Juvenile jollies. Only just now they didn't seem so funny.)

Life was like college. Get your your degree, five credits. Marriage, six. Raise a child, eight credits. Find and hold a good job, six. Make new friends, four. Die of natural causes, graduation.

But goddamn it, *this* wasn't on the curriculum. *This* was a final exam sprung on you by surprise. No previous study allowed.

And if you flunked it, you died.

She stared at the TV screen. A surrogate mother was being sued for giving birth to a Down's syndrome baby. Bizarre . . . but not unthinkable. Not like *this*.

Van Wyck hung up the phone and asked her if she'd like a drink.

"Yeah," she said, "from the waters of Lethe."

He laughed a little, nodding his head. The ancients had been very shrewd to include the River of Forgetfulness in their mythology. "I know where you're coming from," he said. "I think when this is over I'm going to take a week off and get shitfaced every day. But for the time being we ought to try to stay sober."

"I don't think I could get drunk now if I wanted to," said Dorothy. "How long are we going to sit around and wait, Ed? I feel like I'm gonna go bats."

"At least till midnight. You know we can't take a chance on there being any witnesses."

"What if he isn't home?"

"We wait. If he's out, he'll be back before sunup."

If he's out . . . As if he might decide to go to the movies or have a few beers with the boys at Dutchie's Bar.

"Might as well have supper," Van Wyck said, "It'll help pass the time."

Dorothy had no appetite, but she was happy to move on to the kitchen. Whether or not she could eat it when it was done, preparing a meal would help keep her sane a little while longer.

Toby wasn't hungry, either. He waded dutifully through his greens and pork and listened with half an ear to Gramma's commentary on one of the stories on the TV news.

"I declare, people ain't got no *souls* these days! All they got is too much money. How can they let these rich folks buy people's babies? And what kind of woman sells the child that the good Lord gives her? They gotta do somethin' about this, before we wind up with peddlers hawkin' babies on the streets."

Toby didn't answer—although a vision of a pushcart full of babies passed across his mind's eye. He was listening for any sound from Thornall's room that would indicate that the old man was awake again.

But he was also casting his memory back—not far—to his days as a soldier, wanting to make sure he still had what they'd given him in combat training.

He'd been at loose ends, a young kid with no prospects, when he joined the army, which he did not because he'd had any hankering to kill somebody, but because he knew he couldn't afford to wait much longer before he figured out what to do with his life. The recruitment ads he saw on the tube convinced him that the army could point him in the right direction. It looked like the quickest way out of the woods.

Now that he looked back on it, he had to admire the psych job that they'd done on him. In basic training they ground him down, wiped the wiseass smirk off his face, and built him back up again—their way, the army way. It was simple, only they'd kept him too busy and too tired and too hopped-up to see through it at the time; and anyway he'd been too young to understand what they were doing to him.

Why do soldiers die? The politicians and the peace activists agonized over the question, but every soldier knew the answer. You died for your buddies, the guys in your unit. Why? Because they'd do the same for you. No way you could let 'em down. You'd been through too much together. And you were young. *Here, boy,* the army said; *here's how you become a man.* And you went for it. Jesus, how you went for it. Maybe it looked kind of goofy now, from a civilian perspective, but while you were *in* it, there was nothing like it. You *knew* those fuckin' guys in your platoon would put their lives on the line for you. You'd do it for them. Anything less would be unspeakably disgraceful. You couldn't live with it.

And you killed the enemy because he was trying to kill your buddies; and if you didn't kill him, *couldn't* kill him, you wouldn't be one of the guys anymore. You'd be useless to your unit. An outcast. A leper.

Toby knew he could kill this enemy, as long as he could believe he was doing it for others. To save them. For people who would do the same for him. Over and over again he forced himself to watch Felix Frick shrivel in the sun like a worm on a hot sidewalk. It was real. It had happened. And if he didn't kill the enemy, it would happen again. Count on it. Believe it. Maybe it wasn't the same as being with your platoon on the Korean border, but it was close enough. *The reverend, Van Wyck, Mrs. Matthiesen: we're all in it together.* They're *the unit now.* And if he didn't take up the sword and do what the reverend told him, they were all dead meat. *Hey, the reverend came here to do it himself, all alone. I can't do less. Can't look him in the eye and tell him, "I can't do this."*

But that old gung-ho feeling was slow in coming back.

Blanche saw lights on in Van Wyck's house when she drove to the minipark to watch and think. She had, however, more important concerns than the carryings-on of the police chief and his loose woman.

She felt like a child being suddenly offered the freedom of adulthood, and like a child she was both skeptical and fearful of the offer.

Although she'd dreamed of little else for years, she could not truly believe that she would soon become a vampire. Her life had worn itself into a deep groove, and it was almost impossible to imagine that it could ever take a new direction. The Master had always found a way to put it off. Why should this time be any different? After all these years of lording it over her, why should he finally grant her the beginnings of equality? Why should he release her from service? Such a change was virtually inconceivable. Somehow he'd renege on it, and everything would be as it had always been.

But what if he kept his promise? What if he drank her blood and set her free?

Blanche had always pictured herself as a very successful vampire. Certainly not one of those poor shambling wrecks who could neither understand nor accept the transformation and were doomed to perish with the first sunrise. Hadn't she served a vampire for twenty years? There was no living human being who knew more about it than she. No one could be better prepared to make the change.

Yet what did she know? Only what she'd seen, and that from the outside looking in. She'd seen birds all her life, but if she were to be turned into one, would she survive long enough to learn how to fly? And when the master took her blood, and she slid out of consciousness, how could she be sure she wouldn't just slide down into death? What guarantee was there that she would come back as a vampire? And even if she did, would she remember what she had to do?

For all her closeness to the Master, his true state of being was as alien to her as if she had never known him. She could not anticipate what it would feel like to fall into nothingness and emerge as a vampire. Her imagination did not extend beyond the fall, and she feared the fall as she feared death.

She sat across the street from Van Wyck's house and waited passively, as though waiting for a sign.

XV. LAST RITES

One

"It's time."

Dorothy followed Van Wyck out the door. He paused to lock it, wondering if he'd ever be back to open it again. It was an abstract question; worse was another scene his imagination screened for him.

"You went after Dr. Emerson with a sword?"

"Yes, Mr. Prosecutor."

"Why? Just tell me why."

"He was a vampire, sir."

"Your Honor! My client has already answered the question. Surely even the district attorney can see that he's simply not competent to stand trial . . ."

Thus entertained, he didn't try to talk to Dorothy as they drove toward Alabama Road. He took the back roads, country lanes Dorothy hadn't known existed. It was like riding back through time, back to before the developers got their hands on Millboro. Farms and fields, dark clumps of woodland, spring peepers calling. Van Wyck remembered the dirt roads of his boyhood, and walking barefoot for a mile to get to the fishing hole. It came back to him with a sharp pang, memory of a treasure irrevocably lost. There were no more dirt roads in Millboro, and no fishing holes that he knew of. *But we've got vampires.* . . .

He'd given up trying to get Dorothy to stay behind. He was glad she was with him—and at the same time felt guilty for exposing her to danger. He wondered if it signified some taint of cowardice in him. What kind of man drags a woman into the line of fire with him?

But he wasn't dragging her; she had claimed her right to come. And if he wanted to make it through the rest of the night, he'd better stop thinking like a seventeen-year-old. He was too old for macho bullshit. In retrospect, he knew it was one of the factors that had undermined his marriage. There are two kinds of cops, his father used to say: the kind who don't make the same mistake twice, and ex-cops. ("Do you want to save the marriage," asked the marriage counselor, "or do you want to keep on playing Macho Man?" The marriage had proved to be past saving, but the counselor had nevertheless opened his eyes. He gave up playing Macho Man.) If he made the same mistakes with Dorothy he'd made with Helen, he would lose her.

He missed his kids.

Will you get hold of yourself, Van Wyck? He tightened his grip on the steering wheel and tried to shake off the blues. *All you've got to do for now is be a cop. Protect the people, save 'em from the Bad Guy. Do what has to be done. You know how.*

He drove slowly, but before he knew it he was cruising down Alabama Road. A light drizzle began to fuzz the windshield.

Toby Hicks was waiting, the sword cradled in his arms; it was wrapped in rags. He climbed into the back seat when Van Wyck stopped for him.

"How's Thornall?"

"Still alive. But he's been asleep all night. How're you doing, Mrs. Matthiesen?"

"As well as can be expected," Dorothy said. "Which means I'll scream if I don't watch myself."

"You and me both. Chief?"

"There's nothing more to say. We go in, we kill him, we carry away the pieces. And pray."

"Have you figured out what to do about the wife?"

Van Wyck had been agonizing over it all night, and it wasn't because there was a plethora of alternatives. There were only two. Kill her or let her go.

"She walks," he said. "I can't arrest her. No jury's going to convict her of helping a vampire. If anything they'll convict us—for murder. We can't hope to dispose of a second body. Anyway, I can't just walk up to her and shoot her, and I won't let you do it, either. All I want is for her to get out of Millboro and stay out."

"Chief, she might not just stand by twiddling her thumbs while we hack her boss to smithereens. She might try to stop us."

"In that case," said Van Wyck, "she stands a real good chance of getting killed whether I like it or not."

It was the best he could do.

Van Wyck pointed over the steering wheel and said, "That's it. The house with the lights."

Toby could hardly hear him. After working all night to psych himself for this, his body was finally getting the message. The old fight-or-flight reflexes were taking over now. His glands pumped adrenaline, speeding his heartbeat, raising his blood pressure so that the blood almost seemed to roar as it raced through his veins. His stomach contracted. His knees quaked. Sitting motionless in the car was a torment to him.

Hours ago he'd been out in Gramma's backyard, in the dark, taking practice swings with Thornall's sword. It had whistled as it clove the air. He had kept at it just long enough so that he fairly ached to hit something—maybe test the blade against a tree, or thrust it deep into the ground. Then he had stopped.

Now he gripped the handle as naturally as he used to cradle his M16 in his arms. The weapon had become familiar to him. He was comfortable with the heft of it, his hands had settled into the best possible grip. When he looked down at it, he saw that he'd stripped the rags away. He couldn't remember doing that.

Time to take care of business.

Dorothy stared at the house. Lights were on in what was probably the living room, but curtains were drawn across the windows; you couldn't see inside. *But I don't have to,* she thought. The backlit windows held her like the eyes of a demonic hypnotist commanding her to lower her hand into boiling water. She wanted to beg Van Wyck to pass the house and keep on going, but she couldn't.

"He's in there," she said. Just to see windows shining would have told her that, but she would have known it regardless, even with a blindfold over her eyes. To approach that house, even in a car, was like wading in warm water and crossing into cold, wading in shallow water and feeling the bottom suddenly drop. It was just like coming home with Chris waiting in the living room, or walking up to the Schuylerville Nursing Home with Felix Frick cowering in the cellar. Something in their blood called out to something that was in hers.

"I don't see his wife's car in the driveway," Van Wyck said. "Maybe it's in the garage." He turned to Dorothy. "Can you sense whether she's here, too?" It was a lunatic question, but it fit the situation.

"I don't know."

The car rolled to a stop at the curb.

Lamps lit the streets, but this was commuter country and the houses were dark. Here and there an upstairs light shone, nothing more. There were early trains to be caught in a few hours, early buses; the long haul to the big city.

Van Wyck checked his watch and saw that it was going on two in the morning. *The hour of the wolf draws near,* he thought. He killed the engine and let silence reign. It was a minute or two before he broke it.

"We're going to go right in," he said, "and we're not going to fuck around. We don't give him a chance to take us."

Even as he said it, he wondered: *Take us? I've got a gun, Hicks has a sword. How can he take us? This is butchery.*

Toby spoke up. "Don't give him a chance to talk us down. Don't listen to him. That's what the reverend says. He'll kill us if we let him talk."

Van Wyck opened the door and got out, unbuttoning his holster as soon as his feet touched asphalt. Toby followed with the sword.

God, the chief thought, *this is what a criminal feels when he's about to pull off a big job. That feeling of sheer nakedness just before it starts, the sense that any moment every window, every door on the street's going to fly open and a hundred pairs of eyes are going to be staring down on you, and a hundred guns are going to take aim at your nose. The terrible, seductive knowledge that it's not too late, you can still turn away and go home, none of this has got to happen. All you have to do is boogie out of there. But take one more step and you're lost. No more options. You become a character in your own play, powerless to change your lines.*

Van Wyck took that step. It put him on the Emersons' sidewalk.

Dorothy said, "I can't go in."

It was true. Her feet stuck to the sidewalk. She lost all feeling in her legs. She could no more have gone on than she could have stepped off the roof of a skyscraper. She felt strangely calm, but recognized the feeling as a numbness of the spirit.

Van Wyck pressed his keys into her hand. "Go back and wait in the car. Lock all the doors, roll up the windows, put the key in the ignition—and keep watch. If you see anything

409

we ought to know about, hit the horn. We'll come running. And don't let anybody get too close. It might be a good idea to let the engine run. You might only have a second to get moving.''

"Ed, I'm *sorry* . . ."

"It's all right. We'd be crazy to go in there without a lookout posted. You know how to work the radio?''

She nodded. "I've watched you do it.''

"Good. If this turns out to be more than we can handle, call for help.''

Blanche spotted them just in time. She doused her lights and pulled into a vacant driveway a few houses up the street. From there she could watch them without her face being visible through the windshield. She was safe—unless they'd noticed, on their way down the street, that there hadn't been a car in this particular driveway a few minutes ago. But if they spotted her, she was far enough away to drive off before they could reach her.

They palavered on the sidewalk, under a streetlamp—the police chief, the Matthiesen woman, and a nigger. *(Who's he? Where did he come from?)* Then the woman went back to sit in the car, and the two men proceeded up the walk toward the Master's front door.

(My front door!)

The cop had his hand on the butt of his gun. The colored boy was carrying . . . what? She couldn't make it out.

The Master would have heard them. He'd be ready for them. That he might be in any kind of immediate physical danger never crossed her mind. He could snap men's necks like raw spaghetti.

Obviously there was something going on here that she didn't understand. Not that Felix Frick business. If it were that, the chief would be here with some of his men. But

410

what? Who was the nigger, why was he here? What did he have to do with anything?

Blanche's resentment flared in a hot burst. Clearly one of the Master's little schemes had miscarried, and now the police chief was at the door. Some little caper the Master hadn't seen fit to let her know about. And now here she sat without a clue. Hell's bells, was he preying on the coloreds now? Had this coon *seen* him? Knocking on the door at two in the morning, in Royal Oaks II, was hardly likely to be ordinary police procedure in this town.

She hadn't been able to spend the whole night spying on Van Wyck and his fancy lady, after all. She had given it up after an hour or so and gone out of town for a bite to eat, a little drink to calm her nerves, a nice walk to put her thoughts in order. A leisurely drive down Route 37, following the shoreline. And the hours had flown by with the miles.

"Why don't you go out and have a drink, my dear?" Yeah, sure. *I go out for one lousy night and he gets caught slinking around the colored neighborhood. That's why the nigger's here. "Yowsah, Chief, dat's de one, dat's de man I seen sneakin' roun' my backyard!"* And of course the lights were on when the cop came by, so he couldn't play dumb and say he'd been in bed all night.

What would he do now? Try to put them off with some kind of glib answer? That'd be his style. *Damn you to hell! Smash their heads together and let's get out of here!* She tried to hurl the thought across the intervening space and send it ker-chunking through the Master's thick skull.

The men were at the door.

Words were superfluous. Van Wyck drew his gun and snaked his fingers around the doorknob. It turned freely. Before he could talk himself out of it, he pushed it open.

His heart pounded like an engine suddenly kicked to life,

and he leaped across the threshold without a thought, bringing up his free hand to seize the Police Special in a shooter's grip. In the corner of his eye the sword's point glinted as Hicks came in after him.

The foyer was empty. His mind racing, Van Wyck reached around and shoved the front door shut.

Dorothy watched the cruel house swallow her friends, and thrust her hands into her armpits to keep them from going for the radio

Two

"Blanche?"

To the right, four carpeted steps led up to the living room. That was where the lights were. Emerson was out of the line of sight, but the sound of his voice placed him in that room.

They were only in the foyer for a moment, but every detail of it branded itself on Van Wyck's brain: the smooth slate floor, the shiny paneling of the walls, the sheen of a brass knob on a closet door, the darkened family room straight ahead. The place was bare of decoration, as though the inhabitants had not yet moved in.

Van Wyck advanced to the foot of the small stairs and peered up into the living room. A man stood near the top step, looking down at him.

Van Wyck gave his finger a command to squeeze the trigger. It defied him.

The man was huge, a giant—or was it just his elevation, a trick of the eye? But he had to weigh three hundred pounds. His silver hair was disheveled, and he wore a rumpled suit that looked like he'd slept in it. His skin was the color of cold dough.

And he stood looking down on them, a man with a gun and a man with a sword, with what could only be called the mildest curiosity, as if they were two small children who had wandered in from playing in his yard. There was a Police Special aimed at him, and it might as well have been a water pistol.

You're dead, Chief, an inner voice declared, flatly, as if it were the simplest of facts. Already the gun began to respond to the tug of gravity, an implacable hand pulling the barrel toward the floor. And Van Wyck's mind filled with fear like the hold of a ship taking on dark water, the planks stove in on the rock of Emerson's unnatural self-possession.

Jesus God, said Toby to himself, *those eyes!*

Up until this moment he'd been thinking, in soldier's terms, of a human enemy. You always knew, no matter how well they trained you, that the enemy was human. You could waste a village full of slant-eyed yellow dinks or sub-human Iranian monsters, or whoever. Shit, you could blow away a ten-year-old girl, like Sergeant Dawkins did in Nam (*"Now I know she didn't have a grenade on her, but I didn't know it then. Those were funky times, my man . . ."*), and not feel too guilty about it. You could do almost any damn thing to anybody, if you were properly motivated.

But this was different.

There was nothing they could do to Emerson. He was too powerful. His eyes told you that. Looking into them was like being in an airplane way up over the middle of the ocean, and seeing the wings catch fire. You were dead. You had a few minutes, before the ship turned into a fireball, but there was nothing you could do that'd make the least goddamn bit of difference. You were gone.

"Come up, gentlemen. If this is a robbery, I'm afraid

413

you've come to the wrong house. There's nothing of value here."

He doesn't know who we are, thought Van Wyck. *He doesn't know why we're here. Or is he just playing with us?*

Fighting the growing weight of the gun, Van Wyck took the steps one at a time. *Am I going up after him,* he wondered, *or is he pulling me up like a fish on a line?*

Toby came after him, clutching the sword with both hands. He felt an irrational assurance that the sword was not afraid, that as long as he held onto it, it would protect him. He remembered, in a flash, a story about a man who, as he was about to be hanged, lived through a fantasy of miraculous escape that was cut off only when the executioner sprang the trap. Now he understood it.

"I perceive," Emerson said, "you've come here to kill me. You're not robbers, but murderers. I don't know either of you gentlemen. I am sure I never did you any wrong. How have I offended you?"

To Van Wyck no speech had ever seemed so sweetly reasonable, so free of threat or malice. *What am I doing here?* It came to him, with the force of a sudden inspiration, that the whole thing was nothing but a monstrous mistake. But there was still time. . . .

"Don't listen to him, Chief," said Toby.

Emerson's smile bloomed slowly, like a defective flower.

"Ah! You must be Mr. Van Wyck, the police chief. Forgive me for not having recognized you, but you're out of uniform and we've never met. I've heard a lot about you, though, all of it complimentary. The township is in good hands. And who's your companion?"

For an instant Toby suffered the appalling certainty that Van Wyck would slide his gun back into the holster, apologize to this inhuman thing, and turn to leave. It was like knowing that two cars would collide at an intersection. He could see it happening and do nothing to prevent it.

Van Wyck vacillated. You couldn't just shoot someone

who was trying to hold a civilized conversation with you and wasn't armed. A lifetime of police training and tradition rebelled against it. Everything he was rebelled against it.

("He filled a cup with my blood and drank it.")

"You know why we're here," he said through clenched teeth.

"But I don't—honestly!" said Emerson. "You have me completely at a loss. Have I broken some law?"

(Chris Matthiesen, with his heart shot to hamburger, thrashed and screamed as they loaded him onto the stretcher.)

This is bull-shit! thought Toby. Emerson's oily tone aroused him to something akin to fury.

"The chief can't arrest you for being what you are," he said, "but your time is over."

"But *what* am I? What do you say that I am, young man?"

The words tried to cling to Toby's mouth, but he spat them out. "A vampire. A murdering, bloodsucking *thing.*"

Emerson laughed. The sound of it was like the crash of doors slamming shut in Hell.

"Really!" he said. "A vampire! Young man, you've been staying up too late and watching too many horror movies. Who, in this day and age, believes in vampires? But look!" He pulled his upper lip up and bared his teeth. They were as dirty as a wino's fingertips, but otherwise unremarkable. "See?" He let the lip fall back in place. "No fangs. I'm simply not equipped to be a vampire."

(Fangs? Bruce Randall's teeth were normal. Felix Frick said nothing about fangs. You took a knife and cut his wrist, and you drank his blood, you didn't need fangs for that . . . and when the sun came up, he turned into . . .)

Van Wyck squeezed the trigger.

The gun jumped in his hands. The explosion made his ears ring.

No! I hit him, I know I did, up this close I couldn't miss. But

Emerson was coming at him, doughy face stone-hard with rage, and although he seemed to be coming in slow motion, like a close-up shot of a blitzing linebacker on instant replay, Van Wyck couldn't get off another shot. He had all the time in the world, and it wasn't enough.

Toby froze, immobilized first by the report of the gun and then by the speed and suddenness of Emerson's assault. He came at the chief like a pouncing cat, a striking snake, too fast for Toby to react. And his pasty hands closed on the chief's shirt and yanked him a foot off the floor.

Van Wyck felt his feet dance on empty air and tried to bring up the gun for a heart shot, but Emerson slapped it out of his hand . . . then threw him the length of the room. The wall slammed into his back like a gigantic paddle and dropped him to the floor.

And freed Toby. With both hands he swung the sword, the blade going *whoosh* as it sliced the air. But the swing was wild, Emerson dropped back, and the point passed within inches of his shapeless chin.

He took another step back and held up his hands, eyes locked on the sword, trying to smile but not making it.

Toby was filled with the spirit, and the sword weighed nothing in his hands.

"Maybe you ought to turn into a bat and fly away, sucker!" He brandished the blade and had the enormous satisfaction of seeing Emerson flinch. "Only you can't do that, can you?"

"Young man, you're being very foolish. Put that weapon down before you hurt yourself with it."

"You're the one who's gonna get hurt."

Van Wyck tried to get back up, but his head spun and he slipped back to the floor. He couldn't see the gun anywhere.

"You're not being very reasonable," Emerson said. "Suppose I really were a vampire. Wouldn't I just dissolve myself into a green mist and seep through a crack in the door? Confronted by a madman shaking a sword at me, surely I would have done that by now—if I could. The fact that I haven't proves I'm not a vampire.''

But his words were only words, devoid of meaning. Toby swung at him again, driving him back another step. The word was a part of him now, and he was a part of the word.

A grimace of pure rage twisted Emerson's face. He made a quick swipe at the sword.

Toby struck. The blade met resistance but clove right through it. Toby couldn't see what he hit; the force of the blow overtopped his balance and he stumbled across the room.

When he turned it was to see Emerson staring, as if in disbelief, at the stump of his right arm, shorn off just below the elbow. The flesh was dark and mottled, the bone as white as ivory.

Something snapped in Toby's mind. Roaring, he jerked back the sword and charged, and struck again—a desperate from-the-heels swing that cannoned into Emerson and knocked him down. His fall shook the room.

Van Wyck nearly screamed as he saw the rest of the arm fly away from the giant's shoulder. The gun lay on the carpet a mere five feet from him, but he couldn't move to get it. He could barely find words for what he saw.

"Jesus!" he cried. "Where's the blood? *There's no blood!*''

But Toby was flailing away, raining cuts on Emerson as the huge mound of flesh bucked and writhed and tried to dodge the hungry blade. It thumped and tore and crunched as it struck him. Toby was screaming, a wordless, animal cry; and Emerson was strangely silent. He thrashed on the floor like a beached seal, but was too big to avoid the blows. Every one connected.

The blade fell across Emerson's neck and sent the head rolling crookedly to the baseboard. The point bit through the carpet and lodged in the floor, yanking the weapon from Toby's grasp. He lost his balance and fell forward.

Van Wyck had the gun and had regained his feet, but what he saw next stopped him in his tracks. His voice cracked like an adolescent boy's.

"Do you see that? *He's not dead!*"

Toby couldn't hear him. He was on his hands and knees, his mind a swirling chaos, staring down at a disembodied hand and forearm. The fingers made clutching motions eighteen inches from his face.

Around him the floor was scattered with things that stirred like reptiles coming out of hibernation. A foot quivered in its shoe. An arm flexed and reflexed at the elbow joint, a movement that carried it slowly and jerkily and blindly over the carpet. The huge torso heaved. Legs shuddered. Shapeless lumps of flesh trembled fitfully. They were gray and bloodless.

Miniature pools of colorless, viscous matter spotted the rug. A sickly sweet aroma, like that of long-spoiled meat, hung thickly in the air.

Toby's head cleared slowly. He saw Van Wyck's feet and looked up at him.

"Are you all right, Chief?"

Van Wyck pointed to the far wall, to a space between a chair and a rack that held a nice set of stereo equipment.

Toby's eyes followed the pointing finger.

Emerson's head lay on its ear, mouth flopping open and shut like the mouth of a boated fish gulping for oxygen, eyes rolling crazily. A sparse trail of dime-size blots of pus showed the path the head had taken as it rolled erratically to the wall.

Toby groped for meaning. None of this made sense. The place should be awash with blood. It ought to be sprayed across the floor and walls like an explosion of red paint.

Christ, you'd think a vampire would be *full* of blood—so where was it?

Van Wyck screwed his eyes shut and fought to get a grip on himself. His mind wanted to shut down, erase the insane seconds like a faulty videotape. It was a temptation that had to be fought. *This is real,* he insisted to himself. *This is fact. Emerson wasn't human. My God, he wasn't even alive. You can't kill something that wasn't alive in the first place.*

But you can destroy it.

"Come on, Toby. We've got to put this mess someplace where the sun can get it."

Three

Dorothy heard the gunshot and stiffened in her seat. Her hand reached for the radio transmitter. With an effort she pulled it back. *Not yet.*

She shouldn't have been surprised to hear a shot. Ed had a gun, he would use it. A heart shot would disable the vampire, and give Toby Hicks an easy time with the sword.

(Easy?)

Only then did she discover that she'd wet herself.

Blanche heard it, too: muffled and indistinct, and far away, but she knew it for what it was. A gunshot. Not a car backfiring a few blocks away, not a kid setting off a cherry bomb, not a garage door slamming shut. Van Wyck had shot the Master.

But so what? The Master had been shot before. When he was naked you could count the bullet holes. There were

419

bullets rattling around inside his body. They couldn't hurt him.

In a few minutes she would have to go and help him. They would have two bodies to get rid of.

Three, counting Dorothy Matthiesen.

Blanche turned the key in the ignition.

In the Emersons' kitchen they found black plastic trash bags for the fragments.

Van Wyck tugged the sword from the floor and hacked Emerson's thighs from the torso—not for vengeance, but for the sake of practicality. They had a big body to move, and he wasn't sure that he and Toby could carry it unless they took it out in pieces, like a grand piano disassembled for the sake of the movers. Somehow the job made him think of the meat room at the A&P, and standardized chicken parts wrapped neatly in see-through plastic. From time to time he felt faint and giddy, but he kept on with it. He opened the box of Hefty Lawn and Leaf Bags and gathered up pieces of Emerson, dropping them into the bags with fingers that soon were slimy and smelled like a pathologist's.

Toby moved as in a daze. Whatever high he'd been on minutes ago, he was coming down in a hurry. He had to stop almost immediately to vomit into a Hefty bag. His head swam.

They gathered fragments of arms, legs, and flesh, and filled one trash bag after another, tightly tying each one at the mouth and setting them by the steps that led down to the foyer. The black parcels twitched and rustled.

Blanche kept the car in park so that the brakelights wouldn't come on.

The problem was to get close to Matthiesen, close enough

to pull her from the police chief's car, without spooking her. Unless she had nerves of stone, the woman would be poised to bolt like a cornered rat at the first hint of a threat—or to fight like one.

The Master must have finished with Van Wyck and the colored boy by now, Blanche thought. Did he know there was a third enemy waiting outside? Would he come out to get Matthiesen? Or would she start wondering what was taking her friends so long, and venture up to the house to see what was keeping them?

Should I swoop down on her or what? Can't let her get away again. What was she supposed to do?

With the engine running, she tried to work it out.

Dorothy jumped when the Emersons' front door swung open, then relaxed when she recognized Ed and Toby. They didn't bother to close the door but came down the sidewalk quickly, each holding what looked like two full bags of laundry. They came around to the rear of the car, and Van Wyck swung the hatchback open. The Escort rocked drunkenly on its springs as they threw the bags into the luggage space.

"Ed—"

"We did it, Dorothy! But we're not done yet. We have to go back. Keep your eyes open!"

They hurried back to the house and went inside again. Dorothy turned to get a better look at the Escort's cargo. The plastic bags rustled. She saw them move.

She stared at them, her mind refusing to deduce the nature of their contents.

Emerson's head tried to bite him when he reached for it to put it into a black bag. Van Wyck stepped back and closed his eyes, and silently recited the Lord's Prayer to himself. *Our Father, who art in Heaven . . .* He took it slowly, concentrating on each word, and felt better by the time he reached *Amen.* He opened his eyes and looked at the head. It bared its teeth at him.

"Looks like he can still bite," said Toby. "Maybe we ought to chop the head up, too. Or smash it or something."

Van Wyck saw the dead eyes roll wildly, just as if the head could understand Toby's suggestion. Well, why shouldn't it? It still had ears, it still had a brain. Ask *any* disembodied head. . . .

Van Wyck suppressed a crazy laugh that suddenly swam up his throat. "Let's just get it over with, okay?"

He held a Hefty bag open on the floor while Toby used the point of the sword to roll the head into the sack. It didn't roll smoothly, like a bowling ball, but wobbled this way and that, eyes staring, jaws gnashing soundlessly. Toby remembered hearing a story about an Asian tribe that played polo with the severed heads of enemies. *How do they do that? How do they get the fuckin' things to go straight when they hit 'em?* He tried to imagine the thonk of a polo mallet against a flesh-covered skull. A little part of him was able to view the scene objectively. *I look like I'm playing a game. Head-in-the-Bag. All you need is a sword, a chopped-off head, and a garbage bag.* It took him longer than he would have expected to prod the head into the bag. He realized, before he was done, that it didn't want to go.

Van Wyck's stomach was bucking like a spooked horse, but he kept it on a tether as the head finally rolled into the bag. He knotted the bag shut, picked it up, and held it at arm's length. It moved. He remembered a man he'd met once who'd had a rattlesnake in a gunnysack and held it far away from his body as the sack writhed. "Fucker'll bite you right through the bag," the man explained. So Van Wyck held the bag at arm's length and queasily watched the bottom stir. It felt like it weighed fifty pounds. He took it out o the car and let it fall into the luggage space. It thumped when it landed.

"Almost done," he told Dorothy.

"Ed . . ."

"We've got to finish." He turned and walked stiffly back o the house. Dorothy thought he was moving like a sleep-walker.

She knew, now, what was in the plastic bags. They rus-led like a nest of vipers. *Trying to get out, come together again, maybe wriggle up here next to me . . .* It was so much like a dream that she simply sat and listened, unable to accept it as a part of her reality.

The Master had failed.

That was why the police chief and the coon were going back and forth between the house and the car, like two friends loading up for a fishing trip. That was the meaning of the gunshot.

The Master was dead. That which could not die was dead. That which was infallible had failed.

The butchers were taking him out in bits and pieces.

I told him this would happen someday, didn't I? Blanche thought. She felt oddly vindicated. *You never wanted to listen to me, did you? Hell, no, you knew it all. You knew all the angles, had 'em all covered. Nothing to worry about. I told him the police chief has to go, Dorothy Matthiesen has to go. And here they are, like I knew they'd be.*

A deadly chill seeped out of the marrow of her bones and turned her flesh to ice. Out of nowhere came a cold rain that fell upon her soul. Caught short, she coughed out a mess onto her lap. Through her dress, it felt feverishly hot against her numbed skin.

They'll do the same to me if they catch me here.

Without turning on the headlights, she shifted into re-verse and backed slowly out of the driveway.

* * *

The quaking torso wouldn't fit into a Hefty Bag.

They stood over it, watching as it jerked and quivered and palpitated. Emerson's shirt had lost its buttons during the struggle, coming apart to reveal a continent of pallid flesh. Van Wyck counted a dozen bullet holes without looking for more. Some of them looked fresh, albeit bloodless; they were still ringed with powder burns. He thought he recognized the work of his own Police Special, one of the larger, fresher entrance wounds just below the rib cage. It oozed a thick, colorless fluid.

"Shower curtain," he said to Toby. They went to the bathroom and got it, spread it on the floor beside the torso, and used their feet to roll the shapeless burden onto the polyethylene sheet. Using it as a travois, they dragged the body down to the foyer. Like a pair of battlefield medics, they picked it up at the ends and lugged it to the car, panting with the effort. The Escort lurched on its springs when they raised the burden and crammed it into the back.

"We'll turn out the lights and lock up, then come back tomorrow night to wipe out our prints."

"That rug's a mess," Toby said.

Van Wyck pulled the hatchback down. "The hell with the rug. If the county crime lab wants it, they can have it. If they can make any sense out of those stains, more power to 'em."

Dorothy watched them enter the house for the last time, saw the lights go out, and was unspeakably relieved when they came out again, locking the door behind them. Toby carried the sword. He paused once to thrust it into the earth, cleaning it, then caught up to Van Wyck on the run. The car rocked when they jumped into it.

"Ed, Toby—are you all right?"

"We're righter than we thought we'd be," Van Wyck said.

"Ed, just now, while you were in the house . . . I thought I saw a car."

"Where?"

"Backing out of a driveway somewhere up the street; I'm not sure which house."

"Did it come past here?"

She shook her head. "No, it went out onto Suydam Road."

Van Wyck spun the wheel and maneuvered the Escort through a K-turn. "Might've been someone who had to catch an early plane to somewhere," he said. "We can't worry about it now. There's more we have to do."

They went to the place they'd selected earlier, the unofficial dump site in the woods off Cherokee Road.

I just hope it's safe, Toby thought, as Van Wyck turned off the road onto the two parallel ruts in the earth that led to the site. *I just hope nobody stops by this morning with a load of old magazines.* Like clawed fingers reaching for the passengers, branches scraped the car's fenders and windows as Van Wyck negotiated the narrow track.

The headlights shone on a scattering of junk—a broken rocking chair sat crookedly atop a pile of rubbish like a throne—then went out as Van Wyck killed the engine. They all got out of the car.

It's so peaceful here at night, Dorothy thought. *The air smells so sweet.* The light perfume of green leaves mingled with the heavier scent of woodland earth. Far, far overhead, the stars glimmered like the lights of an unattainable city of bliss and peace.

The mood vanished when Ed raised the hatchback and dragged out the first of the Hefty Bags.

Dorothy helped the men carry the bags to the middle of the site. "Be careful," Van Wyck said, unnecessarily. Dorothy took a sack from the car, holding it as far from

425

her body as she could. Its contents stirred sluggishly; she felt as if she were carrying a bag with a dying cat inside it. She put it down, then found that her fingers were too unsteady to undo the tight knot. Toby Hicks slit the bag down the side with a pocketknife. Dorothy jumped backward as a hand and a forearm spilled out. The hand reached mindlessly for her foot. She backed away, feeling ill.

One by one they emptied the bags. The pieces of Emerson twitched amid the rubble, making a sound in the darkness like the foragings of small, clumsy animals.

"Sun'll finish 'em," Toby said.

The men went back to the car for the torso. It was too heavy to carry now; their strength was ebbing fast. They dragged it to the dump and rolled it off the shower curtain. The mound of undead flesh rippled like gelatin. They threw the shower curtain into the bushes.

Toby went back for the bag with the head in it. It was still moving, still working its jaws. He held out the bag and slit the bottom with the knife. The head fell to the ground with a thud and bounced away from him. He wondered if it could still feel anything, maybe even still think—then decided he was better off not knowing.

Van Wyck had a fantasy. His mind's eye saw the disarticulated fragments squirming back to the torso and reuniting with it, the head rolling back to the stump of the neck and welding itself back onto the body, and the whole reassembled bulk of Emerson rising up like a wicked dream and shambling out of the woods to come knocking on his door—and all before the sun rose. Reason told him it was impossible, but reason hadn't been sinking many putts lately. *Eddie baby, your troubles have just begun.*

The sound of Toby's voice snapped him out of it. "What're we gonna do with . . . . this," he was asking, "After the sun kills it?"

"Shit." Van Wyck shrugged. "I don't know. Bury it, I guess."

"Burn it," Dorothy said. *Don't put it underground! Not down there with all the nutrients that're in the soil, sheltered from the sun. Where—if there is just the tiniest spark of life remaining, one single undead cell—it might yet grow again.* "Incinerate it."

"We might be smart to stand guard here until it's all finished," Toby said. "Just in case . . . I don't know. In case something goes wrong."

The idea had its merits, but Van Wyck had his limits, and he had reached them. He didn't want to listen anymore to the pieces of Emerson stirring in the rubbish. He didn't want to stand and watch them shrivel in the sun. Decay had been waiting for this corpse since God knew when. Van Wyck didn't think he wanted to see decay claim its overdue fee.

"We can come back in the daytime," Dorothy said. "If we stay out here much longer, I'm afraid I'll drop. There's still so much to be done. We won't be able to do it right unless we get some rest."

The thought of peaceful rest was like an impossible dream of riches.

"What about that wife of his?" Toby said. "What happens when she comes home and finds him gone?"

"She'll know he's finished," Van Wyck said. God, he hoped so. "She'll take off. I can't see her sticking around to file a missing persons report. What the hell, she might've flown the coop already.

"Eventually the neighbors will start wondering what happened to the two of them, and somebody'll call us. We'll have to investigate. I can handle that, as long as we don't leave our prints behind in the house. There better not be any, once we go back and wipe the place down. I don't ever want to try to tell this story to a judge. I wouldn't even want to tell it to a shrink."

Dorothy came close to Van Wyck, and they held each

427

other. Toby stood looking at the dump site, seeing nothing in the darkness.

"Let's get out of here," he said. Dorothy reached for him and squeezed his hand.

The rustlings followed them as they walked back to the car.

Benejah Thornall woke to find himself standing next to his bed. He felt fine: stronger, healthier, saner that he'd felt in many years.

He saw himself lying peacefully on the bed, eyes closed, lips parted slightly, motionless, soundless. Breathless.

It was given to him to know that his quest had been fulfilled. By another, it was true, but he was thankful for that knowledge.

Smiling, he turned and walked easily from the room, leaving his body behind.

Four

The sky turned gray. Emerson was aware of the sun even before its red rim peeked over the horizon.

His thoughts were disordered. They swirled chaotically, with little bits of coherence sticking out like pieces of flotsam in a whirlpool. Among them was the knowledge that his existence was soon to come to an end. If the sun didn't boil him away, he would still succumb to an inability to procure nourishment.

He felt no pain, yet. And although he could see parts of his body scattered all around him, he wasn't conscious of the separation. He still felt whole, only powerless to move. Knowing it was an illusion, he still felt connected o his lost body. His body never caused him pain, or weariness, or satisfaction, except when he was feeding. There was little difference between its presence and its absence.

He knew no fear. Fear was rooted in pain, in deprivation, and his undead being was a stranger to those—except for those rare occasions when he'd had to go some time without blood. The long years had taught him to bear that.

But he was frustrated, and not only by his utter loss of power. His work was left unfinished. He would never be able, now, to isolate the microorganism that had made his long existence possible, that had rendered him immune from pain and from corruption while leaving him prey to the sun and a slave to his need for blood. He would never learn how to protect himself from the sun, how to become a creature that could function in the light of day. He would never again be able to assuage his cravings.

Spells of regret punctuated the mad rattlings of his blood-deprived brain. He tried to hold back the chaos but could only succeed sporadically.

Now the sun climbed higher. As yet the trees shielded him from the sight of it, but the rosy tint in the sky was poison to him, too. He managed to close his eyes, but they still crept open from time to time, opening the doors of pain. The skin of his cheeks tingled.

The sun rose above the trees. His eyelids became blistering plasters to burn his eyes. He heard his disconnected arms and legs thrash in the rubble like sea creatures left behind by a retreating tide.

His thoughts dissolved completely, leaving only pain. Time became a molten flow of pain without beginning, without an end. He fell into it and was carried helplessly along.

* * *

He became aware of himself again—abruptly, like the victim of a violent accident emerging from anesthesia in a clean hospital bed. His pain had lessened. Darkness sheltered him. He heard a voice inside his head, a crazed imagining, saying *"Doctor . . . Doctor . . . Doctor"* over and over again. Blanche's voice. Wreckage of memory floating on a sea of pain.

But it wasn't memory. Sharply, persistently, something tapped his deadened cheek. Something pale and round loomed in and out of focus before his eyes.

In the darkness he saw Blanche's face.

"Doctor, can you hear me?"

He could hear her. He moved his lips and jaws to say so, but could make no sound.

"I followed them, Doctor. I took you away from that place, I took you away from the sun. I have you now."

He concentrated and was able to see her clearly. They were in a darkened room, and she was holding his head in her hands, close to her face.

"I'm going to give you some blood, Doctor. It'll save you. And I'll become like you. Deathless."

She sat and rested his head in her lap. He saw her take a scalpel and make an incision in her wrist: a small one, avoiding the major blood vessels. Her blood came in a slow trickle.

She held her wrist to his mouth. He closed his eyes and focused what energies he had on the warmth of her blood. In time he was able to move his swollen tongue and press it to the tiny wound. His pain roared up to meet him, then fell back just as violently, like a tidal surge. Absorbed through his tongue, the small amount of blood slowly rekindled his ability to mold thoughts into words. It came to him, then, that the vampire microorganism was concentrated in

430

his brain and ought to be able to sustain itself indefinitely, as long as it was provided with fresh blood.

He sucked until she stopped bleeding. He wanted to keep his lips pressed to her skin, but she easily pulled him away.

"Listen to me, Doctor. If you can understand me, blink your eyes—slowly."

To his mild surprise, he was able to open and shut his eyes as effortlessly as ever. The blood had saved him.

"I know you can't talk," she said. "But you'll probably be able to, once I rig up some way to force air through your larynx. You're lucky it's still there. If they'd cut off your head an inch higher, you would've lost that, too.

"I'm sorry I wasn't able to save your body, but it was hopeless. All chopped to pieces, and too far gone in the sun. But you have your brain, and that's where all your knowledge is. I want that knowledge, Doctor. I'll give you my blood. You'll teach me how to survive my transformation when it comes. And then we'll carry on our work."

He blinked again to show he understood and approved. Had he been capable of it, he would have been exhilarated.

Meanwhile it frustrated him that he couldn't question her. There was much he wanted to know. How had she escaped their enemies? Where were they now? Where were they going? He was sure he would be able to speak if she attached a simple air pump to his larynx.

"I'm glad you agree with me," she said. "I was a good servant to you, wasn't I? Now I'll be your equal. You'll be dependent on me to provide blood for you, but I'll need your experience, your intelligence. We'll be partners. I'm sure we'll work together very well."

He blinked again and tried to smile. Understandably, his face had lost much of its mobility. But he saw no reason why he shouldn't regain it, in time.

She showed him the scalpel.

"For now," she said, "Another drink of blood. And then we'll find a safe place for my transformation. Someplace far from here."